Cast of

Thomas Elphinstone Hambledon.

Sigmund Ulseth. A confidence man posing as a chemist who has invented a revolutionary new explosive. Circumstances force Tommy to assume Ulseth's identity.

Theophilus Hartzer. An alias first used by Tommy Hambledon and then by Sigmund Ulseth, both posing as a commercial traveler for a Swiss manufacturer of railway wagons.

Charles Denton. Another British spy, a special friend of Tommy's.

Weber. A Berlin tobacconist with strong anti-Nazi leanings. Now Denton's father-in-law, he's been of immense help to British intelligence.

Hugo Grautz. A young Dutch chemist and spy who is recruited to be Tommy's assistant.

Erich Landahl, of the Armaments Ministry.

Kurt Bernstein. A Storm Trooper assigned to protect Hambledon/Ulseth.

Wilhelm Eckhoff. Another, far more sympathetic Storm Trooper.

Gibson. A British agent who is one of Tommy's contacts in Berlin.

Joseph Goebbels. Minister of Propaganda and one of the most hated men in the Third Reich.

Hermann Goering. After Hitler, the ranking Nazi of the Third Reich.

Amalie Rielander. A young film actress whom Goebbels is pursuing.

Frau Gerda Clausen. A widow who is being courted by Ulseth/Hartzer.

Herr Kallenbach. A chemist who operates a munitions factory.

Alexia Schneider. A high-ranking Polish spy.

Kapitan Rudolf von Dettmann. Amalie's fiancé.

Plus assorted servants, Nazis, German citizens, spies, and of course Swedes.

Books by Manning Coles

The Tommy Hambledon Spy Novels
Drink to Yesterday, 1940
A Toast to Tomorrow (English title: *Pray Silence*), 1940
They Tell No Tales, 1941
Without Lawful Authority, 1943
Green Hazard, 1945
The Fifth Man, 1946
Let the Tiger Die, 1947
With Intent to Deceive (English title: *A Brother for Hugh*), 1947
Among Those Absent, 1948
Diamonds to Amsterdam, 1949
Not Negotiable, 1949
Dangerous by Nature, 1950
Now or Never, 1951
Alias Uncle Hugo (Reprint: *Operation Manhunt*), 1952
Night Train to Paris, 1952
A Knife for the Juggler (Reprint: *The Vengeance Man*), 1953
All that Glitters (English title: *Not for Export*;
Reprint: *The Mystery of the Stolen Plans*), 1954
The Man in the Green Hat, 1955
Basle Express, 1956
Birdwatcher's Quarry (English title: *The Three Beans*), 1956
Death of an Ambassador, 1957
No Entry, 1958
Concrete Crime (English title: *Crime in Concrete*), 1960
Search for a Sultan, 1961
The House at Pluck's Gutter, 1963

Ghost Books
Brief Candles, 1954
Happy Returns (English title: *A Family Matter*), 1955
The Far Traveller (non-series),1956
Come and Go, 1958

Non-Series
This Fortress, 1942
Duty Free, 1959

Short Story Collection
Nothing to Declare, 1960

Young Adult
Great Caesar's Ghost (English title: *The Emperor's Bracelet*), 1943

* Reprinted by Rue Morgue Press

Green Hazard

by Manning Coles

The Rue Morgue Press
Lyons / Boulder

ISBN: 978-1-60187-032-2

Rue Morgue Press

87 Lone Tree Lane

Lyons CO 80540

Printed by Johnson Printing

Boulder, Colorado

PRINTED IN THE UNITED STATES OF AMERICA

About Manning Coles

Manning Coles was the pseudonym of two Hampshire neighbors who collaborated on a long series of entertaining spy novels featuring Thomas Elphinstone Hambledon, a modern-language instructor turned British secret agent. Hambledon was based on a teacher of Cyril Henry Coles (1895-1965). This same teacher encouraged the teenage Coles to study modern languages, German and French in particular, having recognized Coles' extraordinary ability to learn languages. When World War I broke out Coles lied about his age and enlisted. His native speaker ability in German prompted him to be pulled off the front lines and he soon became the youngest intelligence agent in British history and spent the rest of the war working behind enemy lines in Cologne.

The books came to be written thanks to a fortuitous meeting in 1938. After Adelaide Frances Oke Manning (1891-1959), rented a flat from Cyril's father in East Meon, Hampshire, she and Cyril became neighbors and friends. Educated at the High School for Girls in Tunbridge Wells, Kent, Adelaide, who was eight years Cyril's senior, worked in a munitions factory and later at the War Office during World War I. She already had published one novel, *Half Valdez*, about a search for buried Spanish treasure. *Drink to Yesterday*, loosely based on Cyril's own adventures, was an immediate hit and the authors were besieged to write a sequel, no mean feat given the ending to that novel. That sequel, *A Toast to Tomorrow*, and its prequel were heralded as the birth of the modern espionage novel with Anthony Boucher terming them "a single long and magnificent novel of drama and intrigue and humor." The Manning Coles collaboration ended when Adelaide died of throat cancer in 1959. During those twenty years the two worked together almost daily, although Cyril's continuing activities with the Foreign Intelligence Branch, now known as the Secret Intelligence Service or, more commonly, MI6, often required that he be out of the country, especially during World War II. Cyril wrote *Concrete Crime* on his own but the final two books in the series were the work of a ghostwriter, Cyril not wanting to go on with the series without Adelaide. While the earliest books had shown flashes of humor, it would not be until *Without Lawful Authority*, published in 1943 but set in 1938, that the collaborators first embraced the almost farcical humor that would come to be their hallmark. *Green Hazard* may be their best book written in this mode. For more details on their collaboration and Cyril's activities in British intelligence see Tom & Enid Schantz' introduction to the Rue Morgue Press edition of *Drink to Yesterday*.

To

Michael and Peter

Green Hazard

Chapter I

Peace, 1941 Vintage

"I SUPPOSE," said the old colonel sadly, "that one had come to regard Hambledon as practically indestructible."

"No man," said the Foreign Office head of department, "is indestructible if he is close to a sufficiently violent explosion at the moment of detonation. Poor Hambledon seems to have been in the middle of this one, according to Denton."

"He was getting on, you know," said the colonel, "and he'd lived a pretty trying sort of life. Must have lost his grip a bit, what?"

"I did my best to persuade him not to go," said Wilcox of the Foreign Office, "but he insisted. He said that (a) he was sick of office work, (b) that it was only Switzerland and nobody could come to any harm there if they were careful to avoid precipices, and (c) there was his beard anyway. You know how he used to talk."

"Beard," said the colonel. "Beard? I didn't know he had one."

"He grew one," said the departmental head, "after Dunkirk. You remember Churchill's defiant speech telling the world that we should go on fighting whatever happened and if we were driven out of the British Isles we should continue the fight from overseas? Yes, I suppose none of us are likely to forget it; it looked too much as though it might come true at any moment. Well, Tommy—"

"It may yet," said the colonel.

"It may, of course. Tommy said that if that happened, he would be one of those left behind to make himself useful, and the more unrecognizable he was the longer his usefulness was likely to continue. So he grew a beard. He said it was cheaper than having his face remodeled by plastic surgery, and a lot less painful."

"It grew quite well," said Wilcox. "It's quite a good beard now—that is—"

"Oh, quite," said the colonel. "But what happened, exactly?"

"He went to Scrvatsch—that's a small village between Zurich and Lake Constance–to have a look at a man who was alleged to be making high explosives. We had heard of this fellow, and there seemed to be points of interest about him. Then there was a really startling explosion at a moment when poor

Hambledon is known to have been on the premises, and he has not been seen since. I haven't heard any details yet. We sent Denton out with him and he stayed on to make inquiries. I expect him here this morning."

"He should be here," said Wilcox, looking at the clock. At that moment there was a knock at the door and Charles Denton was shown in. He was a tall, loose-limbed man with a habitually languid manner. On this occasion one felt that the languor was not a mannerism but the result of a depression of spirit too heavy to be thrown off.

"Glad to see you, Denton," said the Foreign Office man.

"Thanks," said Denton in a tired voice, and shook hands all round mechanically, as one thinking of something else.

"This is a melancholy occasion," said the colonel.

"Did you have a good journey?" asked Wilcox.

"Oh, much as usual," said Denton. He threw his hat into a corner of the room and dropped into a chair. "Well, I suppose you want my report."

"Please."

"I may as well start at the beginning and go on straight through. As you know, Hambledon reached Servatsch three days before I did. He was staying at a pub called the Trois Couronnes, and I took a room there too. Foul place; I think they knitted their omelets out of catgut." Denton sighed heavily. "We did not know each other, of course, and we never did more than pass the time of day, as they say. I used to go along to his room in the middle of the night for conferences; he had the end room of a corridor, and the one next his was empty. By the time I got there—to Servatsch, I mean—he had done a certain amount of scouting round Ulseth's place and got the lie of the land fairly well."

"Ulseth," said Wilcox to the colonel, "was the name of the man who was alleged to be making high explosives."

" 'Alleged' is good," said Denton grimly. "Ulseth's place, as I told you before, was a small farmhouse just outside Servatsch on the Zurich road, rather isolated. There was a house and a number of outbuildings all surrounded by high iron railings with barbed wire on the top. Inside this was a wooden fence to prevent rude people from staring in. In fact, the only way to get any view of what was going on inside was to climb one of the local scenic humps and admire the landscape through a pair of binoculars. There was only one entrance–a tall iron gate with spikes on the top. Very private, our Mr. Ulseth."

"What sort of a chap was he?" asked the colonel.

"Only saw him at a distance of about a mile, through glasses. Shortish, gray or fair hair, usual Continental beard; nothing remarkable about him at that range. He never came outside his fortress, so I did not see him face to face. He was waited upon by a man one saw occasionally who used to come into the village to buy his master's chops and potatoes and fetch parcels from the station. He didn't talk either; he was surly and rather stupid. Not a local man; I don't even know what nationality he was. Everyone talks German there, of course. By the way, those snaps I got of Ulseth with the telephoto lens—were they any good?"

"They came out all right," said Wilcox's chief, "but nobody recognized him. They were small, of course, but quite clear."

Denton nodded. "He didn't look to me like anyone I'd ever seen before. I did try to get into conversation with his servant, but he was very unforthcoming. He snubbed me and scuttled away."

"Tell me," said the colonel, "weren't you and Hambledon a trifle conspicuous in a small place like that? You know what villages are."

"Normally we should have been, in which case I should have left at once, or never arrived; but as it happened, we were more or less lost in the crowd. There were quite a lot of people in Servatsch and district taking an interest in our Mr. Ulseth. There were three Swedes, for example. Hambledon got into conversation with them; they were quite friendly. They told him frankly that they represented a firm of armaments manufacturers in Sweden who had backed Ulseth financially on the strength of some demonstrations he had given which had impressed them. Ulseth told them he was on the point of discovering an explosive twenty times more effective than TNT and only wanted some money to complete his experiments, so they had advanced him some. And then some more. Now they wanted to see results, but Mr. Ulseth was never at home when they called, so they were sitting round the place like patient cats round a mousehole, waiting."

"I suppose they hadn't any ideas about his formula?" asked the Foreign Office man.

"None whatever. Hambledon thought of that; it would have simplified the job if they had."

The colonel raised his eyebrows, and Wilcox explained that the British had the formula for an extremely effective explosive, only unfortunately it was so unstable as to be unusable. "Either it won't go off at all or it detonates spontaneously on practically no provocation, and no means has yet been found of making it manageable. It's not new; our chemists have been working on it for years without success. Hambledon's job was to find out if this fellow Ulseth's explosive was the same or whether he'd really got hold of something fresh."

"But Hambledon wasn't a chemist, was he?" said the colonel.

"No, but he went through a short but concentrated course of chemistry before he started, just enough to enable him to recognize the formula if he saw it. I beg your pardon, Denton."

"Then there were the Swiss police, trying to get damages out of him for destruction of the property of a neighbor—to wit, one cow. Apparently the cow was being taken past his premises one day when there was a sudden bang from inside the fence. The cow was in a delicate state of health at the time, and this startled her so that she bolted for a couple of miles and subsequently died, and the owner wants compensation. Ulseth obstinately denied responsibility;

he said he wasn't a cows' midwife anyway and she shouldn't have been walking about in that state, and it was their own fault for bringing her past his place where bangs were liable to occur. So the police wanted to interview him too, as all they'd done so far was to write him polite letters and get rude answers."

"That's two lots of people after this fellow Ulseth," said the colonel.

"There was a third lot," said Denton, "and I think he was more frightened of them than all the others put together. They came and went in powerful cars or on motorcycles and didn't talk to anybody, but they were Gestapo all right. In fact, Hambledon is sure he recognized one of them as a man who used to work under him when he was deputy chief of the German police. I gather that Ulseth used to come into the village occasionally before the cow episode, but since these fellows started hanging about no one had set eyes on him. I suppose they were after this formula too, but they weren't admitted any more than anyone else."

"Gestapo, eh?" said the Foreign Office chief. "I don't imagine Hambledon exactly sought their society, did he?"

"Definitely not," drawled Denton, "but he wasn't peculiar in that. Nobody did. Quite curious to see the way everyone drifted out of a bar if they came in, even though we weren't in Germany. Nobody seemed to like 'em."

"Sons of Ishmael," said the colonel.

"Sons of Cain. Well, as I was saying, here was this bird Ulseth sitting tight in his nest and all these other people revolvin' round outside with nothing to do but wonder about each other. Tommy got fidgety and said something would have to be done and he was going to do it. So he took to going for country walks with a long stick like a young pole. You sent it out to him, didn't you?"

Wilcox nodded. "Looked very Alpine, didn't it?"

"Very. You pulled out a pin at one end," said Denton to the colonel, "and the thing sort of dissected itself and turned into a ladder with rungs about six inches wide. You fitted a hook on the top, hung it on any fence or what not you desired to scale, and there you were."

"Doesn't sound much like Hambledon, somehow," said the colonel.

"His methods were usually so brilliantly ordinary."

"Yes, I know, but there wasn't any alternative. He had managed so far never to meet any of the Gestapo face to face—they made him nervous; he admitted it. But you can't keep up that sort of thing for long in a place the size of Servatsch even though the Nazis weren't actually staying there. They used to come and go, as I said, across the frontier. So one night he slipped out with his pole and made an entry over the fences, neither of which was electrified. I went as far as the first fence with him and then awaited developments. He said he was going to reason with Ulseth. I helped him with the first fence, and there was a certain amount of subdued cursing over the barbed wire atop. Eventually he borrowed my coat to muffle the barbs with and threw it back to me when he was over. The second fence—the wooden one—presented no difficulties; it was merely a screen. I could faintly see him going over; it was a very dark night."

"Nobody saw or heard you, of course?"

"No. I don't think so. We were on the far side of the place, away from Servatsch, at a point where there weren't any outbuildings or sheds near the fence on the inside. This fence of theirs enclosed a fairly big area, about ten or twelve acres or so. I listened for some time and didn't hear a sound, so I went back to the hotel and waited. It was about half-past eleven when Hambledon went over."

"Nothing to be seen? No lights?"

"I shouldn't have seen it if there had been, on account of the fence. But it must have been all quiet, or Hambledon wouldn't have gone in. I went back to the Trois Couronnes and sat in my bedroom waiting for him to come back. The arrangement was that he should come straight to my room if he returned before the hotel awoke. So I sat there reading a perfectly foul murder mystery and the Continental Bradshaw, alternately, and getting up every now and then to look out of the window. There was never anything to see; I don't know why I kept on doing it. It was one of the longest nights I remember, and I began to get fidgety as time went on. Eventually, at about a quarter to five, I was again staring out of my window — with the bedroom light out, of course — when from the direction of Ulseth's place there came a most terrific flash, obviously an explosion. Never seen anything like it since the Vimy Ridge went up, in the last war. A few seconds later there was a very loud boom; the whole house shook and the glass fell out of my window. I hardly knew what to do. I naturally hoped that it was Hambledon who'd blown the place up and that he would presently arrive, so I stayed put. Lights appeared all over Servatsch. In a few minutes car and cycle lights were rushing up the road in the direction of the chateau Ulseth. Disturbed noises took place all over the hotel, and there was an indignation meeting in the corridor outside my room. They said that the British had dropped a bomb. I knew that wasn't right, as I hadn't heard any aircraft. I waited and waited, and when the coast was clear I went along to Hambledon's room." Denton stopped and coughed.

"Have a drink," said the Foreign Office man sympathetically. Wilcox brought whisky and glasses from a cupboard and administered refreshment.

"Thanks," said Denton. "Well, here's luck. I went into Hambledon's room, and it was completely bare and empty — except for the furniture, I mean. His luggage had gone and all his clothes; there was nothing of Hambledon's left. Even his attaché case with the Heroes people's papers in it had gone. There was the hotel's bill for the week lying on the table with the necessary money lying on it, and," said Denton emphatically, "the money was Hambledon's."

"How could you possibly tell that?" asked the colonel.

"There was a five-franc note among it which was filthily dirty and torn almost across. Hambledon showed it to me only the night before, with a few incisive comments upon foreign currencies, and I mended it for him with stamp paper. I recognized it."

The colonel grunted, and Denton continued.

"It could not have been Hambledon himself who came to the hotel, or he would have come to me. Therefore it was somebody else making it appear that Hambledon had left, and since he'd got Tommy's money, something had happened to Tommy. I got out of the hotel and up the road as hard as I could leg it. By the time I got there the place was fair hotching with gendarmerie, villagers, and the unfortunate Swedes in leather overcoats over striped pajamas. I suppose they thought their money had gone up with the bang, and I expect they were quite right, too. The farmhouse was wrecked, the other buildings were damaged, and most of the fence blown flat. They dug the body of the manservant out of the ruins of the house; he was quite dead. The police found Ulseth still partially alive and rushed him off to hospital, where he died later the same day. I did not see him myself, but I see no reason to doubt it. Hambledon simply disappeared completely, and though I hunted round very thoroughly for several days till I was warned off by the authorities, I could find no trace of him whatever. It is true one usually finds something, but not always. If he was close enough to that explosion, one wouldn't. The only thing I found was his scaling ladder where he left it on the fence. I collected that."

There was a short space of silence. As no one seemed to have any comment to make, Denton emptied his glass and continued.

"Besides, if Hambledon had survived he would have got in touch with me, or you, or somebody. Nobody else in the district found a body or a wounded man. I made sure of that."

"It sounds fairly final," said the colonel with a sigh. "Poor old Hambledon. Not to beat about the bush, I suppose he was one of the most brilliant men who ever served the department."

"I should say quite the most brilliant," said the head of the department concerned. "They say that no man is irreplaceable, but I personally regard his death as an irreparable loss. He had a very remarkable career, very remarkable."

"He lasted longer than most people," said Wilcox. "Of course he was lost for years in Germany and turned up again. I wish I could think he was likely to do so this time."

"I'm afraid not," said Denton.

"What was he ostensibly supposed to be doing in Servatsch?" asked the colonel.

"Merely recuperating after influenza," said Wilcox. "He was the Herr Theophilus Hartzer, of Swiss nationality, a traveler for the Swiss Heroas Company of railway wagon manufacturers. The firm is quite real; it is actuated mainly by British capital and some of the directors are British subjects. Even those directors who are themselves Swiss are pro-British in sympathy. After all, before the war we took the bulk of their products. They were very helpful. The British directors knew of Hambledon as a British intelligence agent and did all they could: they provided him with all necessary credentials and a wonderful range of literature—complete with pictures, diagrams, and production charts—about their goods. Hambledon, I imagine, merely knew a railway truck when he saw one before he became Herr Hartzer with a perfectly good Swiss passport. If he'd read all their leaflets, handbooks, and folders he must have become quite an expert before he died. I wish he hadn't," added Wilcox impulsively.

"A very good cover," said the colonel. "I wonder what the firm do with their products now they can't get 'em through to us."

"Sell 'em to Germany," said Denton. "What? A firm must live. Besides, Switzerland can't afford to annoy Germany."

"Looks like being a complete clear-up of the Servatsch problem, anyway," said the Foreign Office chief. "Ulseth is dead, his servant is dead, and I imagine his notes and formulas are literally scattered to the four winds. We can write off this item, I think, unless anything very unforeseen turns up."

"What did the various parties do then?" asked the colonel. "The different people who wanted to interview Ulseth, I mean."

"The Swiss police immediately swept in and tidied up. They said they thought a claim for the cow might be laid against Ulseth's estate; there was enough salvage from the wreck to cover that. They are advertising for his heirs and assignees. I wish 'em luck. The Swedes merely heaved deep sighs when they heard Ulseth was dead, packed their bags, and went away. Back to Sweden, presumably; I don't know. The Gestapo hung around for days, nosing about, asking questions, and picking up any odd scraps of paper they could find scattered over the hillside. I don't think any of it was any good; I got there first. No, it was a clean sweep. The Servatsch problem is solved—dissolved, in fact." He sighed.

"I suppose there is nothing more we can do," said the colonel.

"Nothing, in my opinion," said the Foreign Office man. "We have, as a matter of routine, circularized our agents everywhere, including Germany, to keep a lookout for Hambledon, alias Herr Theophilus Hartzer, but I should be very surprised if we got any result. Very surprised indeed."

"Yes," said the colonel. "But what I want to know is who went into Hambledon's room, packed his things, and took the luggage away? And paid the bill. Why pay the bill?"

"To make it appear that Hambledon had left suddenly," said Denton. "To catch the 4:15 A.M. from Servatsch, for instance. I may as well say that I went down to the station and asked if anyone resembling Hambledon left by that train, though I didn't believe it for a moment. Only one passenger boarded that train, and that was a local Servatsch man well known to the station staff. Various people arrived, but they did not interest me. As for who took the luggage, frankly I don't know."

"It must have been taken out before the explosion," said Wilcox. "I mean, I suppose that somebody could have walked into the hotel unobserved while everyone was running about asking what the noise was; but he wouldn't have had time to pack before you went along, Denton, would he?"

"No. Certainly not. Besides, someone would have seen him. I should think the only person who didn't open their bedroom door and leap out was me. No, the packing was done earlier. I asked the porter if anyone came in between midnight, when I returned, and the time of the explosion, and he said no one at all. But he sleeps in his little chair—I've seen him—and the front door is never locked. Someone came in and went out again without being seen, that's all."

"Someone else staying in the hotel?" suggested the colonel.

"Very few people there. The three Swedes, three or four stray ladies who knitted, Hambledon, and myself. Also I had a look round each of their rooms at a well-chosen moment. Besides, you forget. Whoever it was had been in touch with Hambledon, or he wouldn't have had that five-franc note."

"It looks to me," said the Foreign Office man, "as though Hambledon must have been already dead, since it was necessary to make it appear that he had just gone away of his own accord."

"Then he didn't die in the explosion," said the colonel.

"I don't know anything at all," said Denton in an exasperated voice. "Somebody passed twice within a few yards of my bedroom door, and though I was awake and listening, I didn't hear a sound. I put it down to those Nazi blighters who were always nosing about, but that may be my uncharitable dislike of the Nazis. If it rained on my birthday I should think it was their fault. It's just possible that the fellow whom Hambledon thought he recognized also thought he recognized Hambledon, so they went through his luggage. That's reasonable, so far as it goes, but they wouldn't pack it up and take it away."

"Nor pay the hotel bill," said Wilcox.

"No. More likely to rob the till in passing," said Denton savagely.

"If Hambledon was already dead, who blew up Ulseth?" asked the colonel, but Denton merely shook his head.

"I suppose he blew himself up," said Wilcox. "Hambledon wouldn't have done it. He might have hit the man on the head or shot him, but not blow up the whole place, surely?"

"It would have been a good way of concealing the fact that Ulseth had been brained with a poker," said Denton. He rose impatiently and kicked his chair back. "It's sheer waste of time sitting here arguing when we don't know enough to argue about. Somebody outed Hambledon and evaded me and got away with it—that's all we know. I shall go and put my head in the fountains in Trafalgar Square; perhaps that'll give me an idea. Good-by." He walked out of the room and slammed the door behind him.

"If I hear anything," said the Foreign Office man, "I will let you know."

"Personally," said the colonel, "I shall look forward impatiently to the Judgment Day. I don't think we shall hear anything before that. Poor Hambledon."

As Denton had said, directly after the explosion the Swiss police swept in and tidied up. There were several of them in the neighborhood, in addition to the local gendarme, because the Zurich police were beginning to take an interest in Herr Ulseth. At the time of the cow episode the police were successful in interviewing him once, though their later efforts to see him were all failures. During that interview they obtained from him, as a matter of routine, particulars about himself and his origins. He was, he said, a Swiss citizen by birth, born in Semione in the pleasant canton of Ticino in 1893, that he was educated in Lucerne and took a science degree in the University of Milan and that he was by profession an experimental chemist. The police looked with natural distaste upon a chemist whose experiments were of so violent a character and sought about for means of persuading him to go and live elsewhere, preferably outside Switzerland, With this in view they checked his statements and found that in the village of Semione, where memories are long, there was no trace of any Ulseth.

"Strange," said the superintendent in Zurich. "It's not so long ago, and he said his parents lived there many years."

"I am not myself surprised," said the inspector, who came from the South. "I spoke to him in Romansh and he failed to comprehend me."

"Try the Lucerne school he mentioned," said the superintendent.

But the Lycée of St. Joseph in Lucerne also disclaimed the budding Ulseth.

"He is a liar, it appears," said the superintendent. "I wonder who he really is. It would be helpful to have his fingerprints. Go and try to see him again and see if you can get them. I dislike mysterious people who make explosions."

But Ulseth was not to be seen, and the inspector was giving it up as a bad job when the roar of the chemist's last experiment brought all Servatsch out of their beds in the chilly hour before the dawn. The inspector collected his gendarmes and rushed up to the scene to find the house turned into rubble round a large hole in the ground and a semiconscious man, blackened and dirty and much cut up, lying some twenty yards in front of where the door used to be. Around him were the ruins of a chair.

"Which one is this?" asked the inspector, gingerly turning him over. "Ulseth or the servant?"

"It is Herr Ulseth," said the gendarme from Servatsch. "He has a beard; the servant was clean-shaven."

"He is still alive," said the inspector. "Is there a doctor in Servatsch? No, I thought not. Put him in that shed over there and get that big hire car from the village. He'd better go to hospital in Zurich. Gently, now. Get a door or something to carry him on."

"I have some morphia tablets," said the Servatsch gendarme, "in case of accidents on the mountains."

"Give him one. Tell all these people to stand back and get out of the way; the whole village seems to be in the act of arriving. Tell them we expect another explosion at any moment."

The village recoiled obediently, but certain strangers, refusing to be alarmed, insisted on helping to carry the injured man and asked what was to be done with him.

"Hospital in Zurich," answered the gendarme surlily, for he disliked these visitors from over the German border. "Thank you for your help; that will do. Best get back out of the way now; there's no knowing what may happen next."

The Nazis retired with unexpected readiness, and the police went on searching the ruins by torchlight till the car should arrive. They found the other body in installments, but that was all. The big car arrived from Servatsch, and the wounded man was lifted carefully into the back seat, a gendarme sitting on either side of him. The inspector sat in the front seat beside the police driver, and the car moved off just before a tall man arrived, having run all the way from the Trois Couronnes, and began a vain search for the missing Hambledon.

"Careful over these ruts," said the inspector to the driver. "Take it slowly till we reach the main road. We do not wish to complete upon Herr Ulseth, by shaking, the work begun by the explosion."

"No," said the driver, anxiously trying to avoid the bumps in the road. "He appeared to me to be, in effect, considerably damaged. No Christian would wish to harm the poor man further."

"That is so," agreed the inspector. "Besides, when he recovers consciousness I want him to talk. I was looking, only two days ago, through a number of dossiers of international criminals, and the portrait and particulars of one of them reminded me strongly of this man. Only the name on the dossier was not Ulseth."

"Indeed?" said the driver. "That is interesting, and he must certainly be preserved alive if possible. Though it is a consolation to remember that his fingerprints will be just as good when he is dead."

The car turned on to the main road and gathered speed, with powerful head lamps lighting up the turns and bends as they came.

"Was the subject of the dossier you mentioned a chemist?" asked the driver.

"No. A swindler. A confidence trickster. His career is fairly well known, and if this is the same man, I shall be surprised to learn that he knows much about explosives."

"He seems to have been undoubtedly successful on this occasion," said the driver.

"Any fool with an elementary textbook can make explosives," said the inspector. "It is when one manages to render them controllable that real success is attained."

The car rounded a bend in the road and skidded, with complete disregard of its damaged passenger, to an abrupt stop before a barricade hastily improvised from timber which had been stacked at the side of the road. Several men, in civilian clothes but armed with revolvers, appeared suddenly beside the car.

"Halt," they said imperiously. "No trouble will be made, please. Nevertheless, we are taking possession of your passenger."

"What is this unwarrantable—" began the inspector, but a revolver pushed against his tunic hushed him as by a spell. The men in the road opened the rear doors of the car and said, "Out, please," to the two gendarmes sitting beside the casualty.

One of them obeyed promptly, but the other drew his revolver, or attempted to do so. Before he had it clear of the holster a gun cracked in the road and the unfortunate man rolled out of the car in a heap.

"Lift out the Herr Professor," said the leader, and four men helped Ulseth out of the car and carried him to another which was waiting in the shadows.

"We told you not to cause trouble," said the leader to the inspector. "You have only yourselves to blame for this," and he indicated the wounded gendarme who was rolling about in the dust. The ambush party then climbed into the waiting car with their patient and drove away at a high speed in the direction of Germany.

The inspector got out of his car and made several ineffective attempts to speak, but rage choked him. One of the gendarmes suggested telephoning orders for the car to be stopped at the frontier.

"No," said the inspector unwillingly. "I must obtain authority in Zurich. My poor Heller! Pick him up; we will drive on."

They removed the barricade and drove to Zurich as fast as the road would let them. Heller was rushed to hospital, but he died half an hour after admission.

"Discretion," said the superintendent to the sizzling inspector, "discretion. Incidents are to be avoided at all costs. These are our definite orders."

"Even if the 'incident' includes the murder of our own men?"

"Even so," said the superintendent sadly, "for many more would die if we gave occasion for reprisals—God curse the Germans root and branch! Heller died of an accident, and Switzerland remains at peace."

So when the newspapers announced next morning that the distinguished scientist Ulseth had died in hospital as a result of the fatal explosion at Servatsch which had also killed his servant, nobody corrected the mistake. Heller's wife was told of an unfortunate accident at revolver practice, and the newspaper paragraph which reported it was much shorter than the one relating to Ulseth. For peace was bought in many strange currencies in 1941.

Chapter II

Explosion at Servatsch

TOMMY HAMBLEDON climbed carefully over the wooden fence, left his inconspicuous scaling ladder hanging there in case he wished to leave the premises in a hurry, and looked carefully about him.

"I don't think this was a good idea," he said to himself, for Hambledon was always nervous at the outset of an adventure. "Invading fortresses single-handed is not really in my line, especially at my age. Thank goodness the sky is clearing; it's getting quite starlight now. There's the long barn away on the left there. Denton says it's a store. Denton ought to be doing this, not me; he'd enjoy it. I wonder if the place is festooned with tripwires attached to loud electric bells. It was a good thing that iron fence wasn't electrified, or was it? If it had been I should have bounced backward off it into the edelweiss, or whatever the local weeds are called, and could then have picked myself up and gone home to bed; how lovely. Straight across from here, avoiding the ancient pond, and we reach what Denton says is the blighter's workshop. No, there don't seem to be any wires. I wonder what time Herr Ulseth goes to bed. I have a nasty feeling it's too early; an hour later would have been better. And about ten years later better still. This is where they dump their empty tins. I avoid that with care. Or shall I kick them about and meow loudly, hoping that Ulseth will think the cats are having a night out and take no notice of further noises? Better not; perhaps the Servatsch cats sing differently from English ones. I wonder why I always get such ridiculous ideas on these occasions—wind up, no doubt. Here is a stone wall; what—if anything—is waiting for me on the other side, and if I stick my head over will somebody biff it? Perhaps there's a gap in it round this corner–there is. Good. Now for the workshop. Better work round behind it in case there's anyone about, though I see no light in the windows. Great care is indicated."

Hambledon crouched down and crept round behind the building—merely a substantial outhouse which was once a stable. He felt his way with his fingertips on the ground, in case of unseen obstructions, and reached the last corner abutting on the front of the building. Here he dropped to his knees and put his head cautiously round the corner.

Something cold touched the back of his neck, and he started violently as a harsh voice behind him said, "Hands up! And get up."

The language used was German.

"I can't possibly hands up and get up at the same time," said Tommy plaintively. "I want my hands to get up with."

"Get up, then," said the voice, "but no monkey tricks. Now, hands up. Walk forward slowly— No, not that way. Turn half right, down that path to the house." The owner of the voice switched on a small electric torch, and Tommy's shadow moved before him along a concrete path and up four steps to the front door of the house. At this point the revolver was removed from the back of his neck and placed against his spine in the neighborhood of his waist instead, a move which in Hambledon's opinion was no improvement at all.

"Have I the honor to address Herr Ulseth?" he asked politely.

"You have," said the voice, and immediately shouted, "Joachim!"

"I am so glad," said Hambledon. "I came here on purpose to see you."

"It seemed like it," said Ulseth sarcastically, "crawling round my place on your hands and knees. Joachim! Joachim!"

"Perhaps he's asleep," said Tommy helpfully. "Shall I ring the bell?"

"Keep your hands up!" snapped Ulseth. *"Joachim!"*

There came a sound from within of heavy footsteps down a stone passage, and the door opened.

"In!" said Ulseth. "Turn left. Wait. Joachim, switch the lights on." The servant did so, and Hambledon walked forward into a bare room furnished with a large table and a few hard chairs. Ulseth followed, still menacing him with the revolver, while Joachim awaited further instructions by the door. Hambledon turned and saw Ulseth for the first time: a nondescript, medium-sized man with a beard and fishlike eyes.

"I owe you," said Hambledon courteously, "a sincere apology for my unceremonious entry, but—"

"Don't bother to apologize."

"Oh, but I must. You see, it doesn't seem much good ringing at your gate."

"No?"

"No. Nobody is admitted, are they?"

"Has it not occurred to you that that might be because I do not desire visitors?" said Ulseth.

"Oh, quite. But until you met me you couldn't know whether you would enjoy meeting me or not," said Tommy logically.

"Sit down in that chair," said Ulseth peremptorily. "Joachim, get the rope out of the hall. Just behind you, on the settle. That's right. Now tie him to the chair. Round his waist and round the back of the chair. Now tie his arms to the back of the chair too— Cut the rope, idiot! That's right. Now his legs to the front chair legs. That will do; you may go."

"Will you want me again tonight?" asked Joachim.

"I don't think so; you can go to bed. If I do want you, you can always get up again."

Joachim went out without another word, but as he shut the door he threw a look at his master which was not one of affection, and it occurred to Tommy that here might be an ally.

"Allow me to introduce myself," he said politely. "Theophilus Hartzer of Zurich, traveler for the Heroas Wagon Company of Zurich."

"Really," said Ulseth. "Now what would a fat little drummer of the Heroas Wagon Company want with the Herr Professor Ulseth so badly that he scales fences in the dark to reach him?"

Tommy winced slightly. "Fat" was unfair. More, it was untrue.

"The fact is—" he began.

"The fact is," interrupted Ulseth, "that you are no more a traveler for a wagon company than I am. You are one of these blasted Swiss detectives, that's what."

He walked across to the helpless Hambledon and went through his pockets, taking out all his papers and his automatic.

"I am nothing of the sort," said Hambledon indignantly, "and your behavior is an outrage."

"This is quite a nice passport," said Ulseth, taking no notice. "It seems to have visas for every country in Europe except the principality of Montenegro."

"Naturally," said Hambledon coldly. "Travelers generally travel a good deal. Look here, Herr Ulseth, you are making a big mistake. I have come here with a proposition to put before you."

Ulseth crossed the room to a cracked and discolored mirror on the wall and looked from his own reflection to the passport photograph and back again.

"I have no interest in wagons," he said, "except passenger wagons en route for the nearest frontier. I am going to leave, Herr—what is it?—Hartzer, and I think this will help me. Absurd things, passport photographs, don't you think? Really, this one will do quite well for me if I clip my beard a bit and thin out my eyebrows. Yours are scanty; deficiency of thyroid, you know."

"I have come here," said Hambledon again, "to make you an offer on behalf of a certain government for the formula of an explosive which I understand you have discovered. That is, if upon investigation the formula—"

"So you're the agent of a foreign power now, are you?" said Ulseth sarcastically. "I thought you traveled for a—"

"So I do," interrupted Hambledon. "I am merely a messenger sent here to open negotiations since I know the district well."

"Oh," said Ulseth. He laid down the passport and opened a wallet he had taken from Hambledon's pocket. "Printed cards, introducing Herr Theophilus Hartzer of the Heroas Wagon Company. They might be useful; I'll take those too. A letter from the firm authorizing a fortnight's sick leave on full pay—a nice firm, evidently. I trust your health is now quite restored. Not that it will matter much by tomorrow morning anyway."

"What do you mean?"

"Don't you see? If I resemble you, you also resemble me. Not a startling likeness, but enough to pass, especially after a regrettable explosion. Poor dear Professor Ulseth is going to have a disastrous accident tonight, and his mangled remains can be sorted out by the police tomorrow morning. Any little discrepancies will be put down to the effects of the explosion. I have enough TNT in the cellars of this house to blow the whole place to bits, let alone alter the shape of your nose. Anyway, nobody here knows me well, and the police only saw me once. It is really quite providential—for me—that you should wear a beard. Funny to think that if you'd been clean-shaven you might have lived a lot longer, isn't it? I'll have your automatic too; it might come in useful. It's a nice one; pity to destroy it."

Hambledon was seized with a spasm of remorse, such as had never afflicted him about any of his sins, for having given way to a beard at all. It seemed such a good idea in London, but now—

"I have been considering for some time how to arrange my unobtrusive departure," went on Ulseth, "and have made certain preparations already. The explosion is all ready for use. I did think I should have to be blown to pieces without leaving a trace, but that was not very satisfactory. Some of the people whom I wish to deceive have unpleasantly suspicious minds, and if they did not find anything of me at all, they might conclude that I wasn't here at the time. Then they would go on looking for me, and I don't want them to. I want them to go home satisfied, and when they've examined your remnants I am sure they will. I hope there will be some remnants, by the way. I wonder whether I'd better move you to another room not directly over the cellar?"

"You are a cold-blooded scoundrel," said the indignant Hambledon, "and if I can manage it I'll haunt you. You will look well with a dismembered commercial traveler accompanying you everywhere you go."

Ulseth looked at him and laughed. "Really, I'm sorry I've got to kill you," he said. "You deserve to live for a remark like that. I am quite glad your end will be so sudden as to be practically painless. Would you like to hear how it will be arranged? Just a moment while I run through the rest of your things. Handkerchief—no mark on it. Bunch of three keys—your luggage, of course. I'd forgotten your luggage; naturally you will have to disappear too—abscond is the right word for you. Hotel bedroom key with admirable metal tab, Hotel des Trois Couronnes, Servatsch, p.d. Zurich, Switzerland; room number fifteen. I must visit room number fifteen on my way to the railway station. If your luggage disappears, it will add color to the idea that you have fled. I expect Herr Hartzer is in financial difficulties if one only knew. Gambling or women, Hartzer?"

"Both," said Hambledon without hesitation.

"Well done. I like you more and more. Your sense of—"

"Your sentiments are not reciprocated," said Tommy, "and if I get out of this alive I will look for you till I find you and then I'll saw your head off with a meat saw without an anesthetic."

"Cruel," said Ulseth, "very cruel. Now, I'm not cruel, only practical. You had better have my passport and a few odd letters—bills mostly. If you do come out of this alive, you might pay them, will you? I can't. An appropriate thank offering," he went on, putting his papers into Hambledon's pockets. "You may have my cards too—in fact, my wallet and all. I'll take the money out; you won't want it where you're going, and I shall. Excuse me a moment; I'll fetch the simple apparatus. It might interest you to see how it's going to be worked."

Ulseth walked toward the door and stopped suddenly.

"I am a fool," he said. "I hope no one else ever finds that out, but I am. Of course you have got to have my clothes on, and I had better have yours. The effects of blast are notoriously uncertain: you may be blown into atoms or you may sail through the air all in one piece and finish up on the spire of Servatsch church. I expect your clothes will be blown off you, but they may as well find the right ones if they find any. This means calling Joachim again. He won't like it, but that doesn't matter."

"I think you talk more than any man I've ever met," said Hambledon contemptuously. "Why not discuss the offer I am empowered to make you? It's quite a good offer. Your formula—"

"Because, you poor fool, there isn't any formula. I know no more about chemistry than you could learn from a handbook given away with Our Boys' Chemistry Outfit in a cardboard box. Well, a little more, because I had to talk intelligently to those Swedes. I found it a strain, believe me. No, all this is merely a scheme for getting money out of the Swedes, and quite successful, too. So now you know all my dark secrets, we will get on with the arrangements." He left the room, and Hambledon heard him go down the passage toward the back of the house and call Joachim again. Ulseth's voice sounded hollow, as though the place were bare and empty.

He called several times and then stopped. Presumably there had been an answer, though Hambledon did not hear it. "It doesn't sound as though it would be much good yelling for Joachim from here when Ulseth goes," he said to himself. "My brain's going; of course he'll take Joachim with him." He strained at his bonds, but they did not yield enough to do any good. His automatic had gone away in Ulseth's pocket; otherwise he might have struggled toward the table and got it somehow.

"If I were a pessimist I should think I was sunk," he said, and thrust the thought from him. There were voices returning along the passage. They sounded quite friendly; presumably Ulseth had thought it worth while to pacify the aggrieved Joachim.

"I see," said the servant's voice. "And then we makes off, do we?"

"That's it," said Ulseth. "This won't take long, and then you can go upstairs and pack." The men entered the room, and Ulseth stripped off his suit and stood up in his underwear.

"I wonder whether your underclothes are marked," he said. "If not, this is as far as we need go. We'll have a look in a minute." He leveled his own revolver at Hambledon again and said, "Go ahead, Joachim. Untie him. Not all at once; legs first." He was very careful never to let Joachim get into his line of fire. "You must excuse Joachim if he is awkward; he has not had much practice at valeting. I should not struggle with him, either, if I were you; he is liable to kick if he is annoyed."

Hambledon's trousers were pulled off and the rope round his waist slackened to get Ulseth's on instead; it was something of a struggle, as they were a little too tight. "I can't do up these two top buttons," said Joachim, gasping.

"Never mind," said Ulseth. "Herr Hartzer has put on weight a little during his holiday—it often happens. Now tie his legs again and we'll start at the top."

Hambledon made the process as long and awkward as possible without appearing to do so. There was no sense in resisting violently; they would only stun him or shoot him, and nothing would be gained thereby. Eventually coat and waistcoat came off, and Joachim removed collar and tie to look for marks on them and on the shirt and vest. There were none.

"Good," said Ulseth. "Now dress him up and we're done." When the job was finished and Hambledon trussed up again, the servant prepared to leave the room.

"Just a minute," said Ulseth, in shirtsleeves and Hambledon's trousers with the braces dangling. "I think you deserve a drink — we'll just have one for the road." He went across to a corner cupboard, and Hambledon could hear the chink of glasses and the sound of liquid being poured.

"Well, here's luck on our journey," said Ulseth, and drank.

"Salut," said Joachim, and sipped it. "This is very strong wine, surely."

"It only seems so when you first taste it," said Ulseth. "It has no ill effects."

Joachim drank again. "It is very pleasant. Is this a long journey we are going?"

"No, no. Not really. You will be surprised to find how soon you arrive. Drink up now and then go upstairs and pack."

The servant obeyed. He staggered a little as he reached the door, caught at the doorpost in passing out, and failed to latch the door properly. It swung open again, and the sound of his footsteps could be heard along the passage, irregular and seeming to slow down. They persisted, however, and died away in the distance. Ulseth listened with his head a little on one side and a smile on his thin lips.

"Poor dear Joachim," he remarked. "Stupid, and becoming tiresome. He had outlived his usefulness."

"You disgusting murderer," said Hambledon.

"Oh, don't say that. He is as much a necessary part of the local color of my great explosion as you are — even more so. One must not neglect details, and Joachim's body cannot be missing, you must see that. Besides, he has a chance — a small one. I have not poisoned him, only given him a little something to make him sleep. So it will be no good your yelling for him when you are alone; he will probably hear no more until the Last Trump," went on Ulseth, putting his papers, passport, cards and wallet, pocketknife, and other small items back in the pockets of the suit Hambledon was wearing. "I seem to have wasted a lot of time swapping these things about from one pocket to another, but there is plenty of time. My train doesn't leave till a quarter past four, and it's only half-past one now. I will now explain my simple apparatus; no time to show it to you. You know the German stick bomb? It is a hand grenade with a wooden handle rather like a stonecutter's maul, and in the end of the handle is a string you pull when you are about to throw it. I suppose, the Swiss being neutrals in the last war, you didn't have occasion to meet one. The pulling of the string ignites the fuse, which in due course does the rest. Well, if you have followed me so far, now imagine a stick bomb fastened securely to a board, upon the other end of which is an alarm clock also screwed down. This neat contrivance is placed near the TNT in the cellar below us. The clock is one of those cheap alarm things your countrymen turn out in such quantities; when the bell rings, the alarm winder at the back revolves. Now imagine the string of the bomb tied to the alarm winder, which I shall set for four forty-five. At that moment—some three hours hence—the bell will ring downstairs, and if you listen carefully I expect you'll hear it. The winder will revolve, pulling the string of the bomb. Four seconds later your troubles will, I trust, be over. I shall be in the train heading for Germany, where I might take up your appointment as traveler for the Heroas people unless something better offers itself. I believe you are only a commercial traveler after all; no detective would have been caught so easily, not even a Swiss one. Besides, you had no official card. I wish you had; it might have been fun to use it—outside Switzerland. It wouldn't give one any authority, of course, only a sort of official status."

"If you keep on talking much longer," said Hambledon wearily, "you'll miss the train."

"Oh no. I've only got to wind up the alarm, walk down to the Trois Couronnes and pick up your luggage, and stroll gently on to the station. Still, perhaps it's time I made a move."

Ulseth went out of the room, and Hambledon heard him open a door in the passage and run down some stairs. Five minutes later he came back again and stood in the doorway looking in.

"Well, I think that's all I can do for you," he said cheerfully. "You will be called at four forty-five sharp."

"Does the clock keep good time?"

"You are a cool hand," said Ulseth admiringly. "Er—would you like a drink? I'll get you one if you like."

"No, thanks," said Hambledon coldly. "For a commercial traveler, I've always been rather particular whom I drank with."

"Hell blast you!"

"And remember this. The time will come when you will regret this. Look at this room again a moment, look at me, and remember this scene when you die screaming."

Ulseth turned white, stared round the room, avoiding Hambledon's eye, and bolted out of the house without waiting to lock the front door after him.

"And I hope that comes true," said Hambledon aloud. "Don't know what made me say it; it just seemed to come to me. Now then, I've got three hours to get away from this house." He began very carefully to wriggle in his bonds.

At the end of half an hour he had loosened his right arm enough to move it six inches from the side of the chair at the expense of tying up his left arm so tightly that the circulation left it. Then he began to wriggle his feet down toward the floor. Joachim had lifted them off the ground when he tied the ropes. There was a cuckoo clock somewhere in the back premises which called three times just after he got his left toe on the floor. "If I could hear that thing ticking," said Tommy, "I should go mad." The sweat ran off his nose and dripped on to Ulseth's waistcoat.

At half-past three he had got both feet on the ground and, balancing himself very carefully, he began to shuffle forward, walking the chair with him. It would never do to overbalance forward; if he once fell on his face he was done. He had to stop frequently because his leg bonds constricted with the strain and he lost all feeling in his feet. Then he had to sit and wait for the pins and needles to arise, sting, and subside again before he could shuffle on a few inches more.

When the cuckoo clock struck four he was almost at the doorway, and excitement made him careless. He fell back on the chair's hind legs so roughly that he nearly went over, and his heart almost stopped beating with the fright.

Once in the doorway, it was easier, for he had the wall to help him to balance, and he reached the front door in what seemed like a few moments. Then there came the business of getting the door open. It took him an endless age of struggling to get hold of a handle he could scarcely reach; when he did his hand was so wet with perspiration he could not turn the knob.

At last he managed it, and there came the dreadful business of pulling the door open toward him and getting round its edge. Surely the time must be past; perhaps the alarm clock had stopped. Twice he nearly went over.

He was out of the door at last, on the little platform at the top of the four steps. The night wind blew refreshingly on his face and the stars still shone overhead.

"So far, so good," said Hambledon, drawing a long breath, "though how on earth I'm going to get down those steps—"

At that moment a shrill bell somewhere below him began to ring. Hambledon shuffled to the edge, threw himself down the steps anyhow, chair and all, and tried to roll.

There was a blinding flash and a great heave upward—

Chapter III

A Slight Case of Abduction

CHARLES DENTON was recalled from leave to another meeting at the Foreign Office a fortnight after the first. He found the head of the department sitting as usual in the swivel armchair behind his big desk, on which were three sets of papers; from time to time he glanced at these with an expression of mingled incredulity and amusement not without a trace of exasperation. Wilcox was leaning against the mantelpiece, rubbing his hair with the palm of his hand, and a retired colonel, who had come up from his Sussex cottage on purpose to be present, was sitting staring out of the window at white clouds floating in a blue October sky over St. James's Park. Denton greeted his friends, dropped into the most comfortable chair available, and waited to hear why he had been summoned.

"Now we're all here," said the Foreign Office man, "I will give you some rather curious news I have received. I should like your opinions upon it."

"Hitler got a new secret weapon?" asked the colonel.

"Performing seals trained to tie sponge bags over the periscopes of British submarines," said Denton instantly. "They distinguish British submarines from German ones by the smell of carbolic soap used by the crews."

"It's a lot funnier than that," said Wilcox.

"It could be, easily," conceded Denton.

"That is, if it's funny at all," said their chief. "I am not quite sure. This is it. Four days ago I had a call from one of the British directors of the Heroas Wagon Company of Zurich. He had heard from Zurich that they had received an order from Berlin—a very large order—for meter–gauge contractors' tipping wagons. He wanted to know if they should fulfill it. They are in a position to do so from stock, as they had made them some time ago for an order from England, and of course they can't deliver them here now."

"Those little truck things?" said the colonel. "See 'em when they're making embankments."

"Very polite of them to ask our permission," said Denton, "but wouldn't it be all the same whatever we said? I mean, a firm must live. I said that before, I'm sure I did. It sounds familiar."

"You did," said Wilcox. "Here. Last time."

"I agree," said the Foreign Office man. "I mean that they would have carried out the order in any case. Their politely asking permission was only a pretext for coming here to tell me that the Berlin agent who forwarded the order is Herr Theophilus Hartzer, of Zurich."

"That was Hambledon's alias," said the colonel.

"It can't be Hambledon," said Denton. "It must be the—"

"One moment," said the man at the desk. "I shouldn't have called you back from leave merely to tell you that. I have more. I told you at our last meeting that I had sent out a routine instruction to all our agents to look out for Hambledon or Hartzer. Yesterday morning I got a report from one of our fellows in Berlin that somebody with Hambledon's Hartzer passport is living in an expensive flat in the Uhland Strasse, a turning off the Kurfürstendamm."

Denton sat up. "Tommy's passport? Impossible. He had it on him when he went up to Ulseth's place; I know he did. I saw him put it in his pocket."

"It's in Berlin now. Our man saw it."

There was a short silence, which the colonel broke by remarking reminiscently that Hambledon always did like living in comfort, and Wilcox snorted.

"Even that is not all," said the Foreign Office chief. "Late last night—and this was the point at which I telephoned to you—I got a message from your father-in-law, Denton. He calls himself Weber, Colonel; he keeps a tobacconist's shop in Spandauer Strasse in Berlin."

"I remember," said the colonel. "His real name is Keppel; he comes from Loch Awe."

"Yes. I ought to explain that though this message reached me last it was actually sent off before either of the others. It took some time coming. He said that on Tuesday of last week the Herr Professor Ulseth came into—"

"Ulseth?" said Denton.

"Ulseth came into his shop with a couple of S.S. men as escort-bodyguards, warders, or guides; Weber wasn't sure which. Anyway, Ulseth seemed on the best of terms with them. He asked for American cigarettes, and Weber said he was out of them. Ulseth then introduced himself—Weber hadn't seen him before—and said that though his main interest in life was explosives he still preferred cigarettes that didn't behave—or taste—like fireworks, as most of the German ones do. Or so he said. He said saltpeter is all right in gunpowder but could easily be overdone in tobacco."

"It seems to have been a very full report," said the colonel.

"It was. I got the impression that our good Weber was a little excited. After that, Ulseth made some excuse to send his escort out of the shop and immediately told Weber to ask M.I.5 at once for the name of a reliable laboratory assistant with experience of explosives. The man should preferably come from Holland or Belgium. It was urgent. While he was talking he placed the thumb and four fingers of his right hand, severally and seriatim, on the lid of a polished cigarette box, rolling them slightly as he did so. Then he beamed upon Weber, who does not seem to have said anything—I imagine he was speechless—and asked again for American cigarettes. Weber found him some this time. Ulseth went out of the shop and could be seen outside sharing his cigarettes with his guides—or guards. Then they went away together. Weber photographed the fingerprints and sent them over with the message. Gentlemen, the prints are those of Thomas Elphinstone Hambledon."

Denton shut his mouth, which had been hanging regrettably open, rose to his feet, and took several turns about the room. "Hamble—" he began, swallowed, and started again. "So Hambledon is alive," he said slowly. "He is Ulseth. I suppose he blew up Ulseth and— But why go to Germany? It's the last place he meant to visit; we all know that. He—"

"Yes," said the departmental head. "It's much too dangerous. But listen. Who are the other two? Hartzer with the passport in the Uhland Strasse, and Hartzer of the Heroas Company with an office in the Schönebuerger Strasse buying tipping wagons for the German Government? Is Hambledon all of them?"

"He seems to have been blown into three pieces," said the colonel, "all going strong. I thought you said, Charles, that the Nazis had walked off with Hambledon's luggage."

"I said I supposed it was they. And they are quite capable of impersonating Hartzer in Berlin to get wagons out of the Heroas people," said Denton. "And the commission, of course. This may be the explanation of the wagon agent. But the fellow in the Uhland Strasse flat—a real Nazi wouldn't use a faked passport in Berlin—"

"You're getting mixed up," said Wilcox. "If Hambledon walked out of Ulseth's place before or after blowing it up—"

"Before," said Denton. "Nothing walked out of that place after it."

"Before, then. Why shouldn't he pick up his own luggage?"

Denton merely looked at him.

"And proceed to Berlin by the first available train and start business as the Heroas Company's representative."

"Tommy would never go to Germany of his own free will," said Denton positively. "Not while Goebbels is still with us, anyway. He must have been taken there, and taken so suddenly that he had no chance to communicate with me. I tell you, if he walked up the stairs at the Trois Couronnes he only had to take five paces to the left and he would have been at my bedroom door. It wasn't Hambledon who came that night."

"Unless he saw an opportunity for abducting Goebbels in a tipping wagon and blowing him up with TNT," said the colonel distractedly. "This business makes my head ache. Which is Hambledon?"

"We know definitely that he is posing as Ulseth," said the departmental head. "Fingerprints are definite evidence. He may also be the man in the Uhland Strasse flat, on account of the passport. It is less likely that he is the Heroas man; as Denton has pointed out, that might be any Nazi on the make who had got hold of Hambledon's luggage from the Trois Couronnes. Of course he might have collected it himself, as Wilcox said, but he can hardly be all three, and this one has the least evidence of connection."

"But Ulseth was a chemist," said the colonel. "Hambledon wasn't in spite of the short course you told us about."

"Oh, quite. Hence his demand for a laboratory assistant."

"Have you found him one?" asked Denton.

"Oh yes. A nice young man named Grautz, from the University of Leyden. He has been useful to us before, but the Nazis don't know that, of course. Stevens recommended him."

"Poor Stevens," said the colonel.

"Hambledon must be having a wonderful time," said Denton, "stalling off real chemists who want to talk shop. He doesn't know the difference between a sulphide and a sulphate."

"If anybody can do it, he will," said Wilcox with conviction.

"Is there anything more we can do to help him?" asked the colonel.

"Not at the moment, I think," said the Foreign Office man. "Weber and others have been warned to stand by him, and we are trying to get more details about the two Hartzers. I will let you know at once when I get any more news."

"If I were Hambledon," said the colonel, rising stiffly and picking up his hat, "I should give up espionage after this and take to walking a tightrope across Vesuvius. It would be so much less dangerous."

"I'm afraid you're right," said Wilcox.

As the police car drove off from Ulseth's place Hambledon, between two gendarmes in the back seat, was feeling far from well. He was stunned and shaken by the proximity of that appalling explosion; he was sore and bruised all over by flying fragments and falling debris; he had cut his face and made his nose bleed rolling down the steps, and finally there was the kindly gendarme's morphia tablet. He was, in fact, little more than half-conscious. He was vaguely aware that he was extremely lucky to be alive at all, and he had an indistinct idea that somebody had said something about a hospital. Bed. Nurses. Kindly attentions. Peace and quiet. Excellent ideas; let them be imple—implicated—implemented. That's the word, implemented. Agricultural implements. Speed the plow. If only his head didn't ache so . . .

Hambledon slept.

He was awakened by being thrown roughly forward when the car skidded to a standstill, and only the prompt action of his two gendarmes prevented him from slamming his unfortunate nose again on the back of the front seat. The car door was thrown open, and a rush of cold night air revived him and made him shiver. He shivered again for another reason when he heard a peremptory German voice saying, "Out, please."

"They've got me," said Tommy to himself. "They've got me at last. One of them spotted me in Servatsch, and this is the end." Nevertheless he retained enough self-control to slump back in his seat, and did not open his eyes even when a shot was fired close by and one of his fellow passengers rolled out in the road with a groan.

"Lift out the Herr Professor," said the German voice. Herr Professor? Why Herr Professor? Probably the brutes were being sarcastic. Now for it.

But he was lifted out gently enough, carried across to a waiting car, and deposited, with tender care, in the back seat. Rugs were wrapped round him, cushions were placed where they would do most good; apparently he was not to be shot just yet.

"Is the Herr Professor in much pain?" asked someone.

Hambledon half opened his eyes, moaned feebly, and relaxed again. Still this Herr Professor business, whatever it meant.

"He is unconscious," said the same voice to somebody else.

"Of course he's unconscious," said the rasping voice which had ordered the gendarmes out. "What did you expect? If he wasn't as tough as old boots he would be dead. Drive on, George."

The car moved off in the direction of Servatsch, passed through the village again, and took the left-hand fork two miles beyond it. Hambledon had been waiting for this, but when they actually took that turning he nearly fainted in earnest.

"We shall be in Germany in an hour," he said to himself. "If I had a gun I'd shoot the driver. If I had a hand grenade I'd wreck the car. I should go out too, but not in Germany." He wriggled feebly, and the man beside him patted his arm and said, "Patience, Herr Professor. All will yet be well."

Hambledon sighed and lay quiet again. Who was it who said "the Herr Professor" somebody a little while ago? In a bare room with a big table in the middle, and a man looking at himself in a mirror—Ulseth, that was it. The Herr Professor Ulseth. Got it. "My hat, I believe they think I'm Ulseth. Of course I had his passport and things; besides, that was the idea. To make out I was Ulseth."

The car sped on toward the German frontier.

Hambledon waited till he saw ahead, in the growing light of dawn, a house or two at the side of the road. He then stretched himself painfully, threw up his arms, and slid off the seat. He lay crouched on the floor of the car and whimpered sharply at every attempt his escort made to raise him.

"Stop the car!" said the man beside him. "The Herr Professor is taken seriously ill."

The man beside the driver turned and shone a torch on Hambledon, who squinted alarmingly.

"My orders are not to stop the car till we get to Germany," he said doubtfully, and the driver slowed down a little.

"We could, perhaps, obtain some water at one of these houses," he said.

"No," said their leader decidedly. "No stopping at houses. Pass them and pull up at the side of the road further on."

"Water," said Hambledon feebly.

"There," said the driver. "That's what he wants." He slowed down yet more.

"There is a stream beside the road two hundred meters further on," said the leader. "I have a cup on my flask; he shall have his water there."

They passed the houses, and Hambledon could have cried. When they reached the stream the leader got out with his flask in his hand, dipped the cup, and came back to Hambledon's door with it brimming in his hand. Tommy was still pathetically but strongly resisting all attempts to lift him.

"Better open the door," said Georg, the driver. "It will be easier to get at him."

The door opened, and Tommy immediately rolled out in the road, butting into the man with the cup and spilling the water. Hambledon straightened out as though actuated by a spring and lay perfectly stiff, rolling slightly from side to side.

"It is tetanus, Herr Gruppenfuehrer," said Georg. "I have seen it before." (So had Hambledon.) "I think the Herr Professor is dying."

"I have some brandy," said the Group Leader, pouring from his flask into the cup. "Lift his head, Hans."

Hans, having emerged from the back seat, strained and grunted, and Hambledon rose up a few inches all in one piece like a wooden doll.

"Help him, Georg," said the leader, and between them quite an appreciable dose of brandy went down Tommy's throat. Would nobody come along the road? He could not hold his stiff pose another moment; with a grunt he collapsed so suddenly that the two men holding him banged their heads together, exclaiming "Ach!"

"Quickly!" said the leader. "Back in the car before he stiffens again." Before Hambledon could do anything he was in the back seat again with Hans on one side and the Group Leader on the other, both holding him firmly.

"Get in, Georg, and drive like blazes. There is a nursing home at Singen. The sooner we get him there the better."

"Suppose he dies on the way," said the softer-hearted Hans.

"Then he dies," said the Group Leader. "In any case, it is now the nearest place where he can receive proper attention. What good would it do to lay him out on the roadside? You are a fool."

Hambledon thought he had better faint again, but even this did not affect the leader. As they approached the frontier post the side window was wound down and signals were flashed from an electric torch. The car went through without slowing, and Hambledon really lost track of proceedings till the car turned into the entrance of a large house in Singen and stopped.

Half an hour later, washed and with his more obvious wounds dressed, he was in bed with a doctor and a nurse leaning over him. He murmured something about nitroglycerin which he hoped would be noticed and went to sleep. At least he would now have a little time in which to think. At least he was out of that car and not too far from the Swiss frontier. It might be possible to escape from this place.

But when he woke up in the morning he was so stiff that he could not turn over in bed, and his face was so swollen he could hardly eat. When on the third day he had recovered enough to get up and stagger across the room, he noticed through the half-open door a chair in the passage outside, and on it was seated a man in the uninspired uniform of the S.S.

"Damn and blast," said Hambledon to himself. "Always so thorough, these Germans." He went back to bed.

In the afternoon the Group Leader was permitted by the doctor to pay a short visit, and Hambledon was distinctly snappish.

"Nevertheless, I must myself make search, or I shall never sleep again. Clothes, Herr Gruppenfuehrer, clothes."

"Listen," said the German persuasively. "Why exhaust your valuable energies searching among ruins for what is not there? Why conceal in a remote corner of Switzerland the brilliant intellect which could assist a great nation in its hour of need? Come to Berlin, Herr Ulseth. Your fame has preceded you there—"

"Heaven help me," said Hambledon to himself. "I was afraid it had."

"A welcome awaits you from the most powerful, the most talented sections of our Reich. Facilities shall be placed at your disposal—I am authorized officially to say this—such as could not be equaled in any other capital in Europe. Or the world."

"Very well," said Hambledon after a moment's pause. "A day—two days—to visit Servatsch and say a prayer over the grave of my servant, and lay a wreath to his memory, and I will come to Berlin at once."

"It is inadvisable. I regret. The Herr Professor has forgotten—the Swiss police—"

"What about the police?"

"There was a little matter of a cow."

"Bah! I will pay for the cow. I ought to pay for the cow. I am obliged to you for reminding me. I must return in order to pay for the cow."

"The money can be sent," said the German obstinately. "The wreath also. The Herr Professor is strongly advised to travel to Berlin at once."

Hambledon saw it was no use arguing. He sank into his chair murmuring, "I am fatigued. Leave me alone, please; all this is very agitating. My poor servant! My precious formulas!"

The Nazi rose instantly. "Let the Herr Professor's mind be at rest. He has chosen wisely. Tomorrow the clothes shall be obtained." He left the room, and Hambledon looked anxiously after him.

"They are not going to let me go," he said. "Well, I couldn't very well bolt in pajamas, anyway. Perhaps something will occur tomorrow."

Chapter IV
Nazi Welcome

By THE FIFTH DAY Hambledon was regretfully well enough to be moved, and not the faintest chance of escape had presented itself even though he was once more clothed in garments more suitable for travel than a pair of fawn Jaeger pajamas with pink stripes. He had spent hours trying to compose a telegram to Denton which would not tell the Gruppenfuehrer more than it was advisable for him to know, but had had to give it up. It would have to be signed "Ulseth," and Denton would simply disbelieve it. It would be better to go on to Berlin and try to get in touch with one of the British agents there. All the same, his heart sank at the thought of traveling straight into the heart of Nazi Germany without a further effort to extricate himself, and he beat his brains till his head ached trying to think of some way out. But no solution came to him, and it was even dangerous to appear too unwilling. He gave it up.

"If I have got to be a distinguished chemist visiting Germany," said Tommy crossly, "I will be the most irritable and eccentric scientist that ever stepped out of the pages of a book. The few real ones I've ever met have been singularly mild and unassuming. I'm hanged if I will be. If they annoy me—and they're sure to—I will curse them from Hell to Halifax. I shall merely sneer whenever I'm asked questions I can't answer. Like Professor Challenger with his 'every schoolboy knows' in a horrid sarcastic voice. I only wish I knew as much about chemistry as 'every schoolboy knows.' It is going to be difficult, very."

He got up and looked at himself in the glass. He had been clean-shaven when he was in Germany before, with hair cut short and marks on his face which looked like dueling scars. He had been a soldier when he was a young man, and contact with the militaristic Nazis had kept him in the habit of walking like one. Now the scars on his face had disappeared; his hair was rough and getting long. The beard which had seemed such a good idea was ragged and uneven as a result of the explosion; one side was burned considerably shorter than the other. His eyebrows had been singed off, and various strips of sticking plaster decorated his skull. One of his knees had suffered quite severely, and he walked with a limp in consequence, a limp which he intended to last him throughout his stay in Germany. Hambledon noticed all these alterations with growing confidence.

"I don't look like a leading Nazi now," he remarked to the mirror. "I look like a dilapidated goat. I might get away with it—perhaps. Though I doubt it."

He traveled by train to Berlin accompanied by the Group Leader, who combined the offices of courier, nurse, and, Tommy strongly suspected, warder. For one thing, there was no money forthcoming, though Hambledon did his best. He could not even attempt to escape without any, and Ulseth had left him none.

When the Gruppenfuehrer came to tell him the time of their departure, he said casually, "By the way, I should be glad of a couple of hundred marks or so, if you could oblige me. My own money is doubtless scattered broadcast over the landscape of Servatsch."

"The Herr Professor," said the Nazi awkwardly, "will not be put to any expense on the journey. He is the guest of the Reich."

"I will not insult the Reich by suggesting that they expect me to work for my bare keep. What I want is a small advance to enable me to tip the boots here. He has been civil and obliging."

"That has already been done."

"Thank you," said Tommy coldly, "but I should have preferred to do it myself. I also wish to make some small presents to my kind nurses."

"They have already been more than adequately remunerated."

"But—"

"In your name, Herr Professor, I myself have just given them fifty marks each. This is more than ample, besides the natural gratification they feel at having been of service to the famous Herr Ulseth," said the Nazi in a tone meant to be soothing. But Tommy refused to be soothed.

"My good young man, when you have had a little more experience of life you will learn how narrow a line divides being helpful from being officious. You mean well, no doubt," said Tommy with one of the sneers he had been practicing in the mirror, "but be so good in future as to permit the famous Herr Ulseth to manage his own unimportant affairs. For the last time, I refuse to be treated like a child. I want some money, Herr Gruppenfuehrer."

"I regret—"

"What! Am I to come to you whenever I want a pfennig on the journey?"

"Oh, if it is a matter of a few copper coins," said the German, "that is another matter." He brought a handful of small change out of his pocket and laid it on the table. Tommy promptly picked it up and threw it at him, and the coins rolled about the floor.

"Who do you think you are?" he stormed. "Who do you think I am? A blind beggar at a street corner, I, Ulseth? You insult me!"

"I regret deeply," said the Gruppenfuehrer, rising, "but I have no authority to—"

"Ah! Of course I had forgotten. An underling like you would not, naturally, have access to anything but the smallest petty cash. Send me the local gauleiter at once."

"He is ill in bed," said the Nazi, backing toward the door. "Patience, Herr Professor. In Berlin all will be explained and regularized."

"Yes, I will do the explaining and you will be regularized! Get out of my sight," shouted Hambledon, just in time as the door closed behind the German. "Owl! Donkey! Jackass!" Retreating footsteps sounded along the passage.

"A moral victory, as people always say when they lose elections," said Tommy ruefully. "I may as well have what there is, though." He hunted about for the scattered coins and counted them up. "Three marks seventy-five pfennigs. Not so good. I shouldn't get far on that."

They arrived in Berlin late one evening, and Herr Ulseth was conducted to the Adlon, where the Reich parks its distinguished visitors. The Group Leader took a ceremonious leave of him, saying that one more worthy than himself would come in the morning adequately to welcome him; in the meantime let the Reich's honored guest rest himself and sleep well. Hambledon, who was still suffering from the aftereffects of the Servatsch affair, thought this an excellent idea. He thanked the Gruppenfuehrer in a few kindly if patronizing phrases, had a light supper in his own room, and went early to bed.

The Gruppenfuehrer left the Adlon and went to the Armaments Ministry to report. Yes, he had brought the Herr Professor Ulseth as directed. He described the occurrences at Servatsch with exactness and the explosion with awe. There was no doubt the Herr Professor had got something there. The Herr Professor had not talked about his experiments except to lament the loss of his notes, and the Gruppenfuehrer had not questioned him— Oh, quite. A matter for experts. Not within his province at all. The Herr Professor was without doubt a very able man indeed; he had that authoritative manner one always found in the— Well, a little dictatorial, perhaps. The Gruppenfuehrer had found it necessary to be diplomatic. One made excuses for a certain irascibility in one who had just suffered such a loss— Well, yes, to be frank, definitely hot-tempered. A tendency to throw things. These scientists, these brilliant intellects, no one should be surprised if they exhibited impatience, even to the point of calling one names, when it was unfortunately necessary to refuse some request. The Gruppenfuehrer bore no malice; on the contrary, he would always recall with pleasure his good fortune in being brought into contact with— Oh, certainly. His private opinions were not, indeed, of the slightest importance. No, he had nothing further to report. Heil Hitler!

After which the official at the Armaments Ministry knew what to expect when he called upon Hambledon at the Adlon next morning. He found the distinguished scientist in his bedroom, in dressing gown and slippers, consuming coffee and rolls without enthusiasm. The official introduced himself.

"Obersatz Erich Landahl, of the Armaments Ministry," he said, bowing in the doorway. "I have the honor to address the Herr Professor Ulseth?"

"Heil Hitler!" said Hambledon smartly, with a Nazi salute rather spoiled by the fact that he had a coffee cup in the hand he used to make it. "Uttermost hells, I have now spilt my coffee—"

"Heil Hitler," said the Obersatz, "let me help you to mop it." He rushed forward.

"That is, if you can call it coffee," went on Hambledon irritably. "Roast acorns, is it not? I thought the Adlon would be capable of producing—"

"A mistake has been made," said Landahl, ceasing to mop Hambledon and ringing the bell instead. "I will give instructions that more care shall be taken in future." He looked nervously at the coffee cup which Hambledon was holding more like a missile than a receptacle. "Coffee is becoming a difficulty in our Germany, but there is still enough for those whom the Reich delights to honor. A replacement shall be made."

Hambledon relaxed slightly and put down the cup.

"A cold morning, is it not?" he said.

"We do, indeed, experience the onset of winter," agreed the Obersatz.

"Especially when the door of the room has been left open," remarked Hambledon, and Landahl shut it hastily, with apologies. Having thus established matters on the right footing, Tommy thought it time to be a little more friendly.

"It is a source of gratification to me," he said politely, "that the Herr Obersatz should have honored me with a call in person."

"The honor is bestowed upon me. Moreover, I do not come in my own person, but as representing the Armaments Minister, who has commanded me to greet you in his name, to make you welcome to the Reich, and particularly to ask what can be done to expedite in every possible way the prosecution of your invaluable experimental research work."

"I thank the Armaments Minister," said Tommy solemnly. A waiter came in response to the bell, and Landahl ordered coffee, "real coffee," in a masterful voice. The waiter raised his eyebrows, Landahl glared, and the man withdrew.

"I trust the Herr Professor is completely recovered from the effects of the unfortunate accident at Servatsch?"

"I am recovering, thank you. My burns are almost healed and my bruises are disappearing. I still suffer daily from most devastating headaches," said Hambledon, clutching at excuses for putting off the start of his chemical adventures. "My doctor told me they would pass in time, I must be patient." He added with a laugh, "I fear patience is not my most outstanding virtue."

Landahl thought of what the Gruppenfuehrer had told him.

"Patience and enthusiasm are bad yokefellows," he said tactfully. "Nevertheless, certain preparations can be made. I understand the Herr Professor has lost all his apparatus in the accident?"

"Accident," said Hambledon, becoming agitated. "The Herr Obersatz is mistaken in calling it an accident. It was due entirely to my own carelessness. I blame myself. I blame myself severely. I was engaged in a process of distillation with a small quantity of my product—I call it Ulsenite, Herr Obersatz; forgive the vanity of a creator, Ulsenite—in a laboratory flask. The laboratory was hot, the fumes were somewhat overpowering, I was tired and jaded, I had been working all night—"

"Indeed, I heard that the explosion took place early in the morning," said Landahl, nodding his head.

"I always work at night. No distractions, no interruptions. As I was saying, no doubt fatigue had made me careless. I was gasping for air. I went outside and sat on a chair in the garden to smoke a cigarette, my eyes on my watch— I had a watch then," added Hambledon with a sad little laugh. "The air was cool and refreshing. I remember thinking how brightly the stars shone as I rose from my chair to return to my labors. But the distillation must have proceeded more quickly than I expected, for at that moment—it happened." Hambledon leaned back in his chair and closed his eyes, as one overpowered by a painful memory.

"Unfortunate," said Landahl, "most unfortunate. Had you much in the flask?"

"About half a liter," said Hambledon, still with closed eyes.

"Then the bursting of the flask set off other explosive material in its immediate vicinity?"

"My good man," said Tommy, sitting up sharply, "one does not have 'other explosive material' lying about in the vicinity of such experiments. One isolates them—one segregates them—every schoolboy knows that." ("Got that one off," he added to himself.)

"But—I do not understand," said the Obersatz. "The flask containing half a liter exploded, and—"

"And the explosion took place," said Tommy testily.

"Half a liter—then what blew up the house?"

"I've told you twice!" roared Hambledon. "Half a liter of Ulsenite. How many more times—"

"Half a liter!" gasped the astonished Landahl. "Only half a liter—half a—Merciful heavens, what an explosive!"

"What do you take me for?" asked Hambledon contemptuously. "A child playing with toys?"

"No, no, most excellent Herr Professor. No, no. I was surprised, that's all. Forgive my foolishness. The Armaments Ministry will be most—half a liter—nothing like it has ever been heard of before."

"Naturally. There is nothing like it," said Hambledon with perfect truth. The waiter came with the fresh coffee and poured out a cup. Hambledon tasted it.

"This is better," he said, "though still not equal to that my poor Joachim used to make."

"And what will you require to continue your work?" asked Landahl, when the affronted waiter had gone.

"A well-equipped laboratory situated near the city, yet sufficiently isolated to be private. I shall want to visit makers of laboratory equipment in order to explain my requirements exactly. I shall want some books—my excellent technical library, all destroyed—"

"All these things shall be obtained," said Landahl. "If necessary, a laboratory shall be built. You will doubtless require assistants."

"I will choose my own assistant, thank you," said Tommy loftily. "It is quite bad enough to blow oneself up. I have no wish to be assisted heavenward by ham-handed boneheaded of-the-necessary-experience-not-possessed chemists."

"No, no. I will report to the Armaments Ministry. Is there anything else?"

"The tiresome but necessary money, Herr Obersatz. I am at the moment possessed of three marks twenty-five pfennigs, and until I get in touch with my bank in Zurich—"

"Your salary starts as from today and is payable monthly in advance," interrupted Landahl. "The amount suggested is fifteen hundred marks per month."

Tommy hastily altered his astonished expression to one of politely suppressed contempt. No wonder Ulseth had taken so much trouble to work up this pose; the financial rewards were worth it. Landahl noticed his expression and added hastily that, in addition, the expenses of fitting out and upkeep of the laboratory and the raw materials of his experiments would naturally be supplied by the Reich.

"Naturally," said Hambledon in a bored voice.

"Then I can now tell my colleagues at the Armaments Ministry that Herr Ulseth will proceed with his work as soon as his health is sufficiently restored?"

"Certainly."

"And in the meantime a suitable laboratory shall be found or erected."

"Thank you."

"I will supply you with the names of firms manufacturing scientific appliances."

"Reliable firms," said Hambledon.

"All German firms are reliable since our Fuehrer weeded out the Jewish element in commerce."

"One of the numerous blessings for which Germany has to thank her Fuehrer."

"That is undoubtedly so," said Landahl, rising. "By the way, one small item."

"What is it?"

"An escort will be provided for you. There are too many people who would like to deprive the Reich of the Herr Professor's eminent services."

"But—" began Hambledon, seeing an inconvenient check upon his liberty of action.

"Forgive me," said the Obersatz firmly, "but it must be so. Our Germany is at war—unwillingly, but still at war—and our enemies are bold and cunning."

Tommy thought of the Swedes at Servatsch, patiently waiting at Ulseth's gate. If a mention slipped into the German papers of Herr Ulseth's arrival in Berlin, it would not be long before they arrived, too, and waited at his gate. They had known him as Hartzer, the traveler for the Heroas Company; if they saw him again as Ulseth, they would be naturally surprised, and their surprise might become vocal. Then a spark of doubt might kindle in the Nazi mind, and an explosion follow more fatal to Hambledon than the one at Servatsch. Something must be done to ward off the Swedes. Tommy turned a frank gaze upon Landahl.

"There are some Swedes," he said.

"Swedes?" said Landahl, sitting down again.

"Swedes. They were negotiating with me for the purchase of the formula for Ulsenite before I was—er—approached by your government," said Hambledon. "They insisted upon paying me a sum down as a lien upon future discoveries, and I saw no reason why I should not accept it. They may consider they have a prior right—"

"Pah," said Landahl. "A prior right. Swedes. Pah."

"Oh, quite. But they may come and worry me. I cannot be worried when I am working."

"Fear nothing. You shall never see a Swede."

Tommy felt that it was more important that they shouldn't see him, but hardly liked to say so. If an emergency arose, it must be dealt with at the time.

"You will find these men tactful and unobtrusive," said Landahl. "They have been carefully selected."

"I will give you my opinion of them when I have seen them," said Hambledon loftily. "I daresay I may find them useful."

The Obersatz rose for the second time. "They have been so instructed," he said. "I go now to convey the good news to my colleagues that our Germany has henceforth the collaboration of the eminent Herr Ulseth. I have the honor to wish you good day. Heil Hitler."

"Heil Hitler. The honor is mine," said Tommy politely, but when he was left alone he held his hand up before him and looked at his fingers. They were shaking.

"I have been in some damned tight corners in my time, but never one like this. I'm supposed to be an expert on a subject I know nothing about, in a city where I was once far too well known. I am to have two warders trailing me wherever I go unless I can do something about it. There are three perfectly intelligent neutrals who knew me as somebody else a week ago, and who may be in Berlin a week hence. There is also Ulseth, who said he was coming to Germany; it's a large country, but it would add a lot to the fun if he turned up in Berlin too. As representative of the Heroas Company, this is where he'd make for. Well," said Tommy, setting his teeth, "I think I can deal with Ulseth. As for the other emergencies, perhaps some solution will present itself. Let's hope so. My time may be short, but it doesn't look as though it was going to be dull." He lifted his right hand in the Nazi salute and added, "Blast Hitler!"

Chapter V
Personally Conducted Tour

THE WAITER came in to remove the breakfast things and said that there were two men ready to attend the Herr at any time he thought fit to appoint.

"Send them up," said Hambledon, "in—ah—half an hour's time. I have not yet seen the papers. By some oversight they were not sent up with the breakfast."

"I will bring them at once—"

"Tomorrow I should like them earlier."

"It shall be as the Herr wishes."

"Naturally. Tell the manager that the last brew of coffee was better, but still on the weak side."

"There is a shortage—"

"Difficulties exist, my good man, in order to be overcome. Now the papers, if you please."

The waiter went out with the tray and met the liftman in the passage outside.

"That old rhinoceros in there," said the waiter, "look out!"

"Like that, is he?"

" 'Tell the manager,' he says, 'the coffee's weak.' Weak! Real coffee!"

"Oh well," said the liftman philosophically, "they come all sorts. He's a scientist, or some such, isn't he?"

The waiter was just beginning to say what Hambledon, in his opinion, was, when the door suddenly opened.

"My papers," said Hambledon irritably. "Must I come and get them myself? I thought the Adlon—"

"Immediately, *gnä' Herr*. At once," said the waiter and liftman in duet, and left hurriedly.

"I wonder if this kind of manner grows on one," said Hambledon as he shut the door. "It seems to come unexpectedly easy to me; perhaps it's the Berlin air. Rhinoceros, indeed!"

He received his papers with commendable promptitude from the hands of the liftman, whom he rewarded with his last remaining three marks.

"You work the lift which is nearest to this room?"

"Yes, *gnä' Herr*."

"Good. If you are civil and obliging, there will be more where that came from."

"It will be a pleasure as well as a duty to serve the gracious Herr."

"I sincerely hope so," said Hambledon.

"Rhinoceros, *quatsch!*" said the liftman to himself as he shut the door. "He's a very nice gentleman. It is that Alberich who is a clumsy bear."

"Divide and rule," said Tommy as he opened the *Voelkischer Beobachter*. Banner headlines all across the front page announced the "Annihilation of Soviet Armies Almost Concluded." There were scenes of appalling terror in Odessa; deserters from the Soviet forces were being shot in the back by their infuriated comrades. The Bolshevist hordes were either surrounded in masses and being rapidly pulverized or reeling back in disorder from an unending series of merciless hammer blows which they could not hope to survive. Russia was already defeated. The war was practically won. The liquidation process, so far advanced, had only to be completed, and all the immense resources of Russia would be available for the prosecution of Germany's other wars. *Sieg Heil!* The date was October the twelfth, 1941.

"I don't like it," said Hambledon anxiously. "I don't like it at all. If even one tenth of this is true—and surely not even the Nazis would lie on this scale—it won't be long before the Eastern Front closes down, and then it'll be our turn. I shouldn't have thought the Russians would have collapsed like this, but of course they did very badly against Finland. I hope it isn't true, but I'm afraid it is. Oh damn!" He screwed up the *Voelkischer Beobachter* into a ball and hurled it across the room, only to rise hastily to his feet, retrieve the paper, and straighten it out carefully. He then dropped it in the seat of his chair, sat on it to account for the creases, and was attentively reading the *Berliner Zeitung* when there came a knock at the door.

"Enter," said Hambledon peremptorily.

"The two men whom the gracious Herr wished to see at this time," said the liftman.

"Let them come in."

They came in, two men in the uniform of Storm Troopers; one tall and thin with a long, melancholy face and a long nose red at the end ("Has indigestion," commented Tommy within himself), the other short and rotund, with a round face, bright red cheeks, and very black hair. They introduced themselves.

"Storm Trooper Kurt Bernstein," said the tall, thin one with a polite bow.

"Storm Trooper Wilhelm Eckhoff," said the short man with a similar bow. Then they straightened up and stared at him.

"Chemist–Professor Sigmund Ulseth," said Hambledon in a sarcastic voice, and barked, "Heil Hitler!"

"Heil Hitler!" they chorused, with the appropriate gesture. Hambledon looked at them both carefully all over from head to foot without speaking till Bernstein averted his eyes and Eckhoff shifted his feet.

"Well, now we all know each other," said Tommy after nearly half a minute's silence, "what happens next?"

"Whatever the Herr Professor wishes," said Bernstein.

"I want to go out."

"Jawohl, Herr Professor."

"First to the bank."

"Jawohl, Herr Professor."

"Then to some booksellers' shops."

"Jawohl, Herr Professor."

"Booksellers of a good class, where I can obtain scientific books."

"Jawohl, Herr—"

"Herrgott!" roared Hambledon. "Say something else besides '*Jawohl,* Herr Professor' every ten seconds like a pink-crested psittacotic parrot!"

Bernstein started nervously, but a distinct twinkle appeared in the eyes of Eckhoff.

"As Your Excellency wishes," stammered Bernstein.

"Of course it is as I wish. Wait now while I put on my coat and hat, and we will go out."

Clothes were rationed in Germany, but Hambledon had been supplied with the necessary coupons at Singen by the Gruppenfuehrer. Singen was a provincial town, not a fashionable resort, and Hambledon had taken care to choose clothes of country cut as unlike as possible to the sort of thing he used to wear when he was in Berlin before the war. A flowing green overcoat of a slightly surprising tweed labeled by the tailor "Schottisch," and a broad-brimmed hat "to shelter my poor damaged eyes"—and also to conceal them—together with a beard which looked as though the rats had been at it, combined in a picturesque effect very unlike the trim city figure of Hitler's late chief of police. Also, Hambledon no longer walked smartly; he ambled. He looked at himself in the long glass of his wardrobe when he put his hat on and was considerably reassured. "Anyone who recognizes me now must have second sight," he thought, and pulled the hat brim well down. "Of course there are still my fingerprints . . ." He kept his escort waiting while he put on a pair of thick leather gloves. "Not that this does any good; I can't wear gloves all the time. I just like to feel as completely covered as possible."

He picked up a substantial walking stick—a present from the hospital at Singen on account of his damaged knee—and the curious trio set out; Tommy Hambledon stumping along half a yard ahead of his escort, who followed up smartly behind. At least that was their idea. In practice it was not quite so simple, because Tommy's pace varied from moment to moment. He would stop so abruptly that they almost cannoned into him whenever he saw something that interested him or wanted to ask them the way, and would then start off again at a pace which surprised them till his knee hurt him and he pottered along limping, tapping loudly with his stick on the pavement and glancing keenly about him under the brim of his wide hat. They went first to the bank, where Tommy presented the letter which Obersatz Landahl had given him, interviewed the manager, left a specimen signature, and drew a satisfactory number of marks to go on with. When they left the bank Hambledon stopped and looked about him.

"This street—Mauer Strasse, is it?"

"Yes, Herr Professor."

"Any bookshops here?"

"There is one almost opposite—" began Eckhoff, but broke off with a cry of horror as his impetuous charge immediately dived across the street and had to be snatched from the brink of death under a lorry.

"This traffic is singularly ill regulated," said Tommy, disregarding the lorry driver's remarks.

"Perhaps it would prevent fatigue if the Herr Professor engaged a taxi," suggested Bernstein.

"I have not yet seen one," said Hambledon.

"They are, in point of fact, somewhat scarce," admitted Bernstein.

"Practically unobtainable," said Eckhoff.

"There is, after all, a war on," said Bernstein.

"Young man," said Hambledon, "endeavor not to commit platitudinous imbecilities."

Bernstein looked as though he thought Hambledon had accused him of some new kind of sin.

"The Herr Professor means that he has already noticed the war," said Eckhoff.

Hambledon grinned at him, entered the bookshop, and was directed to the section labeled "Scientific, Technical, etc." He took several books down from the shelves and dipped into them. The mere appearance of their contents appalled him.

"And to think I've got to mug up this stuff to save my life," he murmured. "'O Death, where is thy sting?' "

He selected several with increasing distaste and gave them to Bernstein to carry. There was a section labeled "Elementary"; he drew from this a *Child's First Steps in Chemistry* and a *Beginner's Guide to Chemistry*. They had lovely pictures of apparatus of all kinds, clearly named and described.

"Those are of a very elementary character," said the shopkeeper, who had had a few words with Eckhoff. "The distinguished Herr Professor would scarcely—"

"I have a little grandson, sir," said Tommy with simple dignity. "It is impossible too soon to direct the childish mind into the in-later-years supremely-useful branches of study. Have you a note of those I have selected?"

"I will make out the account in the shortest possible time," said the bookseller, scribbling furiously on a bill pad.

"Good. Send the account to the Ministry of Armaments," said Hambledon, walking toward the door.

"There is one here," said a bright girl assistant with tight hair and immensely strong glasses. "I think the Herr Professor overlooked it. It is the most advanced textbook of chemistry yet published."

Hambledon took it—a solid lump of learning in depressingly dingy covers and crammed on every page with formulas of the most horrifying aspect and in the most painfully small print. The others were quite bad enough; this one was simply frightful. He decided to lose his temper.

"You offer me this?" he roared. "This—this foul outpouring of the most debased Jewish mentality of our century? How dare you?"

"But," began the assistant, "the eminent author is the most—"

"He is a Jew! How dare you pollute your premises with such infamy? Take your wretched book," said Hambledon, and hurled it at the assistant, giving her plenty of time to dodge, for he was a kind man at heart. The book sailed over her head, hit a revolving stand of postcards, and vanished over a counter in a snowstorm of Views of Berlin, real photogravures. Hambledon watched its departure with deep satisfaction and left the shop without another word; his escort followed, sharing his purchases between them.

"Definitely a tiger," said Bernstein out of the corner of his mouth to Eckhoff.

"*Quatsch,*" said Eckhoff, which means "nonsense."

"The man is dangerous," persisted Bernstein. "We were warned about his temper, weren't we?"

"*Quatsch,*" said Eckhoff again. "He's not a bad old boy at all."

"I want some soap," said Hambledon.

"The Herr Professor has his ration cards, of course."

"I have a handful of variously colored permits to buy," said Hambledon, producing a sheaf of cards in blue, orange, green, yellow, purple, and pink. "Very gay. Very enlivening."

They entered a store where the professor was handed a cake about the size of a matchbox.

"Two, please," said Hambledon.

"One only," said the assistant.

"Another next month," said Eckhoff.

Hambledon remembered the shortage of soap in Germany during the last war and did not argue; besides, it would have been of no use.

"Small men have an advantage," he said while he was waiting for his change.

"How so, Herr Professor?"

"Less acreage to wash. The big fat man must find it difficult—Reichsmarschall Goering, for example?"

His two guards laughed, for Goering's size is a joke in Germany as elsewhere, and they drifted out into the street again.

"Now a few smokable cigarettes, and my immediate needs are satisfied," said Tommy.

"The Herr Professor will get as good cigarettes at the Adlon as anywhere," said Bernstein, but this did not fit in with Hambledon's plans at all. There was a certain tobacconist named Weber in Spandauer Strasse whom he must visit soon, but it was a long way from where they stood at the junction of Mauer Strasse and Kanonier Strasse, by the Dreifaltigkeits Church. Spandauer Strasse was more than a mile away eastward across Die Lange Brücke—the Long Bridge—it was the second crossroads on the Konigs Strasse leading out to the Alexander Platz. Some other day, provided it were soon. Tommy felt keenly the need for a little moral support; besides, it was necessary to get into touch with M.I.5. For one thing, he wanted an assistant who did know something about explosives. He must work up to Weber by natural degrees.

"They have no American cigarettes at the Adlon," said Hambledon. "I always smoke American cigarettes."

"So did we," said Eckhoff, "while we could get them. I fear the supply is now exhausted; I have not seen one for months."

"There might be a small, inconspicuous tobacconist somewhere with a few left," said Hambledon.

"There would be no harm in asking whenever we see such a place as the Herr describes," agreed Bernstein.

"The Herr has undoubtedly indicated the only chance," said Eckhoff.

"The Herr is now thirsty," said Hambledon firmly. "Must one walk all the way back to the Adlon to satisfy that craving also?"

The faces of his escort brightened. "By no means, Herr Professor, by no means. But one block further and we reach the Leipziger Strasse, where the Herr Professor's thirst can be assuaged in suitable surroundings."

"I am not interested in the surroundings," said Hambledon. "Only in the beer."

His guards exchanged a few brief sentences. "Gottfried's." "No, he was sold out last night. Friedl's have some." "Friedl's is no good." "The last lot was better."

"Straight ahead, gracious Herr, and turn left. We will show you."

The beer in Friedl's was definitely bad in Hambledon's view, but his escort seemed to enjoy it, and even Bernstein cheered up. They strolled together like old friends up the Wilhelmstrasse to the Adlon, with the two Germans pointing out the government buildings on either side and especially Hitler's new yellow Chancellory.

"Has the Herr never been in our city before?"

"Only a brief business visit some twenty years ago. I have only the vaguest recollections."

"Our city is beautiful," said Eckhoff. "We will show the gracious Herr. It will be a pleasure as well as a privilege."

"Tomorrow," said Hambledon as they parted, "if the weather is fine, we will go on a sightseeing tour."

"The Royal Palaces," said Eckhoff.

"The museum," said Bernstein.

"The Tiergarten—the Sieges Allee," said Eckhoff.

"The Domkirche," urged Bernstein.

"The zoo!" cried Eckhoff.

"It all sounds too with-breathtaking-excitement-filled for words," said Hambledon. "Tomorrow morning at eleven, then? I shall not go out again today. I shall rest and read. The liftman will carry the books if you will give them to him. Thank you. Heil Hitler!"

Hambledon was not by preference a sightseer; baroque architecture, ornate furniture stiffly preserved in uninhabited rooms, and labeled specimens in glass cases afflicted him with a sensation resembling indigestion. He endured about an hour of it and then jibbed.

"If I see too many of your priceless treasures of art and history at one time," he remarked, "I shall get them confused in my memory. That would be regrettable. I would rather see fewer at a time and thus preserve the recollection of them like precious jewels in separate compartments."

"The Herr is right," said Bernstein. "Besides, the contemplation of too many interesting objects at once is fatiguing."

"Undoubtedly," agreed Eckhoff.

"Doubtless the noticeable dryness of the air in these places is deliberately provided to preserve the exhibits," said Hambledon, coughing delicately.

"It affects the throat," said Eckhoff.

"A remedy should be applied," said Hambledon, making for the door.

"*Jawohl,* Herr Professor," said his escort cheerfully, and guided him to a place where a remedy for laryngeal dryness could be obtained.

"This will be quite a good Moselle," said Hambledon, sipping it, "in another fifteen years' time."

"It is pleasant," said the uncultured Eckhoff; "it has a fresh taste."

Hambledon shuddered, and the bartender said apologetically that it was the war. "Our brave troops at the front—they must have the best."

"Certainly," said Tommy. "I absolutely agree. Nothing is too good for them. Nevertheless I am puzzled, because before they went to the war they lived at home, and there was then enough wine for all. I mean, several million full-grown Germans have not suddenly been created."

"The Herr is right," said Bernstein gloomily. "I also do not understand it, now that it is so clearly explained."

"Perhaps the soldiers drink more when they are at war," suggested Eckhoff. "I should."

"Another for my friends," said Hambledon, taking the hint.

When he considered the party had lasted long enough he suggested resuming the search for American cigarettes. The escort took an affectionate farewell of the bartender, and Hambledon led them forth on a round of visits to every tobacconist they saw. In the course of the tour they crossed the Long Bridge, worked up the Konigs Strasse, and came to Spandauer Strasse.

"Left or right first?" asked Bernstein.

Weber's shop was down the turning to the left. "It does not matter," said Hambledon carelessly. "Left today, right tomorrow. It is nearly lunch time, and I am getting tired. We can try again another day."

"Would the excellent Herr Professor not prefer to go straight home from here?" asked Eckhoff anxiously. This professor was definitely a treasure to be carefully preserved. He had the right ideas. This job was a soft number.

"No, no," said Hambledon. "There is plenty of time. We will just walk along here before we give up."

They strolled along the pavement, and Eckhoff pointed out three tobacconists, two on the right and one on the left; this last was Weber's modest establishment. They entered it, and the proprietor shuffled forward to serve them. Hambledon noticed with distress that the man had aged rapidly in the four years since they had last met: his hair had thinned and turned white, and his once sturdy figure seemed to have shriveled. He looked dusty and neglected, too; his coat had not been brushed recently, and his cuffs were ragged at the edges. Hambledon thought of Weber's precious only daughter who ran away with a British Intelligence officer at the time of the Nazi purge. What would she say if she could see him now? Weber looked at his new customer, and no spark of recognition showed in his eyes.

"I am Sigmund Ulseth, professor of chemistry in the service of the Reich," said Tommy pompously. "If you have any American cigarettes, I will make it my business to see that you do not regret having secured my custom."

"I am honored by a visit from the distinguished Herr Professor," said Weber, who had never heard of him. "I regret exceedingly that I am out of stock of American cigarettes. They were sold out some months ago, and fresh supplies appear unobtainable."

"It is the fault of the damned British blockade," said Tommy gloomily, leaning one elbow on the counter.

"Without doubt that is the cause," said Weber. "I have some American-type cigarettes here which have a better flavor than most of those now obtainable."

"They are longer than usual," said Hambledon, looking dubiously at them. "What about the flavor? Saltpeter is all very well in gunpowder, but I object to it in cigarettes."

"Naturally, Herr Professor. These are called 'Johnnies.' The leaves are sprayed with a preparation which improves the flavor."

"And has no harmful effects?"

"As to that I could not say. I have only recently stocked them, and I am a pipe smoker myself."

"I might try them. Give me a packet, please. I am interested in explosives, but I do dislike cigarettes that behave like fireworks and taste like them too." Hambledon paid him and sat down wearily on a stool while he was waiting for the change. There was a cigarette lighter on the counter in the form of a model tank. He picked it up and examined it. "This is a very attractive model. How does it work?"

"One depresses the gun, thus, and the lid flies open and offers a light there," said Weber, demonstrating.

"But it doesn't light," objected Tommy.

"The little machine requires filling with petrol. If the Herr Professor could wait a little—it will not take a moment to fill it," said Weber, fussing about with a small bottle of lighter fuel.

Hambledon turned a tired face on his escort. "I think I will go straight home after this," he said. "If you men would go to the other two shops while this man is making the tank work, it would save time. We can then write off this street."

The men nodded and went out of the shop. Hambledon watched them uninterestedly till they were out of sight and immediately rose to his feet and leaned over the counter. "Weber," he said authoritatively. "This is official. Get into touch with M.I.5. at once and tell them to give me the name of a reliable laboratory assistant as soon as possible. They will know what I mean by 'reliable.' The man must have considerable knowledge of explosives. I suggest a Dutchman or a Belgian."

Weber stood as though he were frozen, with the little tank in one hand and the bottle in the other, looking at Hambledon under his grizzled eyebrows.

"You quite understand, don't you?" went on Hambledon. He drew a varnished wooden cigarette box toward him, pulled off his right glove, and pressed his fingers and thumb deliberately on the polished surface, rolling them from side to side. "The matter is extremely urgent. Please put it through as quickly as possible. The name is Ulseth, Professor Ulseth, and I am staying at the Adlon." He resumed his glove and pushed the cigarette box casually toward Weber. "Now then," he added with a smile, "are you sure you really haven't got any American cigarettes?"

Weber put his hand under the counter and brought out two packets of twenty Chesterfields.

"Thank you very much. That will be a treat. It will also be a good excuse for coming here again. Does the lighter work now?"

The two S.S. men returned to the shop just as Weber screwed the cap down on the tank, waited a moment, and flicked the gun with his thumb. At the third attempt the flame sprang up.

"Good," said Hambledon cheerfully. "Excellent. I will buy that, please. How much do I owe you?"

"We had no luck," said Bernstein mournfully.

"There are no American cigarettes in this street," said Eckhoff.

Hambledon laughed jovially as he picked up his change. *"Auf Wiedersehen,* Herr Shopkeeper. I shall come back another day." Weber bowed as Tommy went out, followed by his escort; just outside the window they stopped.

"Look what I've got," said Hambledon, and produced one of the Chesterfield packets.

"So he had some after all," said Bernstein crossly.

"Hush-sh," said Tommy. "Don't advertise it." He divided the cigarettes and gave his companions ten each. "Make them last as long as possible. Heaven knows when we shall get any more."

"The Herr is a miracle-worker!" said the delighted Eckhoff.

"A thousand thanks, but how did you manage it?" asked Bernstein.

"Aha," said Hambledon mysteriously. "Your friend is right, I am a miracle-worker. And goodness knows," he added to himself, "I shall need to be before I get out of this. Oh dear, what madness possessed me to grow a beard?"

Chapter VI
Reformation of a Crook

WHEN THE ORIGINAL Sigmund Ulseth rushed out of the farmhouse at Servatsch with Hambledon's unpleasant prophecies tolling in his ears, he ran panting down the drive till he reached the gate. Here he stopped and told himself not to be a fool; it didn't matter what that man said; he would soon be dead anyway. The present and future affairs of Sigmund Ulseth were much more important and interesting.

He pushed Hambledon out of his mind and unlocked the gate quietly, for sounds carry far on a still night; he was not far from the village; someone might be about. He slipped through and locked the gate after him, withdrew the key and looked at it.

"They will think it was lost in the explosion," he decided, and carried the key away with him. A few hundred yards ahead the lane crossed a small stream. Ulseth paused on the bridge and dropped the key into the pool below.

He was wearing rubber-soled shoes and padded silently through the starlit night toward the village, considering his plans. On second thoughts, it would be a fool's act to walk into Servatsch station, especially at 4:15 A.M. when there would probably be no other passenger. He had visited the station several times, and someone would certainly notice him. A much better idea would be to collect Hambledon's luggage from the hotel as unobtrusively as possible and thereafter take the path over the hills and get a train on the Schauffhausen line which ran down the next valley. It was not far, only five or six miles. He knew the first mile or two well enough; after that it would soon be light. A much better idea, if only Hambledon's luggage wasn't too heavy.

He had stayed at the Trois Couronnes for a couple of nights while he was moving in to the farmhouse, and he remembered where room fifteen was. Up the stairs and turn right, the last room at the end of the passage. His room had been number fourteen, as luck would have it. Mustn't let anyone see him.

He opened the front door quietly—it was never locked—and slid in, looking for the night porter. There he was, in the little cubbyhole he inhabited, sound asleep in a chair with his feet in the fender. Ulseth tiptoed past him and up the stairs, turned right, and went to the far end of the corridor. Hambledon's key opened Hambledon's door. Ulseth entered and locked himself in.

Six doors away, just on the left of the head of the stairs, the waiting Denton poured himself out a glass of lager, lit another cigarette, and glanced at his watch. "Nearly two o'clock," he muttered. "Wonder how much longer he'll be? He wasn't thrown out on his ear at sight, evidently." Denton got up, turned out the light, and stared out of the window for some minutes, though there was nothing to see but the starlit sky bitten into by the black mountains. "Not so dark as it was. It's clearing and getting colder." He drew down the blind again, switched on the light once more, and looked with distaste at a copy of *The Sky-Blue-Scarlet Murder* (with several pages missing) which he had been trying to read. He threw it across the room and picked up the Continental Bradshaw instead. There is good solid reading in the Continental Bradshaw. How many different ways can one travel from Rome to Copenhagen inside four days?

Ulseth looked for Hambledon's luggage and found only a suitcase and a small attaché case. He packed all Hambledon's clothes quickly and neatly, not forgetting the pajamas on the bed and the toothbrush on the washstand. There remained only the Heroas Wagon Company's literature, illustrated brochures printed on beautiful shiny paper, folders containing schedules of costs, prices, and percentages, model contracts and details of accessories. He put them all in the attaché case, lifted it, and grimaced at the weight. Still, it all had to go, so it was no use grumbling.

He looked carefully round the room to see that he had left nothing behind and noticed Hambledon's bill for the week lying tactfully folded on the table. "I suppose an honest little commercial traveler would pay that before bolting," he said to himself. "Stupid, but one must keep in character. After all, it's his money I'm paying with." He counted out the necessary number of francs from Hambledon's wallet, added a quite inadequate tip, and laid the money conspicuously on the bill. He then switched out the light, picked up his luggage, and walked out of the room, leaving the key in the lock inside.

Getting out of the hotel was a more nervous business than getting in. One is less agile and inconspicuous with luggage than without. Besides, if anyone had caught a glimpse of him coming in they would only have thought it was Hambledon going to bed and thought nothing of it. A guest surreptitiously leaving a hotel at 2:15 A.M. complete with suitcase was quite another matter. Interest would be aroused, surprise caused, and probably remarks occasioned. On no account must remarks be occasioned.

He passed carefully along the passage and froze into immobility by the head of the stairs because Denton had a fit of coughing which seemed to Ulseth to resound along the corridors like the Last Trump. However, it ceased at last and no door opened. Ulseth began to descend the stairs. The fourth one creaked loudly as it took his weight, and he cursed it frantically and silently. If that didn't waken the porter, nothing would. Ulseth put the luggage down at the foot of the stairs and peeped cautiously into the porter's office. The man had been disturbed by the sound; he moved restlessly and muttered something in his sleep.

Ulseth stood like a statue of the Winged Mercury, poised for flight, for what seemed like half an hour but was probably five minutes. The porter settled off again and even began to snore, so the fugitive picked up the luggage once more and got it and himself outside without further incident. He sighed with relief and set off almost at a run for the path over the mountains. The sooner he was out of Servatsch, in the train, and over the frontier, the better.

The path started as a lane between cottages, continued as a track across two or three fields, and then began to climb. Ulseth plodded on, occasionally resting himself by changing over the suitcase in one hand for the attaché case in the other. When even this was not enough to ease his aching arms he laid down his burden for a few minutes and stood looking down at the valley below him. Very few lights showed in sleeping Servatsch: a dull glow from the station where lamps burned high under the roof; an amber oblong in the village, probably the Trois Couronnes' landing light behind its linen blind; a lighted window here and there where someone was ill or could not sleep. No light from his own farm. He could not even be sure where it was in the darkness. Ulseth smiled at the thought of Hambledon still sitting on that hard but strong chair waiting for a bell to ring in the cellar below. He picked up his burden again and went on. The path was clearly marked; even by starlight he could see it well enough.

Some time later there rose from the valley a rattling mutter. Ulseth rested again for a few minutes to watch a string of topaz pass below him, slow down, and come to a stop at Servatsch station. "My train," he murmured. "If I'd stayed there I should now be getting into a comfortable carriage and sitting down on a comfortable seat. Never mind, this is safer though it's damned tiring. Curse this luggage."

Ulseth's watch had a luminous dial; as the time for the explosion drew near he kept on glancing at it and finally stopped, lighting a pipe with a carefully shielded match and keeping his eyes on that part of the valley where his house lay. The time ran on just sufficiently past the moment for him to begin to wonder whether some part of his apparatus had failed him, when suddenly there was a flare of flame, followed thirty seconds later by a dull boom. Lights sprang up all over Servatsch as the startled village woke. Ulseth sighed with relief and continued on his way. Well, that was that, and he was now the only Herr Theophilus Hartzer, agent for the Heroas Wagon Company. Judging by what one read in the papers about Germany's transport difficulties, it should be easy to sell railway wagons in Berlin. It would be amusing to earn an honest living for once.

He wondered whether anyone in Berlin knew the authentic Hartzer; it might be a little awkward if someone did. If the situation arose, it must be dealt with; he had got out of tighter corners than that many a time. "Queer little chap, that traveler, got plenty of pluck. He really gave me the creeps for a moment. Silly." The stars paled before the dawn; gradually the sky grew light and he could see his path more plainly. Ulseth took a fresh grip on his detested baggage and strode out with greater confidence.

He arrived in Berlin six days before Hambledon and took a room in an inconspicuous hotel near the station. He discovered with faint uneasiness that instead of merely registering at the hotel he had to fill in a police report form of some length which, in addition to searching questions about himself and his past, wanted information about his parents, their birthplaces and nationalities. Also his children, if any, their names and ages. Ulseth intensely disliked being asked personal questions.

"Tomorrow," said the hotel proprietor, "the Herr will go to the police and apply for permission to stay for a fortnight."

"Suppose I want to stay longer?"

"Then the Herr applies for further permission to do so."

"Oh," said Ulseth, and decided that the police took altogether too much interest in their visitors. He went for a stroll to see how Berlin was getting on.

The first thing he noticed was that most of the bright, friendly little bars were closed for want of something to sell and that those which remained open were not bright at all but shabby to the last degree. Paint peeling off, broken windows not replaced but blocked with cardboard, stuffing coming out of the seats of chairs. Ulseth went into one of the places which remained open and ordered a cognac; what he received was a terrifying compound rooted in rhubarb. He shuddered and passed on.

He went for dinner to the Pschorr Haus—the Lyons of Berlin—in Potsdamer Platz; he used to enjoy going there; it was noisy and cheerful and the food good but cheap. Now Ulseth hardly recognized it; it was grimy and shabby beyond words, the plaster cracking on the walls, the paint dirty, the elderly waiters harassed and uncivil. Worst of all was the smell of bad fish which hung about in the unventilated air. The place was full, and Ulseth had to wait near the door for a vacant seat. He watched the meals being served at the tables nearest to him; everyone had the same dubious tomato soup and two undersized sausages. Before there was a vacant table Ulseth sickened at the smell; he turned and went out. Berlin seemed to have gone downhill rapidly in this war; it wasn't so bad during the last, at least not till the closing stages. He began to wonder whether it had been a good idea to leave Switzerland.

He went on a tram to the Wedding district, the working people's quarter, hoping to meet some men he used to know—two in particular. He strolled into a public house in the interminable Müller Strasse, obtained a glass of watery beer and a couple of mysterious sandwiches, and looked about him. Apart from the general shabbiness, the place looked much the same and was filled with the same sort of people, though he did not recognize any of them.

Presently an old man came in whom Ulseth did recognize, mainly because his face was hideously scarred where a horse had kicked him and destroyed one of his eyes, hence his nickname, Einauge—One-Eye. Einauge did not notice him and was edging his way toward the bar when Ulseth clapped a jovial hand on his shoulder.

The man spun round with a stifled yelp and turned perfectly white, at least as perfectly white as was consistent with being imperfectly washed.

"Who are you—what d'you want me for?" he stammered.

"It's all right," said Ulseth. "Quite all right, Einauge. You remember me, don't you? I only want to buy you a drink."

Einauge peered closely at him and became reassured. "Yes, I do. I remember you now. Can't remember your name. Haven't seen you for a long time, 'ave I?"

"Not for a long time," said Ulseth. "What's yours? Beer—such as it is?"

The man nodded. Ulseth obtained a second pot of a fluid which owed more to a laboratory than a brewery, and led the way to a fairly quiet spot, uncrowded because it was furthest from the stove and the night was cold for the thinly clad.

"*Prosit,*" said Ulseth, sipping his drink. "Not much change here."

"Prosit," said the old man. "No, this place don't alter much."

"How are you getting on?"

"Oh, fine," said Einauge loudly. "Fine. No unemployment now, you know. We're all doing fine."

Ulseth looked at him. The man's face was yellow, drawn into lines of permanent ill temper, and his one eye was red-rimmed; his teeth had nearly all disappeared, and he would have been better without those that remained. Still, it would obviously have been tactless to comment.

"Glad to hear it," said Ulseth. "Yes, we're not doing too badly considering there's a war on, and when it's over we'll all be fine."

"That's the way to talk," said Einauge. There was a short pause while he looked Ulseth over carefully and then said, "It's odd, but I still can't remember your name."

"Never mind," said Ulseth. "It's not important. I came in here hoping to see Gregor Heppler and Rudi the plumber. Seen 'em lately?"

"No," said the old man, edging closer and dropping his voice. "No, I 'aven't. Nobody 'as."

"Why?"

"They've gone away."

"What, into the Army?"

"No. Oh no. Jus' disappeared." He dropped his voice further toward a whisper and added, "People do, you know. It don't do to ask questions."

"Oh," said Ulseth, unpleasantly impressed. "I see."

"That's why I was so scared when you put your 'and on my shoulder jus' now. We never knows, you see." The old man looked round nervously and noticed two men who appeared to be staring at him, though probably they were thinking about something else and one's eyes must rest on something.

"I'm goin'," said Einauge suddenly. "Thanks for the beer. Watch your step." He added "Heil Hitler" in a louder voice, gave the Nazi salute, and slid out at the nearest door.

"Windy," said Ulseth, thoughtfully filling his pipe. "Very windy. Probably been up to something and thinks the police are after him. Curious. He never used to mind the police. Must have been in and out of jail dozens of times. Getting old, I expect. Losing his nerve."

But the incident left an uneasy feeling behind it; the place looked shabbier and less friendly than it had seemed when he came in; also it smelt, and not of bad fish this time. The severe rationing of soap made itself evident to one fresh from the pure air of Switzerland. Ulseth wrinkled his nose with distaste, lit his pipe, and walked out.

He dropped off the tram at the nearest point to his hotel and had walked only a few yards toward it when two dark figures emerged from an archway and said, "Stop, please. May we see your papers?"

Ulseth stopped at once, though a pulse began to hammer in his throat so hard that it was difficult to speak. Why this? Was it usual, or was this what Einauge meant? These men were in uniform, no use to argue.

"Certainly, *mein Herren.*" He handed over the Hartzer passport, which was examined by the light of an electric torch.

"Your permission to remain, also?"

"I haven't got it yet. I only arrived from Switzerland this evening. I was told at the hotel that it would be in order if I went to the police station in the morning."

"That is so, but do not fail to do so. You are staying—where?"

"At Auguste's Hotel in Sniebuerger Strasse—just along here."

The men nodded, made a few notes from his passport, and handed it back to him.

"You will take that to the police station in the morning."

"Thank you," said Ulseth meekly.

"Heil Hitler," said both men, saluting together like automata.

"Heil Hitler," answered Ulseth, and walked hastily away. Nor did he feel safe till he was back in the stuffy hotel bedroom, for his knees were quivering. When it occurred to him that of course he wasn't safe there either if they chose to come for him, he rang the bell and ordered a drink of some kind–any kind so long as it was good. The landlord for a wonder had a little schnapps, and Ulseth began to feel better. Nothing to be alarmed at; of course they took precautions with a war on. He was obviously a stranger. Hambledon's clothes were made in Zurich and looked foreign in Berlin. The S.S. men were perfectly civil if a trifle peremptory. Yet—yet—there was something cold and terrifying about Nazi Germany.

In the morning the sun shone and things looked brighter. Ulseth scoffed at his overnight attack of nerves and went along to the police station quite cheerfully. He had more forms to fill up and was asked a number of questions.

"Why have you come to Germany?"

"On business."

"What business?"

"I am a commercial traveler for the Heroas Wagon Company of Zurich. I propose to open an—"

"One moment," interrupted the official, taking notes. "The Heroas Company—how do you spell it?"

Ulseth obliged.

"And their products are?"

"Wagons. Railway wagons."

"Oh. And you propose—you were going to say?"

"I propose to open an office in some convenient place and solicit orders for my firm."

"You have credentials, doubtless?"

Ulseth produced Theophilus Hartzer's credentials and put in, for good weight and measure, the firm's letter giving him a fortnight's sick leave.

"Yours are considerate employers, evidently," said the official, reading it. "A good firm, no doubt."

"None better," said Ulseth proudly.

"You can have your *permis de séjour*. At the end of a fortnight, if you wish to remain longer, you will return here and make a further application."

Ulseth left, rejoicing. It was all quite easy. These people were perfectly all right to deal with, provided you knew how to treat them. He must have had a touch of liver the night before.

He spent the afternoon strolling about looking for a vacant shop he could take for an office. There was no difficulty about that; so many small shops were empty that he had an almost endless choice. It should be near the Anhalter goods yards; eventually he decided upon one in the Schönebuerger Strasse and opened negotiations for it. He wired to the Heroas Company details of what he had done, requesting their approval, and returned to his hotel for dinner, happy in the consciousness of a good day's work well done.

The proprietor met him to say that a message had just been received asking the Herr Hartzer to be so good as to remain within the hotel on the following morning as someone would be calling to see him.

"Who?"

The proprietor could not say. The message appeared to be official. It was from the Transport Ministry.

"Oh," said the relieved Ulseth. "Is that all?" He gave an impersonation of one upon whom ministries waited daily, and the proprietor was visibly impressed. Ulseth, however, sat up half the night soaking himself in information about wagons—their sizes, capacities, weights, gauges, materials, prices, habits, tricks, and characteristics. At last he stretched himself wearily and went to bed. Earning an honest living looked like being horribly hard work.

In the morning there came to Auguste's Hotel a fat little man with white hair cut so short that pink skin showed through it all over his head. He introduced himself as coming from the Transport Ministry. "I have the honor to address the Herr Theophilus Hartzer?"

Ulseth agreed with him, and they settled down to business. Before long the spurious Hartzer was very glad he had spent the night studying railway wagons, for the fat man seemed to have been brought up with them as a brother. They discussed wooden ones, steel ones, special containers sometimes refrigerating and sometimes not for (a) liquids and (b) solids. Then they branched off from standard-size wagons for ordinary railways and discussed narrow-gauge railways such as contractors lay down, the small boy's dream of delight, to haul cement, sand, and gravel to wherever these may be required. Just when Ulseth was beginning to feel that this particularly exacting viva-voce had lasted since yesterday and looked like going on till tomorrow, the fat man stopped and took off his glasses.

"There is no doubt," he said politely, "that the Heroas Wagon Company are well served in the person of Herr Hartzer. The Herr has the business at his fingertips."

Ulseth laughed. "My company expect their people to know what they're talking about," he said, "though I think if you'd gone on much longer you would have come to the end of my knowledge somewhere. May I offer you a cigar?"

They were Havanas. Ulseth, unable to bear the thought of their being blown like chaff before the TNT at Servatsch, had snatched up two boxes and brought them with him. Germany's stock of good cigars had all gone up in smoke long before; the little fat man had not had a Havana for nearly a year, he said. He cut the end carefully, lit up and inhaled, and an expression of bliss came over his face.

"Delightful," he murmured. "Exquisite. Ravishing."

Ulseth felt as though someone had presented him with a handful of trumps. These cigars were going to be useful.

"I am glad the Herr approves," he said carelessly. "Myself I fear they are not in perfect condition—traveling, you know—the unavoidable changes of temperature—"

"The Herr is a connoisseur," said the visitor enviously, and made an appointment for Ulseth at the Transport Ministry at eleven-fifteen the following morning.

Ulseth, now on top of his form, strolled in there punctually to the minute. He did not see his fat friend again. He was shown into an office where an oversize man sat behind an oversize desk barking into a telephone. Nobody asked Ulseth to sit down, so he remedied the omission himself.

The telephone conversation came to an end. The big man put the receiver down as though he disliked it and barked at Ulseth instead.

"You are Hartzer from Zurich?"

"I am," said Ulseth easily, and rose from his chair because he had a feeling he was going to be told to stand up. "May I offer you a cigar?"

The transport official glared, grunted, noticed the band on the cigar, and accepted. Ulseth gave him a light and sat down again. There was a short pause.

"Agent for the Heroas Company?"

"Yes, mein Herr."

"Contractors' tipping wagons, meter gauge."

"Yes, mein Herr."

"Can your firm supply them?"

"Certainly. Where to, and in what quantities?"

"What is your price?"

Ulseth quoted him the list price, f.o.r. Zurich.

"Huh. Quote me a price for two thousand delivered at the following French ports: Calais, Boulogne, Dieppe, Havre, Cherbourg, Brest, Lorient, and St. Nazaire."

"Two thousand to each place?" asked Ulseth calmly, making notes on the back of an old envelope, "or two thousand only?"

"Two thousand only," said the big man, somewhat deflated.

"I must consult my firm and will then notify Your Excellency," said Ulseth, tactfully promoting him.

"Certainly." The official drew carefully at his cigar and his expression softened considerably, as Ulseth noticed with inward glee. "Eighty of these trucks will be delivered here in Berlin at once if possible. You will also state the time required to complete the contract."

"Naturally."

"I shall expect to hear from you in the course of the next few days."

"I shall not fail Your Excellency. To whom shall I address my reply?"

"Department D.23. I will give you a reference number. Here it is. MD/46943."

Ulseth repeated it and wrote it down, and the big man relaxed slightly.

"This is a very excellent cigar," he said, waving it in the air and watching the blue smoke drift through a sunbeam.

"I shall give myself the pleasure of sending Your Excellency a box of them," said Ulseth, rising.

"Most kind of you," said the transport man, also rising politely. "Such cigars are rare in our Germany today. I shall accept with pleasure, as an earnest of our good relations in the future."

"I am honored by Your Excellency's cordiality," said Ulseth, retreating toward the door.

"The name is Adler," said the official hastily, for he had no intention of letting his cigars loose upon Department D.23. "Herr Andreas Adler."

"Herr Andreas Adler," said Ulseth, with his hand on the door handle, "I have the honor to wish you a very good day. Heil Hitler!"

When he got outside, only self-control and a sense of the fitness of things prevented him from performing a small dance upon the pavement. He went into the first post office he came to and sent a wire to the Heroas Company about the order. He had to wait six days for the answer, because the company communicated with the Foreign Office in London before they replied.

When the answer came it approved of everything he had done, accepted the order for two thousand tipping wagons, and gave the particulars required by the Transport Ministry. Ulseth sat down on the edge of his bed and worked out the amount of his commission. He blinked at the figures and checked them carefully, but the result remained the same. He shook hands with himself, a gesture he had learned from American films, and went out to look for a small service flat. He found one in the Uhland Strasse.

Chapter VII
Three Gentlemen of Stockholm

IN LESS THAN A WEEK after his visit to Weber, Hambledon received a message from him. It ran: "Grautz, Hugo, University of Leyden." Hambledon said, "Thank goodness," and rang up Major Landahl at the Armaments Ministry.

"Ulseth speaking," said Hambledon. "In the matter of my laboratory—"

Landahl said that an extensive search had been made for suitable premises and three buildings had been selected for the Herr Professor's approval. Alterations could be made if necessary. One was in the Grünewald, another in the Jungfern Heide, and the third out beyond the Weissensee. The Grünewald place was originally a keeper's cottage, which could doubtless be adapted—

"Electric light and power, and main water?"

Well, no. The cottage was remote and had not been occupied for some time. The Herr Professor would understand—

"Next, please," snapped Hambledon.

Landahl explained that there was a disused ammunition store in the Jungfern Heide, close to the Berlin-Spandau Canal. "It is readily accessible, just off the Tegeler Weg, yet private. It is solidly built of stone and resembles a small castle in appearance, having castellations upon the walls and a small round tower at each corner. It—"

"Listen," said Tommy, breathing heavily into the mouthpiece, "I am looking for a workshop, not a picturesque castle in which to spend my declining years cultivating radishes. Has it water and electricity?"

Landahl, who was beginning to wonder whether he would ever be allowed to finish a sentence again, said no, but these supplies were conveniently available and could readily be laid on. The third place, out by the Weissensee, had been a clubhouse and had all modern conveniences. It was at present being used by a band of the Hitler Youth Movement, but they could be transferred elsewhere if necessary. It was not quite so solitary as the other places, there being a few houses in the vicinity.

"I will look at all these places," said Hambledon, "this afternoon. There will doubtless be a car available."

Landahl said that a car would arrive at the Adlon at fourteen-thirty if agreeable to the Herr Professor, and Hambledon said he would be ready then. "About my assistant," he added. "There is a young man named Grautz in the University of Leyden, Hugo Grautz. He was very highly spoken of by a distinguished scientist of my acquaintance; in fact, he was recommended to me if ever I should need a subordinate colleague. Let him be sent for."

"Certainly," agreed Landahl.

"That is all for the moment," said Hambledon, and rang off.

Hugo Grautz was called from his work on the following afternoon by a messenger who said that there were two men desiring to speak to him instantly. "There must be no delay, they said," quoted the messenger, an elderly man who had grown gray in the service of the University of Leyden. Grautz, a thin-faced young man with strong glasses and wearing the white overalls of the chemist, stood in the tiled corridor and looked at the messenger.

"They are Germans," said Grautz, "to send a message like that."

"Yes, Mynheer," said the man stolidly, "our masters the Germans." His face bore no particular expression, but there were beads of perspiration at the sides of his nose.

"As you say, my good Loken," said Grautz gently. He went at once along the corridor and ran lightly down the stairs. He had been expecting some such message for two days now and knew what he had to do; though of course one could not be sure, their errand might be of another kind altogether. Things did leak out sometimes. . . .

However, when he entered the room where they were waiting, his doubts were set at rest. They told him in the fewest possible words that he was honored far above his deserts, he had been selected to act as assistant to the distinguished Herr Professor Ulseth in Berlin. As doubtless he had books and so forth to pack, he need not start at once. A car would call for him at eight-thirty the following morning to take him and his goods to the train.

"This Professor Ulseth," said Grautz. "What is his particular line?"

"It is unwise to question an order. It is only necessary to obey."

"It would be a help in selecting what to take, if I went," said Grautz dryly. "In any case, I cannot go at such short notice. I must see the university authorities, ask for leave of absence, and arrange for a substitute."

"You can see your precious authorities tonight, not to ask for leave of absence but to inform them that you are ordered to Berlin tomorrow morning. They can find a substitute for you if it is really necessary."

Grautz hesitated for a moment and then threw up his head. "My compliments and thanks to the Herr Professor, but I beg to decline the honor. There must be hundreds of chemists in Germany better qualified than I to fill this post."

"Thousands, not hundreds. But for some not-to-be-understood reason it is you who have been selected. Let this futile arguing cease. See that you are ready when the car calls for you at eight-thirty tomorrow."

But when the car came Grautz was nowhere to be found, though search was made throughout Leyden. No one had seen him go and no one knew what had become of him. Grautz had been told to display unwillingness for the post, and he was a very thorough young man.

Landahl, trembling a little at the knees, rang up Hambledon on the telephone.

"A very awkward thing has happened," he said. "I am to express to you the annoyance and distress of the Armaments Minister. The man Grautz has disappeared from Leyden University and cannot be found."

"Cannot?" said Hambledon. "He must be found."

"Yes, Herr Professor. I mean no. We have caused search to be made, but unsuccessfully. It is feared that the young man may have fled the country. He first declined the honor, and then, upon pressure being applied, he disappeared."

"This is ridiculous," said Hambledon angrily. "A solid human being does not disappear like a soap bubble when touched. Your police, or whoever you sent, have bungled the affair. Declined the honor, you say? Absurd. If the matter had been properly explained he would not have either declined or disappeared. Send to Leyden at once someone with a little more intelligence than a cretinous anthropoid ape and get me Grautz without further delay."

"Certainly, Herr Professor. Yet, in the event of Grautz not being available, I am forwarding to you a list of German chemists with details of their qualifications in order that—"

"Dunderhead!" roared Hambledon. "Donkey. Idiot. Fool. Jackass. Double jackass. I said, get me Grautz!" He slammed down the receiver and remarked to himself that this was all very well but he hoped Grautz wouldn't keep it up too long. Hambledon was beginning to feel acutely the need for instructed moral support, not to say prompting. However, it was a fortnight before anything further was heard of the missing Dutchman.

Hambledon was quite accurate in his estimate of Swedish perseverance. A small paragraph appeared in the *Berliner Zeitung* announcing the arrival in the German capital of the well-known Professor Ulseth; it was read with interest in Stockholm. Three surprised and interested gentlemen immediately started for Berlin.

"The paragraph said that he was staying at the Adlon until a laboratory had been made ready for him."

"Then we will inquire at the Adlon."

"He may already have left."

"Then we will ask where he has gone."

Accordingly they arrived at the Adlon and asked if the Herr Professor Ulseth was within. The clerk at the desk said she would inquire, and what name, please? They gave their names and sat in a row in the hall, waiting.

The clerk telephoned to Hambledon, who replied in a weak and pain-wrung voice that unfortunately he was suffering from one of his violent headaches and was quite unable to see anyone. Tomorrow, perhaps tomorrow. He called up Eckhoff and Bernstein and gave them orders to sit in the passage outside his door and admit no one but the waiter with his lunch. He then rang up Landahl.

"Those Swedes," said Tommy irritably. "They are here."

"In your room?" twittered Landahl.

"Heavens no. In the hall or on the doorstep or sitting on the stairs—how should I know? They are asking to see me."

"They shall be removed," said Landahl.

"At once, please," said Hambledon.

"Instantly," said Landahl.

In the meantime the clerk at the Adlon gave Hambledon's message. The three Swedes expressed their disappointment and sympathy in a few well-chosen words and retired into the street outside.

"We will come back tomorrow."

"One wonders whether this headache is genuine or whether this is merely a continuation of his demeanor at Servatsch."

"It is possible. In that case, let us cross the street here in such a way that our departure may be seen if he is looking out of the window, walk round the block, and return to a point where we, unobserved, may watch the door."

So the three Swedes crossed the Unter den Linden as leisurely as was consistent with not getting run over and strolled away. Hambledon watched their departure.

"They have gone unexpectedly meekly," he said. "I wonder whether they really have? I don't think I shall be well enough to *go* out today." He retired to bed with a book.

In the meantime the real Ulseth's affairs had been flourishing extremely. On the day that the Swedes came to Berlin he was summoned to the Transport Ministry and told that the first eighty contractors' wagons had arrived in Berlin, been examined and found satisfactory. He was to wire the Heroas people to proceed at once with the balance of the order. The transaction was entirely satisfactory in every respect, and the Transport Ministry congratulated Herr Hartzer on the firm he represented, the Heroas Company on possessing Herr Hartzer, and themselves upon entering into dealings with them both.

"Have a cigar," said the big man, and offered him one which was definitely not a Havana.

"Have one of mine," said Ulseth with a laugh, and offered him one which was.

"I was wondering," said Adler, "whether it would be possible for you to obtain some more of those so excellent cigars. I have friends—influential friends—who would be more than grateful for a few boxes."

"To obtain them in Switzerland is simple," said Ulseth. "To get them through the German customs is quite another matter."

"It is certainly a difficulty," mused Adler. "Yet, if it could be managed, you would add several grateful persons of high position to the doubtless already wide circle of your friends."

"The knowledge that I had been of use to the distinguished Herr Adler would be more than enough reward," said Ulseth gracefully. "Did I understand you to say that more of these trucks would be required here in Berlin in addition to those already delivered?"

"Certainly. I will give you a memorandum, before you leave, of the exact number."

"If your undoubted influence could be exerted to insure that these trucks were not examined at the frontier," suggested Ulseth, "there is no reason why they should not contain a few boxes of cigars now and again."

"It would be a simple matter to order, on grounds of urgency, that they are to be passed through without the delay involved in examination," said the German. "You would no doubt—"

"Oh, I'll attend to the rest of the business; that's simple. It is, after all, only my duty to check the consignments on arrival at the terminus here."

Ulseth was overwhelmed with thanks, followed up by a promise of further orders for railway trucks of various types at an early date. "We will make your firm's fortune," said Adler jovially, "and as for you personally, you shall find Germany is not ungrateful to those who go out of their way to serve her in her hour of need."

"Serve your fat party bosses with fat cigars," said Ulseth to himself when he got outside. "Other things too, I daresay. I expect there are stocks in Switzerland of brandy and armagnac and stuff like that they haven't seen here for years. They say honesty's the best policy. I never believed it before, but I was a fool. There's more money to be made out of earning an honest living than I ever thought possible. Besides," he added with surprise, "it's rather a nice feeling, to be honest. So restful not to have the police after you." He turned this beautiful new thought over in his mind, and his spirits rose to bubbling point. "This is where I turn over a new leaf in life. Honest Hartzer, that's me."

He decided to stand himself a good lunch somewhere to celebrate the fresh venture, and since the nicest place he could think of was the Adlon, he went there. He arrived early and took his meal leisurely, watching the people and enjoying his new peace of mind. It was while he was in the dining room that the Swedes arrived in the hall.

They left again before he came out. They crossed the Unter den Linden with Hambledon watching them, took the first turning to the right, turned right again in Behren Strasse, and right again in the Wilhelmstrasse.

"If we keep close under the wall we shall not be observable from the windows."

"That is so. Moreover, if we stand well back and appear to be discussing business, no one will notice us."

So they arranged themselves near the doorway of the Adlon, produced notebooks and pencils, and engaged in animated conversation among themselves until the moment when Ulseth, having finished his coffee and alleged benedictine, came cheerfully out and nearly ran into them.

They sprang to attention as one man, removed their hats, bowed politely, and said, "Herr Ulseth, I believe. May we—"

Ulseth, without a sign of recognition on his face, turned sharply on his heel and bolted back into the Adlon. He almost ran through the entrance hall, past the reception clerk at her desk, and down the passage to the back entrance. He had known the Adlon well in former years. He got clear away, jumped on a tram, left it again, dived into the Underground, and did not stop till he was safely back in his Uhland Strasse flat. Here he threw his hat on the floor, sank into a chair, and mopped his forehead.

"Great heavens, what an escape! I'd forgotten those wretched Swedes. I must be careful–I'll never go there again. Just when everything was going so well—"

The Swedes charged into the Adlon after Ulseth, but they were men of dignity and also disadvantaged by surprise. Ulseth was out of sight before they entered. "Herr Ulseth," they said, gasping. "We must see him at once. Our business is urgent."

"I have already told you," said the reception clerk, "that the Herr Professor Ulseth is incapacitated by ill-health today and can see no one."

"Ill-health, nonsense. He has just come out of this hotel and dodged in again when he saw us."

"I beg your pardon," said the clerk icily. "The Herr Professor is ill in bed, as I had the honor to tell you just now. He has not been downstairs today."

"This is madness! The Herr Professor—"

The door opened again, and four S.S. men entered and regarded the scene with curiosity. At this point the unfortunate Swedes made their last and worst mistake. They appealed to the newcomers.

"We are three Swedish gentlemen having business to discuss with the Herr Professor Ulseth, and he—"

"Oh, you are, are you?" said the leader. "Then you're the men we're looking for. Come along."

They hustled the Swedes out of the door and into a large black saloon car which was waiting at the curb. They were taken they knew not where and scolded by someone; they knew not whom. They were guilty of conspiring against the Reich, they were criminals of the worst kind, they were worthy of death. Only Germany was merciful and also anxious to avoid international incidents. They would merely be taken to a Baltic port under escort and put aboard a steamer sailing to Sweden. Let them thank Germany for her clemency and never, never dare to come back.

Landahl rang up Hambledon that evening and said, "Let your mind be at rest. The Swedes are in custody and already en route for the frontier. They will not return."

"Thank you very much," said Hambledon, and meant it.

About a week after this the elusive Grautz turned up in a dockside tavern in Amsterdam. There had been a British air raid, lights had been reported, and the police rounded up everyone in the area and looked at their identity papers.

"Grautz, Hugo," they said when they came to his. "There was something about Grautz, Hugo, a little while ago, wasn't there? Turn it up and see."

Accordingly Grautz found himself arrested, scolded, and sent under escort to Leyden, where he was scolded more violently and threatened with frightful penalties.

"If it were not," said the German police officer at Leyden, "that this professor apparently wants you in good working order, I would show you what it means to defy the Reich. Ever seen a rubber truncheon? Get out of my sight before I lose my temper."

Grautz had a most uncomfortable journey to Berlin and arrived tired, bruised, hungry, thirsty, and disheveled, but intact.

"Thank goodness you've come," said Hambledon as soon as they were alone. "Now you can tell me what to say when they ask me damnfool questions. You can choose the test tubes and things. You can order the chemicals. D'you know I've been reduced to staying in bed with a headache to keep out of the way?"

"But why didn't you order them yourself?" asked the puzzled Grautz.

"Because I don't know the first thing about it," said Hambledon. "Didn't they tell you?"

"No. I was only told to go to Berlin to help a British Intelligence agent and to appear as unwilling as possible, so I did. Aren't you really a chemist?"

"Listen. As a chemist I'd make a good ballet dancer," said Hambledon, and told him the whole story.

"You are in a jam, aren't you?" said the young man thoughtfully. "Something will have to be done about it."

"We will move into that gingerbread castle in the Jungfern Heide as soon as possible. What I want," said the British agent dreamily, "is a nice stout door about three inches thick with a lock on it about two feet square. I want to turn the key and hear it go plonk, with all the rest of Germany outside, and if anyone knocks I shall say, 'Go away. The Herr Professor Ulseth is about to explode.' "

Chapter VIII

Theophilus Meets Romance

DURING THE TIME that Hambledon had been awaiting Grautz, workmen had been busy at the ammunition store in the Jungfern Heide. It was basically a stone-walled oblong thirty feet by forty-five, containing little but cobwebs. It was scraped, swept, and whitewashed. Windows were inserted, partitions put in, electric light and power installed, and water laid on. The result was a large laboratory with smaller rooms opening off it for Hambledon and Grautz to live in; they moved there from the Adlon two days after Grautz arrived. Landahl suggested that Hambledon's guards, Bernstein and Eckhoff, should live there also, but Hambledon objected on the score of disturbance and the guards objected on the score of risk. News of the explosion at Servatsch had drifted round, and though Eckhoff and Bernstein regarded the professor at play with esteem approaching affection, the professor at work was a matter for distant respect and the more distant the better. So a frame hut was erected for them a hundred yards from the laboratory. Bernstein's wife came to cook for them, and Hambledon and Grautz went there for meals. An electrified wire fence enclosed Hambledon's domain, and the guards' hut served as a lodge. A private telephone was provided between the lodge and the laboratory.

"I had no intention whatever of entering Germany," said Hambledon. "These Nazis dragged me in for their own abominable purposes. Well, I now propose that they shall bitterly regret it."

"Couldn't British Intelligence get you out?" asked Grautz.

"I daresay they could, but I don't think I want to go now. Look at the position I've got. Look at the opportunities it offers. It's true I haven't looked at many of them myself yet, but they will doubtless present themselves in droves. Sabotage, for instance. We could make enough explosives in this barn of a place," said Hambledon, waving his hand round his beautiful new laboratory, "to damage half the factories in Germany."

"I foresee a certain difficulty," said the Dutchman stolidly. "If large quantities of ingredients are brought here and there is no obvious result, the Nazis may begin to wonder."

"How right you are. There shall be some obvious results. The first thing, however, is to stall them off from expecting us to produce quantities of Ulsenite at short notice. Unless you have a formula for Ulsenite?"

"No. The argument, however, is simply this. We have produced Ulsenite, but it is dangerously unstable, and that is what we are working to remedy. There is at least one explosive known to chemists of which that is true; I have heard something about that. An explosive, to be of any practical use, must be safe for at least three months, preferably much longer. It has to be loaded into bombs or shells, and these accumulated in quantity and then sent to wherever they are needed. On the Eastern Front, perhaps. When they get there they will be stored again till they are served out to the Luftwaffe or the artillery. Six months would be none too long."

Hambledon nodded eagerly. "That's a good talking point."

"It's more than that; it's true," said Grautz.

"Continue," said Hambledon. "I hoped they would send me somebody helpful, and you look like being the alligator's adenoids."

"Hitler being the alligator? I hope I choke him. Another means of staving off the showdown is by asking for something they haven't got. I've been thinking about this. Palm oil, for instance."

"Oh, bribery, of course," said Hambledon. "That was always easy in Germany."

"No, no," said Grautz laughing. "I've no doubt you're right, but I meant palm oil literally. Oil from palm trees. Coconut oil."

"Oh, ah. No, I shouldn't think they'd have much of that. But what should we want that for?"

"I'll tell you what to say when the time comes. Yttrium, too, for use as a catalyst."

"Come again?"

"Never mind. I'll coach you up in all that later on."

"I hope I take it all in," said Hambledon doubtfully. "But look here, I can't do much good cooped up here. I couldn't meet anybody, for instance, or receive or send messages very easily."

"Ask for a car and a driver," suggested Grautz. "You must be able to go about and get necessary supplies at a moment's notice."

"I'll get a car out of Landahl, but Eckhoff shall drive. He used to drive racing cars at one time, he tells me. I don't want another man hanging about me; he might be more intelligent than our charming guards."

"Or more suspicious."

"Same thing. Another quite serious reason for going out pretty often is to get a decent meal. Bernstein's wife can't cook."

"She can't, can she? That's why Bernstein has indigestion."

"I shall go to restaurants and hotels and get myself elected to clubs. I understand the Press Club serves the best food in Berlin, but I can't think of any pretext for approaching them. I've never written for the papers in my life."

"You might write scientific articles for the comic papers," suggested Grautz.

"You are horribly unkind. But seriously, if I wanted to meet anyone, it would be simple at some of those restaurants down the Kurfürstendamm. One can go at an hour when they aren't crowded. Or when they are; one is less noticeable in a crowd. All the same," went on Hambledon, "I think it would be a convenience if there were some means of getting out of this desirable residential property without our guards being any the wiser. Let us go for a walk round the boundary and look for a possible exit."

The fence consisted of four strands of wire which passed through their supports on insulators. Hambledon regarded it with mistrust.

"Too thorough for words, these Germans," he said. "I suggested having a fence put round to keep out intruders. I never asked for them to be electrocuted. Isn't there any means of switching off the current?"

"There's a master switch in the lodge," said Grautz. "Also the current goes off whenever the gate is opened; that breaks the circuit. Neither is any good if we want to get out without the guards knowing it."

"No. We can hardly ask Eckhoff to leave the gate open one night to let in the fresh air. Let's go on walking round; we might find something."

The ground was rough heath land, but the fence followed its irregularities closely. However, they came at last to a place where a miniature gully ran under the wire, leaving a space under the bottom strand.

"Even this," said Hambledon, "isn't much of an escape route for a well-developed man. We couldn't get under it without touching the bottom wire."

"We could if it were propped up," said Grautz. "With a couple of pieces of nice dry wood. I'll cut some the right length and keep them indoors till wanted. You know, I think the blackout should have one or two chinks in it."

"What for?"

"Not enough to annoy the local wardens. Only enough to show there are lights on inside. It will look as though we are working. We might leave a tap running, too. You can hear it under the grating near the gate. I noticed your bath water this morning."

"Your price," said Hambledon appreciatively, "is far above rubies."

As time went by Eckhoff became used to driving Professor Ulseth about Berlin at all hours, and the police became used to seeing the blue Mercedes. Hambledon went to Weber's in the Spandauer Strasse for cigarettes and to different restaurants and hotels for lunch and dinner. Introduced by Landahl and others, he gathered a circle of acquaintances and received invitations to cocktail parties till the cocktails began to disagree with him.

"I may have to live in a laboratory," he said to Grautz, "but I'm hanged if I'll drink its products. I had some alleged vodka tonight which took the skin off my mouth. If this goes on I shall turn teetotal."

"It's mainly methylated spirit," said Grautz calmly, "with a dash of battery acid, touched up with permanganate of potash. Better be careful."

"Have I been drinking that?" asked the horrified Hambledon.

Grautz nodded. "I know the man who makes it. I meant to have warned you. He's a sort of relation of mine; he's lived in Berlin for years. He doesn't like the Nazis. He says it's great fun poisoning people and getting well paid for it. He's getting quite rich."

"But doesn't it occur to people that there's something funny about his drinks? What do they do to you—turn you bright blue all over?"

"Oh no. You go blind, probably, and it affects the brain too. But vodka isn't a thing you sit and drink all the evening; at least Germans wouldn't. They just have a glass or two to top off with, so they don't know which of what they've had is hurting them. Besides, he charges such a lot for it they're sure it must be all right."

"A bit unscrupulous, isn't it?" said Hambledon. "Practically wholesale murder."

"It doesn't matter," said Grautz. "They're only Germans. I'm sorry you got any of it, though," he added. "I ought to have warned you. Careless of me. How much did you have?"

"Only half a small glass. I upset the rest."

"I expect it took the veneer off the table. I'll get you a glass of milk. I think there's some left over from the coffee. Here you are; sip it slowly. You'll be all right."

Hambledon looked at his assistant with something like awe. Quiet, solid, a trifle literal in mind. The stuff blinds you and drives you mad, but it's all right, it's only Germans. "Is your relation a Dutchman, then?" he asked.

"Oh yes. He was a wine merchant in Berlin before the war; he was rather pro-German in those days. Then he lost his fiancée in Rotterdam, in that big raid while we were still resisting, you remember? So now he makes vodka," said Grautz with his gentle smile.

"Gosh," said Hambledon inadequately.

He received a consignment of cigarettes from the helpful Weber and noticed that one of the packets was slightly torn at the corner. He took this packet out, dropped it in his pocket, and opened it when he was alone, for not even Grautz knew that Weber was other than he seemed. Between the double rank of cigarettes there was a scrap of tissue paper with a message on it which ran: "Germannia Restaurant Kurfürstendamm Thursday twenty hours and after." Hambledon destroyed the scrap of paper.

Soon after 8 P.M. on Thursday the blue Mercedes pulled up outside the Germannia Restaurant and the Herr Professor got out. He told Eckhoff to put the car away and then join him as usual. Hambledon then walked impressively into the restaurant, where he was well known, and the proprietor came to greet him.

"Anything fit to eat tonight, Hagen?"

"The fish is good. Yes, really. I have been fortunate in the fish today. I recommend it."

"Umph. Well, I'll try it."

The proprietor looked a little anxious. Evidently the Herr Professor was not in his more genial mood tonight.

"There is a man at my table," pursued Hambledon in an irritated voice.

"I regret exceedingly—I did not know Your Excellency was coming—he has almost finished his meal—I am so sorry—"

"Who is the fellow?"

"I do not know the Herr. He is a stranger here."

"He looks like an undertaker's assistant," grumbled Hambledon, but he strolled across to his usual table with the proprietor fussing round him.

"Have I the Herr's permission to join him?" asked Hambledon. "This place is infernally crowded tonight." The table was a small one for two only, in the far corner of the room. Hambledon always said he liked it because from there one could watch the animals being fed without having to share a trough with them.

The man rose politely and said he would be honored; the proprietor took Hambledon's coat and hat and retired.

"A nice place, this," said the stranger affably.

"Endurable," said Hambledon, "endurable. They do not poison you here so regularly as in most of the Berlin eating houses."

"Only intermittently, eh?" said the man with a laugh.

"So long as you avoid their conception of minestrone you won't do so badly. That is quite beyond tolerance."

"Thank you. I'll remember that if I ever come again."

The waiter came with Hambledon's soup; the people at the next table finished their coffee and rose, collecting wraps and handbags. Hambledon glanced over his shoulder and saw that Eckhoff had already found a seat at a table nearer the door. There was a girl already sitting there. Eckhoff would not move away.

"The Herr is perhaps a stranger to Berlin?"

"I am a traveler in tobacco," said the man for the benefit of those within earshot. "I come at regular intervals to make contact with my customers."

"If I thought you ever obtained American cigarettes," said Hambledon, "I would ask you for the name of one of your customers." The people from the next table drifted away; the waiter tidied up deftly and prepared to depart.

"Try Weber's in Spandauer Strasse, near the Neue Markt," said the alleged tobacco traveler. "How are things going?" he added as soon as the waiter was out of earshot.

"Not too badly at all."

"I was to tell you that arrangements are being made to get you out. My name's Gibson, by the way. As soon as details are complete, I—"

"I'm not going," said Hambledon decisively. "Tell the department that. Since Grautz came I find I can manage quite well, so I'm stopping."

"But—" began Gibson.

"No buts. I've got a wonderful cover here. I should be able to do something useful. You might as well get those details completed. I might want them in a hurry later, but at present I'm staying."

Gibson grinned. "We rather gathered you were not in any immediate danger. How did you manage it?"

"I didn't. I was kidnapped from Servatsch in mistake for Ulseth. It was his idea that I should be mistaken for him. My corpse, that is, only I didn't become a corpse. I survived, so now I'm Ulseth. Simple."

"And I was to ask you, are you Hartzer too, representing the Heroas Company?"

"What? No, I'm not. Ulseth said he was going to take that part. Why, has he turned up somewhere?"

"Here in Berlin," said Gibson.

"The devil he has," said Hambledon.

"Here's your fish," said Gibson. "Yes, most people have a hobby of some kind. I am prepared to wager that the gracious Herr will not guess mine."

"Matchbox labels, possibly?" said Hambledon in a bored voice.

"No, door knockers," said Gibson. "The variety in door knockers is unbelievable until one studies the subject. Certain patterns are popular in certain districts and never seen in others. The conventionalized hand holding a wreath, for example—" He broke off as the waiter went away.

"About Hartzer," prompted Hambledon.

"He has an office in Schönebuerger Strasse, between the Potsdamer and

Anhalter stations, and a flat in Uhland Strasse, close by here. Quite a nice flat."

"My hat," said Hambledon. "I might have bumped into him at any moment. I wonder if he knows I'm here."

"I couldn't say," said Gibson. "He goes to the Transport Ministry quite a lot; he's got some pretty useful contracts out of them for the Heroas people. When the first one came through they consulted the F.O., but of course we didn't know whether Hartzer was you or who he was. Then we heard from Weber you were Ulseth—"

"Yes. A pretty tangle. But suppose you see fastened upon a door such a door knocker as your soul desires, what do you do?"

The proprietor arrived at Hambledon's elbow, inquired earnestly after the fish, was reassured, and went away beaming.

"I knock at the door and try to persuade the owners to sell it to me. Tell me, are you really going to make explosives in your ersatz castle?"

"Yes, of course. In fact, we shall jolly well have to. Please ask the department to let me have, urgently, the formula for that explosive which is so wonderful but so unstable. They'll know the one you mean."

"Sounds dangerous," said Gibson. "What's it called, d'you know?"

"No. Don't even know if it's got a name. *La Donna è mobile,* perhaps; it seems subject to tantrums. Were you going to say something?"

"Yes. As you know, we've got plenty of agents in Germany now. They came in with the droves of forced labor from the occupied countries, a few of them even volunteered. But for all the good most of 'em are, they might as well be building sand castles at Morecambe Bay. They can't move, they can't get out, and quite a lot of them can't even send messages. But they are potential saboteurs; the difficulty has been to supply them with the necessary wherewithal. If you could make the stuff, we can arrange means of distributing it."

Hambledon nodded. "I think Grautz could manage that. We can't do much at a time, or the gentle Nazi might wonder where all those masses of chemicals have gone."

"Yes," said Gibson earnestly. "For heaven's sake be careful. These people aren't in the least like the old Germans. They are horribly dangerous."

"So am I," said Hambledon cheerfully, "and they don't know it yet, which makes me doubly so."

"I must go," said Gibson, rising. "See you again soon, I hope. Here's your cheese coming. I have the honor to wish the Herr a very good evening. It has been an honor to spend a short half hour in his company."

"To me, also, it has been a pleasure. I wish you many happy door knockers. Is that really cheese, Heinrich? It much more strongly resembles my soap ration."

"It is, nevertheless, cheese, Herr Professor. It will not lather," said the waiter cheerfully, for this guest always tipped well.

"Nor does my soap, my good Heinrich, so there is not even that difference."

Ulseth's flat was on the second floor of the block in the Uhland Strasse; there were two floors of flats above him and one below; the ground floor was occupied by a restaurant, kitchens, and other offices. He was lucky to get it, for Berlin was grossly overcrowded at the end of 1941. He settled in happily and began to enjoy himself.

The people in the first-floor flats were principally middle-aged female relations of Army men; since Ulseth was interested neither in the Army nor in middle-aged ladies he took no steps in their direction. The flat opposite his own was occupied by one of the heads of departments in the Armaments Ministry, a dull man with a dull wife and no children. Ulseth could not see, at the moment, how this man could be of use to him; but one never knows, so the Heroas man made opportunities for exchanging formal civilities formally reciprocated. The families on the floors above were less important and influential, and he took little notice of them. Besides, he hardly saw them until the day when the lift broke down for the last time.

He came in from his Schönebuerger Strasse office one evening in November to find a little group gathered round the lift on the ground floor. There were the manager of the flats, the porter, and a lady whom he remembered having seen in the restaurant once or twice. She was tall and slim and dressed in black. Ulseth had thought when he first saw her that she would be attractive if only she'd look a bit more cheerful.

"It is beyond measure deplorable, *gnädige Frau,*" said the manager. "I regret extremely the inconvenience caused to you and the other tenants of the higher flats. Nevertheless, the mechanic who repaired it before told me that if that part should break again he could do no more. This is an American-made lift, and spare parts are now unobtainable."

"It is not your fault, Herr Schwegmann," said the lady in a particularly pleasant voice. "It is only the extra stairs to climb at the end of a tiring day, but it is of no use to lament."

"I hope all my tenants will take the news as reasonably as the Frau," said the manager, bowing. The lady smiled doubtfully and walked toward the stairs, passing Ulseth on the way. He stood back as she passed and noticed that she was younger than he had thought.

"Lift gone wrong again?" said Ulseth to the manager, who repeated, in exactly the same words, the explanation he had just given.

"What a nuisance," said Ulseth "Do you have to stand there and say your little piece to each tenant as they come in? Must be a bit monotonous, what?"

"It is very distressing," and the manager. "Fortunately for the Herr, he is only on the second floor, which is bad enough. For the poor Frau Weissen with the four children on the top floor—" He made a gesture of despair.

"Is that the lady who has just gone up?" asked Ulseth, dropping his voice although she was probably out of earshot already.

"No, no. That is the Frau Clausen who has no children. She is a widow; her husband was killed by the English on the Albert Canal in 1940."

"Poor soul," said Ulseth, and, having learned what he wanted to know, he too walked up the stairs. Hence the mournful expression, no doubt. The Albert Canal fighting—that was in May 1940, wasn't it? Eighteen months ago; time she began to cheer up a bit. Not that he felt particularly called to do the necessary cheering, but she had a very nice voice. Easy to listen to.

It was some days before he saw her again. He had breakfast earlier than usual one morning; he was in the restaurant by eight, and there she was, almost at the end of her meal. He bowed in passing and said it was a cold morning, and she agreed. When she had gone out he asked the waiter if Frau Clausen was always as early as this, and the waiter said yes, the Frau worked at the Marinamt—the German Admiralty—he understood one began work there at eight-thirty.

"Oh, really," said Ulseth in an indifferent tone. "Eight-thirty to seventeen-thirty, I suppose."

The waiter said he supposed so too and bustled away. Ulseth took the trouble to be in before six that evening; he was on his little landing fussing with the flap of his letterbox when she walked wearily up the stairs. Ulseth smiled and said that in these days one had to do these little repairs oneself, and she agreed that it was indeed unavoidable and passed on.

"She has great dignity," said Ulseth, unwillingly impressed. "She walks beautifully, too." He drew a long breath to encourage himself and added, "I'll take her out one evening if she'll come. Do her good."

Chapter IX

Pattern for a Documentary

THE OBERSATZ ERICH LANDAHL came to the gate in Hambledon's wire fence and tried the latch, but found it locked. He looked about him. Just inside the gate on his right was the sectional hut where the guards lived; a hundred yards further back rose the castellated walls of the Ulseth laboratory. Snow lay upon the ground, pathetic birches shivered throughout their branches, and stiffly frozen clumps of broom stuck up through the snow and rustled crossly in the northeast wind. Landahl's nose turned a brighter pink and he clapped his hands together to warm them; it was not a pleasant morning. He shook the gate, but it remained uncivilly fast, and there was no one about.

"Does one, then, howl like the Valkyries?" asked the fat little major in an aggrieved voice.

"One perhaps rings the bell, Herr Obersatz," suggested his chauffeur. "At the Herr's right hand I see a rope."

There was indeed a rope which connected to a bell of the chapel variety hung from the branch of a tree by the gate. Landahl took hold and pulled cautiously, and the result was a clangor which could easily be heard at the laboratory, let alone the hut. Hambledon had chosen it for that purpose; he liked to know when visitors were arriving. He looked out of the window.

"Friend Landahl from the Armaments Ministry," he said to Grautz.

"Coming to see how we're getting on?"

"I expect so. Well, we know what to say."

The door of the hut opened, and Eckhoff bounced out, buttoning his coat, and ran to the gate. Converse was evidently held, after which the guard ran back to the lodge, leaving Landahl outside the gate, for such was the procedure Hambledon had arranged.

"The Herr Obersatz Landahl to see the Herr Professor," said Eckhoff on the telephone.

"Let him be admitted," said Hambledon.

When Landahl was ushered in, Hambledon was intently watching something boiling in a flask while Grautz stood by in an attitude of respectful alacrity, signaling with his hand for the visitor to wait near the door. Landahl hardly breathed till at last Hambledon moved.

"It goes well," he said to Grautz, "but I am not yet quite satisfied. The emulsification is still too rapid."

"That is so, Herr Professor," said Grautz. "Shall I remove the flask? The Herr has a visitor—"

Hambledon emerged from his absorption like a seal rising to the surface of his pond in the zoo and turned genially to Landahl.

"The Herr Obersatzwhat a pleasure! How long have you been standing there? Forgive my inattention—"

"The Herr Professor is too kind," said the gratified Landahl. "I must apologize for intruding upon his distinguished labors."

"It is impossible for the Herr Obersatz's arrival to be an intrusion. One moment while I wash my hands." Hambledon washed them very thoroughly under the tap in the laboratory sink and thereafter rubbed in glycerin which he poured freely from a bottle. "Lest the Herr Obersatz should think us fine ladies anxious to preserve the texture of our hands, I will explain that many of the chemicals we use have a corrosive effect and we use glycerin as an antidote. In fact, it is sometimes necessary to wash in it. Besides this, glycerin is an ingredient of many explosives, as doubtless the Herr knows, so in one way or another we use a great quantity."

"The Ministry of Supply," said Landahl, "has asked me to impress upon you the difficulty that exists in procuring enough glycerin for all the purposes—"

"Tell the Supply Ministry," broke in Hambledon testily, "that if Germany requires Ulsenite she must provide the ingredients necessary. Actually I asked for palm oil, for which the glycerin is an inadequate substitute."

"The palm oil," began Landahl, who always became nervous when Hambledon began to interrupt him, "the Supply Minister asked me to ascertain for
what purpose you required it. Palm oil is not a product native to Germany, and
the damned British blockade—"

"I will tell you what I want it for. I am nitrating the next homologue above
glycerin—"

"One moment," said Landahl, hastily producing a notebook, "may I write
that down?"

"You can rubricate it in red and blue inks with gold capitals if you like,"
said Hambledon. "This nitrate—"

"I beg your pardon. You said first you were 'nitrating the next'—what was
it? I beg a thousand pardons—"

"Homologue," said Hambledon, and kindly spelt it for him, "above glycerin. This nitrate is obtained by the fractionalization of palm oil. Fractionalization, that's right. By the way, will you ask the supply people to expedite delivery of the colloidal platinum I asked for? It is more than a month since I re-
quested it urgently."

"Certainly," said Landahl, scribbling again. "Platinum, you said, coll— Oh,
thank you. Colloidal. Quite so. Platinum, again, is one of our difficulties. The
Minister wondered—"

"What I want that for, I suppose," said Hambledon contemptuously. "It is
used as a catalyst, and if he wants to know what that is, he can ask the chemist
from whom he buys his liver pills. I don't keep an infant school."

"No indeed, Herr Professor. Certainly not."

Hambledon left off rubbing glycerin into his hands and suddenly beamed
upon the little major.

"It is a cold morning, and here I keep you standing in my comfortless workshop
surrounded by you know not what death-dealing mixtures. Let us go into our
humble sitting room, such as it is," said Hambledon, leading the way, "and we
will see if we can find some liquid more congenial to the human frame. Grautz!"

"Yes, Herr Professor."

"Continue with the process, noting down all variation of temperature at
five-minute intervals."

"Yes, Herr Professor."

"It would be a convenience if you charted the results."

"Certainly, Herr Professor."

"An attentive and intelligent-looking young man," said Landahl, almost
before the door was shut.

"He is very well," said Tommy carelessly. "He is learning fast. A little glass
of schnapps, Herr Obersatz, to keep out the cold. Is there any news today?"

"Has the Herr Professor not heard?" asked Landahl, staring.

"No, my paper has not yet come. Has something, then, occurred?"

"We have sunk the *Ark Royal*."

"What, again?" said Hambledon with a smile.

Landahl looked rather shocked but laughed dutifully in response. "It is really true this time; even the British admit it. They tried to tow her into Gibraltar, but she sank before reaching it."

"How was she sunk? Bombed by the Luftwaffe?"

"No, no. By torpedoes from a submarine."

"It is good work," said Tommy solemnly, and he handed the Obersatz his glass. "The *Ark Royal* has been many times a thorn in our side. Let us drink the health of the gallant and skillful U-boat commander and his crew. Hoch!"

"Hoch! But how comes it you did not hear this wonderful news on the radio this morning?"

"My set has been out of order," said Hambledon. "It has only just come back from being repaired." In point of fact he listened only to the BBC news service, though sometimes he called it names. Regarding the German news bulletins, he told Grautz that if he had to listen to fairy tales he preferred Hans Andersen's. They, at least, had not been polluted by passing through the mind of Goebbels on their way to the world. Goebbels, huh!

"You dislike Goebbels," said Grautz.

"How right you are," said Tommy cheerfully.

To revert to Landahl's visit. When they had rejoiced suitably over the sinking of the *Ark Royal,* the little major returned to the subject of Ulsenite. The Armaments Ministry were wondering whether, at a time and place entirely subject to the wishes of the Herr Professor, a small demonstration could be arranged. Hambledon and Grautz had expected this, and the Herr Professor was ready with his answer.

"Certainly. By all means. At an early date. I shall, however, ask you to make it clear to the Armaments Minister that a demonstration is one thing and production quite another." Hambledon repeated Grautz's arguments about the stability of the explosive and added, "We now have it controllable for a matter of five or six hours. No one knows better than the Herr Obersatz that five or six months would be none too long." Landahl nodded eagerly. "I expect another seven or eight months' work upon it before it is fit to be put into production without endangering the lives of those who handle it. Especially," went on Hambledon emphatically, "when I am hampered by inability to procure what I want, and by having to use substitutes."

"It is understood," said Landahl. "I will make it all clear to the Minister myself. Everything possible shall be done. You will, then, let us know about the demonstration?"

"I will write to you in the course of the next few days," said Hambledon, and showed him out. Hambledon then dived into his laboratory and told Grautz the news about the *Ark Royal.*

"It's a pity," said Grautz, "but you will build many more *Arks Royal*. Was there much loss of life?"

"I don't know yet. I hope not. We will listen in to London tonight; perhaps they'll tell us. Returning to Landahl, these people want a demonstration."

"I thought they would."

"They shall have it. I said I would write and fix a date. How long will it take us to arrange it?"

"Today's November the fourteenth. Next Friday?"

"I'll write and tell him so. I said my little piece about insuring the controllability of Ulsenite. Did I get the other bit right, about nitrating the homologue, whatever that means? Good. You noticed I closed the conversation before he could ask me what a catalyst was. Grautz, if we get out of this with our lives I shall spend the rest of my declining years in a state of perpetual astonishment. It's not in the least likely, you know, that we shall get away with it. It only wants somebody who does know something about chemistry to corner me and ask me some damnfool question I can't answer, and we're done. Sunk. Oh, why did I grow a beard?"

"Cheer up," said Grautz. "If we live long enough to hit them where it hurts, I personally shall be satisfied. It's more than most people have been able to do in this war."

"You're right, as usual. Now, about this demonstration."

"We will hold it on that flat piece of land just behind here. We bury in the ground beforehand two five-liter cans of nitroglycerin complete with detonators, that will make a bang which should surprise them."

"It goes to my heart," said Hambledon, "to waste all that nitroglycerin on a mere firework display when it would do so much more good under Hitler's bed."

"I know, but it must be done. We connect the detonators to a battery with wires running from it to the place where there is a button to press. They will be very long wires indeed. At the time of the show we will fill one of those half-liter beakers with something mysterious looking, carry it ceremonially down to the place where the nitroglycerin is buried, and inter it carefully on the top. When we have regained the starting place you can give the word, your most distinguished guest can press the button, and I trust the result will fulfill their wildest hopes. As a result, they ought to give us everything we want and about a year's grace to work in. Then we can turn out explosives for your friend Gibson, the traveler in sabotage."

"I asked Gibson for that formula, you know, the unreliable one," said Hambledon, "but it hasn't come through yet. What did you want it for?"

"To leave about," said Grautz.

"Eh?"

"I have an idea that our papers are sometimes disturbed," said Grautz. "I think that perhaps our experiments are a subject of curiosity to other firms manufacturing explosives, or it may be the German government, with a panel of chemists of their own, trying to keep abreast of us."

"You didn't tell me this before," said Hambledon.

"No, and I'm not sure now. But I think our invoices of goods delivered here are copied, and probably anything else we leave lying about."

"Who does it? Surely not our guards; they're not educated enough to—"

"Bernstein was a schoolmaster, didn't you know? Only at an elementary school, it's true, but he could copy correctly. He got into some sort of trouble, so he joined the Party to get out of the rain."

"I never did like Bernstein much," said Tommy thoughtfully. "How did you learn that?"

"His wife told me. She thinks they've come down in the world, and it's a grievance."

"Oh. So you're going to leave this formula lying about and see who blows themselves up?"

"I had some such idea. In the meantime we can keep a watch."

"Yes. It is a consolation to remember that, as regards the Ulsenite formula, there isn't anything to steal."

Accordingly Hambledon wrote to the Armaments Ministry proposing to give a demonstration on the following Friday, November the twenty-first. He expected an answer saying that the performance would be attended by a couple of semiretired generals, two or three high officials from the Ministry, and a handful of smaller fry. Instead of the postman with a letter, however, an enormous black limousine drew up at his gate and the driver descended and rang the bell. The usual ceremonies were performed, and Bernstein spoke on the telephone.

"The Herr Minister of Propaganda Goebbels to see the Herr Professor."

"Admit him," said Hambledon in a slightly breathless voice, and turned to Grautz.

"Goebbels," he said, "dear Doktor Goebbels. Well, well. We do move in aristocratic circles, don't we? Or don't we? The slimy little toad. I wonder what the devil he wants." Hambledon took out his handkerchief and mopped his face. "Just time for a small dose of schnapps. I feel hot at the ends and cold in the middle, as it were. I wish I'd had a little more notice of this, though I don't know what I'd have done if I had. Grautz, I've got the wind up. You can't arrange a small explosion as he enters and blacken my face all over, can you? Bernstein is opening the gate. Yes, that's him all right. Just the same as ever, hasn't even put on weight."

"I gather you knew him before," said Grautz, handing the restorative. Tommy gulped it down and returned the glass.

"Yes, I did. Put that where he can't see it. But I look very different now. I wish I was a fairy queen. I'd wave my wand, turn him into a log of wood, hurl him into the stove, boil a kettle on him, and then pour the water down the drain. Thank you, Grautz. I feel better."

Bernstein ushered in their distinguished visitor, and Goebbels was genial, as he can be when he tries. It was a pleasure too long delayed by pressure of business, to meet the Herr Professor, and so forth. Hambledon responded suitably, having arranged himself with his back to the light, and compliments were bounced back and forth until Goebbels tired of it.

"But I must not waste your valuable time in idle chatter," he said. "About this demonstration you are giving us."

"Yes, Herr Minister?"

"You were thinking of something in the nature of a private show before a few experts?"

"I was, yes," said Hambledon, wondering what was coming.

"I have great news for you. Most gratifying news. Astonishing. Our Fuehrer wishes to be present in person."

"I am overcome," said Hambledon, and meant it. "The Fuehrer himself! Why?"

"Your modesty does you credit. The point is this. It is our duty at the Propaganda Ministry to do everything possible to encourage our people by showing them the wonderful inventions Germany is producing for the downfall of our enemies. So far as is consistent with military secrecy, of course. It is good for morale."

"Quite," said Hambledon. "Exactly. Of course."

"There will, therefore, be quite a splash made over your demonstration, my dear professor. You will permit photographers, cinematographers—"

"Heaven help me, Herr Goebbels! I am a poor student of chemistry, not a glamorous what-d'you-call-'em—radio star, is it not? Am I then to make up my poor face and strut before the—"

"No, no," said Goebbels, laughing heartily. "No. Quite a natural out-of-door affair. A feature film, as they are called. You will be shown making your arrangements; you would perhaps consent to say a few explanatory words. The Fuehrer will be seen to press the button, and then the explosion will be recorded. A simple matter, my dear professor. Short. Easy. A quarter of an hour at most. Do not be alarmed; everything will be done to suit your convenience."

"But I am alarmed. I am horrified. To be dragged from the cloistered life of the laboratory into the glare of publicity—no, no. No, Herr Minister of Propaganda. The marvelous not-to-be-believed war effort of Germany must provide many more fruitful opportunities for the uplift of morale than my poor efforts. I must really refuse."

Goebbels' expression hardened. "I see I have not made myself clear. There is no question of refusing, Herr Ulseth. The decision has been made."

Hambledon leaned back in his chair as one overborne by insistence.

"There is only one alteration necessary, the date. Next Friday does not suit our Fuehrer," went on Goebbels. "Tuesday week, November the twenty-fifth, is the appointed date, and the time fourteen-thirty."

"Very well," said Hambledon in a weak voice, and Goebbels immediately beamed upon him.

"You will not find the experience an ordeal," he said. "Instructions will be given to make it as easy and pleasant as possible. You have not to act, only to reveal yourself as you are—patient, brilliant, successful."

"Heavens above forbid," said Hambledon inwardly, and added aloud, "No doubt the terrors I experience must seem ridiculous to you, who are filmed every day. Put it down to my idiotic shrinking from publicity, Herr Goebbels. After all," went on Hambledon with a wry laugh, "is it not the ambition of all bright young people to appear on the films? There must be something fascinating about it."

"Well done, Herr Professor. We shall yet turn you into a film star," said Goebbels, rising. "I have already taken up too much of your precious time—"

"Not at all, an honor—"

"A pleasure, believe me. Some other day may I come again and improve our acquaintance?"

"Delighted," said Hambledon, "delighted." By this time they had arrived at the door; Tommy, holding it open for his visitor, had to face the light. Goebbels turned on the step and looked him full in the face.

"I can't help thinking," he said, "that I've seen you before somewhere."

Hambledon turned perfectly cold.

"Are you, by any chance," went on Goebbels, "the same Ulseth who was one of our party members in the very early days?"

"I am," said Tommy without hesitation.

"During and before the Munich putsch?"

"Even so."

"I thought there was something in your appearance which was familiar. That doubtless accounts for it," said Goebbels, still regarding him in a manner which made Hambledon feel he was being perforated by gimlets.

"I remember Your Excellency very well," said Hambledon with a smile which made his face ache.

"You should have told us this at first," said Goebbels, smiling in return. "One of our earliest members—a welcome would have been ready—"

"One does not presume upon having done one's duty," said Hambledon loftily. "I am now a poor chemist, Herr Minister of Propaganda, but happy beyond words to be following our beloved Fuehrer once more in the service of the Reich."

Goebbels nodded in a friendly manner and went away. Hambledon shut the door and then leaned against it, holding the handle.

"You are shaking," said Grautz, regarding him with interest. "Come and sit down."

"If I let go of this handle I shall probably fall down. Well, I suppose I can't stand here all day; here goes. My legs do support me; curious, must be habit.

One of these days, Grautz, that appalling little squirt is going to remember where he's seen me before, and the results will be interesting. And probably painful. I made a mistake then, overflowing into moral aphorisms. I used to do that when I knew him before, and it may remind him. I don't know why Goebbels should have that effect on me—natural reaction, doubtless."

"Drink this," said Grautz practically.

"You do have the right ideas," said Hambledon, obeying. "Did you hear that last bit of conversation at the door?" Grautz nodded, and Tommy went on, "I wonder what Ulseth did in the Party's early days. I expect he was a rogue; most of 'em were. I don't remember him at all."

"Were you one of the early rogues?"

"Early, but not a rogue, believe it or not. My business was to catch 'em."

"May I ask, without being indiscreet, what you were in those days?"

"I joined the Party at Munich and rose to become chief of police," said Hambledon. "My name in those days was Klaus Lehmann."

"My immortal soul, what a nerve," said Grautz reverently.

"No nerve required; it just happened. I had an accident toward the end of the last war and lost my memory. I recovered it on the night of the Reichstag Fire; that same night our Adolf made me assistant chief of police."

"Are you a German, then?"

"Oh no, I'm English."

"And how did you get out? did you escape?"

"I died," said Tommy in a solemn voice. "I was assassinated in Danzig and accorded a state funeral here in Berlin with an oration by our Fuehrer, may moths devour his underclothing. D'you mean to say you didn't hear about it? I am pained. I thought Europe rang with it."

"I did, of course. I am sorry, I became confused—I did not connect that Lehmann with you."

"Don't apologize, please. It's not a connection which would naturally occur to anyone, at least I piously trust not. I ought to go and visit my grave."

"Lay a wreath on it," suggested Grautz, "of immortelles."

Chapter X
Much Ado about Ulseth

TWO DAYS LATER there arrived at the laboratory gate quite a cavalcade of cars, headed by Goebbels' big car. Hambledon looked at this display of efficiency and his jaw came out.

"They have come to arrest us," he said. "Well, that's that, Grautz. Pleased to have met you."

"Perhaps they have some other purpose," said Grautz, not very hopefully. "Goebbels wouldn't come in person to arrest us, you know. Look, those aren't

S.S. men getting out, they are civilians."

"You may be right; perhaps they've come to arrange the film show." Hambledon opened the door and signaled to Eckhoff to open the gate. "We may as well make a display of welcome, anyway."

Goebbels came up the path accompanied by a fat man in a leather overcoat whom he introduced as "my friend, Herr Kallenbach."

Kallenbach said he was honored. Hambledon looked him over and was coldly polite, wondering who he was and why he had been brought there since Goebbels never did anything without a reason, usually an unpleasant one. The occupants of the other cars drifted about or walked briskly from place to place, viewing the laboratory, the hut, and the adjacent scenery through little wire frames which they produced from their pockets.

"We have come to worry you about this film, Herr Professor," said Goebbels. "We don't want to take up more of your time than can be avoided. If you would just show us where you propose to give this demonstration, the cameramen can make their mysterious arrangements."

"Certainly," said Hambledon. "My time is at the disposal of the Herr Minister of Propaganda; he knows as well as anyone how valuable it is."

Goebbels' smile diminished slightly at this two-edged remark, and Hambledon went on without waiting for an answer. "If you would come this way, Herr Goebbels—is the Herr Kallenbach my film mentor?"

"No, no," said Kallenbach, heartily amused. "My interest in films is confined to taking my good wife to the cinema once a week. Still, I think I'll stay here and see what these fellows are going to do," he added to Goebbels, "if the Herr Professor will permit. It might be amusing."

"I beg the Herr to entertain himself in any manner which my poor resources will permit," said Hambledon. "Grautz! The Herr Kallenbach will perhaps have a little glass of something."

"No, thank you, no," said Kallenbach to Grautz. "A cup of coffee, perhaps, if the trouble is not too great –"

Hambledon left them at it and conducted Goebbels through a screen of birches round the end of the laboratory and over the shoulder of a little ridge of hill behind the building. "An ideal spot, Herr Minister. Close at hand, yet the ridge protects the buildings from blast." They topped the ridge and saw before them a stretch of flat land some half a mile long, covered with snowy grass. "I directed that the fence should enclose this area," went on Hambledon. "I foresaw when we came here that it would be useful for my experiments." In point of fact the suggestion came from Grautz, who said that since loud and repeated bangs would be part of their camouflage they had better have somewhere to make them. "No sense in blowing out the lab windows in midwinter to impress the natives. Besides, the sound will carry further out of doors."

"Very convenient," said Goebbels. "Eminently for-the-purpose suitable. Schafer!"

One of the strangers who had drifted after them came trotting up, and Goebbels presented him.

"This is Herr Schafer of the Ufa Film Studios, who will be responsible for immortalizing you, my dear professor."

"With a camera or a gun?" asked Tommy cheerfully, and the jest was well received. Herr Schafer was almost excessively amused. He was a gaunt young man with black hair which fell in a soft plume over his eyes. He tossed it back frequently with a manicured hand and had the manner of one accustomed to public appearances.

"I can see we shall get on fine, Herr Professor. I like a man with a sense of humor."

"The demonstration will take place here, Schafer. The Fuehrer's stand will be hereabouts, will it not, Professor?" Hambledon nodded. "And the explosion over there, about a hundred meters away?"

"Heavens no," said Hambledon. "Three hundred meters at least."

"But we shan't see anything at that range," objected Schafer.

"Oh yes, you will, my good young man," said Hambledon.

"Surely two hundred meters will be far enough," said Goebbels. "How much explosive are you going to use, for goodness' sake?"

"About half a liter," said Hambledon. "One of those flasks you saw me with the other day, do you remember? Yes. You want to show the Fuehrer something worth seeing, don't you?"

"Certainly. But only half a liter, at that range—"

"Listen, Herr Minister of Propaganda. I wrecked a stone house in Switzerland with half a liter of Ulsenite two months ago, and I have slightly improved it since then. You tell me I am to be honored with the presence of our heaven-sent Leader, and yet you argue with me—me, Ulseth!—about the range at which his person will be in safety. I tell you frankly that either I have my way in this matter or there will be no demonstration," said Hambledon, becoming more and more excited. "Even at the range I have decided upon, I shall have a bank of earth thrown up this side to minimize the blast. You have no notion of the powers with which you are dealing, Herr Minister; we are not children playing with fireworks—"

"Calm yourself, Herr Professor, calm yourself," said Goebbels, yielding gracefully. "I bow to the expert. All shall be arranged as you wish."

"Naturally," said Hambledon with a snort. "Otherwise it will not take place."

Schafer kept in the background during this exchange and walked behind when Hambledon and his visitor returned to the laboratory, Goebbels chatting lightly of this and that and Hambledon making humph noises. At the door Schafer drew Hambledon aside and asked him if he would come to the Ufa Studios on the following morning together with his eminently-to-be-respected assistant.

"Whatever for?"

"Because we should like to take some interior shots of you and him working in your laboratory, and the lighting is better there."

"But am I supposed to bring my laboratory fittings?"

"By no means, Herr Professor. Not necessary at all. We have a permanent set representing a laboratory which will serve admirably as a background."

"Background to what?" said Hambledon impatiently.

"To your impossible-to-be-overestimated labors. In the studio—"

"But, my good young man, you don't seriously suppose I should transfer my chemicals—some of which are highly dangerous—to your imitation laboratory even for—"

"No, no. I was thinking that if you could be seen boiling something in a flask—water would do—while your invaluable assistant took notes, or whatever he does—"

"Oh, I see. Pretend to be working."

"Even so, Herr Professor. Then if you could be heard discussing with him the future of Ulsenite—"

"While waiting for the kettle to boil?"

Schafer laughed. "Think it over, Herr Professor. Regard it as a welcome relaxation from your so-arduous labors."

"I will discuss it with Grautz and telephone to you."

Schafer thanked him and retreated hastily to make way for Goebbels and his Kallenbach, who took their leave. Hambledon withdrew into his laboratory and watched through the window the party climbing into their cars again; at last the procession drove away. Then he turned on Grautz and said, "Well? Who and what is Kallenbach?"

"I don't know who he is. He is a chemist and knows quite a lot about explosives. I think he came here to pump me while you were out of the way. The ingenuous young assistant overflowing with enthusiasm might easily let something slip, you understand. He did it rather well," said Grautz thoughtfully.

"How did you deal with him?"

"Talked a lot and said nothing."

"Here's Eckhoff coming for the coffee cups and to tell us dinner's ready, I hope," said Hambledon. "Nervous exhaustion always makes me hungry."

Eckhoff entered with his usual cheerful grin, saying that dinner was now being served for the gracious Herren. He gathered up the coffee cups and added, "Is this Herr Kallenbach's? I'll give it an extra wash."

Hambledon paused in the act of opening the door and said, "That sounds as though you didn't like the man. I didn't know you knew him."

"Actually, I've never spoken to him. It's his partner who sometimes speaks to me." Eckhoff put down the tray and became serious. "I have been wishing to tell the Herr Professor, but no opportunity offered. They are paying me money to find out anything I can about what you are doing."

"Oh, are they? And who are 'they'?"

"Kallenbach's firm. They make explosives. A small firm, but they get good orders. It is said that Herr Goebbels has a controlling interest—is that how to put it?"

"And what do they want you to do?"

"Send them copies of anything I find lying about. I nearly told them to go to hell, then I thought again. It is unwise to disoblige the big bosses of the Nazi party; besides, the money is good and my pay isn't much," said Eckhoff frankly. "On the other hand, the Herr Professor—it is an honor to serve him—Your Excellency is always kind, I couldn't bring myself—"

"Very good of you, Eckhoff."

"I really mean it, Excellency," said Eckhoff, actually blushing with earnestness. "Then it occurred to me to put the facts before the Herr Professor."

"In order that I should pay you instead of Kallenbach?" said Hambledon sternly. "A clever scheme, Eckhoff, but—"

"No, no," broke in Eckhoff. "Not at all. That would be foolish, for you have only to dismiss me, and I like this job. No. I only thought that perhaps you could sometimes leave something about that looked interesting but didn't matter. Then Kallenbach would be happy and pay me, and I should be happy serving Your Excellency, who would be happy knowing he was not being betrayed, and thus everyone concerned would be contented."

Hambledon burst into a roar of laughter.

"What do you think, Grautz? Shall we have Eckhoff shot at dawn?"

"I think it would be a waste of an intelligent man," said Grautz.

"So do I," said Hambledon. "After all, trying to learn one's competitors' trade secrets is a thing that is done all the time in peace as well as war. Now we are forewarned, we can be careful."

"But sometimes there might be a little something," urged Eckhoff.

"After this, Eckhoff, you will be welcome to anything you may find left about. Come on, Grautz. My stomach is ringing the dinner bell."

When they were alone again Hambledon told Grautz about the Ufa man's suggestion that the interior scenes should be taken in the studio.

"I think it's a good idea," said Grautz. "We don't want people poking about in here. We can say so openly and no harm done."

"I should agree," said Tommy, "only the last thing I want is to have my face, form, and movements brilliantly photographed and displayed to the entire population of Germany. I shrink. I nearly shrivel. The proverbial violet is a peony compared to me."

"But you can't get out of this film, can you?"

"No. Blast Goebbels and all his Ministry. That's an idea, by the way; we might do it one day."

"Yes," said Grautz. "This film, though—I think the only thing to do is to go through with it. You could avoid facing the lights as much as possible because they hurt your eyes."

"Already damaged in the Servatsch affair. I couldn't wear an eyeshade, I suppose? Why not? No one except Landahl has ever seen me working at my chemical researches, and if I keep my wits about me no one ever will. Get me an eyeshade when you go into town this evening, will you? What do we do in their chromium-plated laboratory?"

"We will get out a script," said Grautz. "We shan't have to learn it by heart, because we can have it in notebooks and refer to them whenever necessary. I expect Schafer will want to see it, and possibly the censor also."

"You can write it while I ring up Schafer."

"By the way," said Grautz, "I have been thinking about this demonstration of ours. Ulsenite should be different from all other explosives."

"God knows it is already," said Tommy. "What d'you suggest?"

"Adding colloidal copper to the nitroglycerin. The result should be a vivid green flash. I'll try a few small experiments for quantity; there's plenty of time before the twenty-fifth."

"I'll ask for some colloidal copper," began Hambledon, but Grautz interrupted him.

"Better not. I'll go and buy some tonight. We don't want to let the Ministry into all our secrets."

"Buy some? What's it sold for?"

"Spraying fruit trees," said Grautz.

"Oh. So long as it doesn't spray us over the adjacent trees, that's all right."

"I want to make it clear to you," said Grautz earnestly, "that that is quite likely to happen. Nitroglycerin is the most touchy stuff imaginable, and if we get it into the ground without blowing ourselves up I shall be agreeably surprised. I don't think adding copper will make it any worse, but frankly I don't know."

"Oh," said Hambledon rather doubtfully. "Couldn't you mix up something else?"

"Not in the time. Guncotton would take much longer to make."

"Well, we must chance it. We've got nothing to lose but our lives, and I couldn't insure them for twopence each without defrauding the company. I like your idea of a vivid green flash. Green for danger, eh?"

"A soft apple-green," said Grautz placidly. "Very pretty."

Hambledon looked at him in silence for a moment and then went away to telephone to Schafer.

Tommy had never been a motion-picture enthusiast and regarded the whole performance as an unavoidable nuisance. He had a hazy idea that film studios were full of glamorous young females being temperamental and long-haired young men being self-important in a strong atmosphere of grease paint and publicity. Much ado about nothing, in short. He arrived at the Ufa Studios prepared to be patronizing and bored. To his surprise he found the place buzzing with hard-working people doing a highly technical job with marked efficiency and lack of fuss. Schafer with his foot on his native heath was very different from the obsequious attendant upon Goebbels at the Ulseth laboratory.

"I am delighted to receive the Herr Professor," he began, "and the Herr Grautz. The laboratory set is over here. We have the cameras and the lights all in position already, in order not to waste your valuable time. Will you look over it and see that everything is as you like it? Please tell me if you want anything altered."

Hambledon looked at the white laboratory bench, the polished pipes, flasks, and tubes shining with cleanliness, the Bunsen burner already alight, the sink tap very slowly dripping, and said frankly, "I think it's wonderful. I had expected something much more—how shall I put it?—makeshift. Eh, Grautz?"

"It all appears to me completely satisfactory," said the unemotional Grautz.

"Good," said Schafer. "This your script? Thank you. It will have to be submitted to the censor, but I don't expect he will raise any points. I will just run through it while you are putting your white coats on, then we will go through it once to see how it runs and afterward try it with the camera. I don't want to bother you more than I can help, and what's more, we don't want the film to look professionally acted. We are eavesdropping on two men working, not watching a stage play, if you see what I mean." He sat down on a chair and read rapidly through Grautz's neatly written dialogue while Hambledon and his assistant changed into linen overalls. Schafer looked up as Tommy was adjusting his eyeshield.

"Oh, I say! Must you wear that thing?"

"I fear it is unavoidable," said Tommy mildly. "My eyes have not recovered from an accident I had in Switzerland. I always wear a shield when I'm working, otherwise they become inflamed."

"Oh. In that case it can't be helped, but it conceals so much of your face, and that's a pity. Perhaps you could remove it for a close-up at the end, just for a few moments."

"We will see when the time comes," said Hambledon, adding, "Not if I know it," to himself. When the lights were all turned on he gasped and blinked without artifice.

"I could not bear this for a moment without the shield," he said, and Grautz, scowling against the lights, said he wished he had one too.

"You will get used to them in a few minutes," said Schafer. "Try not to frown. Now, let's have a preliminary runthrough." He looked at his watch and they began.

By the time they had gone through the script twice without the camera and once with, leaning over the boiling flask above the blue flame of the Bunsen and talking in measured sentences with an air of profound concentration,

Hambledon was dripping with perspiration and his head was beginning to ache. Schafer noticed it.

"Knock off for a few minutes and sit down," he said. "I'll get a mug of beer for you. It is trying when you're not used to it, I know."

"It's the heat as well as the light," said Hambledon, removing his shade to mop his face. "I can't think how anyone ever gets used to it."

"Oh, you do," said Schafer. "Come over here; it's cooler. There isn't much more to do. I just want to take one or two shots again that I'm not quite satisfied with. That place where Herr Grautz is measuring stuff out; you got in front of him, and people won't see what's happening. Again, at that point where the flask comes to the boil you get in each other's way. Sit down here, won't you? May I present you to the Fräulein Amalie Rielander? The distinguished Herr Professor Ulseth, Herr Grautz. Excuse me a moment."

Fräulein Rielander was young, slim, and attractive, with a mop of dark curls and very blue eyes. She smiled upon Hambledon, who sat beside her with Grautz upon his further side.

"You are doing this documentary about explosives, aren't you?" she said. "I was watching you for some time. I think you're going to be good."

"I feel as though I were going to be bad," said Hambledon. "The atmosphere under those lamps is just like the onset of influenza. Heat to the head, cold to the feet, and lights unbearably bright."

"One gets used to it," she said.

"That's what Schafer keeps on saying, but I don't think I want to."

"You haven't got to earn your living that way," she said with a laugh.

"Heaven forbid. Besides, I have been unfairly handicapped in the matter of a face. Now, Grautz here—"

The girl leaned forward and regarded Grautz critically. "A nice face," she said, as though he were not within earshot. "Clearly cut features. Good width across the eyes. Not bad at all."

Hambledon laughed, and Grautz said he had always been told he was the image of his grandmother when she was young. Tommy asked Fräulein Rielander if she was making a film at the moment.

"Oh yes," she said indifferently. "An awful thing all about young heroes in E-boats. I haven't much to do but stand about in admiring attitudes and be suitably delighted when they come home again. Part of the decorative background, you know."

"Then the background is the best part of the film," said Hambledon with conviction.

"You have a discerning mind," she laughed.

"There cannot be much scope in war films for such as you," went on Hambledon. "There's no place for charm and beauty in war. Don't they produce anything but war films now? I should have thought people would want something different."

"They do, but we aren't encouraged to make anything else," she said. "Here's your beer now. That is a lovely sight, don't you think?"

A messenger boy arrived with two steins of beer on a tray, and Hambledon took a long pull at his before replying.

"Ah, that's better," he said. "I begin to hope I may yet live. May I offer the *gnädiges Fräulein* a cigarette?"

She took one and offered Hambledon a light from a gold lighter with her initials in rubies. Hambledon remarked on it.

"A present from Doktor Goebbels," she said in a noncommittal voice. "There is a shortage of matches."

"Very useful," said Hambledon. "Very thoughtful of him."

She glanced quickly at him and away again. "Yes. There are, of course, various kinds of thoughts, kind and otherwise."

"Wise thoughts and foolish ones, Fräulein," said Hambledon in order to check her. He was not sure whether she was trying to pump him or on the point of pouring out undesired confidences to see how he would react. Goebbels would not give a girl an expensive present like that unless she was useful to him. Apparently she took the hint.

"Do you often go to the cinema, Herr Professor?"

"Not six times in my life, though, as it happens, I saw a film in Berne about three months ago."

"What film was that? Who took the star parts?"

"I don't know whether you would say there were any star parts," said Hambledon. "It was very interesting. It was a documentary called Atomic Energy."

She laughed at that. "I'm afraid I should have found that very dull. Come and see my awful film when it comes out? Oh do, you must. It's not so bad as some, really. I spend most of my time clutching an infant in my arms and waving good-by with a handkerchief."

"Perhaps," said Hambledon, "it would be an improvement if you clutched the handkerchief and waved the infant. It would at least make people laugh. But surely the Fräulein has had better parts than that?"

"This is my first lead," she said frankly, and, noticing Hambledon's puzzled look, kindly explained. "The first time I've had the leading part, you know. I've played in much better films. My first small part was in *Die Schwedische Nachtigall* with Gottschalk," she added, her face clouding with sadness. "It was a lovely film all about Hans Andersen. Gottschalk was wonderful–poor Gottschalk."

"He committed suicide the other day, didn't he?" said Hambledon, with a vague idea of having seen the name in a paper.

Amalie Rielander nodded and turned eyes bright with tears upon Hambledon.

"He married a Jewess," she said in low and hurried tones. "She was beautiful; they were terribly happy. They had one child. Then Goebbels wanted to run him for propaganda purposes—the great German film star, you know. So he tried to persuade Gottschalk to part from his wife and child, and he flatly refused. So then he was told she and the child would be exported to Poland and he would have to stay behind; they had an hour in which to pack. When the police went to get them, there they were waiting, all three dead. He'd killed his wife and child and then himself."

"What a frightful affair," said Hambledon, visualizing the unnaturally silent room.

"They are saying," she went on with a wry laugh, "that he's killed Goebbels too, only the Herr Minister of Propaganda hasn't found it out yet."

"You Berliners are terribly cynical," said Hambledon cautiously.

"Here's Schafer coming for us," said Grautz.

"You are giving a demonstration of your new explosive, aren't you?" said the girl, recovering herself. "I should love to see it. May I come? Do send me a ticket, do!"

"I have no tickets to send, Fräulein. The Herr Minister of Propaganda is arranging it all. I merely perform-like a trained seal."

"I adore trained seals," she said, laughing. "I shall certainly come. I will get hold of a ticket somehow."

"*Auf Wiedersehen,* then," said Hambledon as Schafer descended upon them and hurried them away.

Chapter XI
Green Flash

ON THE MORNING of November the twenty-fifth Hambledon, with Grautz beside him, watched a small party of workmen erect a platform for the Fuehrer. It was merely a wooden dais about two feet high, just enough to raise the Leader above the herd. On the dais was placed a wooden table with a chair behind it. Grautz was holding in his hand a switch of the press-button type; twin-flex wire leading from it ran down to the ground and across the frozen grass to a bank of raw earth some four hundred yards away. Grautz put the switch down on the table and tied the flex to the table leg with a piece of string.

"What for?" asked the workmen, watching interestedly.

"In case someone should trip over the wire and pull the switch off the table."

"Would that make it go off?"

"Probably."

"Oh. Well, there's all sorts of jobs," said the workmen philosophically and went away. Hambledon and Grautz walked along the wire to the place where the soil was thrown up. Here two loose ends of wire waited to be connected; they waved uncertainly in the east wind.

"Sure you'll be able to find the other ends?" said Hambledon anxiously.

"Without doubt. Here they are," said Grautz, delving with his hand in the loose earth of the trench from which the bank had been dug. He brought out two more ends of wire from underground. "I have only to twist the wires together in pairs, and the rest is with the divine Fuehrer."

"I hope it goes off."

"Oh, it'll go off all right. The only pity is that it is here instead of under the Fuehrer's dais."

"It is," agreed Hambledon, "but they would spot it when they come to inspect the place. They have thought of that one, you'll see. In fact, here they come."

Four S.S. men, conducted by Bernstein, came over the ridge and descended upon the dais. They looked all over it, round it, and under it.

"There you are," said Hambledon. "What did I tell you? Very thorough, these Germans."

The S.S. men lifted the switch and examined it; they followed the wire down to the ground and across the grass toward Hambledon and Grautz. The second pair of wires had disappeared into the earth again.

"It will not be a good idea if they stamp about over all that nitroglycerin with their heavy boots," said Grautz.

"I'll tell them not to," said Hambledon, and turned to meet the approaching men. "Heil Hitler," he began, with the regulation salute. "I shall want a man on duty here to see that nobody tramps about on the bank and crushes it down. There is a wire here which must not be tampered with."

"I will put a man here on duty," said the corporal in charge. "Where would the Herr wish him to be stationed?"

"Here," said Hambledon, indicating a spot on the further side of the bank. "No one else is to approach nearer than those birch trees upon any pretext."

"Certainly, Herr Professor. Hans! On guard."

Hans obeyed, though he did not look as though he liked it much. "There is nothing there yet, is there?" he asked, with an apprehensive glance over the bank.

"Don't stand on the wire, you oaf!" roared Hambledon, and the unhappy man leaped into the air. "Stand there. Don't move." They left him there alone and strolled back together toward the dais. "One cannot be too careful when dealing with high explosives," said Tommy sententiously. "The smallest mishap and—" He gestured upward.

"The Herr is more than right," said the corporal earnestly.

Soon after two o'clock cars began to arrive. Hambledon, looking out of the laboratory window, saw the cameramen being escorted to their appointed places. Some of them were plainly arguing with the corporal because they would be too far away from the explosion.

"If they knew what there was under there," said Hambledon to Grautz, "they wouldn't be so eager. I think they are rather close as it is."

"They are only Germans," said Grautz indifferently. He held up a beaker he was stirring with a glass rod. "Looks pretty, doesn't it?" It was a viscous liquid of a beautiful deep green; tiny flecks of gold floated in it.

"Reminds me of Christmas trees for some reason. Here's Goebbels. Now the Fuehrer won't be long. Where are the notes for my speech again? Ah, here." Hambledon pored over them, muttering.

"Here's Adolf," said Grautz irreverently.

"Now for it," said Hambledon. "I wish I didn't perspire so readily. Well, here goes."

He opened the laboratory door and advanced to meet the Fuehrer, Grautz following respectfully behind with the beaker of Ulsenite in one hand and a metal container in the other. Goebbels came forward, shook the professor warmly by the hand, and led him to Hitler.

"Mein Fuehrer, this is the distinguished Herr Professor Ulseth." Cameras clicked; sound-recording apparatus buzzed happily.

"I remember the Herr Ulseth," said Hitler in the orator's carrying voice, "from the old days of the inception of Our Party. I welcome an old comrade and party member."

"I am honored beyond my deserving," said Hambledon, bowing jerkily, "to have retained the smallest niche in the memory of Adolf Hitler."

Hitler smiled and nodded and immediately turned restlessly away. "The place—where is it?"

"This way, mein Fuehrer, this way," said Hambledon, and the party proceeded at a rapid pace up the path through the trees and over the ridge. Hitler kept glancing at Hambledon as they went past the cinematograph machines, and Tommy ambled along in as un-soldierly a manner as possible.

"All old comrades," said Hitler, who was apparently bent upon amiability that morning, "are dear to me."

"Everyone knows that," interjected Hambledon, thinking of Ernst Roehm and others.

"You have been too long absent from the Reich, Party Member Ulseth."

"I have spent studious years fitting myself to be of use to the Reich," answered Hambledon. They arrived at the dais. Hitler sat in the chair with his arms on the table before him in the familiar attitude; Hambledon stood in front facing the Fuehrer, and the rest of the concourse grouped itself around. The day was clear and sunny, and the cameramen continued to enjoy themselves. Hambledon drew a long breath.

"Mein Fuehrer, on this, the proudest day of my life, I have the honor to lay at your feet the results of a lifetime of labor. Here before you in this beaker"— Grautz handed it to him—"is Ulsenite, the new explosive, ten times more violent, volume for volume, than nitroglycerin or trinitrotoluol. It looks harmless and even beautiful, does it not?" said Hambledon, holding it up to the light. "Beautiful it is, but harmless?" Hambledon laughed scornfully. "In a few months, when I have perfected it, let Moscow say if it is harmless. Let London say. Let Leningrad say—if there is a voice left in any of those cities to say anything except 'Mercy, Hitler!' "

There was a murmur of approval from the crowd.

"Imagine," went on Hambledon, "the effect of a bombing raid when one hundred-kilogram bomb will do the work of one thousand-kilogram bomb. When a thousand kilograms will equal the effect of ten thousand kilograms. This, mein Fuehrer, is the gift I lay at your feet."

The Fuehrer, without actually recoiling, showed no inclination to inspect Ulsenite more closely.

"Nor is this all," said Hambledon, warming to his subject. "By no means. I look forward to the day when Victory shall crown our German Eagle and the world shall acknowledge the rule of Adolf Hitler from east to west and north to south. When we shall lay aside the arts of war and cultivate the arts of peace. Shall Ulsenite then be laid aside with the sword in the scabbard and the bomb in the—in the bomb rack? No, mein Fuehrer, no. Your acute mind has looked beyond these shadows and seen before I speak the future of Ulsenite in the internal-combustion engine."

Hitler left off fidgeting with the press-button switch and gave Hambledon his surprised attention.

"Here," said Hambledon, tapping the beaker with his fingernail, a performance which caused those nearest to him to retire several paces, "here is the ideal concentrated motor fuel. Men will fly to America and back on as much Ulsenite as would fill the familiar and useful beer mug. When I have perfected my explosive I lose interest in the production of war material. Let the manufacturers work. I, Ulseth, will cloister myself and not seek your august presence again until I have produced the Ulseth carburetor. Then let Adolf Hitler say if Sigmund Ulseth has lived in vain!"

Hambledon ceased amid applause. When it had died down he said, "I will now go and connect up this sample. Grautz! The detonating container."

Grautz handed over his can, which had two terminals soldered on the top and a screw cap at one corner. It had been painted black to conceal the fact that it had once held a liter of motor oil.

"Inside this container," said Hambledon, continuing to address the class, "is a fulminate-of-mercury detonating cap. I will attach these wires to these terminals. When our Fuehrer presses the button, a spark will detonate the fulminate of mercury and that, in its turn, the Ulsenite. I will now pour it in."

Grautz unscrewed the cap; Hambledon poured in the Ulsenite, gently glittering in the winter sunshine, handed the empty beaker to Grautz, and screwed the cap firmly on again.

"Now I will go to the explosion point and connect up," said Hambledon.

"When, exactly, do I press the button?" asked Hitler.

"When we return here, Excellency, when we return," said Hambledon hastily. "Not before, if you have any further use for your servants!"

"You shall yourself give the word," said Hitler kindly. Hambledon bowed, turned smartly, and walked in a processional manner beside the wire, holding the container of Ulsenite in both hands and followed by the faithful Grautz half a pace behind. Cinematograph machines followed them, focusing upon their faces, their hands, their feet. One observant young man picked out a stiff clump of grass; one saw Hambledon's feet approaching it. Would he avoid it? Would he trip over it? He did. He recovered himself.

"For heaven's sake, look where you're going!" hissed Grautz. "Remember what you're carrying."

"Sorry," said Hambledon. They were at that moment out of earshot, and he added thoughtfully, "Ulsenite, of course. Ulsenite. A dignified name. You know, I think it would have been much more appropriate if we'd called it Poppo. You see, don't—"

"Shut up!" snarled Grautz, covering his mouth with a careless gesture. "We're still being filmed, and some of the cinema audiences may be lip readers."

The rest of the journey to the explosion point was made in silence. Hans, still on guard by the bank, saw them coming and stood to attention. Grautz impatiently motioned him away. He obeyed at a speed which would have done him credit at the Olympic games. Hambledon and his assistant climbed over the bank and down into the hollow behind it, Grautz connected up the wires while Tommy partially embedded the tin in the loose soil.

"Can they see us talking from here?"

"No, but keep your head down, just in case."

"I was getting quite carried away by that speech," said Hambledon. "I nearly said Ulsenite was a certain cure for baldness and invaluable for the cleansing of false teeth. What is that stuff, incidentally?"

"Some of my cousin's homemade crème de menthe with a small bottle of gold paint stirred in. Attractive, wasn't it?"

"It might even be explosive."

"I shouldn't wonder," said Grautz. "Inflammable, anyway. Well, I think that'll do." He stood up.

"I only hope dear Adolf doesn't put his bony elbow on the switch before we arrive," said Hambledon, appearing to blow his nose behind a large handkerchief. They returned to the dais much more quickly than they went. Hambledon saw the film actress, Amalie Rielander, among the crowd as he came nearer. Evidently she had managed to obtain admission somehow.

"Well," said Hitler, with his front-teeth smile, "is it all ready now?"

"Whenever mein Fuehrer pleases," said Hambledon, and turned to look toward the explosion point just in time to see the cinema men nearest to it pick up their machines and race toward it. "Stop!" he yelled at the top of his voice, "stop, you damned fools—"

He was too late. Hitler had pressed his hand on the button and kept it there.

One man tripped and fell; the others ran on a pace or two before the earth opened and there was a vivid green flash plainly seen even in the sunlight. There followed an earsplitting roar, and debris flew up in a dense cloud, blotting out the scene; the ground jerked beneath their feet. There was a chorus of cries from the crowd. Hitler ducked instinctively and clung to the table; small pebbles and fragments of soil rained down upon them all. Even Hambledon turned rather white. The only man unmoved was Grautz, who watched the scene with exactly his usual air of placid interest. One felt that he was about to smile; Hambledon looked at him and shivered suddenly.

When the air cleared a little the cameraman who had tripped and fallen picked himself up unsteadily, supporting himself with his tripod; the others lay where they fell and did not move at all.

"They are stunned," said Hitler hoarsely. "Send a doctor to revive them. Hagen, will you see to it?" Several men ran; Hitler turned to Hambledon and said, "Remarkable! Astounding! Incredible! I congratulate you, Party Member Ulseth, on an amazing success. Please continue your so-wonderful work to its triumphant completion."

Hambledon bowed again and said he was happy to have satisfied his Fuehrer; Hitler showed his teeth again in his nervous grin, which had even less of mirth in it than usual, and left at once, accompanied by Goebbels and the more important of his companions. Hambledon stood uncertainly for a moment, and Amalie Rielander came from the small group which remained, to speak to him.

"I know I ought to congratulate you," she said, "but I can hardly speak. I've never been so frightened in all my life."

"If I had told you not to come, Fräulein," said Hambledon, "would you have taken any notice?"

"Probably not, but I certainly shall another time. Those poor men, are they much hurt?"

"I don't know, Fräulein. I am just going to see."

"I must not keep you," she said hastily. "I really wanted to ask you to come to the premiere of my film. Oh, do! It's at the Ufa-Palast next Monday at eight."

"Fräulein Rielander—" began Hambledon.

"Amalie."

"Fräulein Amalie, I am a very busy man, and cinematograph displays are hardly—"

"Oh, Herr Professor, don't be a grump. Bright green explosions aren't in my line at all, but I came to your premiere, didn't I? So you must come to mine. Do; it'll be such fun. Goering will be there with his Emmy, but there will still be room for you. Everybody will be there. I shall be so disappointed if you aren't."

"I could not disappoint the gracious Fräulein," said Hambledon, wondering why on earth she wanted him. There was only one way to find out why, and that was to go. Hambledon was incurably inquisitive.

"Oh, good! I am so glad. I must go; they are calling me. I'll send you a card. *Auf Wiedersehen,* dear Herr Professor."

She hurried away, and Hambledon walked across the grass to the place where the men lay; just before he reached it the doctor came to meet him.

"They are quite dead, Herr Professor. Not from their injuries, which are slight. It is their lungs which are collapsed."

"I am horrified," said Hambledon, "but they disobeyed orders—"

"No one can possibly blame the Herr Professor. I will convey what you have said to their families. Here, there is nothing to be done. I will arrange for the removal of the bodies at the earliest possible moment."

"Please," said Hambledon. He walked rapidly back to his laboratory, speaking to no one, went inside, and shut the door. Grautz was waiting for him.

"A great success," said the Dutchman cheerfully.

"Well done," said Hambledon. "I think a small drink is indicated; my head is still singing. I admired your 'soft apple-green' color immensely; it showed up well. In fact, I thought a distinct reflection of it lingered on the face of our Fuehrer for several moments afterward."

"Goebbels was the one," said Grautz, "only he didn't quite match. He was more the color of cabbage."

"Diseased cabbage. Well, here's to Poppo."

"Ulsenite," said Grautz firmly. "If you think Poppo, one of these days you'll say Poppo, and that won't do at all. Here's to Ulsenite."

"All right, Ulsenite. By the way, the gracious Amalie Rielander buttonholed me just now and insisted I should go to the premiere of her new film. I accepted to pacify her. I don't want to go. I can't even remember what the beastly thing's called."

"Wolfhounds of the Deep," said Grautz. "When is it?"

"Next Monday, at the Ufa-Palast. Goering will be there, she says, and everyone else who is anyone, I gather. Perhaps I'd better go; it's time I started doing something else besides providing the comic relief while you do all the work. Something might transpire. Besides, I want to know why she wants me. It's a trifle mysterious, and I don't like mysteries unless I make 'em myself."

"Perhaps she likes you," suggested Grautz.

"Heaven defend me," said Hambledon. "Life is quite difficult enough without being complicated by film actresses."

In the meantime the real Sigmund Ulseth was settling down well into the job of earning an honest living, answering to the name of Theophilus Hartzer and brightening the life of the widowed Frau Gerda Clausen. He made one trip to the Swiss frontier—not over it—and met a friend of his with whom he had a long talk. Thereafter, among the numerous deliveries from the Heroas Company which arrived at the Anhalter goods yards were many trucks containing wooden cases plainly marked "Spare Parts. Heroas Wagon Company, Zurich, to Herr T. Hartzer, Schönebuerger Strasse, Berlin." Ulseth sorted these out personally, and a railway delivery van brought them to his office. Here, after closing time, they were opened in private, and the Herr Andreas Adler of the Transport Ministry and his friends received cigars, liqueurs, cognac, and chocolate, but principally cigars. Their gratitude naturally expressed itself in more orders for the Heroas Company, and Ulseth's bank balance grew like grass in summer pastures.

Ulseth was of the type which becomes bumptious with success; that he did not do so was due to Gerda Clausen, and sometimes it annoyed him. He used to sit in front of the fire in his comfortable flat and make up imaginary conversations with her in which he was sparkling, irresistible, and a trifle condescending. "Little woman," he called her in his aspiring mind. "Come along, little woman; what about a spot of dinner and a show tonight, eh?" and her eyes would light up. "Oh, Herr Hartzer! How kind you are!" "Not Herr Hartzer," he would say. "Theo to you. Just Theo. Let me hear you say it, little woman." Then he would get out of his chair, walk up the two flights to her door, since the lift was still not working, and knock. This time he would really call her "little woman."

But every time the same thing happened. There came the quick tapping of high heels inside the door, she opened it and looked at him with those deep blue eyes of hers, and immediately his self-confidence evaporated.

"G'n abend, Herr Hartzer."

"G'n abend, gnä' Frau. I was wondering—if you are not too tired—if you have nothing better to do—whether you would honor me with your company this evening? We might—" And he would suggest one of the quieter Berlin resorts, or a play, or an opera. Sometimes she excused herself on the plea of fatigue and sometimes she accepted, whereupon he went downstairs to wait on his own doorstep for her coming, his breath uncontrollably light and his palms damp with excitement. All the evening he would squire her about, "If the *gnä' Frau* would care to—" "Would the *gnä' Frau* like—" This or that amusement or item on a menu. Seated opposite her at table, he would talk of places he had seen and adventures he had had, carefully edited for her ears; and Ulseth could talk well if he chose. After all, he had made his way in life by being able to talk. She was a good listener; she had little to say herself. A question at the right moment, a subdued exclamation of surprise, a suitable comment at the end of each story, that was all. But Ulseth felt himself well rewarded by a flash of amusement in her eyes and sometimes by her rare soft laughter.

When the evening was over he would escort her home, walk up the stairs again to her door, and kiss her hand like any stranger. "Thank you very much,

Herr Hartzer. A very pleasant evening." "The pleasure entirely mine, Frau Clausen. So kind of you to consent to come."

After which he would return to his room, stare discontentedly at himself in the mirror over the mantelpiece, and determine that next time it would be different. Next time, always next time.

On the evening of the day when the Ulsenite demonstration took place Ulseth was waiting in his sitting room with the door open, listening for Gerda Clausen's step on the stairs. They were going to dine at the Bristol — Ulseth still avoided the Adlon for fear of meeting the Swedes again. She had said she would be ready in twenty minutes. While Ulseth was waiting he remembered that he had an unread evening paper in his pocket. He took it out and opened it.

Headlines confronted him. "Ulsenite, the great new explosive. Beware the green flash, England! Famous scientist demonstrates before the Fuehrer." There was a photograph, in the center of the page, of Hambledon bowing before the Leader. The caption read, "Adolf Hitler greets an old comrade, Professor Ulseth, the explosives expert." The photograph was, needless to say, basically a portrait of Hitler. Hambledon presented a three-quarter back view of a man in a white coat who might be anybody; even a house decorator, thought Ulseth distractedly.

He put the paper down, rubbed his hands over his face, took a turn across the room, and stared at himself in the mirror. He looked quite normal, if a trifle wild-eyed; everything in the room was perfectly normal. He even pinched himself — yes, he felt that, but one could presumably pinch oneself in a dream. He returned to the paper, picked it up again, and went on reading.

Gerda Clausen, standing in the doorway, had to speak to him twice before he heard her. He considered for a moment asking her to put off the dinner; it would be no lie to say that he did not feel well. He felt very queer indeed, rather as though he had suddenly become twins. But even at a moment like that the sight of her exercised its usual spell. He could not disappoint her; besides, he felt he needed comforting. He crushed the paper into his overcoat pocket and they went out together.

The Hotel Bristol was full as usual of light, color, and animation. Famous people passed by. Gerda Clausen knew them all by sight much better than Ulseth did; she pointed them out. There was Ribbentrop, the Foreign Minister, with the regalia of an order across his chest, advancing to greet an elderly man who, Gerda said, was the Rumanian Ambassador. Himmler, unsmiling and apparently in a hurry. Emil Jannings, the film star, making a stage entry.

"It is very interesting to see all these famous people," said Gerda Clausen in her gentle voice.

"I am glad you are enjoying it, *gnä' Frau*," answered Ulseth, and immediately fell back into the press of his own thoughts. Who could this fellow be who was impersonating him? That man he had left tied to a chair in the farmhouse at Servatsch — impossible. He died, all right; there was a notice of his death in the Swiss papers. He died in hospital at Zurich; the servant was killed outright.

"Are you sure you are feeling quite well this evening?" asked Gerda Clausen compassionately. Ulseth pulled himself together.

"I beg your pardon; I am dull company tonight. I saw in the evening paper the death of a man I used to know," lied Ulseth. "The news brought back the old days, you understand. I did not mean to bore you with the story—"

"Tell me," she said, leaning forward across the table. "To me your stories are always interesting."

Ulseth recalled a few anecdotes for her entertainment but found it an effort to keep his mind on what he was saying.

"Do you not find this noise and glitter unwelcome tonight? Would you not rather we went home again?"

That did wake him up for a moment. "We went home." Dear intimacy; dear little woman. But already she seemed to have slipped away again, watching the people. "Look, there's Goebbels. I wonder who the woman is who's with him' it's not his wife."

"It often isn't with Goebbels," he answered. Goebbels: he was mentioned in that newspaper article; he was there that morning talking to the other Ulseth, shaking his hand, presenting him to the Fuehrer. A wild idea crossed Ulseth's mind of going up to Goebbels and asking him outright. "Who was that man you were talking to this morning? He's not Ulseth, because I am." Ridiculous idea; Goebbels would probably have him arrested then and there. Besides, he was Hartzer now, the Heroas Company's man; he could not unmask the other Ulseth without betraying himself. Ulseth passed his hand over his eyes; his head was beginning to ache.

Gerda Clausen saw it and cut the dinner short; Ulseth did not argue; he wanted to be alone and read that newspaper again. He wished her good night absentmindedly, let himself into his own room, and locked the door.

A newsreel film of the Ulsenite demonstration would be shown, said the paper, at the following cinemas in Berlin and district tomorrow, one of them was the Ufa-Palast in the Kurfürstendamm. Ulseth hurried away from his office and saw the film the next evening. When Hambledon turned away from the Fuehrer's dais, holding the can of Ulsenite reverently in both hands, he looked straight at one of the cameras for a second. Ulseth, sitting in the stalls at the Ufa-Palast, met the eyes of the man he had murdered in Switzerland seven weeks before.

He went straight back to his flat in Uhland Strasse and opened a case of Herr Adler's cognac. At ten o'clock that night he rolled out of his chair on to the floor, blind drunk.

CHAPTER XII

Next Sunday's Headlines

"IF ONLY my beard were a little longer," said Hambledon, struggling in front of the glass, "I shouldn't have to bother with an evening tie, should I?"

"Let me," said Grautz, and tied it expertly. "After all, a little deshabille is expected of eminent professors."

"And to think I had to part with precious coupons to acquire a dress suit. Grautz, why am I going:?"

"To enjoy yourself," said Grautz stoutly. "Remember to keep off the vodka and all will be well."

Hambledon arrived at the Ufa-Palast cinema in the blue Mercedes with Eckhoff driving and Bernstein sitting up beside him. Amalie Rielander was receiving her friends in a corner of the foyer. She gave him a dazzling smile and said she would look for him at the reception afterward. Hambledon was then conducted to a seat in the stalls and proceeded to sit through the show. In the event, it took more than all his patience to do this. The film was violent, trashy, and without subtlety; not even beautifully photographed sea scenes could give it dignity, and only when Amalie Rielander herself appeared was there anything worth seeing. "The acting's good," said Tommy to himself. "It's the characters that are so obnoxious. Too immaturely adolescent for words. Oh, why did I come?"

The reception was held in a gilded hall somewhere at the back of the stage, and with the help of a glass or two of excellent Rhine wine Hambledon began to recover his temper. He bowed over Amalie's hand and said all the right things in the right voice, exchanged a few words with Landahl of the Armaments Ministry, and talked amiably with a few acquaintances. Presently a booming voice behind him said cheerfully, "Well, Party Member Ulseth, did you enjoy the show?"

Hambledon turned and found Goering just behind him.

"Immensely, thank you, Herr Reichsmarschall."

"Especially when our young friend here was on the stage, eh?"

"She was by far the best actor in the whole cast."

Goering glanced round to see who was near him and spoke in a sort of stage whisper. "The only one of the whole menagerie who can act worth a damn, in my opinion."

Hambledon laughed and agreed with him. Goering handed his glass to someone inconspicuous with a tray, beamed down upon Hambledon, and said bluntly, "You know, when I first heard that you were one of the old gang in the early days I couldn't remember you at all, but now I see you I do. Quite distinctly."

"It is a long time ago," said Hambledon calmly. "There has been nothing to remind you of me for nearly twenty years."

"D'you mean to tell me you've been sitting in a laboratory making stinks and bangs ever since?"

"Incredible, but true."

"Well, well. You seem to have done it to some purpose, from what I hear. I couldn't get to your show last week, wish I had."

"I expect you'll have plenty of opportunities for studying Ulsenite in the future," began Hambledon, but Amalie Rielander interrupted him.

"Herr Reichsmarschall, did the Herr Professor tell you what he said about my poor film?"

"No, m'dear, what was that?"

"That it would be much funnier if, instead of clasping the baby and waving my handkerchief, I clung to the handkerchief and waved the baby."

Goering gave one of his famous roars of laughter. "Wave it round your head by its long petticoats, eh? I quite agree with him. Ulseth, you and I had better collaborate in a farce, I think. I'll suggest the low comedy—very low—while you provide the wisecracks. What?"

"Why not appear in it while we're about it? A new Laurel and Hardy."

Goering guffawed again.

"What about a part for me?" said Amalie. "I can't be left out of this."

"We will find something for you to wave, if only a baby," said Hambledon. At that moment the crowd parted a little and disclosed Goebbels watching them with malicious black eyes. Goering saw him and added pointedly, "Or a monkey. I could suggest an actor for that part."

Amalie Rielander followed his glance and said, "Thank you. On the whole I think I'd rather have a real one."

Goering laughed again. "I agree with you." He added in a lower tone, "All the same, be careful, my dear. The animal is dangerous."

Hambledon thought the subject had better be changed and offered Amalie a cigarette. "A real American one, Fräulein."

"Oh, how nice. Where on earth do you get them?"

"That would be telling," laughed Hambledon. "May I offer the Herr Reichsmarschall one also?"

"Have a cigar in exchange," said Goering. "These also are not ersatz. Curious how one picks these things up here and there, isn't it?"

"Yes, isn't it?" agreed Hambledon. "Though there's no particular mystery about my cigarettes. I happened upon a tobacconist who had a few left. I fear these are the last."

"I shall have to ask my tobacconist if he can get you some more with my next consignment of cigars," said Goering.

"Thank you, it would be kind of you," answered Hambledon, and made a mental note that there was evidently a little favored smuggling going on. Probably the information would never be of any use, but one never knows.

Goebbels arrived unexpectedly at Amalie Rielander's elbow and said, "Good evening, Herr Professor. Did you sleep well last night, Goering?"

"With the help of a good conscience, yes, thank you."

"Splendid. I was afraid you had been kept awake by echoes from Hamburg. What do you think of the British air raids, Professor?"

"I prefer them elsewhere," said Hambledon dryly. "They rattle things, and I live surrounded by substances which resent being rattled."

"You know whom to complain to, don't you?" said Goebbels. "The head of the Luftwaffe." He indicated Goering, who scowled, and Amalie Rielander intervened with immediate tact.

"Must we discuss such horrible things at my party?"

"Your pardon, *gnä'* Fräulein Amalie," said Goebbels. "Your glass is empty, Herr Ulseth. Let us find the Niersteiner. I can recommend it." He led Hambledon toward the bar.

Tommy refrained with an effort from saying that the habits of one's early youth tended to persist and merely answered, "Have you tried the vodka? Or is it unpatriotic to drink it now that they are no longer our allies?"

"I don't care for spirits," said the Minister indifferently. Having detached Hambledon from Amalie Rielander, Goebbels appeared to lose interest in him and introduced him at random to the nearest man at hand, an elderly general whose name Hambledon did not catch.

"Delighted to make your distinguished acquaintance," said the general politely. "I had the privilege of seeing your so-remarkable demonstration last week. Most impressive."

"Excuse me," said Goebbels, "a man there I ought to speak to—" He went away.

"I am reasonably satisfied myself with the explosive as such," said Hambledon carelessly. "The problem of making it stable for an adequate period is the difficulty at present. It is a great difficulty and will probably take some time to solve."

"How long?" asked the general anxiously. "Have you any idea how long?"

"Some months at least," said Hambledon. "One tries one expedient after another, you understand. We might hit on the right thing tomorrow, or not for seven or eight months."

"So long as that—"

"My dear sir," said Hambledon impatiently, "I can't remember offhand how many years it was after the discovery of nitroglycerin before Nobel found out that the addition of diatomaceous earth—"

"It's no good hurling scientific names at me," said the general simply. "I don't understand a word of it." Hambledon warmed toward him. "All I know," went on the soldier, "is what to do with the stuff when I get it. The point I was trying to make was, the sooner the better."

Hambledon pricked up his ears. "I should work double tides," he said. "Night and day. Good night. I am going back to work."

"Good night," said the general. "I wish you luck from the bottom of my heart."

"Not luck, General. Inspiration," said Hambledon, and took his leave.

After breakfast next morning the Herr Professor made a public fuss in front of Eckhoff because he had apparently run out of cigarettes. He was certain he had some. Where were they?

"I expect you gave away a good many at the reception last night, *gnä' Herr,*" said Grautz.

"Here is a packet with two left in it," said Eckhoff, producing it from behind a photograph of Hitler on the bookcase.

"Two, huh," said Hambledon, lighting one of them.

"If I were to get out the car at once," said Eckhoff, "it would only take a very little time to drive to the shop in Spandauer Strasse."

"I suppose that's the only thing to do, though I wanted to start work at once."

"If I were to go alone," began Eckhoff.

"He would say he was out of them," said Hambledon. "He may be, of course. And it's no good my writing a note, because he'd think the Gestapo had forged it."

"Personal shoppers only," said Grautz.

"Quite. Yes, get the car out, Eckhoff. We'll go at once, not to waste time."

"A run in the cool morning air," said Eckhoff kindly, "will refresh the Herr Professor before he starts upon his labors." He left the laboratory to get out the car.

"Anybody would think I was on a binge last night," said Hambledon, "to hear my chauffeur recommending the fresh morning air."

"Our Eckhoff is positively paternal," said Grautz.

"Our Eckhoff isn't at all a bad fellow," said Hambledon, "for a German."

By good fortune the shop was empty when Hambledon went in. He passed behind the counter into the stuffy little sitting room which had heard so many secrets. Gibson, whom he had met at the Germannia Restaurant in the Kurfürstendamm, looked up from the *Berliner Zeitung* as Hambledon entered.

"Good morning, eminent Professor," he said. "How's Ulsenite this morning?"

"Just as green as ever," answered Hambledon. "How are the door knock-ers? And what's the news this morning?"

"Not much," said Gibson, "except that I've got that explosives formula you asked for. Here it is. I was to tell you for heaven's sake to be careful, it's horribly dangerous."

"Oh, I'm not going to use it. I don't know who is, but if there's a resounding bang one afternoon I might be able to guess, mightn't I? How's my twin brother Ulseth-Hartzer getting on?"

"Very nicely indeed. The Heroas people must be pleased with him. He is well in with the Transport Ministry. He gets cigars and other trifles into the country for them, and they respond by giving him orders."

"Cigars, eh?" said Hambledon. "Then I think I probably had one last night, only Goering gave it to me, not one of the transport people. How does he — Ulseth, I mean — get them in, d'you know?"

"In the trucks, in wooden cases marked 'Spare Parts.' We have some fellows working as porters at the Anhalter, among other places, and one of them thought the boxes were rather light for spare parts. So he investigated, and lo! Havanas."

"What about the customs?" asked Weber. "They're my principal worry."

"I expect the transport people have squared them," said Gibson.

"I wish we could induce Herr Hartzer to replenish my stock," said Weber. Hambledon emerged suddenly from a cloud of thought.

"Cigars," he said. "Explosives."

"Eh?" said the surprised Gibson.

"Look here. You want materials for your saboteurs. If I can induce Ulseth to bring them in, can you get them put in his trucks in Switzerland and collect them at the Anhalter goods yards?"

"No doubt," said Gibson. "It'll take a little time to arrange, but doubtless it could be done. I thought you were going to make the stuff at your place and —"

"This is a better idea. You can order just what you want and get it. You see, if we get in a lot of materials without any results to show for it, and if a lot of bangs and pops occur all over Berlin, somebody — probably Goebbels — might begin to wonder. Goebbels doesn't like me already. He never did, though he doesn't know it. Whereas, if I can get the stuff into the country some other way, Grautz and I can go on playing with a few ounces of this and that and it'll be obvious we've had nothing to do with the sabotage. Much better. Thank you, Weber, that was a whale of an idea. Nothing else of any interest, Gibson?"

"There's a lady," began Gibson.

"The world is full of them," said Hambledon. "What does this one do and who is she?"

"I don't know, to both questions, and I should like to. Her name is Alexia Schneider, and she lives in a flat in the Charlottenburg district."

"German?"

"I don't think so."

"Don't say she's a beautiful Russian," said Hambledon. "All my life I've wanted to meet a beautiful Russian spy, and I never have."

"She may be Russian," said Gibson, "but I fear she isn't beautiful. My own idea is that she's possibly a Pole. She's a thin, dark woman of about forty, I suppose, a bit haggard but extremely well dressed. She seems to have plenty of money."

"What's queer about her?" asked Hambledon. "There are hundreds of women like that in every town in Europe. Somebody's widow, is she?"

"Presumably. She's the Frau Schneider, and there doesn't seem to be any complementary Herr. She makes friends with girls and gives them presents."

"Oh gosh," said Hambledon with distaste.

"Always girls who work at the War Ministry," said Gibson pointedly.

"Oh. That's different. Typists and clerks and so forth?"

"Yes. She gives 'em frocks and bits of jewelry and so forth—usually when *der liebe* Fritz is coming home on leave, I think. I've seen one or two of these girls out with their boyfriends in clothes they'd hardly have bought for themselves."

"And you think she's collecting information?"

"I just wondered. I can't imagine her cultivating these girls for the pleasure of their company. I think they'd bore her stiff. She's witty and cultured and very entertaining to talk to."

"Oh, you know her personally, do you?"

"Slightly. I shall improve the acquaintance."

"Well, be careful," said Hambledon, rising. "I don't know why I tell you to be careful, because I'm sure it's quite unnecessary. It is merely the automatic reaction aroused in me by the word 'woman.' I must go now or my driver will begin to wonder what I'm doing all this time. What a curse is the human capacity for wonderment in the wrong place. Think over that suggestion about the explosives via Ulseth. I'll see you again soon. These my cigarettes? Thanks awfully, Weber. What I should do without you I can't think. Good-by."

Chapter XIII
Ulseth Visits Ulseth

ULSETH'S OFFICE in the Schönebuerger Strasse had been a small shop devoted to the sale of sweets, tobacco, and newspapers. The window looked so bare with nothing in it that he had obtained some models of trucks from the Heroas Company, together with short lengths of track, and arranged them in place of the cigarettes and chocolate long since retired to the darkest recesses of the Black Market. Behind the window a net curtain preserved the privacy of the office while enabling the inmate to see out. Ulseth was at his desk one afternoon checking consignment lists, when he heard a car stop outside. He looked out and saw a blue Mercedes with two uniformed S.S. men in the front seats and a bearded gentleman in a wide-brimmed hat sitting behind. "This is somebody very important," said Ulseth to himself. "Fancy having a car to drive round Berlin in these days—and such a car!"

One of S.S. men sprang out as soon as the car stopped, opened the office door, and said, "Heil Hitler! Herr Theophilus Hartzer?"

"Heil Hitler. Right first time," said Ulseth cheerfully, supposing his visitor to be another candidate for his most-favored-bosses list for special imports. The man retired, opened the car door, and saluted smartly as the bearded gentleman got out. The next moment Ulseth felt as though someone had hit him hard in the midriff, for his visitor was that distinguished scientist the inventor of Ulsenite, friend of Hitler, hobnobber with Goebbels and other great ones, impersonator of Ulseth himself, mystery man and general nuisance.

Hambledon walked into the shop and shut the door behind him; Bernstein returned to his seat in the car. Ulseth rose; he did not wish to stand up because it might be taken as a sign of respect, but he felt better on his feet.

"Good afternoon, Herr Ulseth-Hartzer," said Hambledon.

"Good afternoon, Herr Hartzer-Ulseth. I thought I might see you sometime," said Ulseth impudently.

"You may sit down," said Hambledon, and took the other chair. Ulseth hesitated and then obeyed. He felt it was a mistake to do, but for some reason he could not avoid it. There was something unpleasantly compelling about his visitor; there had been even when he was helplessly tied to that hard kitchen chair at Servatsch. Ulseth pulled himself together.

"I am really quite glad you're not dead," he said condescendingly. "I was sorry to have to kill you. I said so at the time, if you remember."

"So you were expecting to see me," said Hambledon, disregarding this. "Why?"

"Why? I should have thought that was obvious."

"Not to me," said Tommy, uncrossing his legs and crossing them the other way.

"Oh, surely," said Ulseth. "Here you are, apparently in quite a nice position, drawing a damn good salary too, I bet, calling yourself Ulseth the chemist and getting away with it. It must have been rather a blow when you found there was a man in Berlin who could blow your pretty story kite high—as though with Ulsenite," he added with a grin. "My congratulations on that name. I wish I'd thought of it myself."

"Is there such a man?" said Hambledon.

"Don't be ridiculous. Me, of course. It's no use your fencing with me, you know. I thought better of your intelligence."

"Tell me," said Tommy, lighting a cigarette, "what did you think I came here for?"

Ulseth uttered an exasperated sigh. "What's the matter with you? Since you insist, what happened was this. You found out I was here in Berlin—how, I don't know, but it doesn't matter. You probably discovered I'd got a pretty good position, too. You said to yourself, 'This won't do. I must see that fellow Ulseth and persuade him not to blow the gaff on me.' Whey not? We're both businessmen. Why shouldn't we come to an arrangement? I don't mind how far you fool these blasted Nazis. Why should I? Live and let live's my motto."

Hambledon laughed scornfully.

"Whenever possible," amended Ulseth. "You're thinking of Servatsch. I didn't see any alternative then, but maybe things have turned out for the best. One of these days you shall tell me how you escaped. I should be interested to hear it."

"I'll tell you that at once," said Hambledon. "I got up and walked out."

Ulseth stared. "You're not Houdini's twin brother, are you? I suppose someone came—"

"No one came. Go on with what you were saying before."

Ulseth gulped. "Well, you're a marvel, I give you that. You came here this afternoon, of course, to see what I'd take to hold my tongue."

Hambledon began to laugh. He was very much amused; he rocked in his chair and had to wipe his eyes. Ulseth watched him with a sort of creeping horror.

"You think," said Hambledon, recovering himself with an effort, "that you have only got to go and ring Himmler's doorbell and say, 'That fellow Ulseth's a fraud,' and the Gestapo will do the rest?"

"Well, I can prove it, can't I?"

"Can you? How?"

Ulseth said, "But I'm Ulseth; you aren't."

"Can you prove it? Suppose you go and say, I'm Ulseth, professor of chemistry, or whatever you called yourself. 'This fellow has merely stolen my formula.' Then they'll—perhaps—say, 'All right. Here's a laboratory complete with all necessary trimmings. Now go ahead and make Ulsenite.' Could you?"

Ulseth stared unhappily at him.

"Complete with a nice green flash?" went on Hambledon. "You know perfectly well you couldn't; you told me so at Servatsch. You'd be unexpectedly lucky if you ended up in a lunatic asylum instead of one of the Gestapo's Quiet Homes for Harmless People. Well?"

Ulseth had nothing to say.

"Whereas," pursued Hambledon, "I have made Ulsenite, and very good stuff it is, though I say it myself. You're in the cart, not me. I've only got to arrange for one of the Heroas Company's directors to come and have a look at you, and you're sunk. We're not really much alike, you know."

"But," began Ulseth, "I have been getting orders for them, lots of orders—"

"A blind, semiparalyzed village idiot could get orders for rolling stock out of the German government just now. It's their greatest shortage; everybody knows that. By the way, I suppose you practiced my signature?"

"Of course," said Ulseth sulkily.

"And Heaven reward the man who invented typewriters."

"There are those three Swedes," said Ulseth, in the manner of a man finding in his hand a trump card he'd overlooked. "You used to talk to them at the Trois Couronnes, didn't you? They knew you as Hartzer. You might find them rather a trouble."

"I did," said Hambledon calmly. "They came worrying at the Adlon when I was staying there. So I complained to the authorities and had them thrown out of the country. Besides, you forget. If they knew me as Hartzer, who are you? I think you owe them some money, don't you?"

Ulseth abandoned the Swedes.

"Who the devil are you, anyway?" he exploded.

"Theophilus Hartzer of the Heroas Company," said Hambledon with an impish grin. "Don't tell anybody, will you?"

"I wish I'd brained you at Servatsch," said Ulseth.

"Alas for wasted opportunities. But now I trust I have made our relative positions clear. You are entirely at my disposal, Ulseth, not vice versa, and I will now tell you what is going to happen. You can carry on as you are doing for the present—during good behavior—on condition you do what I tell you. I have got a little job for you, Ulseth."

"What is it?" asked Ulseth in a choking voice.

"Merely to get me some cigars."

Ulseth gaped at him.

"All this fuss over a few cigars? But I get those—"

"I know you do," said Hambledon gently, "and now you are going to get some for me. I'll let you know the details later. Good-by, and don't to anything rash. It won't pay you."

Hambledon went out to be saluted and waited upon by his smart servants and drove away in state and the blue Mercedes.

There followed three or four weeks which Hambledon always reckoned as among the most miserable he had ever spent. An evil dawn rose and fell upon Pearl Harbor; Shanghai and Hong Kong were names to make the heat ache. Siam admitted the invader; two days later *Prince of Wales* and *Repulse* went down off the Malay coast. The U-boat war in the Atlantic was an appalling menace; as the new year got into its stride, Manila fell and the name of Singapore began to have an ominous ring about it. The Germans, naturally, rejoiced openly, and Hambledon had to join in the general jubilation. He made pressure of work an excuse for not appearing in public and remained, fretting and irritable, in the laboratory.

"I told you it would be death and damnation," he said to Grautz. "I wish to God I wasn't so often right. Here am I shut up in Berlin and not doing a damn thing about it. Posing and capering like a buffoon 'and nobody seems one penny the worse.' "

"Patience," began Grautz.

"Patience!" exploded Hambledon. "I didn't come here to be patient. I think I'll go and call on Hitler with a bomb in my pocket. There'll be one scab the less on the—"

"They search Hitler's visitors," said Grautz with infuriating calmness. "There'd be one British agent the less, that's all. Besides, if you did kill him it wouldn't do any good. He would become the national Martyred Saint, and the war would go on just the same."

"St. Adolf surrounded by a halo of Merry Widows," snarled Hambledon.

"You are losing your sense of humor," observed Grautz with justice. "Merry widows don't usually wear halos—or compose them."

Hambledon laughed. "You are quite right, and I beg your pardon. It's sitting here doing nothing that gets on my nerves."

"When the stuff begins to come through from Switzerland you'll feel better. By the way, I forgot to tell you. I left that very explosive formula you got from Gibson on the floor under the bench again last night, and it was gone this morning."

"At last," said Hambledon. "How often have we left that out for Eckhoff to find? I thought he would never find it."

"I expect he was afraid it was something really important left out by mistake and didn't like to take it. We should have had to hand it to him personally if it had stayed there much oftener."

"Couldn't do that," said Hambledon. "So inartistic. Not playing the game. Eckhoff wouldn't have liked that. Well, I hope Goebbels' dear Herr Kallenbach blows himself into a cloud of pale pink dew."

Hambledon had completed his arrangements with Ulseth for the delivery of what Ulseth still thought were cigars, thought he was a little surprised to find what large quantities were wanted. "You smoke more than Winston Churchill," he said, and Hambledon smiled amiably. "I also have friends," he said. Ulseth was a little annoyed to find that his agents in Switzerland were not expected to purchase the cigars, as there was naturally a nice little profit to be made on them. All Ulseth's men had to do was to refrain from interference when they found wooden cases marked "Spare Parts" already in the Heroas Company's wagons when they came from the works. These cases were clearly marked with a five-pointed star burned into the wood. Many of them disappeared from the wagons wherever the goods trains stopped en route to Berlin, and still more vanished on arrival at the Anhalter goods yards. Very often there were none left by the time the pilfering gang of porters at the Berlin terminus had finished unloading them. If there were, Ulseth would ring up Hambledon, and Eckhoff would come with the car to fetch them away.

Soon after these consignments began to arrive, things started to happen in Berlin, and Hambledon cheered up. There was a cherubic old gentleman, something like Mr. Pickwick in appearance, with gold-rimmed spectacles and an umbrella, who traveled about a great deal on Berlin's transport system by train, bus, and tram. He explained to any friendly traveler who got into conversation with him that he was a chartered accountant whose business it was to go round to different firms and audit their accounts. "Very interesting work. So much psychology in it. So many human documents!" He carried a dispatch case and sometimes small parcels wrapped in paper. He was a careless old gentleman, for he used to leave these parcels behind when he got out of the crowded carriages. Some time later the small packages would burst into inextinguishable flame or just burst with a shattering report. It was all very bad for civilian morale.

Then there was the night when the tramway depot caught fire and the trams blazed furiously. The fire started right in the middle of the parked trams, so that those behind and round it could not be got out. This was pure luck, as the shabby workman who had pushed the incendiaries behind the seat in the tram could not possibly tell where it would be left.

There came a night when the sirens howled over Berlin, and presently the steady roar of many aircraft could be heard. Hambledon and Grautz went outside and looked up at the sky, bright with hundreds of searchlights. A few minutes later the antiaircraft defenses of the city went into action, and the uproar was deafening. It was increased when the bombs began to fall, and in several directions a white glare appeared, turning to red as the fires took hold.

"A pleasant sight," said Hambledon cheerfully.

"It is not yet so impressive as the bombing of Rotterdam," said Grautz regretfully.

"Never mind. It will be, presently. It's a long way from Britain, you know."

"There's a big flash," said Grautz, pointing. "They touched off something that time."

"I could watch this all night, couldn't you?" began Hambledon, and broke off abruptly as something passed near them with a noise like "whee-aouw plonk!"

"Everything that goes up," said Grautz, pushing Hambledon toward the doorway, "must come down. I think it would be silly to be brained by stray bits of antiaircraft shell."

After a time the raid came to an end; the searchlights went out, and only the flickering red of fires illuminated the night sky and the smoke which billowed up and hung like clouds over the city. Hambledon and Grautz went to bed, but all through the night and the next day occasional explosions proclaimed the presence of delayed-action bombs. The following evening Hambledon went to dinner at the Adlon as a change from Frau Bernstein's uninspired cooking. He was having a preliminary sherry at the bar when he was greeted by Goering; they had met several times since the premiere of Amalie Rielander's film.

"Kept awake last night, were you?" asked Goering.

"It was a little noisy, wasn't it?" said Hambledon. "Your gunfire caused most of the uproar, I think."

Goering nodded. "Have you got a shelter out there? You ought to have, if it's only a trench with a sheet of iron over it and earth piled on the top. I'll send a gang out and fix you up."

"It is thoughtful of you," said Hambledon, "but I think the certainty of rheumatism is worse than the chance of a direct hit. My walls are pretty solid."

"Yes, but your roof isn't. Besides, you must have a shelter; it's compulsory. Going into it is compulsory too, you know. There are also your guards at the lodge."

"There wasn't much damage done, was there?" said Hambledon, to change the subject. "Apart from the fires, I mean. There seemed to be a lot of explosions and not much to show for it."

"It's always like that in a city," said the Reichsmarschall. "London has had a frightful hammering, and yet I'm sure you could drive through street after street and not find anything worse than broken windows. Houses shield each other from blast, you know."

Hambledon agreed. "Actually, the only damage I've really seen in Berlin was at the place where I buy my laboratory glass. I went there this afternoon for something, and the place was in ruins. Very annoying. They knew me there. Curious, the other houses round about didn't seem much the worse."

Goering emptied his glass and had it refilled; it occurred to Hambledon, looking at him carefully, that he had done that several times before.

"Between ourselves," said the big man quietly, "it isn't all bombing. Some of it is sabotage, and it's a little annoying."

"I should think so!" said Hambledon indignantly. "But how can you tell? One heap of ruins looks like another to me."

"Yes. But if you have a building damaged on the ground floor by explosion or fire, and there isn't a hole in the roof, it makes you wonder how it got there, doesn't it?"

"I see. But how do they do it? I thought everyone had to leave their houses and go into shelters in the city—"

"Not the air-raid services—firemen, wardens, and so on. The houses are left open; any of these men could walk in. It is almost impossible to keep a check on all of them."

"It's difficult to believe any man would do that in his own city."

Goering laughed and made a gesture with thumb and forefinger. "Money is great persuader, and sometimes people have private grudges to pay off, you know. You are too innocent for this wicked world, Ulseth."

"I do indeed lead a rather retired life."

"Sometimes I could envy you. No, what's worrying me is not that people can be found to do it, but where do they get their supplies from? Tell me that."

Hambledon could have done so, easily. Instead he said, "I suppose it's stolen from the various factories where it's made, isn't it?"

"No doubt," said Goering gloomily, "but there was a hell of a lot of it about last night."

"Would it not be possible—I'm no businessman—to order a check to be taken? A sort of stocktaking in the various firms. If any of them were much short you would have something to go upon."

"Yes," said Goering. "That could be done. An awful job, though, with stuff coming in and going out all the time. Still, I think it will have to be tried. I'll turn the Armaments Ministry on to it."

"You could start with me," said Hambledon in a lighter tone. "We keep our books very tidily."

Goering smiled. "I think I'll keep you as a last resort," he said. "You haven't had enough materials in for a tenth of what happened last night. Besides," he added, laughing, "there was no green flash that I've heard of."

"Then there's Goebbels' factory," went on Hambledon in the same tone. "The Kallenbach concern out at Spandau."

Goering looked at him. "Oh, you know that, do you?"

"Herr Goebbels brought his friend Herr Kallenbach to my place when we were arranging my demonstration. He did not walk round with us; he stayed behind talking to my assistant."

"Doing a little pumping, eh? The dirty dog."

"So I naturally wondered who he was," said Hambledon.

"Naturally." A slow smile broadened upon Goering's face. "It would be funny if there was a leakage there, wouldn't it?"

"It would amuse me," said Hambledon frankly.

"I should laugh for a week," said the Reichsmarschall. "Popular little fellow, G., isn't he?"

"So I've noticed."

"But dangerous, Ulseth, dangerous. Watch your step."

"I can't believe," said Hambledon, "that anything I do is important enough to annoy the Herr Minister of Propaganda. If Ulsenite turns out a success, his firm can have one of the contracts for making it. I don't mind. I told the Fuehrer I wasn't interested in manufacture, and it's true."

"Queer bird you are," said Goering.

"I didn't say I wasn't interested in a small percentage," said Hambledon hastily. "I only mean I didn't care who made it, or where."

"Ah," said Goering with a laugh, "that's more human. If you'd meant you didn't want to make any money out of it, there would indeed have been something queer about you."

"Why?" said Hambledon. "Am I regarded as being a little—" He tapped his forehead.

"I don't mean queer in the head. I mean—what was the expression?—a trifle mysterious, I think."

"Whose expression was that?"

"Goebbels', of course. That's what I meant just now when I told you he was dangerous."

"Oh," said Hambledon rather blankly. "But I still don't know what I've done to—"

Goering began to laugh. "You're altogether too modest, Ulseth. Amalie Rielander, of course."

"Delectable heavens," said the horrified Hambledon, "at my time of life—"

"She always talks about you whenever she sees Goebbels. Perhaps the little devil only does it to annoy him. I told her to stop it. Have you been seeing much of the lady? No business of mine—"

"I have met her once or twice," said Hambledon rather stiffly. "In any case, it would not have occurred to me to ask Herr Goebbels' permission—"

"No, no," said Goering in a soothing voice; perhaps he also had heard of the famous Ulseth tantrums. "Of course not. Don't let it annoy you. I only thought it would be neighborly to drop you a friendly hint sometime as to how the land lay."

"It is extremely good of you, and I'm very grateful," said Hambledon. "Again, I can't think what I've done to deserve your kindness."

"I don't know," said Goering rather vaguely. "You remind me of someone I used to like not so long ago, but for the life of me I can't remember who it is."

"Some chance resemblance," said Hambledon, and took his leave forthwith. He even found he had lost his appetite for dinner.

Chapter XIV

Pink Cloud over Spandau

HAMBLEDON went straight home from the Adlon to the laboratory and found Grautz sitting over the fire and working out chess problems on a pocket chessboard.

"Things are getting sticky," said Hambledon. "I'm beginning to wonder how long we shall last."

"Not 'beginning,' " said Grautz. "You always did. What's happened?"

"Goering says I remind him of someone he knew not long ago and he can't remember who. And Goebbels has got his knife into me over Amalie Rielander."

"Amalie—"

"Don't laugh; it's true. Apparently the little hussy goes all moony over dear Professor Ulseth—I bet she calls me Sigmund—whenever Goebbels shows signs of going moony over her."

"Trying to eclipse him with you?"

"Do be serious, because it is. Besides, at my age and with my beard—if Goebbels had the faintest sense of humor he wouldn't believe it. It isn't respectable," said Hambledon indignantly.

"Never mind," said Grautz. "You aren't chief of police now."

"What d'you mean?"

"No need to spend your days setting a good example."

"You have no sense of decorum," said Hambledon. "By the way, I think I've caused some Nazi headaches tonight." He told Grautz about his suggestion to Goering that stocks of explosives in the possession of manufacturers should be checked. "I can't imagine how they'll do it, with raw materials of all sorts coming in at all times, and the product in all stages of manufacture."

"The best way," said Grautz, "would be to stop production for a couple of days. Just as they close shops for stocktaking, you know."

"They'd never do that in the middle of a war. Or would they? It would be typically German. If I've stopped all local production of explosives for two solid days by a few idle words—"

"You have not talked in vain," said Grautz solemnly.

Far away to the east, between Mojaisk and Moscow, a German battery was shelling a Russian position. The Russians were on the slope of a hillside slightly above their enemies, so the German gunners could themselves see their shells falling instead of having to rely upon telephoned reports. The subaltern in charge of the battery was watching through field glasses and occasionally cursing fluently.

"Another one, Herr Leutnant?"

"Another, yes. This is a rotten batch of shells we've got."

"That makes fifteen today so far," said the sergeant, "besides all those we had yesterday. Would it not be possible to note the markings on these shells in order to make a complaint?"

"An excellent idea, Feldwebel. An even better one would be to send back some of the dud shells for examination."

"If we take the position, Herr Leutnant, we could pick some of them up, no doubt."

"Whereas if we don't take the position, they are uncomfortably out of reach. Let's hope we take it."

As it happened, they did take it, and the lieutenant with his sergeant made a point of going to the spot to look for dud shells. They had to dig them out of snowdrifts unpleasantly littered with the debris of battle, but they managed to find six before the Russians got their range and began to shell them.

"If you fellows have quite finished building snow castles or what ever you're doing," said an infantry officer from the hole in the ground where he was sitting, "you'd better clear out of this. The Bolshevik Menace is coming on again."

They went, taking their treasures with them, and reported what had happened. Since theirs was by no means the only complaint on this subject which had recently been received, the defective shells, with others similarly obtained, were sent back to Germany for investigation. They proved to be full of sand and cement powder, and could not possibly have injured any Russian unless they had actually collided with him.

"Sabotage," said the experts accurately. "Now, where did those shells come from?"

The cases were stamped with the code number of the factory of origin and a date. The lieutenant's six shells were turned out at the Kallenbach works, Spandau, in October 1941; others came from various places. In each instance an immediate investigation of the most stringent description was ordered, and a song of sorrow arose from each of the factories concerned.

"Infected with Bolshevik poison," said one manager. "The workmen have no conscience. So long as they can produce so many filled shells, they care not what they fill them with."

"It is all this rotten foreign labor," said another, with some justification. "One can't trust any of them for a single minute, and it's impossible to watch all the workmen all the time."

"It is the Jews," said yet another, and when it was pointed out to him that there were no Jews working in his factory he said he didn't care, it was the Jews. They had managed it somehow.

Goebbels sent for Kallenbach, and the interview was stormy.

"What the hell do you suppose I put you in as manager for, Kallenbach? For decoration? If there is a factory in Germany whose products are above suspicion, it ought to be mine. I thought it was. I had a right to think it was. Now, here am I standing up to have mud thrown at me because I have an incompetent, idle, muttonheaded fool at the head of it, who allows shells to be filled with sand under his nose and can't see it!"

"Very few people," stammered Kallenbach, "know that Your Excellency is the owner of—"

"Don't blether! Quite a lot of people know. If only one knew, it would be one too many; he'd talk now. How was it done?"

"It was sabotage—" began Kallenbach.

Goebbels exploded with wrath; Kallenbach backed away a couple of paces and tried again.

"It was the French workers. I will arrange a new system of overseeing and inspection—"

"You'd better. Where do they get the sand and cement from to fill them with? Wheel it in in wheelbarrows when you're not looking?"

"Materials for the additional buildings, Excellency," said the agitated Kallenbach. "When we added the two extra filling shops. There was a good deal left lying about—"

"Have it cleared away at once. But the first thing to do is to inspect every single one of the shells completed and awaiting dispatch."

Kallenbach blenched. "But there are thousands of them; as it happens, the bays are almost full."

"All the better. If there are any more, perhaps we shall find them. If there are any more after that, I'll have you shot. Get out of my sight."

Kallenbach fled.

The bays to which he referred were long, narrow, semi-subterranean storage rooms with concrete roofs, having solid banks of earth between them to localize the effect of any possible explosion. In these rooms the boxes of shells were packed away, as soon as they were filled, to await dispatch. Owing to transport difficulties there had been no delivery from the factory for a longer time than usual, and, as the manager had said, the bays were nearly full.

Kallenbach returned to his factory in misery and haste, sent for the two undermanagers and several foremen, and unfolded his packet of woe. The undermanagers lamented loudly; the foremen knew their places too well to speak until they were asked for their views, but their expressions of face equaled anything the undermanagers could say.

"Is it, then, necessary to unpack every one of about twenty-five thousand shells, open them up and examine the contents?" asked one undermanager.

"It will take weeks," said the other.

"It would seem so," said Kallenbach.

There was a painful pause which the manager broke by asking whether any of the foremen had anything to suggest.

"I was wondering," said one of them, "whether they got the weights right."

"Ah," said Kallenbach hopefully. "Go on."

"We'd 'ave to 'unt through one by one till we found a case with a dud one in. Then we weighs it, and if, as I expect, it's a bit too 'eavy, we 'as only to weigh the others and we'd know. At least we'd know which 'ad duds in; we'd 'ave to examine each shell in them cases as was too 'eavy."

"That'll be a long job," said the second undermanager.

"But not nearly so long as examining them all," said Kallenbach. "Thank you, Muller, that was a helpful suggestion. Get on with the job at once. Select trustworthy men to help you and start now. Also, put a gang of laborers at once on the job of clearing away those dumps of sand and stuff. Cart it right away outside the works. If Herr Goebbels sees them still here when he comes again—"

The foreman Muller was right. The first case in which they found a sabotaged shell weighed nearly a kilogram more than the perfect ones. Goebbels came, saw, and approved.

"Get all the cases out of the bays at once," he said. "Get a dozen weighing machines going. Keep at it night and day till you've done them all. Then we shall at least have some ready to send away as soon as transport is available. There will probably be some at the end of this week."

Kallenbach said, "Certainly, Excellency," but one of the undermanagers demurred.

"It is not safe," he said with truth. "Suppose the smallest explosion occurred— Besides, it is against the safety regulations, which forbid—"

"I thought I gave an order," snarled Goebbels. "Besides, it will only be for two or three days. You can pack the cases away again as they are weighed."

Kallenbach agreed again. "We have never had the slightest trouble here before. Why should we have any now?"

"Exactly," said Goebbels, and drove away, leaving the undermanager muttering to himself.

There was a large open space in front of the bays. On the far side of this, away from any other building and enclosed by a bank of earth all to itself, was the experimental laboratory attached to the factory. Here were three painstaking gentlemen in white overalls working diligently upon a new formula which had been presented to them. This formula had been carefully and accurately copied from a piece of paper which Eckhoff had found under a bench in the Ulseth laboratory. The three gentlemen were not fools, and they did not like the formula at all. They said so to Kallenbach.

"It is not safe," said one.

The second agreed with him. "There is nothing in it to provide the not-to-be-dispensed-with stability," he said.

"It cannot be Ulsenite," said the third. "There is nothing in it to cause a green flash such as the Herr described."

Kallenbach was a factory manager, not a chemist. He hesitated before this unfavorable expert opinion and said he'd think it over. The next morning, however, Goebbels rang up asking for a report on the formula, and Kallenbach was considerably more afraid of Goebbels than of any explosive, however unstable. Moreover, his own office was a long way from the experimental laboratory, which had a good bank of earth round it anyway, and in any case there are plenty more chemists in Germany.

"Get on with the job," he said. "How can you tell what it's like till you've made it? Take all necessary precautions, but get on with it."

The chemists shrugged their shoulders, looked resignedly at each other, and got on with it. They took so many precautions, however, that progress was extremely slow, and in the agitation caused by the sabotage discovery Kallenbach forgot all about them and their protests.

The big open space between the bays and the laboratory filled rapidly with boxes of shells as lines of men, busy as ants on moving day, carried them out of the bays, dumped them down on the ground, and went back for more. The three chemists, returning from the canteen after lunch, observed this with mistrust.

"What's our intelligent management playing at now?"

"Heaven knows. It is entirely contrary to safety regulations."

"Never mind. It won't make any real difference to us. We can't be more than blown to pieces."

They returned gloomily to work.

Later that afternoon Hambledon and Grautz were startled by the violent and sudden rattling of the laboratory windows, which leaped in their frames as though kicked by a bad-tempered giant. The two men rushed outside in time to hear a loud, uneven roar which lasted for several seconds. The guards and Frau Bernstein came hastily out of the lodge by the gate to hear it, pointing excitedly toward the west, where a bulbous toadstool of smoke appeared suddenly in the sunset sky.

"What lies over there?" asked Grautz.

"Difficult to tell how far off it is," said Hambledon, "but Spandau is in that direction."

"Oh, it is, is it?"

"But it's an unexpectedly big explosion," said Hambledon thoughtfully.

"Yes. Well, no doubt we shall hear in time," said Grautz placidly.

As for Kallenbach, the three chemists, and most of the factory hands, they found that there are, after all, some things even more fatal than Goebbels.

The Minister of Propaganda was very seriously annoyed indeed, and his annoyance rose to fury during the inquiry, which was held in private, into the disaster at the Kallenbach works. One of the few survivors was the undermanager who had protested against the Minister's order to move all the shells out at once, and he gave evidence to that effect. Not even Goebbels' exalted position saved him on that occasion from Hitler's censure and the pointed remarks of his colleagues. Goering offered consolation, of a sort.

"There's one good thing about your explosion," he said.

"And that is?"

"You are spared the trouble of an elaborate stocktaking to check pilfering. You saw the new order?"

"Of course. I was arranging to have it carried out."

"Well, now you won't have to bother, will you?" said Goering in unpleasantly cheerful tones. "Maybe it's a blessing in disguise, eh?"

Another point emerged at the inquiry from the evidence of eyewitnesses. The explosion appeared to start at the experimental laboratory and to spread from there, by detonation, to the shells. Goebbels did not give evidence, and though the question was raised as to whether the laboratory staff were engaged upon any work more precarious than usual, no answer was returned.

The late Herr Kallenbach, recently transmuted into a faintly pink cloud in the sunset sky, had not told his employer what his chemists had said about the Ulseth formula. Nonetheless, Goebbels knew what they were about and where their formula came from, and he thought it over night and day. This fellow Ulseth— Of course accidents will occur sometimes in such a dangerous trade, and probably this was just one of those things which happen. Still, Ulseth— who was he? Have him looked up. No, that would be a waste of time. The fellow was certainly genuine; for one thing, he had not attempted to plant himself on Germany, quite the contrary. Goebbels knew all about Hambledon's abortive efforts to get back to Switzerland instead of coming to Berlin. Besides, there was the Ulsenite demonstration. Most convincing.

All the same, there was something faintly familiar about the situation which irked him. He had stolen the formula, and the result had come back and slapped him where it hurt. Sometime, somewhere, there was somebody else with whom it did not pay to meddle; unpleasant consequences always ensued. Who it was he could not recall, beyond a vague idea that the fellow was dead. Probably some absurd subliminal association of ideas without any logical foundation, like the way he always thought of cats whenever anyone spilt hot water, because of meddlesome Matty in the Struwelpeter picture book in his nursery. Better have Ulseth looked up. "No," said his subconscious mind, "better not."

Nevertheless, curiosity was too much for him, though he tempered it with caution. He did not apply to the police for information; he preferred not to foregather too closely with the police till the echoes of the Spandau explosion had died away into a further distance. He knew very well that if anyone but himself had given the order about the shells, that person would have gone straight into a concentration camp and found it only a gateway to the hereafter.

There is a very comprehensive information bureau attached to the Ministry of Propaganda. Goebbels applied to it for any information available about the past, present, and probable future of the Herr Professor Ulseth. The intelligent young man who was given the job remembered the Ulsenite demonstration at once and all the favorable publicity it had received. Doubtless the Herr Minister of Propaganda wanted the facts laid freshly before him for an article in *Das Reich*. Accordingly, all Goebbels got was a well-arranged bouquet of testimony to the virtues of the Herr Professor. In Switzerland he had a great reputation as a fearless and untiring research worker; his life was spared in an explosion which took place at Servatsch on the night of the 3rd/4th October last. He arrived in Berlin on October eleventh and started work some three weeks later–laboratory in the Jungfern Heide — demonstration November twenty-fifth attended by Fuehrer — Ulsenite — green flash — old friend of Der Fuehrer–assistant, Hugo Grautz of Leyden —

Goebbels skimmed through it and hurled it, with a gesture of disgust, into the tray labeled "Out." Even to his own department he could hardly explain that what he wanted to find was a purple patch or two in the career of the Herr Professor, the purpler the better. He took up his hat and strolled along to the Adlon; some better line of inquiry might present itself.

However, when he entered the crowded bar that infernal professor was already there, talking to Goering. It occurred to Goebbels that the obnoxious Ulseth was rather frequently to be seen talking to Goering.

"Here's Little Josef," said Goering in a low tone.

Hambledon turned round and said, "Good evening, Herr Minister of Propaganda."

Goebbels greeted them both rather sourly, and Goering offered him a drink. "You look as though you want a little soul-brightener, for some reason."

"The Herr Minister has been overworking, perhaps," suggested Hambledon in a kind voice.

"How's your stuff getting on?" asked Goebbels. "Got through its teething troubles yet?"

"Not quite. It is a matter in which mistakes—"

"It's taking you some time, isn't it?" said Goebbels. "Your demonstration was on November the twenty-fifth, wasn't it? And it is now March."

Conversation in the bar dropped appreciably. Goering glanced at Hambledon with a faintly amused expression, but the Herr Professor only looked even more earnest than usual.

"I dare not let there be any possibility of error," he said. "The consequences are too fatal—as, I fear, you know to your cost. Accept my sincere condolences on the unfortunate fatality at your Spandau works the other day. It must have distressed you beyond measure."

Goebbels glanced round to see how many people were listening. There seemed to be at least a dozen carefully looking the other way.

"That—oh, the Kallenbach works," he said. "Why do you refer to them as mine?"

"Forgive me if I am mistaken. My assistant understood from Herr Kallenbach that you were the presiding genius in his affairs," said Hambledon blandly. "Some misunderstanding, no doubt."

At this point the voice of a page boy was heard chanting, "Herr-Professor-Ulseth, Herr-Professor-Ulseth, Herr—"

"What is it?" asked Hambledon, and the boy said that one desired speech with him on the telephone. Hambledon excused himself and left hastily. As a matter of fact, he had arranged to be called away if at any time he were involved in a conversation with Goebbels. Discretion suggested it and wisdom endorsed it. There would have been a row in another minute.

"Nice fellow, Ulseth," said Goering casually. "Very able. Painstaking."

"Friend of yours?" said Goebbels.

"Oh, quite. A coming man, my dear Goebbels. A rising star. He's got something there, with that explosive of his, you know. Only the other day," said Goering, dropping his voice not quite enough, "Adolf Hitler told me how highly he esteemed him. Going away all these years and working like a beaver on purpose to present Germany with a discovery like this—rather fine, what? Hitler said—"

"He doesn't seem to have quite pulled it off, does he? Ulseth, I mean."

"He didn't mean to come here till he had finished it. He told me so himself. We practically abducted him from Switzerland, you know. Apparently we were a bit previous."

Goebbels emptied his glass and put it down. This was not getting him anywhere except in the wrong direction.

"Have another?" said Goering.

"No, thanks. I've got a headache coming on, I think."

"Yet he's not one of your dull dogs, our professor," said Goering with a laugh. "Quite a lad, actually."

"Really?"

"I can't think why, whenever I see him, I should be reminded of Amalie Rielander. He's a nice fellow, but heaven knows he's no Adonis. His beard looks as though it had had the moth in it. Are you sure you won't have another?"

"No, thank you. I—"

"You do look a bit green. Still worrying over the Spandau affair?"

"I have got one of my sick headaches," said Goebbels, "that's all. It's no use struggling with it; I shall go home."

Information concerning Ulseth must be sought elsewhere, evidently. There must be something worth knowing. Nobody could be so impeccable as this fellow appeared to be. . . .

Chapter XV
The Case of the Golden-Haired Typist

THERE WAS a little typist, aged nineteen, who worked at the War Ministry. She was golden-haired, blue-eyed, fluffy, and more than a little silly, but she did love her Stephan. He was one of the nation's darlings of the Luftwaffe, and he was due for leave. He had written to tell her so; he was coming to Berlin mainly to see her, since his home was in Mainz. He had ten days' leave; could she not get a holiday also at that time? They could go about together here and there; they might even run down to Mainz and see his people.

This was exciting, this was marvelous, this was beyond-all-previous-experience soul-uplifting. Sun, moon, and stars shone together for the little typist, and birds sang in the corridors of the War Ministry. This looked like business; he would hardly take her all that way to see his family unless he wanted to be really and truly betrothed. Betrothed to Stephan! O sweet mystery of life, *du meine Seele, du mein Herz.* A lovely dream enfolded her mind, and she made seven mistakes in one page of indents for clothing, warm, winter, soldiers, for the use of.

Then she looked at her wardrobe and her face fell. Shabby. Old-fashioned. Faded. Fancy greeting Stephan's family in clothes like these. "Who," they would say, "is this walking rag bag our Stephan's brought home?" Tears filled her eyes and overflowed down her thin serge frock.

The girl who shared her boardinghouse bedroom came in at this point and said, "Why, Lottchen! What on earth's the matter? Stephan not coming?"

Lottchen explained her troubles between sobs. He was indeed coming, but it was all going to be spoiled; look at those horrid old things hanging up there. Only fit for a jumble sale, and Stephan always so smart. Perhaps it would be better if he didn't come at all or if she refused to go to Mainz. His people— Sobs extinguished her voice.

"Oh, cheer up," said the other girl. "Won't they clean? If the cleaners will take them," she added doubtfully. "They don't take in much work these days."

"He's coming next week; they'd never be done in time. Besides, they're so old," wailed Lottchen.

"Haven't you got any clothing coupons?"

"Hardly any. I gave them to my sister Liese for the new baby."

"Oh, blow the baby."

"He can't help it," said Lottchen indignantly. "He's a dear little baby. No-body can help it—oh, oh!"

"Let me think," said her friend, and sat down on the bed, considering. "Who was that lady who gave Karen that lovely coat with the fur collar? Perhaps she'd give you something. She's got cupboards full of things she never wears, Karen says."

"I can't ask a lady I don't know to give me things," said Lottchen. "What a cheek—I wouldn't dare!"

"Offer to pay for them, then. You can do that; it's only the coupons."

"D'you think she would?"

"I'll ask Karen tomorrow morning. Do cheer up. We'll manage somehow. I'll lend you my silk scarf Mother gave me for Christmas—"

Two days later Lottchen was introduced to a dark, rather haggard-looking woman whose name, it appeared, was Schneider, Frau Schneider. She was very kind and understanding. Of course Lottchen must have a new frock; two would be better still. That was quite a nice coat she was wearing; if it had a new fur collar it would look very well indeed. Frau Schneider thought she had a fur collar she bought somewhere and had never used. Lottchen had better come along to her flat and see what could be done. Normally Lottchen would have hesitated to go to the house of a stranger; it was just the sort of thing Mother warned her against when she left home. But she would have entered a lion's den to obtain new clothes to wear for Stephan, and this lady seemed so nice–not that sort, you know—

"Oh, she's ever so nice," said Karen. "No nonsense like that. You go; you'll be all right."

Karen was quite right— there was nothing about Frau Schneider to which anyone's mother could object. She talked away cheerfully while Lottchen tried on frocks and stockings and even, by a stroke of luck, the right size in shoes. So Lottchen worked at the War Ministry. Very interesting.

"Not very," said Lottchen. "Only typing out lists of things for the soldiers."

"Rifles and bayonets and things," said Alexia Schneider. "I think that blue frock is the one for you; it exactly matches your eyes."

"Oh, are you sure you can spare it? It's so lovely; it's real silk," said Lottchen in awed tones.

"Of course I can. Blue's not my color at all. I can't think what possessed me to buy it. You must have to be very careful and accurate in your work, dealing with all those weapons. So important."

"Our branch doesn't deal with weapons," said Lottchen. "Boots and vests and pants and things."

"You might as well be in a gentlemen's clothing store," laughed the lady. "Let me help you get this over your head. Nice thin vests and shirts, I suppose, for the African campaign."

"No," said Lottchen in a slightly puzzled voice. "Thick warm ones, with long sleeves. I can't reach this hook; could you— Oh, thank you so much. And fleece-lined leather jerkins. I can't think what they want so many for, because the Russians are really defeated, aren't they?"

"I expect they'll have to keep garrisons in Russia to make them work for us, you know," said Frau Schneider. "Though you'd think they would make the Russians supply them, wouldn't you?"

"There's more than enough for a few garrisons," said Lottchen frankly. "I've worked there long enough to know that."

"I belong to a Guild of Ladies who make comforts for the soldiers," said Frau Schneider. "In fact, I'm the secretary."

"How good and clever you are," said Lottchen with shining eyes. "You seem to spend your life doing kind things for people."

Frau Schneider laughingly disclaimed any special virtue. "And, after all, what are we put into this world for? What I was going to say was that if you could give me some idea of how many soldiers they are ordering warm clothing for, I could start my ladies working in good time."

"Oh, I don't know how many soldiers," said Lottchen doubtfully.

"How many fleece-lined jerkins, then? You see, that would give me an idea, wouldn't it?"

"I ought not to tell you, but since it's only so's you can knit enough socks and things, I'm sure it won't matter. Four and a half million," said Lottchen.

"Oh, really? Thank you so much. Of course I won't repeat it, but the Guild must evidently start working at once. Returning to something more important, you'll have the blue frock, won't you? And the warm brown one and that fur collar for your coat. Three—yes, three pairs of stockings and those shoes. Now I hope you'll have a very happy holiday. Look, I'd like to give you this handbag too, it goes so well with your coat, and Stephan's family will admire your good taste. Please."

"But I couldn't—how much do I owe—you must let me—" stammered Lottchen.

"Nothing at all," said the lady firmly. "No, nothing. Please, I insist. Once, Lottchen, I had a daughter who died. You remind me strongly of her. How old are you? Nineteen. She was nineteen when she—she went away from me. I love giving things to girls; it reminds me of the happy days when I had a girl to give things to. I'm sure you won't hurt me by refusing. Good-by, dear; have a happy holiday with your Stephan. Come and tell me all about it when you return."

Lottchen ran home, almost too happy to breathe. The lady smiled benignly after her and took immediate steps to inform an interested party that Hitler did not expect to finish the Russian campaign that summer of 1942 whatever he said, since he was already ordering winter supplies in large quantities. Four and a half million leather jerkins lined with fleece. . . .

Lottchen and her Stephan had a wonderful leave. They went to Mainz and were formally betrothed, exchanging rings. Stephan's family were charming to her, especially his mother. One felt terribly shy, of course, being introduced to one's future in-laws, but being nicely dressed was a great help. It gave one confidence. When Stephan's mother said, with a faint reserve in her voice, that the blue silk dress must have cost a lot of money, Lottchen admitted frankly that a lady had given it to her. One could not be thought extravagant. Only one minor disaster occurred to mar her otherwise incredible bliss: she lost her handbag in Berlin. She went to the police and gave a description of it, but they had no such bag among their treasure-trove. They would make a note of it and let her know if it was brought in to them.

Hambledon went one evening to a performance of Wagner's *Flying Dutchman* at the State Opera House. That is, Eckhoff drove him as near as possible to the principal entrance, but there was quite a long line of cars waiting to deposit music lovers, and Hambledon became impatient.

"I'll get out here and walk along the pavement," he said through the speaking tube. "You know what time the show is over? Pick me up then. We are only wasting petrol, dawdling like this."

Eckhoff agreed. Hambledon slipped out of the car and was immediately lost to sight in the crowd. He crossed the road and walked rapidly away in the darkness over the Long Bridge and up the Konigs Strasse. Ten minutes of brisk walking brought him to Weber's, where Gibson was waiting for him.

"Glad to see you," said Gibson. "Managed to evade your keepers for once?"

"I am at Goering's Opera House listening to one of Wagner's operas, believe it or not," said Hambledon. "I didn't tell anybody I was coming, so I shan't be missed. I came to say that I'm going to get out as soon as I can think up some means of doing so without leaving my body in a dishonored grave. I haven't found out how to do so yet, but doubtless some method will present itself."

"Things getting a bit sticky?"

"Goebbels is after me. Amalie Rielander told me that he is digging into my past wherever he thinks he can get a spade in. One of these days he'll succeed. My identity isn't so cast iron as it might be if I was really Ulseth, if you see what I mean. Besides, Grautz and I can't keep on playing with chemicals indefinitely."

"Assassinate Goebbels," suggested Gibson.

"I have that under consideration, but even that wouldn't produce Ulsenite. Though if anything would burn with an unquenchable green flame, I should think it would be Goebbels' immortal soul—if he's got one."

"It's a pity," said Gibson. "The stuff you're getting through from Switzerland for us is most useful."

"If I were to get in a really large consignment, a whole trainload of it, could you remove it and store it away?"

"I could, I suppose. Yes, I could, but it would take some weeks to arrange. The main difficulty will be in finding storage space. I shall have to hunt round. Empty cellars of bombed houses, and so forth. A bit here and a bit there."

Hambledon nodded. "We are having a big delivery of full-size railway wagons—closed trucks—before long. I got that from the Heroas people, so I know it's true."

"It must be put off for at least four weeks," said Gibson.

"That can be arranged. I think you'd better find out how much you can deal with for a start, then we'll see about getting it sent through. It all has to be flown to Switzerland to begin with, you remember, and one can't bring too much at once or the Swiss authorities will notice something and be seriously annoyed."

"I don't see why they should be, really," said Gibson. "The Germans send stuff through Switzerland to Italy by train, and troops too."

"I know, but tact is necessary. Well, you work it out and let me know, will you? How are things going with you—seen your lady friend Schneider again?"

"Several times. We talk music. In fact, I was taking her to the *Flying Dutchman* tonight, only you wanted to see me. I am in bed with a bilious attack," said Gibson.

"I think I'd as soon have a bilious attack as listen to Wagner all the evening."

"You're not musical, then? Or do you just not like Wagner?"

"I only know two tunes really well," said Tommy. "One of them is 'God Save the King,' but I'm not sure which."

"The Schneider woman is on to something," said Gibson. "I'm going to have a private look round her flat one day when occasion offers. I'd like to know who and what she is. Besides, if she's picked up any bits of news, we might as well have them too."

"Why not? We have scriptural authority for the doctrine that one soweth and another reapeth. I hope you will have a plenteous harvest. By the way, I meant to have asked you before—what on earth did you want kegs of molasses for?"

Gibson began to laugh. "Did you see the parade of tanks through the city the other day?"

"Not see them, no; I heard about it. Didn't some of them break down and have to be borne away in tank carriers?"

"Yes. Molasses looks very like thick lubricating oil and works all right till the engines have been comfortably hot for a little while. Then they cease to be tanks and become toffee-making machines, after which everything stops. We thought a public demonstration in Berlin would be good for morale."

"What an excellent idea. But wouldn't it be better applied on the Russian front—or in the desert?"

"So we thought. We couldn't get at the tanks going to North Africa, as they're finally serviced in Italy or France. But those going to Russia are tested in Germany—with real oil—and then have the oil changed at the last moment before being put on the train for the Eastern Front. We attended to as many of those as we had molasses for. I hope the Russians like toffee."

"What a frightful job," said Hambledon cheerfully, "cleaning the toffee out of the engines."

"Not even so simple as that. I hope the engines themselves are damaged. I am not a motor mechanic, but I think they ought to be. In any case, they will have to be dissected into their component parts and boiled. Have you heard any complaints from your Nazi friends about the wholesale theft of sugar from storage depots?"

"No. Why? Where has it gone?"

"Into the petrol," said Gibson. "Aviation spirit, for choice. It renders it practically harmless."

"You know," said Hambledon, laughing, "if I didn't dislike the Nazis so much I could almost be sorry for them. Fancy Goering wrestling with non-inflammable petrol."

"You get on pretty well with Goering, don't you?"

"I don't like him, if that's what you suggest. He has one thing the others haven't got, and that's a sense of humor, if of rather a crude description. If somebody sits down on a chair that isn't there he laughs till the pictures fall off the walls, and if they really hurt themselves he laughs louder still. He's a cruel brute, you know. I don't suppose he lost a moment's sleep over Rotterdam, Warsaw, and Belgrade all put together."

"The 'blond beast,' " said Gibson.

"Oh, quite. No, what Goering and I have in common is a loathing of Goebbels. It's certainly a bond. I must go back," said Hambledon. "I should think the *Flying Dutchman* is preparing to return to base by now. Good night, and good luck with your girlfriend."

Three weeks later there was a British bombing raid on Berlin and considerable damage was done.

After the rain the gnats come forth and sting; after the bombers leave, the looters creep out and steal. It happens in every bombed city to a greater or less extent, and Berlin was no exception. It is difficult to check, because as a rule people just grab some object they want and use it up in the privacy of their homes, but sometimes operations are upon a larger scale, properly organized by thieves and receivers of stolen goods. In these cases the produce goes to the black market. The Berlin police were rewarded at this time for much patient work: they fell upon a receiver with his cupboards full. The receiver came to a bad end, and his unlawful collection was spread out upon tables for identification.

"This is not entirely the result of looting," said the superintendent. "Some of it's the proceeds of robbery. Here's the diamond bracelet stolen from the Bristol last month, if I'm not mistaken. Go carefully through the lists of everything reported missing for the last three months. Make a note of anything which you think you can identify, and we'll get the alleged owners in to have a look at them."

Among the items were several handbags, and two were almost exactly alike. The description tallied with that of a handbag which the wife of the deputy chief of police had lost in a restaurant some time before. The superintendent was naturally delighted.

"I'll notify him at once," he said. "He will be pleased. She's been worrying him bald over that for weeks, and he can't get another like it. He'll know which is hers."

The deputy chief of police and his lady arrived together, and the Frau Deputy picked out her bag without hesitation.

"This is mine," she said. "There is a mark on the lining where my lipstick slipped out of its case one day. I could not entirely remove the stain."

"I thought lipstick was not permissible for good German wives," began her husband, but she curtailed him without hesitation.

"If anyone supposes I am going about with a mouth like a door scraper every time the wind's in the east, they're wrong, that's all."

"Try petrol," said her husband. "That might get the stain off."

"Besides, here's my handkerchief in the pocket; that settles it. I wonder who the other one belongs to; let me look. A nice bag; it's newer than mine. It's got a flapjack in it—a nasty cheap thing." She opened it. "Horrid cheap powder, too. And a funny cotton handkerchief. One would think it belonged to a shop-girl."

"The shopgirl's got a wealthy boyfriend, then, judging by what I paid for yours, my dear," said the deputy chief. "It would be interesting to know who is the owner of the other bag."

"Yes sir," said the superintendent. "I will make further inquiries personally."

A day or two later Lottchen received a card telling her that a bag which answered the description of the one she had lost was now in the possession of the police. It was desirable that she should come to the police station as soon as possible to identify it. She went, and recognized it with joy.

"Oh yes, that's mine! Look, that's my flapjack my sister gave me for Christmas, and my handkerchief with L in the corner."

"It's a very expensive bag," said the superintendent. "Where do you work?"

"At the War Ministry. Why?"

"I am asking the questions, not you. Who gave it to you?"

"A friend," said Lottchen, a little frightened at his tone.

"A man?"

"Oh no. A lady. She's a very kind lady."

"Why did she give you this bag?"

"I don't understand," faltered Lottchen. "There's nothing wrong in accepting presents from a lady, is there?"

"Have you known her long?"

"No. I only met her once."

"Why did she give you this bag?"

"B-because Stephan was coming home—"

"Did she give you anything else?"

"Two frocks and some stockings," said Lottchen, beginning to cry.

"Don't blubber! What is her name?"

"What are you so cross about?" sobbed Lottchen. "I haven't done anything wrong."

"That's for me to say. What's her name?"

"I—I forget," said Lottchen, anxious not to get her kind friend into this incomprehensible trouble.

"What's her name?"

"I tell you, I—"

"What's her name?" roared the superintendent, and poor Lottchen collapsed.

"Fräulein Schneider."

"Schneider. Address?"

Lottchen gave it.

"Tell me the truth or you'll regret it. Did she ask you any questions?"

"She—she asked me how old I was—"

"About your work, you little fool. Did she ask you any questions about your work?"

"I don't think so. Oh, only how many jerkins we were ordering for the troops in Russia."

"Did you tell her?"

"Well, you see, she's the secretary of a guild of ladies who make comforts for the troops and—and of course she wanted to know how many things to knit—"

"Did you tell her?" Lottchen nodded miserably. "You wretched little half-wit! You, at the War Ministry! You'll be scrubbing floors in a concentration camp tomorrow, if I'm not mistaken."

"Oh, please! I didn't mean it. Please, can I go home?"

"No. You'll stay here while I look up the Schneider woman. If she's really only knitting for the troops, you'll both be punished for talking. If she's not, you'd better say your prayers—you'll need 'em."

Chapter XVI
Quick Worker

GIBSON had to choose carefully his time for looking through Frau Alexia Schneider's flat. He cultivated her acquaintance and took her to a Brahms recital instead of the performance of the *Flying Dutchman* of which they were disappointed by his unfortunate bilious attack. There came an afternoon when he knew she would be away from home for some hours. He went to the block of flats where she lived, walked up the stairs, and rang the bell.

There was no answer, which did not surprise him. The door was locked, but he knew how to deal with that. He walked in and closed the door behind him without locking it. There was a sitting room, a couple of bedrooms, bathroom, and kitchen; he started with the sitting room and worked methodically through the flat. The furniture was good if a trifle old-fashioned; drawers slid open easily; doors had solid but simple locks. He looked between and underneath everything, even beneath the white paper lining the drawers; putting every-thing back exactly as he found it, not a crease where no crease should be, papers in precisely the same order, stockings apparently undisturbed. He worked quickly and thoroughly for half an hour and found absolutely nothing.

"She carries the stuff about with her," he said, standing in the sitting room and looking round it, "either on her person or, more probably and wisely, in her head. I have wasted my time. I think I'll go home."

He dropped into an armchair for a moment to consider whether there was any probable place he had left unsearched. Books in the bookcase, yes, he'd looked into all those—

There came a thunderous knock at the door, the knock of authority, official authority. Gibson's eyes widened for a moment, but he knew there was no other exit. He lit a cigarette and shouted, "Come in!"

The door opened and there entered four men of the Gestapo. They looked quickly about them, but there was no one in sight but a bored-looking gentle-man lounging in an armchair with his legs crossed.

"This is the flat of the Frau Alexia Schneider," said the first man. It sounded like a statement, not a question, but Gibson agreed that it was, indeed, her flat.

"What are you doing here?"

"Waiting for her," said Gibson.

"Your name and address?"

Gibson gave the name under which he passed and showed his papers. One does not argue with the Gestapo.

"Get on with it," said the man to his companions, and they began to search the flat as thoroughly as Gibson had, but, he noticed, not nearly so tidily. Things were thrown about or bundled up anyhow to be out of their way.

"Where is the Frau Schneider?"

"I wish I knew," said Gibson. "I've been waiting for her for half an hour or more." They might have been watching the place and have seen him arrive. He rose to his feet as one preparing to go, but the Gestapo man told him to sit down again and wait. Gibson sighed patiently and lit another cigarette from the end of the first. Matches were, after all, scarce.

"You smoke a good deal, do you?"

"I do, yes," admitted Gibson.

"Yet you've been waiting here half an hour and the ashtray is practically clean."

"That was a bad break," said Gibson to himself. "I must be a lot more careful than that; this man's intelligent." Aloud he merely murmured, "Lady's flat, you know. Didn't like to smoke without permission. I just felt I couldn't go without any longer."

"You know Frau Schneider well, do you?"

"Not well, really. I've known her some time. We are both interested in music."

"You have been here before—how many times?"

"Two or three," answered Gibson, speaking the truth, since they would probably ask the concierge of the flats to confirm it. "Three times. Twice just calling for her when we were going out together."

"Have you ever met anyone else here?"

"No."

At this moment the Frau Schneider turned the corner from the Kaiser Friedrich Strasse into her own street and saw the official car standing outside the block of flats in which she lived. There was a man in uniform standing beside the car. Fortunately he was looking the other way. She did not hesitate or even change her pace. She turned almost at once into an alley which admitted tradesmen to the back doors, turned left again and regained the Kaiser Friedrich Strasse, having merely walked round a block of houses. She went, without hesitation or undue haste, to the Stettiner Station and took a ticket for Eberswalde. Even when she had three quarters of an hour to wait for the train she remained outwardly perfectly calm, though it is possible that the time seemed to pass rather slowly. However, the train started at last with the Frau Schneider in it, unmolested. Perhaps she had friends at Eberswalde or perhaps she never went there at all. However she managed it, the Gestapo never saw her again. It was very unfortunate for Lottchen, but Frau Schneider was not thinking of Lottchen. She could not have helped her, if she had. Stephan, unfortunately, was killed on his first operational flight after he returned from leave, so he could not inquire after Lottchen either. His mother wrote to her once or twice, got no answer, and let the matter drop. Lottchen never returned to the War Ministry or to the shabby boardinghouse bedroom she shared with another girl. Nobody asked why; it is better not to ask questions in these cases.

To return to Gibson. He waited patiently till the Gestapo had finished their investigations and then said that if he could be of no further assistance to the police he would be glad to be allowed to return home. He had business which required his attention.

"I regret," said the leader of the party, "it is at the moment impossible to permit the Herr to return home. There are some questions which must be asked."

"Then surely they can be asked at my house. I am a Berlin businessman of some years' standing. I shall not run away. I have my living to earn."

"All that is undoubtedly true. Nonetheless, the Herr will accompany us to the police headquarters. It is probable that the delay will not be serious."

Gibson could have torn his hair, for the trainload of explosives, which Hambledon was providing, was due in five days' time and no one but himself knew what arrangements had been made to deal with it. The mere fact that the man was so polite—for the Gestapo—showed that they had nothing against him at present except his acquaintance with Alexia Schneider, and he could explain away that in a manner guaranteed to convince Himmler himself. All the same, "detained for inquiry" might mean detention for hours or days or weeks; perhaps being questioned daily, perhaps not being questioned at all, just dumbly held till one day the cell door opens and one is simply told to go. Or perhaps one is never seen again.

However, it was no use fussing. Gibson merely pushed up his eyebrows, assumed an expression of bored annoyance, and said that in that case he was at the Herr's disposal. The Gestapo leader thanked him civilly, and that was that.

The concierge was called in and questioned. When did she expect the Frau Schneider to return? She did not know. Where had the Frau gone that afternoon? She did not know; the Frau often went out in the afternoon. The Frau did not confide in the concierge; why should she?

"You will find it pays to be civil to the police, woman!"

"Yes sir," said the concierge.

Gibson was taken down to the police car while the woman was further interrogated. No doubt she was being asked about him, how often he had been there before, and so on. He congratulated himself on having told the truth. He sat in the car looking along the street. Frau Schneider should be here at any moment. Perhaps she'd been run over. It would probably be better for all concerned if she had. She did not come. The Gestapo leader left a man on guard at the flat and himself came out; they all drove away together. The car slowed down at the main road, and a man selling newspapers glanced uninterestedly in at the window. Gibson did not even look at him.

Hambledon received an apparently harmless message from Weber about a supply of fuel for his cigarette lighter, but the wording of it was a prearranged signal meaning "Come at once; urgent news." Hambledon wasted no time in obeying.

"What's the trouble?" he asked as soon as they had the shop to themselves, Eckhoff being outside in the car. "Something gone wrong?"

"Very wrong indeed. Gibson has been arrested by the Gestapo."

Hambledon looked at him in silence.

"At Alexia Schneider's flat yesterday evening," Weber went on. "He has been taken to that new detention camp out at Schöneberg, not far from the Tempelhof airport."

"You don't know what he's charged with?"

"Not yet. I have made arrangements with a man who goes in there with the rations every day, to get a message to Gibson. This is only a place where people are detained for inquiries, you know; it's not what you'd call a really serious prison. It is possible to talk to the inmates through the wire fence in places with ordinary care and, if necessary, a bribe to the nearest sentry to look the other way. I have told Gibson to be at that spot at fourteen-thirty today. I thought you would wish to speak to him yourself. I will show you where the place is and how you get to it."

"This is frightfully inconvenient," said Hambledon. "Today's Tuesday. That stuff ought to arrive on Saturday or Sunday, and I've no more idea than Goering's lion cub what arrangements he's made to deal with it."

"They will have gone through his flat," said Weber.

"They won't find anything if they have. Gibson never wrote down anything; he has a marvelous memory. He must be got out, Weber."

"They may not keep him long," said Weber without much conviction.

"He may be able to tell me how to deal with this consignment. If not, he must be out on Thursday night at latest. Tomorrow night better still, but I can't make any plans till I've seen him and the place. Have you got any ideas for covering him up if I do get him out?"

"I've got a nice set of papers here, and the luggage belonging to them. They were the property of a Spaniard who has now no further use for any of them. But—"

"I know. The position is as full of 'buts' as a goat. I wonder why the Gestapo pitched on the Schneider woman; at least I suppose that's what they did. Looked for her and found him, I mean. Have they got her too, d'you know?" Weber shook his head. "Not that it matters," went on Hambledon. "They must have been after her. If they merely wanted Gibson they wouldn't have gone to her flat for him."

"I expect she was careless," said Weber. "Gibson had noticed something unusual about her, and the Gestapo are good at noticing, too."

"I mustn't stop," said Hambledon. "I don't want to arouse Eckhoff's curiosity. How do I find the place you spoke of?"

"Here's a street map. Here's the camp. Look, the entrance is there. If you turn off here, go behind those houses—there's a path behind them—and across those allotments; there's a hut near the wire. Wait there and he'll come. The hut nearest to the wire. I don't think you'll have any trouble. If the sentry does turn up, give him twenty-five marks and he'll go away again."

At half-past two that afternoon Hambledon crossed the allotments toward the wire fence at the appointed spot and leaned against the wall of somebody's tool shed, waiting. The detention camp consisted of a large area of neglected grass with small bushes here and there and a number of ugly wooden huts; all surrounded by an eight-foot fence of barbed wire on iron stanchions. In the distance he could see men moving listlessly about or standing in groups, talking. Presently Gibson came, strolling casually along as though on a tour of inspection.

"Good afternoon," said Hambledon. "This is a nice mess, what?"

"Yes, isn't it? Of all the awkward times to arrest a bloke—"

"Any idea how long they'll keep you?"

"Absolutely none. Over the weekend, anyway. I do know a little more than I did last night. They are quite civil to me, even pleasant, because there is nothing against me except knowing Frau Schneider. The man in charge here is an acquaintance of mine, as it happens, so when I was taken before him I adopted the 'look here, old man, what is all this nonsense' attitude. He was apologetic but firm. It appears that Frau Alexia was a Pole—I thought so myself, if you remember—and rather a kingpin in Polish espionage. Or should it be queenpin? I am held for questioning because even the smallest piece of information might be of a value unsuspected by the innocent me. I asked why I should be kept locked up, as I was perfectly willing to come along and answer anybody's questions at any time. He humped his shoulders and merely said 'It is the rule.' I argued, but it was no good. You know what these Germans are when they've got a rule."

Hambledon nodded. "Mustn't complain, really. It's a great help sometimes, knowing beforehand exactly what they'll do. Look, here's a sentry coming."

"Oh, that's all right. You have come to see what I want in the way of shirts and shaving tackle. It's the done thing, here. No prisoner is allowed to receive visitors officially, but unofficially they realize that man wants clean collars now and again. So practically every new prisoner has one interview with his friends through the wire, and they don't report it. There'd be a row if it was repeated. This man isn't a bad fellow. Give him twenty-five marks and a few cigarettes if you have them. Not all you've got; I want some myself. Good evening, Schultze. This is a neighbor of mine who's come to see me about collars and vests and things."

"Not allowed, you know," said the sentry perfunctorily, "talking through the wire. Don't be long about it or I shall have to report you."

"It is very kind of you," said Hambledon, "to allow us to talk at all. Please permit me—a few cigarettes—"

"Thank you," said the sentry. "Very 'andy. I was almost out of 'em, and I can't get leave tonight." The cigarettes were handed through the wire with a twenty-five mark note wrapped round the packet. The sentry glanced at it, grinned, and dropped it in his pocket. "Don't you be still 'ere when I come back, that's all," he said, and walked on.

"As easy as that," said Hambledon.

"Yes. But I shall be searched for wire cutters the moment you turn your back; they've thought of that one. Look, Schultze is watching us."

"About this consignment," said Hambledon hastily. "Can you tell me what arrangements you've made and I will see that they are carried out?"

"Impossible," said Gibson. "For one thing, it'll take far too long; for another, you'd have to write it down, and I won't have my people's names written down on any account, and finally, they wouldn't believe you. They'd just look blank and decline to play. I must get out, Hambledon."

"When are you to be interrogated, d'you know that?"

"Not till next week. Himmler's coming himself—it's as important as that—and at the moment he's enjoying himself after his fashion in Poland. You've got to get me out. Any ideas?"

"I wandered round and had a look at the place on my way here," said Hambledon. "What do they do with you during air raids? Any shelters here?"

"Lord no. The prisoners just lie flat on the floors and pray. We're rather too near the Tempelhof airdrome to be healthy."

"The guards at the gate?"

"I don't know. I expect they've got something, if only a slit trench. I've only been here one night, you know," said Gibson.

"Lights?"

"During raids? All out except the one which illuminates the gate. They used to put that out too, they tell me, only they lost some prisoners once, so now they leave that one on. It's hooded."

"Can you get out of the huts at night?"

"Only by permission. One goes to the sentry on the door and says 'Please may I be excused?' or words to that effect, and he lets one out. We can only go along the one path and back; if we wander off it we're liable to be shot at."

"Where's the path?"

"From my hut, near the gatehouse. My hut's the first one east of the gate, and my destination would be that row of sheds just west of the gate. So I should cross behind the gatehouse about twenty yards back."

"Thank heaven for its first mercy," said Hambledon. "If you'd been parked in the middle, I don't know what I'd have done. Listen, if there was a handcart standing close to the gate, could you see it by the light on the gate?"

"I should think so," said Gibson doubtfully. "I noticed last night that one could see the pavement and a bit of the road—Hurry up; here's Schultze coming back."

"If there's a raid on, get out of your hut. Got your watch? Good. Get as close to the gatehouse as you can when you see the handcart arrive. When the men pushing it let go of it and run, throw yourself flat," said Hambledon, talking faster and faster as the sentry drew near. "After the explosion get up instantly and dash out over the wreck of the gate. I expect the light will go out; anyway, there will be clouds of dust. Go to Weber's. When you get your soft collars, wash them. All right, I'll see to it," he added for Schultze's benefit, and drew back from the wire as in the act of departure.

"And the soap," said Gibson anxiously. "Don't forget the soap."

"On no account will I forget the soap. Good-by, and keep your heart up. You will be at home again soon, I'm sure," said Hambledon, and departed with a friendly nod to the sentry. He had managed to be out, for once, without Eckhoff and the car; he returned to Weber's thinking deeply.

"Get this message off tonight," he said. " 'Please arrange small nuisance raid on Tempelhof district as near as possible Tempelhof detention camp without hitting it next Thursday twenty-three forty-five acknowledge.' "

"I'll see to it," said Weber. "What are you going to do, if I may ask?"

"Wait till the raid begins and then blow in the main gate. Gibson will, I trust, be lurking in the offing and will dash out before the dust settles. I want a handcart, Weber. A very shabby one with wobbly wheels, but not so wobbly as to fall off."

"I think I can manage that," said Weber.

"It will have a false bottom, Weber. Can you do that, or get it done? All that's necessary is four blocks, one in each corner, about six inches high. Four small firewood logs will do. The handcart should have rather high sides. An old door, or some rough planks nailed together, will drop into the cart and rest on the four blocks, thus leaving a space underneath."

Weber nodded. "I had better do it myself, I think. There is a man who comes round here with such a cart as you describe; he sells firewood. I will hire it from him tomorrow morning for a couple of days. I will say that I want it to help an old servant of mine to move his furniture—what's left of it. My old servant has been bombed out, I think. It is a fact that it's nearly impossible to get any carting done now."

"And yet some people say there's no such thing as thought transference," said Hambledon. "That is exactly what's going to happen. A poor shabby old man—that's me—assisted by a dilapidated nephew—that's Grautz—is going to move his broken home on a handcart. Their way will take them past the gate of the detention camp. They lived, I think, in the Neukoln district. There has been some bomb damage there, I believe, Weber?"

"Oh yes. It's near the Tempelhof. They get the 'overs.' "

"The false bottom of the truck will be filled with explosives. Can you manage that, or shall I—I don't quite know how I could manage to convey it—"

"Leave it to me," said Weber. "I can lay my hand on a few slabs of guncotton, if that will do."

"I don't care what it is," said Hambledon, "so long as it doesn't give off a green flash. Detonate them in the usual way. Grautz and I will provide the exploding apparatus. At least, Grautz will while I stand well back and admire him. Something that will give us about fifteen seconds to get clear in, and I hope neither of us steps on a bit of orange peel while in the act of departing. Do not stint the guncotton, Weber."

"No, I won't. Will you want identity papers?"

"No, I don't think so. They were destroyed in the wreck of our poor but honest home, and we are going to the police about it next morning—I don't think. On the top of the truck, over the false bottom, is piled a selection of the sort of salvage one sees being rescued from bombed homes. Dirty bedding, a few bits of carpet, a damaged chair or two, a fender—you know the sort of thing."

"Leave it to me," said Weber again.

"You are a tower of strength. Will you do all that in the time?"

"I can do a lot tonight, and there's all tomorrow and Thursday not touched yet. Besides, the later it's done the better, so long as it's in time. We don't want that handcart standing about for some inquisitive body to investigate. I will meet you with it myself, I'll show you where, I know the Neukoln district well. Anything else you want?"

"A couple of shabby overcoats and two disreputable hats?"

"I have those here. I'll make them into a parcel. Will you take them back to the laboratory with you now?"

"Please. By heaven, Weber, if this comes off I'll get you out of this filthy city and back to England, home, and grandchild. You deserve it."

"Thank you," said Weber, "but I'm not going home yet. The grandchild will keep, God bless him, till I've seen the Allied Armies marching down the Unter den Linden."

"With the bands playing 'Oh, I do like to be beside the Spree-side'?" suggested Hambledon. "God send it soon. Well, I think that's all for the present. Gibson will come to you here if and when he gets clear away."

" 'When,' " said Weber. "Not 'if.' "

"Beat on, stout heart," said Hambledon appreciatively.

Early next morning Hambledon was rung up on the telephone by Weber.

"The gracious Herr Professor will forgive my presuming to interrupt his labors," said the tobacconist humbly. "The fresh supply of cigarettes will be here tomorrow, Thursday, evening definitely. The Herr Professor wished to be informed as soon as—"

"Thank you, Herr Shopkeeper, thank you," said Hambledon loftily. "I will call for them when I am next in your district."

"Whenever the Herr Professor pleases," said Weber, and Hambledon cut him off.

Gibson received a brown paper parcel containing toilet necessaries but no shaving tackle and a change of linen which included some soft collars. It would appear that he did not think them clean enough, for he took them into the washroom at a moment when it was empty and washed them himself. Brown letters came up on one of them; they read, "Thursday night twenty-three forty-five."

"Quarter to twelve tomorrow night," said Gibson to himself. "I always heard Hambledon was a quick worker."

Chapter XVII

The Gentleman from Spain

SHORTLY AFTER ELEVEN on that Thursday night two shabby men with an ancient handcart took leave of a friend near some bombed houses in the Neukoln district of Berlin and proceeded through the dark and silent streets in the direction of the Tempelhof detention camp. One was an elderly man with a ragged beard which looked as though it had not been combed for weeks; it also contained cobwebs. The other man was younger but no smarter; both were as dusty and dirty as is natural when one has been grubbing for salvage among the debris of ruined houses.

"How far is it?" asked Grautz.

"About a mile," answered Hambledon. "This is really very awkward. I didn't want to leave it any later, in case we are stopped on the road, on the other hand, we ought not to be too early. It would be unwise, one feels, to trundle this horrible contraption up and down in front of the camp gate waiting for the raid to begin."

"I don't think half an hour is any too long to push this cart a whole mile. It never runs straight for two minutes together."

"That's because the tires are flat. Two motorcycle wheels, I fancy," said Hambledon. "Come up, you cow! It's the camber of the road which makes it so bad just here."

"What did you tell Eckhoff?" asked Grautz.

"I told him that we were engaged upon a most delicate and crucial stage in our experiments and were not to be disturbed on any account whatever. I said it wouldn't be any use ringing us up on our telephone from the gate, either, because I was going to take the receiver off. I also rang the girl at the telephone exchange and told her not to put any calls through before morning. The Herr Professor Ulseth is engaged upon work of national importance tonight. How excessively true. You made sure there were a few chinks showing light round the blackout, did you?"

"I did. Not enough to get us into trouble. You can just see that there are lights on inside."

"Yes. We don't want to be investigated by air-raid wardens. Eleven thirty-five. Ten minutes from now the raid should begin. D'you think this thing would run any better if we pulled it instead of pushing?"

"Sh-sh!" said Grautz. "Somebody coming behind."

"Two somebodies with official tread," said Hambledon. "Probably police. Look miserable, you worm."

The footsteps drew nearer, overtaking them, and a torch was switched on.

"Halt," said the newcomers, who were policemen. "Who are you?"

Hambledon supplied names for himself and nephew.

"What are you doing?"

"Moving our things, Herr Polizei, just moving our things."

"So I see. Why, and where to?"

"Because we were bombed out. We had nowhere to go. Then we heard of a—"

"Show your papers."

"We haven't got any, Herr Polizei. They were destroyed. We are going to the police station about them tomorrow."

"Oh. Where are you going now?"

"We've found a hut on some allotments the man it belongs to doesn't want. He's going to let us live there."

"Sounds pretty miserable," said the policeman who had not previously spoken. "Can't you get anything better than that?"

"Presently, Herr Polizei, with luck. The shed's better than nothing."

"You are moving very late," said the first policeman. "Better get on or you won't get to bed tonight." He laughed not unkindly. Hambledon and Grautz put the truck into motion again, and the police strolled along beside it.

"I was looking for my money," said Hambledon in a tearful voice. "It was in a tin."

"Didn't you find it?"

"No."

"Now don't you go upsetting yourself over that again, Uncle," said Grautz. "There wasn't much in it, anyway."

"You save your breath for pushing," said Hambledon fiercely. "You don't know what was in it."

"Poor old buffer," said the second policeman, and gave him fifty pfennigs—about sixpence. Hambledon took it gratefully and said he was a real gentleman and probably a baron.

"You'll have to find another tin and start again," began the first policeman, but his voice was drowned in an inhuman howl which rose and fell and rose again—the air-raid warning. Hambledon sighed with relief; the detention camp was almost in sight. Searchlights flashed up; the road became almost light.

"You'll have to leave that thing and go to shelter," said the policeman, and they all began to hurry.

"What?" said Hambledon. "Lose the little I've got left? Not likely! It's not far now. Come on, Hans," he added to Grautz. They bent over the truck's handle, and the crazy thing yawed from left to right. There came the sound of aircraft overhead and a whistling followed by a crash as the first bomb fell. The policemen broke into a run and disappeared down a side turning.

"Thank goodness," said Hambledon from the bottom of his heart. "I thought they were never going. Now for it."

Three more bombs fell as they struggled along the last hundred yards to the camp gate, and flashes helped the searchlights to illuminate the scene. The gatehouse was a small brick lodge with a slate roof; two or three men could be seen running toward it and diving inside. Another man came from a row of sheds beyond the gate and stood at their corner, hesitating. He saw the truck coming and broke into a run toward the gate.

"That's Gibson, I hope," said Hambledon. "As near the gate as we can get it, Grautz." The truck gave a violent swerve and ran on the pavement as another rising whistle began. Grautz fumbled at the truck for an instant and jerked a string as Hambledon turned away; both men ran at top speed across the rather wide road, round the corner of a building, and threw themselves flat. Neither heard the bomb fall, for the noise it made was drowned in the deafening roar from the gate as Weber's slabs of guncotton blew up. Debris flew up in the air and fell all around, together with slates from neighboring houses and glass out of adjacent windows. The two men picked themselves up and leaned against the wall. Hambledon started to speak but realized he was stone-deaf for the moment. Grautz saw his lips move and gestured toward his own ears. In the complete silence that held them there was a ghostlike quality in the sight of a man who passed within a few inches of them, running like a stag, with soundless steps. Hambledon nudged Grautz, indicated the runner, and gestured with both thumbs upward.

Then they put their hands in their pockets, humped their shoulders, and started the ten-mile walk back to the laboratory in the Jungfern Heide.

The two policemen who had stopped them ten minutes earlier came upon the scene and looked unhappily about. The gatehouse was in ruins; the gate had disappeared, and there was a gap in the wire, but one of the guards had come unhurt from the reinforced cellar where they had been sheltering and was already patrolling the gap. Nothing was left of the truck but one crazy wheel lying in the roadway with its tire burning. The younger policeman pointed it out.

"Poor old buffer," he said again. "Fancy bein' killed for that pile of rubbish. Must have come right down on 'em."

"You might have saved your fifty pfennigs," said the other.

When the raid was over, the guard on Gibson's hut reported that he had given one prisoner leave to go out of it and that said prisoner had not returned. The roll was called and the missing man identified. Another warder testified to having seen one prisoner, presumably the missing one, come out of the sheds and run toward the gate just before the bomb fell. No, he did not see what happened to the man; he himself was flat on his face, hoping for the best. He could not see anything directly afterward on account of the dust, which rose in a thick cloud and hung about for several minutes. The sentry who took up his post in the gap where the gate used to be said that no one could possibly have escaped before he got there. The explosion, he said, was not really over before he, realizing that there would be a breach, sprang into it. The camp commandant may have thought the man was exaggerating a trifle here, but he did appear to have acted very promptly. Considering the scale of the explosion and the fact that Gibson was last seen running toward it, the commandant had no doubt as to what had happened to the missing prisoner. He reported accordingly, and Gibson was eventually written off.

Gibson threw himself flat as soon as he saw Hambledon and Grautz run across the road; even so, he thought the explosion had killed him. He had run nearly a quarter of a mile before he was quite sure he was still alive and really running. He stopped and leaned panting against a wall, trembling from head to foot, deafened and shaken, and with a violent headache. Somebody came up to him and said something Gibson did not catch. The man was an air-raid warden, not a policeman, thank goodness.

"Eh?" said Gibson. "I can't hear very well."

"You ought to be in a shelter," said the warden loudly.

"I was making for one," said Gibson, "when that happened. Where am I—where's the nearest shelter?"

"You've been shook up, I can see," said the warden, and took his arm. "Come and have a sit-down and I'll get you a drink of water."

"I'm all right," said Gibson, but the warden persisted in leading him away. He took him down some steps into an underground shelter full of people and made room for him on a bench.

"You sit quiet," he said. "You'll be all right. I'll be back in a minute."

"What's happened?" asked the people round Gibson. "Are you hurt?"

"No, thank you," said Gibson feebly. "Only blown over by blast. Let me just stay quiet a minute. I'll be all right."

He leaned back, closing his eyes, and kindly people left him alone. Before the warden returned the all-clear sounded, and people began to stream out of the shelter to return to their homes. In the confusion Gibson managed to give his kind friend the slip and walk away, lost in the crowd in the dark.

"That was a short raid," said one.

"I hope they don't come back again later on," said a woman's voice.

"We drove them off, that's what," said a man.

" 'Ear that big bang?" said another. "That was a bomber blowing up. I've heard that before; you can always tell."

By the time Gibson reached Weber's house in Spandauer Strasse he was recovering. His hearing had returned, and the walk in the night air had cured his headache. Weber had the door ajar and was standing just inside, waiting for him.

"Thank goodness," said the tobacconist. "I was getting horribly anxious about you."

"Not half so anxious as I was," said Gibson. "Give you my word I thought I was dead and it was my ghost running away. Let nobody say Hambledon isn't thorough. I'm sure he broke every window for miles around. Next time I have to be rescued, let it be by a company of commandos. I think they'd be much less violent."

"Come and sit down," said Weber. "There is time for a glass of wine and a cigarette before I start operations on you."

"Sounds alarming," said Gibson. "What are you going to do—remove my appendix?"

Weber laughed. "You speak Spanish, don't you? Of course, you were in Madrid for some years. You are the Señor Rodrigo de' Arueta. You haven't shaved since you were arrested, I notice."

"No," said Gibson. "There were no facilities for shaving in the parcel I received, so I took it I wasn't meant to. Who is the blighter and why doesn't he shave?"

"Señor de' Arueta wore sideburns," said Weber, sketching with a gesture a strip of hair running down in front of his ears. "I didn't mean you to shave; that's why there wasn't a razor in the parcel. I packed it myself. I think you've got enough hair there now to lock convincing when the rest of your face is shaven. It's very fortunate you are fairly dark."

"I'm not so dark as a Spaniard."

"You will be by the time I've done with you. I shall stain your skin and dye your hair black instead of brown."

"Sideburns," said Gibson with distaste. "Well, well. What do I do when the dye begins to grow out of my hair?"

"Leave Berlin," said Weber simply.

"Just like that. Who was our Rodrigo—I notice you used the past tense— and what is he supposed to be doing in Berlin?"

"Having a holiday. I think I'd better start work on you now; then I'll find you something to eat and you can lie down for a few hours before going to your hotel. I'm afraid I must stain you all over to start with and apply a second coat to the sunburned parts. This is very good stuff; it won't wash off. I'll switch the fire on while you undress."

"This is just like the spy thrillers," said Gibson, removing collar and tie. "But about Rodrigo—"

"De' Arueta was one of Franco's men and commandant of a camp where a number of the International Brigade were imprisoned. I fear he was not very tender with his prisoners. Apart from that, he had no very strict views about sanitation and facilities for washing. He also economized on their food if all I've heard is true. The death rate in that camp was rather high, and when the Civil War came to an end the survivors remembered Señor de' Arueta. They returned to their homes, still remembering; quite a number of them live in Paris. Last week De' Arueta went to Paris on the first stage of his journey to Berlin. He was—sorry! This stuff is cold. I ought to have warmed it."

"Never mind," said Gibson. "It was only the first dab that startled me. Carry on."

"De' Arueta was much in favor with the Nazis. I think he has been very helpful to them lately. He was boasting in Paris about what a wonderful time he was going to have in Berlin. He was great on night life, hitting the high spots as they say, and all that sort of thing."

"Oh, look here," said Gibson. "Did he chase the ladies too?"

"I fear so."

"D'you mean to say that in addition to wearing sideburns like a blasted Dago I've got to chase skirts round Berlin in the small hours? Look here, Weber—"

"Cheer up," said Weber. "Your reputation may have been exaggerated, and surely you can manage a few mild indiscretions."

"Go on," said Gibson gloomily.

"De' Arueta was supposed to spend a night or two in Paris; in point of fact he stayed there for a week. I shouldn't enjoy Paris under the Nazis myself, but he apparently found it to his taste. He was coming to Berlin by the night train on Tuesday, and his heavy luggage actually did so. De' Arueta himself was just having a last look round, I suppose, when he met some of the ex-International Brigade men from his old camp. I'm not clear what happened, but he's at the bottom of the Seine and unlikely to rise again in our time. One of our men was more or less involved in the affair—he says it was an execution, not a murder. He collected all De' Arueta's papers and hand luggage. They were sent to me here on the chance they might be useful; there are even the tickets for the heavy luggage now waiting at the station to be called for. Well, I think that's all right for the first coat. You can get half dressed again now, and I'll shave you and put the second coat on your arms and legs. And manicure your hands, too. He had highly polished nails."

Gibson moaned fluently, but Weber pointed out that De' Arueta's alias was undoubtedly sent by Providence and it would be ungrateful not to use it. De' Arueta had apparently gone into the Seine in his birthday suit, for a complete set of clothes was there, even to a hat. Gibson objected violently to the hat. "I've never seen such a thing. Even in Madrid they don't wear hats like this."

"It is rather distinctive, certainly," said Weber, looking inside the hat. "Made in Buenos Aires. A favorite hat. He was well known in it."

"I wish he'd been—something—well drowned in it. Good heart alive," said

Gibson, studying himself in the looking glass, "I don't recognize myself. What a frightful-looking— Oh well. What we do suffer for an ungrateful country. Did this fellow know anybody in Berlin, d'you know?"

"Don't think so—nobody who matters. A few fellows in the Luftwaffe, possibly."

"Some of the Guernica boys? I will shun the Luftwaffe. I shall get through my business as quickly as possible, Weber, and then get out. I don't approve of my new personality. I shall be recalled to Madrid by the serious illness of a relative from whom I have expectations. You will arrange about that, won't you? I mean the telegram, not the relation. I don't think I want to adopt the De' Arueta family. This coat is too big round the middle and so are the trousers. Rodrigo was running to fat in certain well-defined zones. Also the sleeves are a trifle short."

"I can alter that a little while you lie down," said Weber. "You must want some sleep. If the suit is a little loose, you lost weight in Paris, that's all."

"All this dual-identity stuff may be very well for Hambledon," said Gibson, "but it doesn't suit my style at all. I'm not used to it. 'Lawk-a-mussy on us, this be none of I.' Well, lead me to bed, and I hope I wake up and find I'm in Somerset and all this is an evil dream."

Gibson went in the morning to the hotel at which De' Arueta had booked rooms, and from there to the police station to obtain his *permis de séjour*. Here he was cooed over and given to understand that Berlin was his to play with.

"I meant to have been here some days ago," said the Spanish gentleman nonchalantly, "but I was delayed in Paris." He spoke German with a Spanish accent, a mixture which he regarded as a simply horrible noise.

"Yes, yes," said the police. "Quite so. We quite understand. It is of no consequence, the delay. We hope the Señor will enjoy his visit to our beautiful capital."

"Oh, I expect so. There is fun to be had in most places if one knows how to look for it. By the way, my hotel manager tells me there is a difficulty about getting my baggage from the station."

"A permit to engage a taxi. Certainly, I will make out one. There is a labor shortage, señor, which is an inconvenience to us all."

"The war," said Gibson carelessly, "the war. In Spain we are accustomed to war. Thank you, gentlemen. I have the honor to salute you." He strolled out.

"Bit of a lad, eh?" said one policeman. "He'll make the sparks fly before he goes home, I'm sure of it."

"Nasty piece of work, in my opinion," said the other. "Yet, unless he does anything too outrageous, we are to look the other way. It is an order. He's got a pull somewhere. No business of ours. Next applicant, please."

Gibson spent the following week working harder than he had ever worked in all his life before. There was a certain porter in the Anhalter goods yards who had an attractive daughter, blue-eyed and flaxen-haired like the typical

Gretchen of German folk tales. Since opposites attract, she caught the roving eye of the gallant Señor de' Arueta. He made an opportunity to enter into conversation with her, and when she walked away he followed her. The policeman on point duty near by observed with disapproval.

"That Spaniard," he said when he returned to the section house. "De' Aroota or whatever his abominable name is. He is running after that little Annchen Muller. If I was her father I'd knock his face out through the back of his head and give her a good hiding. Several hidings. Bread and water for a week."

"Money," said his cynical friend. "The dear Señor has money. Muller's only a goods porter, and they're not very well paid."

"Which of us is? Before I'd let a girl of mine run about with a skunk like that I'd—I'd drown her."

Annchen Muller hurried nervously through the streets toward her home, followed by the self-conscious De' Arueta. She reached her own door and scuttled inside; the Señor calmly reopened the door and followed her in. The neighbors stared and nudged each other.

"It is too bad," one said. "She was always respectable."

"Her father is at home," said another. "You wait. Next time that door opens that man'll come flying out and not touch the ground till his head hits the house opposite."

But the door did not open for some time, and when it did the parent Muller was seen parting from the stranger with obvious cordiality. He explained to his neighbors that the Spaniard had known Annchen's brother who was killed in Spain, fighting with the Falangists. He recognized her from a photograph her brother used to carry.

"Is that indeed so?" said the unbelieving neighbors. "She did not behave as though he was one with a right to speak to her."

"My daughter has been well brought up," said Muller. "When he spoke to her, saying, 'You must be Annchen Muller,' she told him he must speak to me and not to her. He came here in order to do so. His behavior was most correct."

"You think so," said the neighbors. "You be careful. One never knows with these foreigners."

"He was my son's friend," said Muller obstinately, and the neighbors gave it up. In point of fact they need not have worried. Once inside the house, Annchen was banished to the kitchen while Gibson and her father sat in the stuffy parlor, going through lists of names, places, and amounts.

"I don't like throwing all this upon you, Muller," said Gibson. "I think I'd better put on overalls, dirty my face, and come to the yard for a job this week. Or, better still, drive one of the vans."

"Your face would have to be very dirty indeed to disguise those fascinating little side whiskers," objected Muller. "There is not their like in Berlin. If you were once recognized—" He threw up his hands.

"I suppose you're right," said Gibson unwillingly. "We must manage without. Let's have the map again. You see this narrow street here, it has been completely wrecked by bombing, and evacuated. The four last houses have cellars under them—"

Señor de' Arueta paid several visits to the Muller household during the week that followed, and at night he displayed himself in various places of amusement such as might be expected to appeal to a broad-minded foreigner. Gibson hated the whole performance so violently that one night he gave himself a holiday from more raffish entertainments and had dinner early in his own hotel, intending to go to the opera afterward. In a corner of the dining room there was a dinner party in progress; one of Gibson's fellow guests was entertaining friends. Gibson bowed politely in passing, saying *"Bue' noche"* to the company at large, and went on to his own table. He became at once aware that he was the subject of comment at the dinner party; he could not hear what was said, but he thought he heard his name, and there was no mistaking the interested glances thrown at him. One lady in particular fixed a stern, unwavering gaze upon him, and it was not the gaze of admiration. She was a large, muscular young lady, definitely a Brünnehilde with a strong dash of schoolmistress. She was, in fact, a leader in athletics among the Hitler Maidens, and looked it. Gibson quailed inwardly, but preened himself and returned the glances with discretion.

Presently she arose with grandeur and stalked across to his table, and Gibson rose politely.

" Señor Rodrigo de' Arueta?"

"At your service, most charming Fräulein."

"From Madrid?"

"The same, most excellent—"

"Stop that. How long have you been in Berlin?"

"I am flattered," began Gibson, "that my unimportant affairs—"

"You have been here several days; my friend tells me so," said the lady. "How is it you have not yet been to see my sister?"

"I was not aware that—I have not the honor of knowing your distinguished name?"

"You know my sister's well enough; she is Brigitte von Eisenbaum."

"Ah yes," said Gibson. "Yes, of course. I should have known. The likeness—"

"Don't be ridiculous!" snapped Brigitte's sister. "We are not in the least alike. You are coming to call upon her tomorrow morning at eleven-thirty."

"I regret—" began Gibson.

"Regret, nonsense. You are going to marry her."

"Impossible, gracious Fräulein. I have the misfortune to be already married," said Gibson untruthfully, but with considerable presence of mind.

"You were, you mean. Your wife is dead. Do not deny it; we still have news from Madrid."

"Ah, but since that unhappy event I am married again," urged Gibson. "Last week, in Paris," he added.

"You liar!"

"Most entrancing señorita—"

"You are either a liar or a worm."

"I am a very worm at the feet of the charming señorita and her delightful sister, but—"

"You centipede!"

"I beg a thousand pardons—"

"You crawling thing! You louse. Are you coming tomorrow morning?"

"It is wiser not to reopen old wounds," said Gibson thoughtfully. "The heart is—"

She dealt him a slap on the cheek which rang like a pistol shot, and the unfortunate Gibson staggered and clutched at his chair. He became aware that the whole room, including the waiters clustered round the service door, were watching, entranced.

"I am unworthy to approach your sister—"

"That's the first true thing you've said!"

"And I'm leaving Berlin tomorrow morning, and that's the second," said Gibson desperately. An immediate retreat was indicated; this couldn't go on. She was quite capable of putting him across a chair and spanking him. He bowed low and took a step back. "I kiss your hands and feet," he murmured, in the formal Spanish leave-taking.

"If you kissed my boots I'd burn them," she retorted. "Get out of my sight!"

Gibson fled.

Chapter XVIII

One Hundred Cigars

THERE WAS A MEETING in Stockholm of the directors of that firm of armament manufacturers who had unwisely financed Ulseth at Servatsch and whose delegates had been so unceremoniously deported after their attempt to interview the Herr Professor at the Adlon. After this failure they had let the matter slide for some months, but it had not been forgotten. On the contrary, it rankled. At every directors' meeting since then, somebody was sure to bring up the subject, but nothing was done about it. Indeed, it was not clear that there was anything effectual to do, and the matter was dropped. At this meeting it cropped up again.

"That fellow Ulseth—"

"I have here," said the chairman, "a cutting from a Berlin paper about Ulseth. I will read it. It is headed 'Green Flash Soon? Inventor Dines with Goering,' and goes on: 'Considerable interest was occasioned last night when the

Herr Professor Sigmund Ulseth, the inventor of Ulsenite, the new explosive, was seen at the Adlon dining with the Reichsmarschall. They were in obviously good spirits. The Herr Professor, approached after dinner by our representative, said he hoped before long to be able to make a pronouncement on the subject of Ulsenite. He has spent the whole winter in his laboratory in the Jungfern Heide wrestling with the outstanding problems involved, and is now in hopes of reaching a satisfactory solution at an early date.' "

"It is perfectly useless," said another director, "to attempt to obtain the formula, and we deceive ourselves if we retain any such hope. Germany will never release it."

"I think that has been obvious for some time," said the chairman, and there was general agreement.

"I was no longer considering the formula," said the director who had first spoken. "I was thinking about our money. This fellow Ulseth is doubtless well paid by the German government. In common honesty he should return us our two hundred and fifty thousand kroner."

"Any sort of honesty," said the chairman, "is very uncommon indeed in Germany today."

"I think another attempt should be made to obtain it," said the last speaker obstinately. "In view of the deliberate rudeness with which we were treated, I am not disposed to let the matter drop. We know where to find him now, at this laboratory of his."

"I think it is a waste of time and money to pursue the matter further," said another director. "We shall only be insulted again. The firm can stand the loss; let it go."

"No," said the other man. "It is a matter of principle." He banged the table.

"Any other views on this question?" asked the chairman, and a discussion followed. Eventually the first speaker proposed a motion, "That two representatives be sent to interview Herr Ulseth and make a last attempt to induce him to repay us the loan we made him." It was seconded and carried by a majority of eight to seven.

"It shall be as you wish, of course," said the chairman, "though I admit frankly that I have little confidence in the outcome."

Accordingly, there came a day when the bell rang at Hambledon's gate and he looked out of the window as usual to see who was there.

"Strangers," he said to Grautz. "Not lordly strangers, either, since they come on foot. Square, stocky men. I wonder what they want?"

"No vacuum cleaners being sold in Germany these days," said Grautz. "Perhaps they want to insure our lives."

"I think they'd do better by telling our fortunes," said Tommy. " 'Danger surrounds you. Beware of a dark man with a clubfoot. Nevertheless I think I see you rising suddenly to great heights. A green light is all about you.' "

The bell of their private telephone rang from the gate; Eckhoff, at the other end, said that two gentlemen wished to speak to the Herr Professor on business.

"Their names?" said Hambledon.

The gentlemen had said that their names would convey nothing to the Herr Professor.

"Their business, then?" asked Hambledon, but Eckhoff replied that they would not tell him that either. They would themselves disclose it to the Herr Professor.

"Oh no, they won't. I don't allow people to come barging in here when they won't tell either their names or their business. It's ridiculous. I'm surprised at your ringing me up with such a tale, Eckhoff. Either they'll say who they are and what they want or they can make a noise like a Heinkel and dive away. Tell 'em so." Hambledon put down the telephone and returned to the window. An argument was obviously in progress through the bars of the gate; even at a range of a hundred yards he could see Eckhoff obstinately shaking his head while the two gentlemen outside continued to talk. Eventually the guard left the gate and returned to the lodge; the telephone rang again.

"Well?" said Hambledon, lifting the receiver.

"They want to see you about some money," said Eckhoff. "I couldn't get out of them whether they want to pay it to you or get it out of you. I'm sorry, sir."

"Are they Germans?" asked Hambledon. "Or, if not, what are they?"

"They're Swedes, sir, I'm sure. They speak to each other in that, and though I don't know it well enough to understand what they say, I know what it is when I hear it, if you understand me, sir."

"Swedes, eh?" said Hambledon, and paused for thought with a glance at Grautz. "Listen, Eckhoff. There's a lock on the door of the dining room at the lodge, isn't there? Yes; well, show them in there and tell them I'll see them in half an hour's time. Then lock the door."

"*Jawohl,* Herr Professor."

Hambledon turned to the public telephone and rang up the Armaments Ministry.

"Please put me through to the Obersatz Erich Landahl. Professor Sigmund Ulseth speaking. . . . Oh, good morning, Landahl. Heil Hitler! Ulseth here. The pleasure is mine, or it would be if I wasn't being pestered by two tiresome men. . . . I was sure of it; that's why I rang you up. You remember that Swedish firm of armament makers I told you about, with whom I had some dealings before I came to Berlin. . . . Yes, yes, they came to the Adlon, and you kindly removed them. Unless I am much mistaken, these are two more of them. . . . No, not actually in the laboratory; the guards are holding them at the gate. I told them to lock them up in the lodge. . . . I am very busy this morning, and I don't want to be— Quite so. Neither now nor at any other time."

"They shall be instantly removed," said Landahl. "What is more, I will arrange for stringent instructions to be issued to the police that any Swedes inquiring for you or about you or making any attempt whatever to come into contact with you shall be deported forthwith. It is intolerable that you should be pestered—Germany will not tolerate—"

"I am greatly obliged to you," said Hambledon. "You will act at once, then? It is inconvenient to have them here a moment longer than is unavoidable. Besides, they are occupying our dining room."

"A quarter of an hour," said Landahl. "Twenty minutes at the outside. And I will undertake that the annoyance shall not recur—"

Hambledon rang up the lodge, and Eckhoff said the men were sitting patiently waiting; at least he supposed they were waiting patiently; there was no disturbance arising from the room.

"They will be removed before the half hour is up," said Hambledon. "The police are coming for them. Let them have them."

"*Jawohl,* Herr Professor."

"Well, that's that," said Hambledon, putting down the receiver. "I can't, at that range, actually identify either of those two as being any of those I met at Servatsch, but I can't risk it. They are the only people who could say 'This ain't Ulseth' and be believed."

"Except Ulseth himself," said Grautz.

"Not even except Ulseth, for if he did say it nobody would believe him."

"It would be a bit rough, wouldn't it," said Grautz, "on any innocent visiting Swede who happened to mention Ulsenite in the course of conversation? He would find himself immediately collared, I suppose, hurled into the first available transport plane, and thrust out of the country. These Germans are so thorough. He would be surprised, wouldn't he, if he was only selling scrubbing brushes or arranging tours for variety— What's the matter?"

"What a perfectly marvelous idea," said Hambledon slowly.

"What for?"

"For getting out of the country, of course. I have been racking my brains for a means of escape. I am a fool. Don't attempt to escape from Germany, Grautz. Get yourself thrown out. A far better scheme."

Hambledon made an opportunity to visit the useful Weber. "Would it be possible to get Swedish papers for Grautz and myself, d'you think?"

"I've no doubt I could. It would take some little time, probably. How soon will you need them, do you know?"

"No definite date. The scheme is this. Any Swedes asking for us are to be thrown out of the country instantly without argument. So if Grautz and I can pose as Swedes for a few hours and demand to see me, I hope we shall be assisted to depart. What?"

"The plan is simple, anyway," said Weber. "You will have to alter your appearance a little, both of you."

"Yes, but only for a few hours, and with luck we ought to be able to avoid meeting anyone who knows us well. I have made a point of not coming into contact with the police any more than could possibly be avoided. I was afraid of meeting someone who knew me before. Well, if I shave off my beard, retaining a flowing mustache, and wear a monocle, that should alter my face a good deal; enough to pass, I think. It's wonderful what a monocle does to your face besides making it ache. That, with different clothes and a different walk, should do me, I think. Grautz, now—"

"I haven't seen Grautz," said Weber.

"He appeared in that Ulsenite film, of course. Apart from that, not many people have seen him to know who he is."

"I'd forgotten the film," said Weber. "I saw him in that, of course. A thin young man in glasses, isn't he?"

Hambledon nodded. "Nothing very noticeable about him. He's very fair-haired, almost flaxen. Colorless eyebrows and eyelashes."

"Simple makeup," said Weber. "We darken his hair and his eyebrows too. Are they strong glasses he wears?"

"Yes. Thick lenses; he's very shortsighted. Gold rims."

"He'd better have horn-rimmed ones, then. If he goes without any, he might fall over things; besides, there's usually a mark on the nose. Got any passport photographs?"

"I have," said Hambledon. "I think Grautz has too. Of us as we are, of course."

"Let me have them. They will be enlarged, your beard painted out, and Grautz's hair darkened and horn-rims put in, then rephotographed and reduced to passport size. Any particular names?"

"No prejudice about names; anything you like. It won't be for long, and probably in the dark, too, if I can manage it. Not that names matter in the dark; I was thinking of our looks. Well, that's fine. I shall have a lot to tell the department about you when I get back to London, Weber. Any other news? How's Gibson getting on?"

"He's gone," said Weber with one of his rare chuckles, for life presented the tobacconist with few occasions for laughter. "He left Berlin two days ago. I expect he is now passing through Spain on his way to Lisbon and England."

"Gone already," said Hambledon. "Rather sudden, wasn't it? What's the joke?"

"He came across the sister of one of the late Rodrigo's love affairs, a large, athletic woman—the sister, not the affair. She told Gibson he was going to marry her sister at eleven-thirty the following morning, and when Gibson demurred she clouted him in a restaurant full of people. Gibson said he never knew a slap could sound so loud or hurt so much. He left early the following morning."

"Don't blame him," said Hambledon. "I only hope he doesn't come across any more sticky bits of Rodrigo's past on his way through Spain. He made all the arrangements about those explosives before he left, I hope."

"Yes, that was all settled up. They've got enough stuff now to keep them going for a couple of years, if the war lasts so long. It will, in my opinion."

"I'm sure it will. There's no particular object in my remaining after this, and I can't stall off the government much longer over this Ulsenite business. Even Goering's getting restive about it. It's time I went home, Weber."

Weber nodded. "I'll get those papers through as soon as possible. You'll want Swedish clothes, too. Let me have Grautz's measurements, please. You must have some luggage too."

"Only hand luggage, Gladstone bags or whatever they use in Sweden. I'd like to do one more little job before I go."

"What's that?"

"Oh, nothing definite. I mean, I've no definite idea yet. I only feel that some parting gesture would be fitting. I'll think up something. Do what I will," said Hambledon earnestly, "I never feel I've annoyed Goebbels enough."

"He is a loathsome little beast," said Weber thoughtfully. "How women put up with him I don't know."

"He is morally verminous," said Hambledon. "Why did you say that about women—any particular reason?"

"I heard that he was running after that little friend of yours, Amalie Rielander. I don't know if it's true."

"He was taking a certain amount of interest in her some time ago," said Hambledon rather anxiously. "I hadn't heard that the siege had been intensified; I haven't seen her for some time. In fact, I have not seen much of anyone lately. I thought a period of seclusion was advisable."

"I am always in favor of caution," said Weber firmly.

"Are you picturing me rushing to Amalie's rescue? I'm afraid she'll have to look after herself; knight-errantry of that sort doesn't fit in with the job. All the same, it's an additional reason for bumping him off, if only I could find a way. Perhaps some scheme will present itself. If only I could hypnotize Ulseth and send him in a state of trance to assassinate Goebbels, two birds would be killed with the same stone in a most literal manner. I still owe him one for blowing me up at Servatsch. How is Ulseth these days? I haven't heard anything of him for a long time."

"He is leading an industrious and upright life selling railway wagons and courting a widow. Her name is Clausen, Gerda Clausen. She lives in the same block of flats as he does, and works at the Admiralty."

"Oh. Sounds a thoroughly admirable and rather dull life for an international crook. Middle age must be creeping over Ulseth. What a pity we can't induce Goebbels to run after Frau—what's her name? Clausen, and then Ulseth could shoot him for us with an automatic disguised as a box of cigars. Disguised as a box of cigars," repeated Hambledon dreamily, and looked out through the tobacconist's dusty back window with eyes which evidently did not see what they rested upon. Weber watched him with interest, and there was a pause.

"The idea," said Weber, "has it come?"

"I can see a distant possibility in faint outline. I think I'll go home and have a chat with Grautz. He is getting most horribly bored. He says he is a chemist, not an intelligence agent. He wants to get to England and find a job in a real laboratory where men are men and flasks are full of genuine chemicals and not ersatz crème de menthe with gold paint stirred in. Well, I must go. I'll see you have those photographs and Grautz's measurements. On second thoughts, I'll send Grautz, and you can measure him yourself. He still doesn't know that you are other than you seem. I am a firm believer in keeping separate things apart."

"That's why you're still alive," said Weber.

"Incontrovertibly," said Hambledon.

He went home and repeated to Grautz the substance of his talk with Weber, and the Dutchman was very interested.

"Weber, eh?" said Grautz. "You know, I have sometimes wondered whether there was more in Weber than cigarettes."

"You have, have you? I hope I haven't been indiscreet. I should never forgive myself if I brought suspicion on the excellent and useful Weber."

"Oh no, I don't think so," said Grautz simply. "Even I, knowing who you are, hadn't thought of that."

"What had you thought about him, then?"

"If I may be forgiven, I wondered whether he had, perhaps, a daughter."

"Grautz!"

"Or a niece."

"At my age—" began Hambledon.

"Your age, my foot," said the Dutchman cheerfully. "Look at Amalie Rielander."

"I haven't done so for a long time. Weber tells me she is having a little trouble with Goebbels."

"I heard that too," said Grautz. "I met Schafer the other night, you remember, the fellow from the Ufa Studios who made the Ulsenite film. We met in the Underground, actually, and went and had a drink together. He says Amalie is engaged to a young officer in the 71st Panzer Division, at present somewhere near Stalingrad."

"Bless their young romance," murmured Hambledon.

"But Goebbels doesn't approve of his rising stars becoming engaged. He says it takes their minds off their work."

"Off Goebbels, he means."

"Same thing," said Grautz. "Goebbels has practically got the Berlin film industry in his pocket."

"I gather they kick and struggle a bit," said Hambledon. "Like a bag of ferrets."

"I've never seen a bag of ferrets, but no doubt you're right. Anyway, Goebbels does not bless the young romance."

"Perhaps the Panzer officer will clout him," said Hambledon hopefully.

"There was another matter I wanted to discuss with you. It is this. I dislike Goebbels, as you may have noticed. I also owe Ulseth for the Servatsch affair, and I'd like to settle up my accounts before I go. I was considering a scheme for using Ulseth to destroy Goebbels, then the Nazis can destroy Ulseth, and everybody will be happy."

"Your mind is full of beautiful ideas," said Grautz. "How did you propose to carry it out?"

"Could one, d'you think, make up a cigar box containing a bomb? If it would burst on being opened, it would be rather nice, don't you think? I don't know whether Ulseth supplies Goebbels with cigars, but even if he doesn't he might send him one, mightn't he? A sample, you know. Touting for custom."

"You mean to exchange boxes somewhere, don't you? It means finding out exactly when and how Ulseth sends out his boxes."

"We know how. He sends 'em round by an old fellow with a horse and cart—a sort of Berlin Carter Paterson."

"You would get hold of the one addressed to Goebbels—if there was one at all—and exchange it after it was on the cart," said Grautz in a rather doubtful voice.

"If there wasn't one addressed to Goebbels, it would be only courteous to remedy the omission, don't you think?"

"Why confine it to Goebbels? There are also the Admiralty, the War Ministry, Air, Supply, Transport, and the rest," said Grautz placidly. "Besides, one only might fail to act, or go astray. It would be much safer to send eight or ten to different places."

"I do like the calm voice in which you suggest all this," said Hambledon admiringly. "To hear you, one would think you were merely planning to issue chocolates all round. Except that if you did they would probably be poisoned."

"What is there to get excited about? They are only Germans. In any case, it's no good sending poisoned chocolates; it's the men we want to get at, not their wives. There is this to remember—cigars are very light. You wouldn't get enough explosive into them to do more than kill the nearest people and damage a few others."

"About as much effect as a Mills bomb."

"Or a little less. You could pack some incendiary material round the explosive; then, when the bomb went off, the stuff would blow all over the room and start fires. Some incendiary stuff is very light in weight."

"Blazing curtains ought to help a lot," said Hambledon. "Most disconcerting. Besides, they might be prosecuted for infringing blackout regulations if it happened after dark. That would be really funny."

"Another idea which might be good," continued Grautz, "would be to include a simple form of time detonator. I gather that you are thinking of boxes that would detonate by opening the lid. Cigar-box lids are usually fastened down with one small nail in addition to any labels which may overlap the edges. One runs a knife through the labels and then slips the blade under the lid, forcing it up? I am not myself a cigar smoker."

Hambledon nodded. "That's the usual method, though occasionally one finds boxes with a metal catch."

"It doesn't matter how they're fastened; opening the lid will set it off. That can be arranged quite simply. I was only thinking that it might be useful if unopened boxes would also go off after a short lapse of time, possibly in cupboards and, with luck, at a moment when nobody was about. A small detonator of the acid type would do; one has to consider keeping down the weight."

"You'd better talk to Weber when you go to be measured for your suit. Gibson introduced him to one or two useful men who make up the explosive parcels which are left about in trains and so on. Weber will have plenty of empty cigar boxes too, no doubt."

"They would probably be able to do the whole job, though I could help by making up some of the detonators if necessary," said Grautz. "I shall take pleasure in talking to Herr Weber. You will choose a moment when a consignment of cigars has just arrived, I suppose."

"Yes. Ulseth makes a practice now of ringing up his customers and telling them the goods are coming. He lost rather a lot, I hear, in transit. I expect they went into the black market. With regard to the Propaganda Ministry, however," went on Hambledon, "I think we want something a little more drastic than a cigar box. They will be pleasingly annoying, but when I think of Goebbels I feel positively destructive."

"A parcel of some kind?" suggested Grautz.

"Yes. Looking like papers or books, perhaps. With a suitable label on it. They must have lots of such parcels arriving at that office."

Grautz nodded. "About the cigar boxes—how will you arrange the exchange? Distract the attention of the old man with the horse and cart?"

"Weber and his friends will see to that. If I were doing it I should have a cart that looked like his and take his place. 'Poor old Hans is ill today, so I'm drivin' for 'im.' There are several ways it could be done; leave it to them."

"And they will, of course, dispose of the real cigars?"

Hambledon laughed. "I imagine the underground movement appreciate good cigars as much as anybody, and don't get many of them."

" 'The laborer is worthy of his hire,' " quoted Grautz. "So long as they aren't smelt smoking them."

"Oh, they won't be. It is also written," said Hambledon solemnly, " 'Thou shalt not muzzle the ox when he treadeth out the corn.' "

Chapter XIX
Osberg the Carrier

"They will be ready by the end of the week," said Weber. "My friends are working on them now. Except that one parcel, they won't, of course, cause a very big explosion because of the small amount of ammonal inside the boxes; we can't put more on account of the weight. But the blast effect of even a small quantity is surprising if it's effectively detonated, as I am assured these will be. Grautz's time fuses are, I am told, jewels of their kind; small, light, and efficient."

"He has been happier than for months past," said Hambledon, "working over them with the loving care of a medieval craftsman producing a master-piece. I am glad your friends like them. What I really came to tell you about was a conversation I had with Goering last night. It all started because he was out of cigars; he said he hoped that a further supply would come in shortly on account of some conferences arranged for next week. Early next week; they start on Monday."

"Conferences?" said Weber.

Hambledon nodded. "He told me that I might be asked to attend one or two of the meetings to testify to the virtues of Ulsenite. I said I was, of course, entirely at their disposal and no doubt the cigars would help to dispel the tedium of my remarks. To cut a long conversation short, I did a little pumping, and it transpired that the Russian war is going to be gingered up. A new scheme has been outlined, and the various ministries involved are to fill in the out-lines—War, Air, Supply, and Transport principally. They are to work out their separate plans for meeting the demands on them; then there will be a grand general meeting of the various heads with Hitler in the Chair, to collate all the reports and make the final arrangements. The Russians are going to be finally squashed this time—maybe."

"I seem to have heard that before," said Weber thoughtfully. "Some months ago their final liquidation was imminent, wasn't it?"

"Last October, when I first came to Berlin," agreed Hambledon. "I was scared stiff; I really believed it. It's turned out to be a much more serious matter than Germany expected."

"The Russians are fighting with their souls," said Weber. "These warring ideologies—"

"Ideologies are all very well if kept in their place," said Hambledon senten-tiously. "It's when they become ideolatries that the trouble begins. However, to return to these conferences. Ulseth has no doubt got a supply of cigars on order, probably en route. If they haven't already arrived, Weber, I want them held up till early next week. We know there are none about at the moment. I am hoping that if they're delivered to the right place at the right moment, they will be taken straight into the conference rooms and opened there. It would be the natural thing to do. One can't imagine conferences without cigars."

"Except the one Hitler attends. I don't think he'll permit smoking, especially if he is going to speak. His throat, you know."

"I suppose not," said Hambledon regretfully, "but one can't have everything."

"Suppose they open one in your presence? You said you might have to attend, didn't you?"

"At the slightest sign of any intention to open a cigar box I shall drop my fountain pen under the table and go on my hands and knees to look for it. If there's a footstool handy, I shall hold it over my head. In any case, I shan't attend whole sittings, you know. I shall only be called in to give evidence and answer questions and then be politely dismissed again. It's a slight risk, not worth considering."

"It is for you to decide," said Weber. "I will pass the word for the real cigars to be held up till early next week. They will then be delivered to Ulseth to address, and he can notify his clients, as usual, that they are coming. Then the carrier will call for them at Ulseth's office, again as usual, and take them round to the various addresses. There will only be about a dozen explosive ones; the rest will be perfectly normal cigars. We can't fix up more than a dozen or so in the time. Our principal difficulty is not the explosives or the detonators, but unbroken labels; they are put on in South America by the manufacturers. When I think of the thousands of labels I have lightheartedly slit open, I could cry."

"Never mind," said Hambledon cheerfully. "A dozen or so will create sufficient distraction to take people's minds off Russia for a few days, I hope. Put as much incendiary stuff in as you can; there will be papers at these meetings which would look pretty all in flames, to my mind. How does Ulseth address his parcels? In his own handwriting?"

"No. Wrapped in brown paper with a typewritten label stuck on. Give me a list of people you want them sent to, will you?"

"I've got it here," said Hambledon, and gave him a half sheet of paper. "About our Swedish passports and so on—"

"About another fortnight, if that will do. There are a good many things to arrange, clothes and luggage included. I like Herr Grautz," added Weber. "Not easily upset, I imagine."

"Good chap, isn't he, though I find that placid manner rather terrifying sometimes. I know 'the only good German is a dead German,' but he enjoys killing them; I don't. What's a duty to me is a pleasure to him. Those poor devils of cameramen with their lungs burst at the Ulsenite demonstration—ugh! He merely smiled calmly and said it was a great success. He's not quite human."

"The answer to that problem," said Weber, "is Rotterdam. When Germany begins to break and the garrisons in Holland begin to withdraw, we shall see something nasty, I think. I wouldn't like to be a German straggler cut off in Holland then."

"Well, they didn't ought to have done it, as my old nurse used to say," remarked Hambledon cheerfully. " 'For all these things there cometh a judgment.' "

The real Ulseth, known to Berlin as Hartzer, sat in his office in Schönebuerger Strasse typing addresses on adhesive labels. On the opposite side of the table Gerda Clausen, no longer dressed in black, was deftly wrapping up cigar boxes in brown paper. There was a faint color in her face and laughter in her voice; her eyes no longer mourned. Ulseth had promised himself to cheer her up and had succeeded, though her dignity still overawed him. He had never yet called her "little woman" to her face, but he had broken through the hedge of her reserve and cheerfulness had crept in through the gap. They were very good friends; he told himself that soon they would be more than that. This was the sort of woman a man could marry and not regret it, nor hanker after the exciting, unsettled life of an adventurer. Gerda Clausen never took the smallest step toward a closer fellowship, but her eyes were kind when she looked at him.

"Am I doing these well enough?" she asked.

"Very nicely indeed. Very neat."

"This paper is so bad it's difficult to do it as well as I could wish. It's soft in places and stiff in others."

"You are doing it much better than I should," he said. "As for the paper, it's all we can get. It is uneven like that because the rollers are worn at the paper mills."

"How do you know that? Do you know all about papermaking too?"

"I know a little."

"You know so many different things, it must make life very interesting."

"There is one thing I wish I knew, that I haven't found out yet," he said with a sudden rush of courage.

"What is that?"

"How to make you happy," he said, and pushed the typewriter away.

"But you have made me happier than I have been for a long time, Herr Hartzer," she said, reaching for another sheet of paper.

"Herr Hartzer," he repeated. "Don't you think—couldn't you manage to call me Sigmund?"

"Sigmund?" she said in a surprised tone. "I thought your name was Theophilus."

"So it is," he said hastily, and could have kicked himself. "Only—my mother used to call me Sigmund to distinguish me from my father; his name was Theophilus too," he went on readily. "It was a sort of pet name. I think she wanted me to be called that, only for some reason I wasn't."

"It is a nice name," she said calmly. "There, I think that is the last box. Shall we stick the labels on now?"

"I have one or two more to type out," he said, and returned to the typewriter. "Must be more careful," he said to himself. "I shall let the cat out of the bag one of these days. She's evaded me again; she always does. I wonder why. I'm not her class, I know, but—"

"When will these arrive?" she asked. "I see there's one for my chief at the Marinamt."

"Sometime tomorrow," he answered. "The carrier is calling for them tomorrow morning, and I suppose he takes them round at once."

"I asked because there is an important conference tomorrow and I'm sure they will like to have them. I will tell the commissionaire to bring the box to me as soon as it comes, and I will take it in myself. I'll remind the admiral that they come from you," she added with a smile.

"That will be very kind of you. It will be good for business, no doubt. Don't lick the labels! Heaven knows what the gum is made of. Here's the roller thing to wet them with."

"They taste sweet," she said, laughing at his horrified face. "They will help out the sugar ration."

"Please don't. I'll get you some more sugar, or some chocolate—anything you want you've only got to tell me. You know that, don't you?"

"You do far too much for me already. That is really all now, isn't it?"

"Yes. Don't go. You aren't going, are you?"

"I must," she said, looking at her watch. "I've promised to go and see a friend this evening, and the time's getting on."

"I was hoping you'd stay a little while and talk to me," said Ulseth in a disappointed voice. "Wouldn't some other time do to see your friend?"

"I'm afraid not. She's just lost her husband; he was killed in Russia. I've known her for years. We were at school together, and she was very good to me two years ago. I must go; she is expecting me."

"Tomorrow evening, if you will," said Ulseth, detaining her, "we might perhaps dine somewhere?"

"Thank you, I should enjoy it. Till tomorrow, then, Herr Hartzer."

"Sigmund," he said, unwillingly releasing her hand.

"Sigmund, then," she answered, and the door closed behind her.

"Well, that's something," he said, watching through the window to see her cross the street. "How beautifully she walks. Damn silly, but I couldn't have her calling me Theophilus. What a name, Theophilus. It won't matter if she does call me Sigmund; a hundred men can have the same Christian name. I got out of that rather neatly, must be careful not to slip up again. Queer how I hate telling lies to her. I never minded lying to anyone before. Gerda. Wasn't Gerda the Snow Maiden in the fairy story? Must get her some sugar." He took a notepad from the drawer of his desk, wrote on it, "Sugar for G," and looked at it with a smile. "Very suitable," he said. "Sugar for G. We're getting on."

He locked up the office and walked home, whistling cheerfully.

Nearly forty years ago Franz Osberg started a carrier's business in Berlin with one horse and one cart. He prospered; his horses increased in numbers and his carts in size. He married and had four sons who came into the business when they were old enough and changed their horse-drawn vehicles for motor lorries. The eldest son was killed in the earlier Great War, and the slump hit them hard. Together with the rest of Germany they struggled slowly out of the mire and were nearly as prosperous as before when war came again in 1939. The three remaining sons were called to the colors, and the old man, now more than sixty years of age, did all he could to keep going. His best lorries were commandeered for national service; the one old wreck left to him kept on breaking down, while spares became more difficult to get. Eventually he was told that, owing to the services' need for petrol, no more could be issued to him.

"It doesn't matter much," he said to his wife. "The old bus is done for anyway, and I can't get another. I'll go back to horses."

In a disused shed at the back of his empty yard, once full of lorries, still stood the last of the horse-drawn vans which used to be his pride. He dragged it out with the help of his wife.

"Not too bad, really. There's dry rot in some of the spokes, but they can be replaced. Clean up and grease and a coat of paint, that's all it wants."

He bought a white horse and started all over again where he began forty years before, finding plenty of errands in a Berlin starved of transport facilities. He fetched luggage from stations, carted coal and wood, removed furniture, and delivered goods of all kinds. He engaged a boy to help him and bought another horse.

"You can tell the lads when you write," he said to his wife, "that their old dad's not done for yet. There'll still be a business going when they come home. Osberg and Sons aren't dead yet."

Ulseth rang him up on the afternoon when Gerda Clausen packed up the cigars and told him to call the following morning. Osberg promised he would, but much later that night there came a heavy knock at his door. He opened it to two men who stood impatiently on the doorstep. By the light of an electric torch he saw that they wore the uniform of the S.S.

"Franz Osberg, carrier?" said one.

"At your service, gentlemen," said the old man politely.

"Get your horse and cart out and come with us at once. There is a job for you."

"I have shut up everything and the horses are stabled for the night," he began. "Tomorrow morning early—"

"At once," they insisted, and since one does not argue with the S.S., he agreed. He went and told his wife, who was already in bed.

"Merciful heavens," she said, sitting up, "are they going to arrest you?"

"Calm yourself, Hanna," he said, struggling into his coat. "They would not arrest Snowball and the cart also. Don't be foolish."

"No. No, I won't. But the S.S.—"

"Want luggage or furniture removed just like other people. Sleep well. I'll be back soon, no doubt."

But he did not return until nearly midnight the following night, by which time she was nearly frantic with anxiety. "Where have you been—what happened to you? Couldn't you let me know?"

"I have been nowhere except to a house behind a yard I never noticed before. Nothing happened except that I was locked in a room all the time. I couldn't see out because the window wouldn't open and the panes were whitewashed. A man brought me food and drink but wouldn't talk. An hour ago one of the same men who came last night walked in and said they'd changed their minds and wouldn't want me after all. They took me down passages and into this yard, and there was Snowball already harnessed. I asked if she had been fed and the man said yes, well fed. He told me to drive home and not hang about. He warned me not to talk about the affair or it would be the worse for me. So we will not mention it again, Hanna. Such things are best forgotten."

"Yes, yes. But where did they take you to?"

"I have already forgotten," he said, shaking his head, "and if I remembered I wouldn't tell you. Better not, with the S.S."

"Better not," she echoed.

"The customers I was to have called on today will be annoyed. I will tell them I was ill. It is true I don't feel at all well. I'll go to bed, Hanna."

"Lean on me," she said, seeing that he was shaking. "It will be all right; we will never mention it again."

"No. I'm getting old. The war, and then this. I wish the lads were home again. Things worry me. I didn't argue, Hanna, I just sat there and waited."

"Come to bed," she said, "and I'll warm up some soup. Don't shake like that—"

The next morning he went round to the various clients upon whom he ought to have called the day before and apologized for having failed them. He felt so unwell when he got up, he said, that his wife persuaded him to have a day in bed. His clients were kind to him, naturally, since there were few carriers available. "It is the weather," said one. "It is the food," said another. "It is the war—the anxiety—the overwork. You must be careful at your age." Only at the Heroas Company's office in Schönebuerger Strasse was there no response. Herr Hartzer was out and the place was shut. Old Osberg waited about for some minutes, but he was busy and had to leave without seeing Ulseth. "Can't be helped," said the carrier. "If he wants me he must ring up, that's all. I'll tell him how it happened, next time. Probably got someone else to take his boxes." He drove off on his next errand.

Ulseth had not, however, been disappointed. At about noon on the previous day, while Osberg was sitting unhappily in the room with the whitewashed windows, the familiar cart drew up at the office in the Schönebuerger Strasse and a man came in and said he had come to call for the parcels.

Ulseth looked up and saw a stranger. "Hullo, where's old Osberg today?"

"He's bad abed," said the man. "I'm doin' his round for him."

"Poor old chap," said Ulseth carelessly. "Well, be careful with these boxes. Mind you take them all to the right places. The addressees know they are coming."

"The who?"

"The addr—the people they are addressed to."

"Oh. Well, they'll get 'em all right."

"This afternoon?"

"Sure. I don't want to keep 'em hangin' about. I've got too much to do as 'tis."

"Oh. Well, here's the money," said Ulseth, and paid him. It would be nice when old Osberg came again; this fellow was grumpy.

The man piled up the boxes and carried them out, steadying the top one with his chin. He put them into the cart and drove away. The same afternoon all the parcels were delivered; if they were not all quite the same parcels, at least they looked the same.

The commissionaire at the Marinamt took in the parcel addressed to Frau Clausen's admiral and remembered the instructions she had given him about it. He called one of the messengers.

"Here! Take this box to Frau Clausen in room seventy-five, first floor, and give it to her personally. If she isn't there, go and find her. If she's in the conference room, wait till she comes out and give it to her then."

The messenger found Frau Clausen in her own room waiting, with a note-book and several sharpened pencils, to be called to the conference room to take notes. She put the box on the desk in front of her and looked at it. The admiral wouldn't want to be bothered to undo the wrapping; she unpacked it herself. It would save time if she opened it too. She took a penknife from the drawer, inserted the blade under the lid, and then stopped. No, on second thoughts, better leave it; men liked to open cigar boxes themselves. She would put the box before the admiral, telling him that they came from Herr Hartzer. Herr Hartzer. Sigmund. If she called him Sigmund she must allow him to call her Gerda; it would be only fair. He was so kind, so thoughtful, if only he didn't bore her so. There was no one else at once so kind and so deferential, but she knew perfectly well that he did not want to remain at arm's length much longer. It was foolish to throw away a good chance like this in the middle of this awful war. So few men, so many widows. "If only he wasn't so—so doglike," said Gerda Clausen irritably," I should like him so much better. Oh dear! . . . I wonder whether I'd better open this box. The admiral will be busy talking to people and not want to be bothered with it."

She picked up the penknife again but at that moment a messenger came to the door and said, "Frau Clausen wanted in the conference room, please." She slipped the knife in her pocket and went quickly along the passage.

The conference room was an imposing apartment with paneled walls decorated with large oil paintings of Germany's naval heroes for several generations. Holding telescopes, or with a background of naval glory, they stared down from the walls or gazed capably into the distance. Below them their successors, seated round a very large table, were discussing in low tones the decisions which had just been made. Gerda Clausen entered the room and walked up the whole length of it to her own small table against the wall; the eyes of several of the officers present followed her. Before she sat down she laid the cigar box before one of the admirals present.

"The cigars from Herr Hartzer."

"Eh? What–who? Oh, I know, the cigar chap. Good. Have you opened it?"

"No sir. I thought you would prefer—"

"Thanks. Just slit it open, will you? Do it here, there's more room."

She took out her knife again and ran the thin blade through the labels which sealed the box, then pushed it in at the middle where the nail was placed and gently levered up the lid.

It did not appear to the officers present, all accustomed to gunfire in enclosed spaces, that the resultant explosion was so very loud. "A sharp crack," was how one of the survivors described it. It was the blast which killed those nearest to it, and, worse than the blast, was the immediate flame which filled the room, as though fire were squirted over all parts of it at once. The curtains were instantly alight; the papers blown off the table were flaming while they were still in the air, and men were tearing off burning coats and beating out flecks of fire which had caught their hair. As for Gerda Clausen, who had been bending over the box, it was as well she was the only woman in the room, for when the fire was extinguished no one could have said that what remained was this woman or that, or if she had ever been graceful and pleasant to the eye. Her admiral had presumably no more need of a capable secretary, since he also had passed at once beyond the enterprise of war.

Chapter XX
Mein Kampf, Japanese Edition

ACTUALLY, the explosion at the German Admiralty was not the first in point of time, and several others occurred upon the same afternoon. At the Air Ministry the box was opened by a junior clerk in an outer office, who had no knowledge of the way of a man with a box of cigars. He thought only of attracting the attention of the great Goering, who was to him only a little lower than the Archangel Michael, if indeed he was lower at all. The clerk's idea was that he would have the box all opened ready and take some opportunity to slip into the conference room with it. He would lay it, swiftly and deferentially, at Goering's elbow, murmuring, "Your cigars, Excellency," or "I understand Your Excellency wished for cigars." No, better leave out "I." "Your Excellency wished for cigars?" with a faint suggestion of a question in the intonation, as though if Goering wished for the moon an enterprising junior clerk would get it for him. Then the great Reichsmarschall would look up and say to somebody, "Smart fellow, that. What's his name?" and remember him in future. So the clerk waited till he was alone in his little office with the door shut, for fear some blighter slightly senior to himself should rob him of his glory, and then took up a knife and opened the box.

It so happened that there was a parade of tanks going by at the time, and in the uproar of their passing the sound of the explosion in a closed room was unnoticed. It was not until a messenger, hurrying along the passage, smelt the more than distasteful smell of burning carpets that the affair was discovered. The messenger looked in and saw the room was on fire. He shut the door quickly again and ran shouting for fire extinguishers, which were used to such good effect that the flames had no time to spread beyond the room. When the blaze was quite out and the smoke had cleared, they found an unrecognizable body lying in a corner. Goering was, of course, informed, but no one knew what had caused the explosion, how it had happened, or why. The commissionaire who took the cigars from the carrier never knew they had not reached the Reichsmarschall and completely forgot about them when questioned; Goering never knew that the box had ever arrived; the junior clerk, of course, had no business to have had it at all. The affair remained a complete mystery.

"By the way," said Goering, "the fellow who was killed—who was he?"

"It is not yet definitely established, Herr Reichsmarschall. It can only be one of the junior clerks–a roll is being taken—"

"So long as it wasn't anybody important," said Goering, and turned again to matters of more consequence. This incident, therefore, was a failure in every respect. No damage worth mentioning was done at the Air Ministry at that time, and Goering never heard the junior clerk's name after all.

At the War Ministry things went better from Hambledon's point of view. Several generals were literally removed in a flash from the active list to the Roll of Honor. Even more serious was the destruction of important papers impossible to replace without much delay. One bright consolation there was for Germany: the hero Rommel, home from Gazala to detail his plans for the imminent push toward Egypt, had just left the room when the explosion took place.

The Armaments Ministry lost papers and also some civil servants, but what are civil servants? Landahl escaped without serious injury, though he was in the room at the time. News that the latest consignment of cigars was not all it should be reached the Transport Ministry in time to prevent a disaster there.

The box delivered to them was taken away by soldiers to a piece of waste ground and detonated by rifle fire. Herr Andreas Adler of Department D.23 had a box of his own which he distrusted so much that he sent it to be detonated with the other. The soldiers duly shot it to pieces, and Adler nearly wept when they returned him the shattered remnants of one hundred entirely innocent Henry Clays.

But the occurrence which mystified the police most of all took place in the coding room of the Air Ministry in the middle of the night. It will be remembered that the Air Ministry did not know why their junior clerk had been so unaccountably destroyed, and when the chief coding officer, a civilian named Renzow, received the box he was expecting to receive, he did not suspect it. Why should he? That fellow Hartzer had telephoned to say it was coming, and here it was. He did not want to take it home with him. Frau Renzow made such ridiculous fusses about the smell of cigar smoke hanging about the curtains. He was certainly not going to leave it about to be stolen. He put it in the safe where the code books were kept and locked it up. He also locked the steel fireproof doors of the coding room when the day's work was done and went home with the keys in his pocket.

Between 2 and 3 A.M. one of the night watchmen on his rounds at the Air Ministry heard a really resounding bang from the coding room. He rushed along the passage and knocked foolishly at the door; there was, naturally, no reply. He reported the matter at once, and since there was no means of seeing through the doors—Yale-lock keyholes are no good—the staff went outside and looked up at the windows. They were filled with flame. It is all very well to make a room completely burglarproof, but it does tend to hamper the fire brigade. Even the windows were covered inside with a close steel grille which could not be removed. . . .

By the time Herr Renzow was brought in haste and pajamas from his house everything inflammable was burned. In fact, the coding room resembled the inside of the garden incinerator when it has been going well. It is filled with the ashes of mainly organic matter, but which is tea leaves and old newspapers, and which is dandelions from off the lawn, who can tell? In the coding room there was wood ash where the desk and chairs had stood, and paper ash all over the room, but to no part of it could Renzow point and say, "Ha! These were the code books."

All these different events were, however, in the nature of side lines compared with the attempt Hambledon made upon the Propaganda Ministry. Adolf Hitler, anxious to pay every possible courtesy to his allies the Japanese, had *Mein Kampf* translated into that language. Goering, when he heard of it, murmured something about school prizes, but even he was careful not to let the Fuehrer hear him; the joke, however, went round Berlin and reached Hambledon. When he found out that the Japanese translations would be ready at about this date he could not forbear to improve the occasion.

A parcel arrived at the Ministry of Propaganda, a heavy square cardboard box such as authors receive whenever they are lucky enough to have a book published, for such parcels contain the Presentation Copies, Not For Sale at Less Than the Published Retail Price. This parcel carried the label of a well-known firm of Berlin publishers who worked for the Propaganda Ministry, and across the top of the label was typed, "*Mein Kampf*. Japanese Edition."

Nobody hurried to open it, for *Mein Kampf* is no novelty to anyone in that Ministry even if he could read Japanese. It lay on a cupboard in the outer office until the late afternoon, when Hitler came to discuss with Goebbels the exact amount of publicity to be given to the conferences. When he had finished his business he looked about the office and said jerkily, "Is that all? Nothing else for me to decide?"

Goebbels said there was nothing else with which it was necessary to burden the mind of his Fuehrer and added, as an afterthought, that the sample copies of the Japanese *Mein Kampf* had come, if Adolf Hitler would care to look at them.

Hitler relaxed somewhat from the pressure of great affairs and said he would like to see a copy. It was an amusing idea to be unable to read a word of one's own work. Goebbels agreed and ordered the parcel to be opened and a copy to be brought in.

Two minutes later it seemed as though the entire building got up and sat down again amid a blast of sound such as stuns the mind which suffers it. In Goebbels' own room the windows were snatched out bodily and the ceiling split like starred ice and fell dustily upon their heads. Plaster falling seldom kills anyone, but it can be painful; also it is suffocating. The Fuehrer and his Minister rushed gasping from the room down the nearest stairs into the courtyard at the back, where the S.S. guards on duty disgraced themselves by failing to recognize their masters coated and caked with plaster. Hitler was furiously angry and seemed to Goebbels unreasonably to think that he should have prevented it.

Late in the day when these explosions took place two members of the Gestapo came to Gerda Clausen's flat in Uhland Strasse on a formal investigation of her effects. Formal because she was naturally not suspected of any complicity in the affair, since she had been killed; but there might be some trace among her letters which would help in discovering the guilty persons. It was unlikely, but had to be pursued. They had orders also to bring in for questioning Theophilus Hartzer, who had supplied the cigars. They found nothing helpful in Gerda's flat and were in the act of leaving when Ulseth knocked at the door. He had been in his office all day and had heard nothing of what had happened.

One of the Gestapo opened the door, and Ulseth, expecting to see Gerda Clausen, merely gaped at him.

"Well?" said the man sharply. "Who are you?"

"Theophilus Hartzer of Zurich, importer," said Ulseth, getting out his identity papers.

"Oh, are you? That's fortunate; we were just coming to call on you."

"What—what for?" stammered Ulseth. Had this terrible organization found out that he wasn't really Hartzer?

"You've got to come to headquarters for questioning."

"What about?"

"Cigars," said the Gestapo man grimly.

Ulseth cheered up. A small misunderstanding about smuggling, tiresome but not serious. A few well-placed donations and a little help from his influential customers, and the affair would be settled.

"Oh, is that all?" he said unwisely.

"All!" said the man, and paused impressively. "What did you come here for?"

"To see Frau Clausen."

"What about?"

"Merely to take her out to dinner," said Ulseth mildly. "May I leave her a note? She will wonder what has become of me—she is expecting me."

"Oh no, she isn't."

"What?" said Ulseth, suddenly frightened. "Why not?"

"Because she's dead."

Ulseth staggered and turned so white that the man caught him by the arm, thinking he was going to fall. "Here, you can sit down if you like. We've got nothing against you—not yet." Ulseth fell into a chair and covered his face. "What happened?" he said thickly. "Was there an accident?"

"No accident. There was a bomb went off."

"Bomb? Where?"

"In a cigar box. At the Marinamt. She opened it, and it exploded and killed her."

"*Lieb Gott,*" said Ulseth softly, "and tonight I was going to ask her to marry me."

He fell back in the chair. One of the Gestapo agents turned to the other and said in a low voice, "This fellow's innocent, anyway."

The other agreed, but added, "He's got to come along for questioning, all the same. Here," he said, addressing Ulseth, "pull yourself together. You've got to come with us; we can't wait all night. Got to get to the bottom of this, you know."

Ulseth got up, and his face was so changed that the men stared at him. It looked at once much younger and much less reasonable, as though masks had been torn off and exposed something naked and elemental. The fact was that for possibly the first time in his life Ulseth was not pretending.

"Damn you all," he said slowly, "you've killed her with your filthy wars. If there wasn't a war she wouldn't have died. Curse Hitler, the blasted little paper hanger who thinks he's an emperor; curse the Admiralty and the War Ministry and everybody who made the war; curse this rotten country—"

"Here," said one of the men weakly, "you can't—"

"Why did I ever come back here to have my life smashed for me—I, a German—"

"What?" said the quicker-witted of the two. "I thought you were a Swiss."

Ulseth laughed, and it was an unpleasant noise.

"Stop that at once," said the Gestapo man authoritatively. "You are coming with us, now. Franz, you go first. Now then, Hartzer, down the stairs. March!"

Ulseth subsided at once and walked meekly away between them. They had no car, and it did not seem worth while getting one; it was not so far, and perhaps the walk would cool the prisoner's head; it seemed to need cooling. Ulseth was barely conscious of what he was doing; he was thinking too deeply to notice. Someone had worked this trick, someone who knew that he traded in cigars. None of his customers would attack that conference at the Admiralty.

His brain clicked suddenly into clearness. There was someone else, of course there was, an outsider, a mystery, his other self, the Herr Professor who called himself Ulseth. He had ordered cigars too, but were they cigars or something else? He knew a lot about explosives, the Herr Professor Ulseth—the Herr Professor Ulseth—

"What's that you're muttering?" said one of his guards sharply, and the prisoner realized he had spoken aloud.

"He did it!" he shouted. "I see it now. God, I'll kill him!"

He broke away from them and started to run.

"Here, come back! Halt! *Sakrament*, he'll get away!" The Gestapo man pulled out his automatic and fired. Ulseth gave a sort of leap and fell.

They rushed to him and found him gasping for breath.

"The Herr Professor," he said, rolled over on his face, and died.

"You've done it," said the man who had not fired. "He can't talk now he's dead. There'll be trouble over this."

"I fired at his legs," said the other agitatedly. "Can I help it if he puts his spine in the way? We can but report it and hope for the best."

They accordingly reported it to their immediate superior, who said, "Accused the Herr Professor? He was raving mad." All the same, he passed on the report to the chief of police, who in his turn handed it on, with the rest of the evidence such as it was, to Goebbels in his capacity as gauleiter of Berlin.

"The Herr Professor Ulseth, eh?" said Goebbels. "That's interesting. Very interesting."

Hambledon spent the afternoon and evening fidgeting about the laboratory till even Grautz got tired of him. "It's not knowing what's happened that's so trying," said Tommy.

"Go out and see, then."

"Most unwise. I never go out in the afternoons, and I don't think I'd better go tonight either. I am working, as a rule. Aren't I?"

"Well—anyway, you seldom go out," conceded Grautz. "Look here, what are you going to do with this place when we leave?"

"I don't mind," said Hambledon. "Just leave it, or blow it up if you like. You know, I'm becoming a man of one idea–blow it up. Let's burn it down for a change."

"I've got quite a lot of stuff accumulated here," said Grautz. "It would be a pity to let the Germans have it back. I think we might set a booby trap of some simple kind; at least making it will give me something to do. Plenty of colloidal copper for a nice green flash. The great Ulsenite—positively its last appearance—"

"Do anything you like. We might try and insure that we don't catch Eckhoff; not that it really matters, but I like Eckhoff. Otherwise, the more the merrier."

By the next evening Hambledon could not bear it any longer. He went out in the Mercedes, called on Weber, and heard some of the news; Weber had his own means of collecting information. Disappointing not to have liquidated Goebbels; on the other hand, it was an unexpected piece of luck to have shaken up Hitler. Weber added that the most severe disturbance was that occasioned in the minds of the Berlin police, secret and otherwise. According to him they were rushing round like a bunch of heifers before a storm, headed by the chief of police in person. On the whole, not a bad day. Hambledon decided to go out and celebrate and try to pick up a few more details. He went to the Adlon and found Goering already there, looking anxious and perplexed. Hambledon greeted him, adding, "You seem worried tonight."

"I am. Haven't you heard the news?"

"I heard that there was an explosion of gas or something at the Admiralty yesterday and several people were killed. Surely it's not true?"

"It wasn't gas; otherwise it's true enough. That wasn't the only one, either," said Goering, and gave him a brief summary of the previous afternoon's events. "This is a score for British Intelligence, blast 'em."

Hambledon's spirits rose; it is not often that one is personally congratulated by the opposition. His face assumed an expression of sympathetic exasperation; he took Goering by the elbow and said, "Come over here." He led the Reichsmarschall to a small table against the wall, produced a flask from his pocket, and poured into glasses a generous portion of real scotch whisky.

At that moment there was a stir near the entrance and people looked round. Amalie Rielander walked in accompanied by Goebbels. He looked much as usual except for a strip of sticking plaster across one side of his forehead, but her face was clouded by a look which suggested unsuccessful defiance. She waved to Hambledon and Goering when she saw them, and Goebbels nodded. He appeared to be offering her a drink, with a gesture toward the bar, but she shook her head and led the way into the dining room.

"Fräulein Amalie doesn't look as happy as usual," said Hambledon.

"She looks as though she didn't want to come," said Goering bluntly, and reached for the water jug.

"Not too much," warned Hambledon. "It'll do you more good if you don't drown it."

Goering tasted it and said, "*Herrgott!* Where did you get this?"

"Ah," said Hambledon mysteriously. "It wasn't made in my laboratory, anyway."

"I believe you. Do you think if I drank enough of this it would dawn on me how the trick was worked?"

"I thought you said," said Hambledon with a puzzled frown, "that the bombs were disguised as boxes of cigars. Where did they come from?"

"Ostensibly from a man named Hartzer, a Swiss importer. He'll have to answer a few questions, of course, but we don't suspect him. He's all right. There was an exchange made somewhere; the Gestapo are working on it. That's fairly simple." He returned gloomily to his glass.

"Simple, you call it," said the unsophisticated professor of chemistry. "To me it sounds like black magic."

"Oh no. That sort of thing's been done before and will be again. It's what happened at my place—the Air Ministry, not my house—last night that's worrying me."

"Tell me," said Hambledon with the keenest interest, for Weber had heard nothing of this one.

Goering explained how the coding room was locked for the night soon after eight, and described the fireproof and burglarproof arrangements. "Yet in the small hours of this morning a time bomb exploded inside the safe and set the whole room alight. How did it get there, Ulseth? The room door was locked and had not been tampered with. The safe door, ditto. The place is watched all the time. Still, somebody got in and put a bomb in the place and got out again, all without being seen."

"The coding officer, whoever he is—"

"Man named Renzow, a civilian."

"Herr Renzow left everything all right—nothing in the safe that shouldn't have been?"

"Of course not," said Goering. "He assured me of that himself. Most reliable man." In point of fact, as soon as Renzow heard how the other disasters were caused he guessed that his own alleged Coronas were responsible, but was much too frightened to admit it. Hambledon also guessed correctly; he remembered the name of Renzow on a certain list. . . .

"You've got other copies of the codes, of course?"

"Yes," said Goering, hitting the table, "but were they burned or were they stolen? Renzow's been raking through the ashes with a table fork and can't find a bit of them. Now all the codes will have to be changed." He stared unhappily at his empty glass, and Hambledon hastily refilled it for him. What a fluke!

"Exasperating," he murmured. "I suppose that's a complicated business?"

"How did they get the keys? That's what I want to know, because what's to stop them from doing it again?"

Better and better. Far better than slaughtering the inoffensive Renzow and causing a mere uproar in the coding room just like the others. This would keep them worrying for months to come. All the same, Hambledon thought it kinder to change the subject.

"I am horrified," he said in low and earnest tones, "to hear what a narrow escape our Fuehrer had."

Goering gave a perfectly genuine shudder, which surprised Hambledon. He always found it difficult to believe that any normal person could really be attached to the pasteboard Napoleon with the comic mustache.

"It is terrible to think of," said Goering, and then smiled. "Goebbels is very upset about it. He turned quite white, they tell me." He laughed. "All over, like a snow man. Then his guards didn't recognize him and tried to arrest him."

Hambledon nearly choked. How blessed are the moments when Fortune lends a helping hand. Even he would never have thought of that inspired climax.

"It is funny, isn't it?" said the Reichsmarschall, watching him. "But the whole business is anything but funny. Here we are in early May. The Russians are going to attack in the south in six weeks' time. So we were going to attack first, naturally; that's what all these conferences were about. Now the loss of life and of still more valuable data has set the whole scheme back three months at least. That makes it July, August, September—at least September before we could get going, and that will be too late. Too near the Russian winter."

A page boy passed through the room, calling in a loud, toneless voice, "Fräulein Amalie Rielander. Fräulein Amalie Rielander. Fräulein Ama—" Somebody caught him by the arm, directing him toward the dining room, and the monotonous cry ceased.

"I suppose paging is the best way of finding people in a crowd," said Hambledon, "though personally I hate being cried as though I were cabbage for sale. Returning to what we were saying, surely the data already assembled is still available?"

"But not the decisions based on it. Men don't make copies of notes so important as that, you know. In fact, most of 'em wouldn't make notes at all; they'd carry them in their heads. So when they're dead—" Goering broke off. "I can't think why I inflict all this on you," he added. "It's not your headache. You've got more time to perfect Ulsenite, that's all."

"It is much more serious than I'd realized," said Hambledon with perfect truth. "Even if the Gestapo do manage to find those responsible—"

"We can make them regret it," said Goering, with a grate in his voice which made Tommy look at him. "But we can't undo the damage."

"The police—" began Hambledon.

"The police are nearly going mad. I am sorry for the chief of police; he's quite an able fellow. His deputy is one of these office wallahs—files beautifully kept, you know—but no more good in action than a toothless Pekinese in a dogfight. Oh well—"

Amalie Rielander came with a rush from the dining room and swept through the crowd to their table. Goering and Hambledon rose to receive her. She was flushed and sparkling, a very different Amalie from the sullen young woman who had stalked through the room a quarter of an hour before.

"Isn't it lovely," she babbled, "isn't it wonderful? Rudolf's come—my fiancé, you know. He must have arrived at my flat the moment we were out of sight. Isn't that car ever coming?" she added over her shoulder to Goebbels, who made an impatient sign to the commissionaire at the door. "You know, it is queer, I didn't want to come out tonight at all; I felt it would be a mistake. I told you so, Herr Goebbels, didn't I?"

"You took a little persuading, certainly," said Goebbels sourly. "You didn't tell me you were indulging in feminine premonitions."

"Would you have believed me if I had?" Goebbels shook his head, and she went on, laughing, "That'll do for another time, then. You'll have to believe it after this, won't you?"

Goebbels snarled, and Hambledon thought it wise to intervene. "Who is the beyond-measure-to-be-envied young man, Fräulein? Have I the honor of his acquaintance?"

"Not yet, but I'll bring him to see you. Kapitan Rudolf von Dettmann—"

"Son of my old friend Oberste Auguste Heinrich von Dettmann?" said Goering. "I remember him as a boy. May I congratulate you, Fräulein—a charming family—"

"The car is here, I think," said Goebbels, and Amalie turned at once to go. "I will bring him tomorrow, shall I?" she said to Hambledon, who answered, "Do, *gnä' Fräulein*. I shall be more than delighted."

"Going to see the lady home, Goebbels?" said Goering.

"Naturally," snapped Goebbels. "Why not?"

"Be tactful and don't stay too long, then," said the Reichsmarschall impishly, but the laughter died out of his face as they left and his mind reverted to his troubles. He turned to Hambledon, saying, "Thanks very much for the drink; it's done me good. I must go back to work, I suppose, and see if I can clear up some of the muddle." He leaned clumsily on the table, a huge bulk of a man. Hambledon thought suddenly that he had never seen him look menacing before. "If I catch the fellows responsible—"

"I trust for their sakes you won't," said Tommy, forcing a laugh. Berlin seemed increasingly to become a good place to leave.

"I daresay you're right. Besides, it wouldn't do any good. Only relieve my feelings. Good night, Ulseth."

"Good night," said Hambledon, "till I see you again."

Goering nodded and went away. Hambledon sent for his car and went home.

"It is time we left," he said to Grautz. "We've done something drastic this time." He repeated what he had heard and added, "I don't like Goering in this mood. He's as dangerous as a mad elephant. Frankly, he terrifies me. He's such a nice companion for an evening out, as a rule; but tonight, with the mask off—ugh!"

"I never believed in your amiable giant idea," said Grautz. "We in Rotterdam—"

Hambledon changed the subject. It was possible, he felt, to have enough of Grautz on Rotterdam.

Chapter XXI
Black for Amalie

RUDOLF VON DETTMANN, the fiancé of Amalie Rielander, was a tall young man almost handsome enough to be a film star himself, and theirs was no ephemeral wartime romance; they had known each other since childhood's days. He had never liked her being mixed up in this film business, although he knew it could not be helped; she was the only support of the widowed Frau Rielander, and even a wellborn German maiden and her mother cannot live on air. His marriage would not be permitted until he attained the rank of captain. Till then he kept himself entirely in the background of her private life; she did not bring him to the studios or talk about him to her fellow artists; she did not even wear his engagement ring in public. Von Dettmann disliked the publicity of her life; he disliked most of the people with whom she had to associate, and most of all he disliked Goebbels. Rudolf and Amalie almost quarreled on his previous leave about the ruby-studded cigarette lighter which the Herr Minister of Propaganda gave her.

"You should not accept valuable presents from such an ill-bred little beast," he said. "It is putting yourself under an obligation to him."

"I don't think so," said Amalie, laughing. "It is very good of me to take any notice of him, you know."

"It is, but I don't like it. He will think—"

"Then he'll find he's wrong. Seriously, Rudolf, I'm sorry, but if I snub him too violently I shall lose my job, and then what will become of Mother?"

"As soon as I'm made Kapitan," he said, "we'll get married, and then it'll be my business to see after you and your mother."

"As soon as you're a Kapitan," she said, "we'll announce our engagement and—"

"Announce our wedding day."

"Very well, we will. And I'll send Herr Goebbels back his lighter for a wedding present. In the meantime, Rudi, I daren't. He's a dangerous man to annoy. Goering warned me to be careful."

"Oh, Goering will be all right with you, he knows my father—he's one of us. But Goebbels—"

"I know, Rudi darling. Don't worry, I'll manage Goebbels. How long do you think it will be?"

"How long what?"

"Before you're a Kapitan?"

"It just depends."

"On what?"

"Oh, various things. On the colonel's temper, for one thing. And on the casualties, for another."

"Casualties—Rudi—"

But time passed, and Von Dettmann survived to get his promotion. Amalie Rielander had found it increasingly difficult to stave off Goebbels, whose reputation became steadily more notorious; by the time Von Dettmann came on leave again she was almost at her wits' end. Rumors of Goebbels' attentions to his fiancée had reached him on the Eastern Front; he came on leave determined that the practice should cease forthwith, the wife of Rudolf von Dettmann would be secure from such persecution. It was therefore very exasperating to be told by the concierge at her flat that she had gone out only five minutes earlier with the man in question. "Gone out to dinner," said the concierge. That meant a hotel in all probability. Von Dettmann went to the telephone and tried the Hotel Bristol without result; he was more fortunate at the Adlon. The Fräulein would return immediately, and the concierge, who knew him well, let him into her flat to await her.

He walked up and down impatiently for a quarter of an hour, then there was the sound of a key in the lock and voices at the door.

"Thank you, Herr Goebbels. I am sorry to have interrupted our dinner so suddenly, but I'm sure you understand. Good night, and thank you again."

"May I not come in for a few moments? I should be happy to renew my acquaintance with Von Dettmann."

Damn the fellow's impudence, pushing himself where he wasn't wanted, at a moment like this—

Amalie Rielander could have slapped him. "Some other time—tomorrow, perhaps—"

"Oh, come," said Goebbels obstinately. "You owe me something for spoiling my dinner."

"Since you insist," she said, and walked in flaming with anger. What a cad to spoil their first meeting. "Rudi—I am so delighted to see you," she went on awkwardly, giving him her hand. "Herr Goebbels kindly brought me home at once. I am so sorry to have been out when you came."

"I could not let you know," said Von Dettmann. "Never mind, it couldn't be helped." He saluted Goebbels. "Heil Hitler! I am grateful, Herr Goebbels, for your courtesy to Fräulein Rielander, my betrothed."

"It is always a pleasure," said Goebbels, "to do anything to oblige the charming Amalie."

Von Dettmann scowled; Amalie bit her lip; Goebbels lit a cigarette without the formality of asking permission, and there was an awkward pause.

"How are things going on the Russian front?" asked the Minister of Propaganda.

"Very well, thank you," said Von Dettmann stiffly.

"Indeed? I thought I understood— Amalie, may I sit down?" She could not refuse, and Goebbels dropped into an easy chair while the two young people stood side by side upon the hearthrug and looked daggers at him. "I thought I heard rumors of crack German troops being pushed back by the half-trained Bolshevik hordes. Not true, eh?"

"The Bolshevik hordes, as you call them, are very good fighting men indeed," said Von Dettmann.

"Oh. I gather that is an admission. Were yours among the troops who— what is the phrase—retired according to plan?"

"Have a drink, won't you?" said Amalie desperately. Anything to stop this scene, but neither man took any notice of the suggestion. Von Dettmann was white with anger.

"My men," he said with a violent effort at self-control, "retired when they were told to and stopped when told to, also."

"Ah," said Goebbels, nodding. "That's what they all say when they go back."

"Herr Goebbels," said Amalie loudly, "if you would kindly excuse us now— we have many things to discuss." She might as well not have spoken.

"I understand on my part," said Von Dettmann angrily, "that things aren't going too well in Berlin."

"What d'you mean?"

"You are Gauleiter of Berlin, aren't you? Yet I hear of sabotage here, there, and everywhere. Explosions in trains, trams set on fire, bombs even in the ministries— Wasn't there a munition factory at Spandau which blew up some time ago?"

Goebbels rose as though a hornet had stung him. "This impertinence—" he began, and at that Von Dettmann hit him in the face. The Minister reeled back across the room, snatched something from his pocket, and there was a loud crack, followed by a scream from Amalie.

"It's all right," said Von Dettmann calmly. "He's missed me." He put his arm round the girl. "My very dear—"

The door opened suddenly and Goebbels' two S.S. guards rushed in. Goebbels pointed one finger at Dettmann and said, "Arrest him. Take him away. Be careful; he is probably armed."

"You beast, you devil," shrieked Amalie, "you can't do this!"

"Oh, can't I?" said Goebbels. "Your fiancé has just reminded me that I am Gauleiter of Berlin." He dabbed his eye delicately with his handkerchief.

"My revolver is not loaded," said Von Dettmann contemptuously. "I do not find it necessary to go armed into the presence of ladies."

"Remove him," said Goebbels.

The guards hesitated, if only for a moment. Amalie Rielander was clinging to Von Dettmann as one distraught, and she was the idol of Berlin. Goebbels definitely was not, but his orders could not be disobeyed.

"With your permission, *gnädiges Fräulein,*" said one of them.

"It is no use, my darling," said Von Dettmann. "I must go with them—it will not be for long." He kissed her and unclasped her hands. Goebbels touched one of the men on the arm and gave him an order in a low tone.

"But—" began the man.

"No buts. It is an order."

Von Dettmann walked out of the room, followed by the two guards. He turned in the doorway to smile at Amalie, and then the door was shut behind them.

Amalie turned her eyes slowly from the door toward Goebbels and said, "I hope you are satisfied with your evening, Herr Minister of Propaganda. A nice homecoming for a soldier, to spend the night in jail."

"I do not think the gallant Kapitan will spend the night in jail."

"Where, then?"

"Listen," said Goebbels, and as though the word were a signal, there came the sound of a shot from outside. "That is what happens to young cubs who think they—"

"They have—they cannot have shot him!"

"I can hardly believe they would miss at a range of about a yard," said Goebbels calmly. "Or possibly less. Console yourself; it is unlikely that he suffered." Amalie stared at him with horror in her eyes, a horror which grew and increased till she looked almost insane. She ran her fingers through her hair, and it seemed as though even the dark curls were quivering with hatred. Goebbels watched her with admiration and sat down again to enjoy the scene, though his eye continued to trouble him.

"You look quite magnificent when you are angry," he remarked. "It is really a pity to waste this performance on an audience of one."

"You crawling thing," she began in low tones, "you cheap little upstart, you dare to—"

"Bravo, bravo," he said, and applauded as though he were in a theater.

"Do you suppose the Herr Kapitan von Dettmann has no friends? What do you think Goering will say when he hears you have had Von Dettmann shot?"

"He won't. Von Dettmann got himself involved in a vulgar brawl over some town wench and was shot by a drunken sailor. His body will be found in appropriate circumstances in the morning. A grief to his distinguished family, I fear—and what a horrid snub for his charming fiancée! On his first night on leave, too."

"My friends will believe me," she said with dignity. "His friends know him better than to believe such a story. Your credit doesn't stand so high as you imagine."

"Do you seriously suppose," said Goebbels, "that you will be allowed to run about Berlin telling your story to everyone you know? You must be half-witted. You aren't Amalie Rielander, the famous film star now, you know. You're only the Rielander woman on her way to a concentration camp. I'm afraid you won't look so pretty or so neat in a month's time. As for your friends—that reminds me, there's another one I must deal with. The dear Herr Professor Ulseth, the celebrated chemist, you know. You found him rather charming, didn't you? I seem to remember being kept waiting on several occasions while you entertained the Herr Professor. I don't like being kept waiting, Rielander. I've got him where I want him now, too. So I'll just dispose of you and then attend to him." Goebbels rose awkwardly from the deep armchair.

"You repulsive clubfooted ape," she said, and struck him with all her strength. She was taller than he and had not played tennis for nothing. He was caught off balance and went over, hitting his head violently against the corner of the table. He dropped to the floor and lay still.

"And I hope I've killed you," she added. "Now they can come and kill me. I don't care."

But he was still breathing, and it was necessary to get away before he revived. He must not revive too soon, either, or she would be caught and brought back. She looked hastily round the flat.

It was a very modern flat, and the sitting room was as bare of concealment as a dinner plate. In the bedroom, however, there were roomy built-in cupboards with doors paneled to match the paneling of the walls. Amalie forced back the disgust she felt at touching him and dragged him into the bedroom. She pressed an inconspicuous knob and a cupboard door flew open. She bundled him in anyhow, doubled up and head downward, and forced the door shut with her knee. Now to get away. She ran a comb through her hair and made up her face again, thinking rapidly. Goering and the Herr Professor were at the Adlon when she left; possibly they were still there. It was imperative to find Goering and tell him the story, and to find the professor and warn him, before Goebbels was free again. Rudolf's name should not be blackened by slander; Goering would see to it and protect her also. Not that life held any charm for her now, but it still held an object—to insure that Goebbels should pay for this.

She walked unhurriedly out of the flat, releasing the spring catch on the outer door so that it locked behind her. Outside, Goebbels' limousine still waited; the escort car had not yet returned from its errand with the body of Von Dettmann. It was dark; she wondered but could not see whether there was blood upon the pavement.

The chauffeur came quickly from his seat to open the car door and looked past her for his master.

"The Herr is bathing his face, which was injured," said Amalie calmly. "He wishes to remain quiet for a little while; his head aches. You are to drive me to the Adlon, please, and then to come back here for him."

The man suspected nothing and drove her to the Adlon. She thanked him and got out, and the car went off again at once.

Amalie entered the hotel and spoke to the commissionaire, that great man who knows everybody.

"The Herr Reichsmarschall and the Herr Professor Ulseth, are they still here?"

"They have gone, *gnädiges Fräulein;* they left soon after you did. The Herr Reichsmarschall went first and the Herr Professor a few minutes later."

"Tiresome," she murmured, with a finger at her lip. "I have a message for them from the Herr Minister of Propaganda. Do you know where they went?"

"I could not say where the Herr Reichsmarschall went, but I heard the Herr Professor tell his man to drive straight home."

Amalie considered this. There was no knowing where Goering might be, and she might spend half the night hunting for him. The Herr Professor's case was the more urgent, since he was still alive and might be saved, whereas Von Dettmann . . .

"Thank you very much," she said, and slipped out again into the dark street.

"While you were out this evening," said Grautz, "I finished the booby trap."

"Where is it?" said Hambledon, looking nervously round the laboratory.

"In that pile of boxes by the door. It's all right; it's quite safe at the moment."

"On this trip," said Hambledon earnestly, "I have had enough of explosives to last me the nine lives I might have had if I had been a tomcat instead of me. If I ever get out of this mess I will never listen to a bang again if I can help it. Even the harmless and mirthful Christmas cracker will be bored from my festal bard."

"Eh?"

"Barred from my festal board. Sorry. That just shows you, my brain's giving way under the strain. How do you adjust your practical joke?"

"Simple," said Grautz. "We just join these two wires here by the door. Then the act of opening the door will ignite the two-second fuse and up goes the lot. There is in those boxes all the high explosive I have left or—"

"But—" began Hambledon.

Grautz was not listening. "—or have been able to make up out of the material at my disposal. There is also—"

"But, Grautz—"

"Just a minute. There is enough colloidal copper in there to provide a green flash that will light up Berlin. I thought we might as well go out in a blaze of glory while we were about it. Don't you agree? What are you laughing at?"

For Hambledon was rocking in his chair with laughter and mopping his eyes. "Nothing," he said between gasps. "Only, how are we to get out? There's only one door."

Grautz looked at him. "The windows—" he began doubtfully.

"Are all barred. Like my festal board. All except the bathroom, and that's not big enough."

"It will be big enough for me," said the thin Dutchman. "It's got to be. You'll go out by the door. I connect up the wires and join you through the bathroom window."

"I'll go round and stand by to pull you if you stick. All right, then, if you think you can get out through a hole a foot square."

"It's a little more than that."

"You'd better go and rehearse your act, I think. Hullo, the telephone. Who on earth's this at this time of night?"

It was Eckhoff speaking on their private line from the gate. "A lady to see you, sir. She says it's very urgent. She has a message for you."

"Oh," said Hambledon doubtfully. "Can't she tell me down your telephone?"

"She says not, sir. I did suggest that."

"Who is she, Eckhoff?"

"The Fräulein Amalie Rielander."

"Alone?"

"Yes sir."

"Oh. Well, you'd better bring her up, I suppose."

"*Jawohl,*" said Eckhoff, and rang off. Hambledon replaced the receiver and said, "Our Amalie to see us. All by herself on the first evening of Rudolf's leave. Something wrong here, Grautz."

"Perhaps they've quarreled," said the stolid Grautz.

"And she's come here to get me to act as peacemaker? Possibly. Let's hope it's only that."

A few minutes later Amalie Rielander was shown in, and one look at her face convinced even Grautz that there was indeed something very seriously wrong.

"What's happened?" asked Hambledon quietly.

Amalie looked at the door. "Has that man gone?" she asked in a whisper. "Nobody can hear us?"

"Go and look, Grautz," said Hambledon.

Grautz went into an adjoining room without turning on the light, lifted the blackout, and looked through the window.

"He's gone, all right; I can see his torch. He's nearly back at the lodge."

"Sit down, Fräulein," said Hambledon, "and tell us what's troubling you."

"You must get out," she said bluntly. "Go at once; don't wait for anything. Can you get out of the country? If not, go and hide somewhere–change your names—"

"Why?"

"Goebbels is after you. He told me so himself"–she glanced at her watch–"an hour ago."

"What did he say?"

"He said he'd got you where he wanted you and he was going to deal with you as he'd dealt with Rudolf."

"Rudolf–Von Dettmann? What—"

"Goebbels shot him dead," she said in a hard, metallic voice.

"God above!" gasped Hambledon.

"Had him shot, rather. It's the same thing."

"My poor little girl—"

"Don't pity me, don't," she said, biting her lip. "Please don't. If I start to cry I shall never stop, and I've got such a lot to do. I must find Goering and tell him before they find him."

"Before who finds who?"

"Before the police find Rudolf." She told Hambledon what had happened as briefly as possible. "So you must get away. Don't stand here talking; go. It can't be long before they find Goebbels and let him out. I wish I'd killed him, and I can't think why I didn't. I could have cut his throat quite easily; it just didn't occur to me. How stupid." Her eyes filled with tears of vexation.

"Of course you couldn't," said Hambledon. "Don't be silly. What are you going to do?"

"Find Goering."

"Where is he at this moment?"

"I don't know."

"But if you're going to run round Berlin looking for him, Goebbels' police will pick you up, and then where will you be?"

"In a concentration camp," she said simply.

Hambledon swore under his breath. "Look here," he said sharply, "you must try to think clearly. It's no use hunting for Goering tonight. Haven't you any friends you could go to who would hide you for a few days?"

She thought for a minute and then nodded like a child. "There's Marianne at Tegel. It's a big house; she could, easily. She was at school with me; she knows Rudolf."

"You're going out there in my car. Eckhoff will take you. He won't tell anyone about it, either, if I tell him not to. He doesn't like Herr Goebbels either."

She rubbed her forehead and spoke more intelligently. "I'm not in much danger really, once Goering knows. If Goebbels could have made me disappear tonight he could have made up some story to account for it. Once Goering has heard all about this, he wouldn't dare."

Hambledon nodded. "That's settled, then. I'll tell Eckhoff to get the car out at once and drive you to Tegel. It's only about half an hour's run." He went to the house telephone.

"But you and Herr Grautz," she said. "You'll want the car to get away."

"No, we shan't. Between ourselves, I've been expecting this and I've made arrangements. Don't you worry about us. You stay quiet at Tegel till you've got in touch with Goering, then you'll be all right." He rang up the lodge and gave Eckhoff detailed instructions.

"You can tell him where the house is when you get there, can't you?" he said, putting down the telephone.

"He'd better not know, had he? He can put me down by the church and I'll walk to it. I shall be all right. Thank you a thousand times for all your kindness. I only want to live for one thing."

"What is that?" said Hambledon, though he guessed the answer.

"I want to see Goebbels die."

Hambledon looked away from her convulsed face only to see what was almost as shocking—Grautz in the doorway smiling placidly. Oh, to be in London where people don't hate so wholeheartedly.

"I can't begin to thank you for what you've done for us," began Tommy. "You have certainly saved our lives; at least, it will be our own fault if you haven't. Someday, perhaps, we shall be able to repay at least some part of the debt we—"

But she was so obviously not listening that his voice died away. She looked as though she were listening to something quite different—another voice, perhaps.

Chapter XXII

Sweden First Stop

TWO HOURS LATER the deputy chief of police was summoned from his bed to go at once to the Ulseth laboratory in the Jungfern Heide. There had been a dreadful accident: the chief of police was dead; Professor Ulseth was dead; others also. The deputy chief must go and take command immediately.

He groaned dismally as he struggled into his clothes. "I am not the man for these violent scenes," he said. "I am not of-a-suitable-disposition-by-nature formed. They must find somebody else for the post."

"Nonsense," said his wife, sitting up in bed with a pale blue sleeping cap over hair curlers. "You are perfectly capable if you will only exert yourself."

"No. You are wrong. Women do not understand these matters. Oh, the devil is in these braces, they— Ah, that's it. I am a civil servant by training, my dear. My office work is second to none, though I say it of myself. My files are quite impeccable— Where is my tie?"

"On the dressing table."

"Thank you, so it is. But when it comes to giving savage orders— 'Shoot that man!' 'Fire on that crowd!'—I repeat, I am not the man."

"I shouldn't think you will be called upon to shoot anybody tonight," she said. "According to the message, most of them seem to be dead already."

"I also dislike corpses," he said, and unwillingly left the room.

He arrived at the Ulseth laboratory with more police, in case they should be wanted, and found a scene of considerable wreckage. The stone walls still stood, but the rafters of the roof were sticking up in the air, the windows were missing, and the doorway a ragged hole. The deputy chief advanced cautiously and peeped inside with the help of several electric torches held by his assistants. The wooden partitions which had formed the private apartments were smashed to matchwood, and the laboratory was unrecognizable as such. He drew back, muttering, "Dreadful, dreadful."

"Careful where you step, Herr Deputy Chief," said one of his men. "There is here—"

His torch illuminated some debris of the kind which the deputy chief most disliked, and he shied violently.

"Cover it up, for goodness' sake. Let us go somewhere where we can sit down—the lodge, yes, the lodge. We can do nothing more here till daylight. In the meantime I will take statements from all witnesses. Fully detailed statements," he continued, trotting down the path toward the lodge. "They can then be properly collated and filed. Send in a shorthand typist to take them down."

Eckhoff gave evidence first. He said that the Herr Professor had sent him out on an errand with the car, and before he left—

"What was the nature of the errand?"

"Merely to take a visitor to the Stettiner railway station," said Eckhoff untruthfully. He had a romantic admiration for Amalie Rielander, and Hambledon had told him frankly that she was in danger and going into hiding.

"What was his name?"

"Pardon?"

"The visitor's name."

"I do not know, Excellency," said Eckhoff without hesitation.

"Oh. Well, I daresay he can be found if necessary. Continue."

"Just as I was starting," said Eckhoff, "the Herr Professor spoke to me at the gate. He said that he was not to be disturbed again that night upon any account, that I was not to go to the laboratory whatever happened, and not even to ring him up on the telephone. He said his experiments had reached a very— a very something stage, I've forgotten the word—

"Crucial?"

"That was it. Even the telephone bell ringing might jar something off—I think that's what he meant."

"Dreadful," said the hater of violence. "Continue."

"So when I came back I put the car away and just looked up the path toward the laboratory. I didn't go near, not me! But I could see they'd got the lights on; there's a chink always shows down the side of the blackout. They'd got a tap running a bit too; I could hear it trickling past the grating outside here. So I said 'Good luck to 'em' and went to bed."

"Have you got all that?" said the deputy chief to the police shorthand typist. "Include my questions also."

"Yes sir."

"Continue."

"I was wakened up by the gate bell ringing, so I got up, it being my turn on duty. It was just after midnight. I went to the gate, and there was the chief of police with six men. He said, 'Open this gate.' I said, 'What for?' He said, 'Don't argue. Open it.' I asked him if he wanted to see the Herr Professor, and he told me to mind my own business. So I begged his pardon and told him what the Herr Professor had said."

"About its being dangerous to disturb him, you mean?"

"Yes sir. But he wouldn't have it. He said he'd heard that tale before, and I could either open the gate at once or have a bullet through my head, whichever I liked. He threatened me with his automatic."

The deputy chief shuddered. If this was the kind of thing expected of him in the future, he would definitely resign.

"So I opened the gate," said Eckhoff. "They'd have forced it if not, and it wouldn't help the Herr Professor, me being shot. The chief left two men at the gate and walked up the path with the four others. I stayed by the gate; I didn't want to be mixed up in it. They had torches, and I watched them go up to the door and knock on it. Nothing happened."

"No answer from within?"

"I couldn't tell, sir. I shouldn't have heard from here if there had been."

"No. Probably not."

"Then they knocked again, and I heard the chief shout, 'Open, in the name of the Reich.' They waited a minute or two, and then I heard them kicking the door in. After a bit it gave way and the light streamed out from inside. The chief rushed in first—I knew it was him because he was the biggest—and then—"

"Well?"

Eckhoff gulped, for he was quite sincerely attached to the Herr Professor.

"Then there was a brilliant green flash as lit up the whole place, and an awful bang, and that's all I know, sir."

"A green flash. That is a characteristic of Ulsenite, I understand."

"Pardon?"

"Ulsenite always explodes with a green flash."

"Yes sir. That is so."

"That proves," said the deputy chief to his shorthand typist, "that this re-grettable affair was, in fact, caused by an explosion of the materials and—er—stock on the premises, and not by a bomb or other fulminatory matter surreptitiously introduced upon the scene by subversive elements engaged in sabotage."

"Yes sir," said the policeman.

"Type that last sentence on a separate sheet of the report, headed 'Conclusions Drawn.' There will doubtless be others arising in the course of the rest of the evidence. Well, my man," to Eckhoff, "have you anything further to add which will help to clear up this dreadful affair?"

"No sir. Except I'd like to say I did my best to stop it, short of gettin' shot myself. Not only 'cause this was a good job, either, believe it or not. He was a nice old cuss—gentleman—so he was," said Eckhoff, very red in the face.

"Your sentiments do you credit, and your actions shall be duly placed on record. Next witness."

The next witness was the senior of the two policemen who had been left with the car at the gate when the chief of police took his four unfortunate comrades to meet their fate at the laboratory door. This man said that he was on duty at headquarters that evening when, at about a quarter to eleven, the Herr Minister of Propaganda came in demanding to see the chief of police at once.

"The Herr Minister of Propaganda," said the deputy chief. "Oh dear. Do not put down that involuntary exclamation," he added hastily to the shorthand typist.

"No sir."

"If I may add something else not for the record," said the witness, "the Herr Minister was in a state. He had a lovely black eye coming and a bump on his head sticking out like half a duck egg; his clothes were all rumpled up any-how, and he was in a rage. Oh dear!"

"Most unfortunate. Most alarming. What happened then?"

"I showed him in, the chief being still there going through reports about these cigar-box outrages. Before I could shut the door after me the Minister says, 'Take a squad of police; go at once and arrest Professor Sigmund Ulseth. Now, at once.'"

"Put that down very clearly," said the deputy chief. "It is very important; it absolves the department from responsibility in the matter. I will give you a further note on that later for the 'Conclusions Drawn' memorandum. Continue."

"I didn't hear any more, sir; it wasn't my place to stay. Five minutes later the chief came out with Herr Goebbels and saw him to his car. He then came back in and said to me, 'Get five other men and the big car; there's an arrest to make.' When I'd given the orders and come back the chief was locking up something in the safe. He says to me, 'I got this order in writing, and that's it. Can't be too careful.' I don't know if that had better be noted down, sir?"

"Omit 'can't be too careful'; the rest is important."

"Yes sir."

"On the way here," continued the witness, "the chief seemed a bit uneasy but he didn't say anything. We arrived at the gate . . ." The rest of the evidence confirmed Eckhoff's in every detail.

The deputy chief of police took statements also from the only other witnesses available, these being the other policeman, Bernstein, and Bernstein's wife. They added nothing to the story. He then contributed a few more comments to the list of "Conclusions Drawn," rose stiffly to his feet, and stretched himself.

"It is nearly three o'clock," he said. "I shall go home and get an hour or two of sleep. Get those statements typed out; they can be signed in the morning. I shall be here at seven-thirty in order to finish off this business and be at my office by nine."

"Yes sir," said the police shorthand typist, looking ruefully at his pages of notes. He also had a home, but it would be no use mentioning it.

The deputy chief arrived at the laboratory gate punctually the following morning. To outward appearance he was as businesslike as usual, but inwardly he shrank from the unpleasant tasks awaiting him. It was, therefore, with considerable pleasure that he found one of the highest of his subordinates already in the lodge, a younger man, of stronger stomach than himself when it came to untidy corpses.

"Good morning, Klopp," said the deputy chief. "I am glad to see you here — I was going to send for you. You will take over this inquiry and arrange for the identification of the remains, if possible. The statements I took last night have yet to be signed by the witnesses concerned, and — "

"Excuse me, sir," said Klopp. "I have to go into the Wedding district at once to investigate a case of assault which took place there early this morning. It is a serious case; the victim is a member of the S.S. I am only here because — "

"I will go direct to headquarters and arrange for someone to take your place there. This disaster, involving such distinguished persons, is more important than — "

"With your permission, sir," persisted Klopp. "I know the Wedding district better than anyone else of my rank on the staff. This case here is, as you say, of such outstanding importance that none but you could adequately deal with it. Particularly as the Herr Minister of Propaganda is coming — "

"What?" said the deputy chief feebly.

"Herr Goebbels will be here very shortly. That is why I came out here so early without awaiting your instructions, I was afraid he might arrive and find only subordinates present."

"Why is he coming?" said the deputy chief agitatedly. "I would be understood to say, what is he coming for? So early, too, after last night . . ." His voice trailed off.

"I myself received his message on the telephone at headquarters," said Klopp. "In fact, he spoke himself. It appears that a mistake was made last night. It was never intended that the Herr Professor should have been forcibly arrested. He was only—"

"But," said the deputy chief, "I have evidence that—"

"The witnesses must be mistaken. Herr Goebbels was very definite about it, not to say annoyed."

"Oh dear!"

"He had discovered a plot to assassinate the Herr Professor with one of these cigar-box bombs. The chief of police was to rush out here before it could be carried out, warn the Herr Professor and remove him to a place of safety. He was too late, and the bomb exploded. That is all."

"But—"

"At least that's the story," said Klopp with something nearly approaching a wink.

The deputy chief looked at him despairingly. "But all the statements I took," he burst out, "prove that the explosion was that of Ulsenite and no other."

Klopp shrugged his shoulders. "So now, sir, if you will excuse me—the assault case I spoke of—"

"I myself," said the deputy chief desperately, "have an overwhelmingly important appointment at the other end of Berlin."

Klopp permitted himself the ghost of an insubordinate grin. "The Wedding district," he began, "is the most disorderly and intractable area—"

He was interrupted by the entry of one of the constables on duty at the gate. "If you please, sir, there are two gentlemen at the gate demanding to see the Herr Professor on urgent business. We told them they couldn't, but they won't go away."

"Tell them again," said the deputy chief.

"We have, sir, but they still won't go."

"Who are they?"

The constable mentioned two names which conveyed nothing to his superiors and added, "We have looked at their papers, which appear to be all in order. They are Swedes."

"Swedes!" cried the deputy chief. "Swedes. I know what to do with Swedes asking for Professor Ulseth. There was a special instruction on the subject circulated to all branches. They are not to be allowed to approach the premises, but to be instantly deported."

"But the professor is dead," said Klopp.

"All the more reason why they can't see him. They must be removed at once, or there will be more scandal. I will see to it myself," said the deputy chief, hurrying out of the lodge. "There has been too much scandal in connection with this case already; more must be prevented at all costs. If I take them away at once I shall be in time to put them on the morning plane for Sweden." He trotted toward the gate, accompanied by the protesting Klopp.

"But the Herr Minister—"

"You will remain here to receive the Herr Minister. Explain to him that only the most urgent call of duty— Start up the car, men! Two constables as well as the driver— Only urgent duty precludes me from the privilege of receiving him in person. Are these the Swedes?"

Two men stood near the gate with expressions of indignant protest upon their faces. One was a solid elderly man with a monocle and a large fair mustache turning gray. He held himself stiffly upright and was obviously laboring under a sense of outrage. His companion was a younger man, dark-haired, with black eyebrows and a sallow skin uncommon among Swedes; he wore large horn-rimmed spectacles and walked with a limp and a stick. The deputy chief looked them over, and the older man opened his mouth to speak.

"Silence," said the police official imperiously. "No argument is permissible. Into the car!"

They were hustled in with a constable each to keep them in order. The deputy chief took the seat beside the driver and gave the word. The car drove rapidly away.

"You artful old—so-and-so!" said the disgusted Klopp, and returned to the lodge to await with misgivings the arrival of an infuriated Goebbels.

Inside the police car, Hambledon settled his monocle more firmly in his eye—it persisted in trying to escape him—and leaned forward to address the deputy chief of police with what he hoped was a strong Swedish accent.

"May I take it we are now being conveyed to the presence of the distinguished Herr Professor Sigmund Ulseth?"

"No. You may not."

"But I insist—"

"Within my proper sphere of influence," said the deputy chief with dignity, "it is I who do all the insisting."

"This is an infamy," said Hambledon angrily.

"No."

"But I say it is. I demand—"

"Be quiet, prisoner," said the constable opposite to Hambledon, and pushed him back in his seat. Tommy thought it best to relapse into silence until the car reached the center of the city and turned south down the Wilhelmstrasse, when he tried again.

"Where are we going, Herr Policeman?"

The deputy chief turned in his seat. "In pursuance of an order made necessary by the tiresome pertinacity of some of your fellow nationals, you are being taken to the Tempelhof airport for immediate deportation," he said sternly.

Hambledon's soul filled with glee, but no sign of it showed in his face. "I protest," he began indignantly.

"It is useless."

"I absolutely refuse."

"It is unavailing."

"But it is a business matter of the highest importance. The Herr Professor—"

"Silence," said the deputy chief appropriately.

The car turned into the Tempelhof airport and stopped. Hambledon and Grautz got out and stood obstinately beside it, making no attempt to move. The passenger plane for Sweden was standing out on the tarmac with its engines slowly ticking over; intending travelers were climbing the steps and disappearing inside the small doorway.

"The money for your tickets," said the deputy chief peremptorily.

"I refuse to pay," said Hambledon bluntly. "If the Reich chooses to treat the nationals of neutral states with such unheard-of incivility, the least it can do is to pay their fares."

The deputy chief lost patience. "Take these two men into one of the waiting rooms and search them," he said to the police escort. "I have no doubt you will find enough money on either or both of them to pay their fares."

They were pushed into an adjacent waiting room and searched. In the waistcoat pocket of each was found the return half of an airline ticket to Sweden.

"Look at that," said one policeman to the other. "Giving all that trouble for nothing!" They scowled at Hambledon and Grautz and went out, taking the tickets and locking the doors after them. Hambledon looked out of the window.

"That airliner looks as though it's filling up," he remarked anxiously.

"I hope they'll find room for us," said Grautz calmly. "If not, it may be a little awkward."

The door opened again, and the deputy chief said, "Come out!"

They thought it best to obey, and were being escorted toward the machine when an official of the airline came running up.

"A thousand apologies, Herr Deputy Chief of Police," he said, "but the plane is full—all the seats were taken days ago—I regret infinitely, but—"

Hambledon's knees became unsteady, and even Grautz turned sallower than was accounted for by his makeup.

"Room must be made," said the police chief. "Turn out two non-priority travelers."

"There are none. They are all of the highest possible priority."

The deputy chief sighed impatiently. "Take these men back to the waiting room," he said, and the escort removed them and locked them up again.

Hambledon and Grautz, once more alone, looked at each other. "I'm afraid you've overdone it," said the Dutchman with less than his usual placidity. "My complexion won't last indefinitely, and if they hold us up for two or three days—"

"I'm sorry, Grautz," said Tommy penitently. "I overacted a bit, I'm afraid. Try not to perspire," he added helpfully.

"They are still arguing," said Grautz, looking out of the window.

"So long as they keep that up, there's hope."

"And so long as the plane doesn't go off without us."

They waited, and the time dragged.

"They are turning toward us," said Grautz at last.

"There's the police car still waiting," said Hambledon. "We shall pass it on our way to the airliner—if we do pass it and are not hustled into it again."

"Did you say something about not perspiring?" said Grautz. "I daren't wipe my face; this stuff might come off."

"Don't. If you had different complexions in streaks, they might suspect something. They are coming this way. My knees want starching."

The door opened once more, and again the deputy chief said, "Come out!" They followed him across the concrete expanse toward the car; they neared it, reached it—passed it—and walked on toward the aircraft. Hambledon drew a long breath and stepped out with more assurance.

By the steps which led up to the door in the side of the airplane were two gentlemen protesting and one airline official endeavoring to pacify them.

"Most urgent and immediate business—first-class priority—"

"Tomorrow, without fail, definitely, seats shall be found."

"Today we must go, not tomorrow."

"An unheard-of infringement of contract. I shall complain to the company."

"Gentlemen, the company regrets—only the service of the Reich could—"

Hambledon, followed closely by Grautz, entered the aircraft without bidding farewell to the deputy chief. Tommy offered him a haughty stare from the window, but the anxious little man was not looking. Doors closed and the steps were removed; the engine revolutions increased and orders and signals were given. The airliner began to move, slowly at first and increasingly faster, bumping on the runway. Presently the bumps ceased; they were airborne.

An official came down the narrow gangway between the seats, and Hambledon stopped him.

"Does this plane touch down again in Germany?" he asked.

"No sir. We go right through to Sweden."

Hambledon and Grautz did not glance at each other. They leaned back in their seats, stretched out their legs, and relaxed comfortably.

THE END

About the Rue Morgue Press

"Rue Morgue Press is the old-mystery lover's best friend,
reprinting high quality books from the 1930s and '40s."
—*Ellery Queen's Mystery Magazine*

Since 1997, the Rue Morgue Press has reprinted scores of traditional mysteries, the kind of books that were the hallmark of the Golden Age of detective fiction. Authors reprinted or to be reprinted by the Rue Morgue include Catherine Aird, Delano Ames, H. C. Bailey, Morris Bishop, Nicholas Blake, Dorothy Bowers, Pamela Branch, Joanna Cannan, John Dickson Carr, Glyn Carr, Torrey Chanslor, Clyde B. Clason, Joan Coggin, Manning Coles, Lucy Cores, Frances Crane, Norbert Davis, Elizabeth Dean, Carter Dickson, Michael Gilbert, Constance & Gwenyth Little, Marlys Millhiser, Gladys Mitchell, James Norman, Stuart Palmer, Craig Rice, Kelley Roos, Charlotte Murray Russell, Maureen Sarsfield, Margaret Scherf, Juanita Sheridan and Colin Watson..

To suggest titles or to receive a catalog of Rue Morgue Press books write 87 Lone Tree Lane, Lyons, Colorado 80540, telephone 800-699-6214, or check out our website, www.ruemorguepress.com, which lists complete descriptions of all of our titles, along with lengthy biographies of our writer